DEATH
AT THE
DOORSTEP

A Karin Niemi Novel

Linda W. Fitzgerald

ISBN: 978-1-4834-4044-6 (sc)
ISBN: 978-1-4834-4043-9 (e)

Lulu Publishing Services rev. date: 04/26/2016

*"If you ignore a ghost,
it will only grow bigger."*

--Old Greenlandic proverb

ACKNOWLEDGEMENTS

This book couldn't have been written without the expert knowledge of others. My thanks to Lieutenant Michael Logghe of the Ann Arbor Police Department and former Michigan State Police Officer Thomas Garvale for their patience and professionalism in answering my many questions. Special thanks as well to Professor Elliott Solloway, Research Professor Peter Honeyman and former University of Michigan graduate fellow Leilah Lyons. Also, a deep bow to the late Qi Master Gabriel Chin. Any factual or technical errors that appear in this book are mine alone.

Heartfelt thanks to all the friends and relatives—you know who you are—who encouraged me and cheered me on when I doubted that Karin Niemi would ever complete her adventure. Sincere gratitude as well to Paula, Penny, Lucille, Eva, Ellie, Frederick, Catherine, Julie, Raven, Grace, Steve, Judy, Jane and Jeanine for their intelligent, insightful and helpfully critical readings of the manuscript. Special thanks to the late, great Albert the MagnifiCat for agreeing to this limited return engagement.

A large measure of gratitude to Steve Maggio, Kris Kourtjian, Chris Ellinger, Terri Devall and, of course, Judy Seling for moving the cover art forward. Appreciation also to Mark Shaw for his warm encouragement and practical suggestions. And to Jane Cleland and Rosemary Harris, belated thanks for their no-nonsense advice.

Above all, thank you to Tom, who—although he's never actually read a mystery novel himself—was quietly and completely supportive as I endeavored to write mine.

This book is dedicated
to my parents, Mary and Arthur Wirtanen,
and to Steve Maggio,
who left too soon and too suddenly.

PROLOGUE

Friday – November 15

From the far corner of the ceiling where she'd been floating for what seemed like minutes but could have been hours, Dana looked down at her body sprawled across the wide oak floorboards.

She studied the silver hair matted with sweat. The smears of vomit around the mouth. The startled, staring eyes. The hands that had finally relaxed their grip on her favorite kilim.

So this was death.

Then the voices were right after all.

As usual.

Across the room, water from an overturned vase pooled across an oversized desk, mingled with a spray of coral tea roses and dripped onto the floor in a slow, relentless rhythm. An empty teacup, handle missing, rested under one of the armchairs. Papers and books littered the room like oversized confetti.

Half a dozen small glass vials formed a random pattern next to her body, surrounded by the tiny white homeopathic tablets they had once contained. Nearby, an embossed silver case had released a handful of business cards announcing that Dana Lewis, MA, MSW, was available for individual and group counseling.

I should have listened.

The voices had been with her for as long as she could remember. Her mother and her mother's mother had been gifted in the same way. That was her grandmother's word for it. Gifted.

"Burdened," was what her mother called it. "I've prayed it away and you can, too," she would say, her voice ringing with a Presbyterian confidence. "God will take it from you if you ask."

But Dana had never asked. And over time, she'd discovered that both women had been right. It was a gift. And a burden.

Early on, she had learned to disregard the voices at her own peril. But this morning, weary and exasperated, wanting just for once to be separate and ordinary and free even if it meant blundering through the day like everyone else, she shut them out.

Dana let herself drift back in time.

Waking late, feeling heavy and dull despite the rare promise of a sunny November day, she lay under the comfort of her favorite quilt for a few minutes and listened to her racing heart, wondering at the source of the unease.

Then she remembered, like a cancer patient who for a brief time had forgotten the disease she carried. It was that terrible business with Chaz, of course. Something had to be done. Somehow she had to convince him to talk to the authorities. Of course, it would create an unholy mess. She made a mental note to call Bill. What a dear man he was, for a lawyer.

Dana glanced at the small wind-up clock on the night table. Just seven a.m. She forced herself to think. Her first appointment was at ten. Surely she could pull herself together by then. A cup of the herbal infusion she always kept in the refrigerator, a homeopathic cocktail of arnica, ignatia, maybe a few pellets of aconite and a dose of Rescue Remedy. That should do it.

In robe and slippers, she made her way downstairs, arguing silently with the voices.

You must listen, Dana.

Not now.

Yes, now. For your own sake.

She stood for a moment in the middle of the kitchen, palms pressed against her forehead. First, the tea. A nice big comforting cup of herbal tea.

Dana, no. There is danger.

She froze from force of habit. Then, slowly and deliberately, she shut the trapdoor in her mind with a firm click.

Danger? She opened the refrigerator, took out a jar of amber-colored liquid and filled her favorite cup. Danger? What could they possibly mean? Most likely the danger of a migraine. Or the danger of going back to bed, burrowing under the quilt and canceling the rest of the day.

Sipping as she walked, Dana crossed the living room, stopping to pick up a large rosewood box. The infusion seemed more bitter than usual. Probably too much elecampane in this batch, she decided. Carrying the cup in her left hand and crooking her right arm around the box, she nudged open the double doors leading to her office, then paused.

It was a room that never failed to give her pleasure. The high-coved ceiling, the walls painted in a whisper of green that always made her feel safe and welcome. She loved this room.

And yet for the past week or so, the atmosphere had been all wrong. Dark. Heavy. Almost sinister. In fact, the energy of the entire house felt somehow tainted. As to the source, she was certain of the who but not the why. Later in the day when she felt stronger there would be time to check in with the voices, make sure she wasn't mistaken in her suspicions.

She made a mental note to call Sharon Gladstone and schedule a cleansing ceremony. There were very few dark energies that could hold out against the power of sage, lavender, juniper and sweet grass, especially in the hands of an Ojibwa medicine woman.

Dana crossed the room to a desk wedged snugly under triple windows and gazed out at the back garden. Even in this season it had a certain bleak beauty. After a few more sips, she placed her cup carefully on a coaster then stopped, her fingers still clutching the handle.

She always kept her appointment book under the coaster, but it had been missing now for nearly two days. Where could it be? She ransacked her memory, willing herself to remember, then shook her head. No matter. It would come to her.

As Dana lifted the catch on the box, a tremor ran through her body. Feeling the vibration snake down her spine, she hunched her shoulders. "Someone walking on my grave," she thought. It was one of her grandmother's sayings and for a few seconds she could have sworn the old woman was standing at her side.

Dana lowered her shoulders and rubbed the back of her neck. Still feeling uneasy, she picked up a small brown bottle, squeezed the rubber top to fill the dropper and released the contents into what remained of her tea. Next, she opened three glass vials, measured out half a dozen white globules from each and tipped them onto her tongue. She waited until they dissolved before finishing her tea.

Now—where was that appointment book? In the bookcase? Unlikely but possible. Dana moved her tongue around in her mouth. It felt thick and slightly scalded. And such an odd taste. Metallic. Like hot aluminum.

As she moved toward the bookcase, a violent surge of dizziness sent her staggering backwards against the desk. With exaggerated, puppet-like movements, she gripped the edge and, arms shaking, pushed herself upright. Above the drumbeat of her heart, Dana could hear the wheezy whistle of each breath, feel the strength ebbing out of her muscles. As she clutched uselessly at the smooth wooden surface of the desk, her body began its slow descent to the floor.

Cheek pressed against the cool indifferent wood, she retched, gasped for air. Her cell phone. It had to be here. It was always here. Fighting pain and panic, with all the will she could summon, she dragged herself along the floor in a vain search.

And now…now she floated weightlessly in this upper corner of the room. Floated on warm eddies of air. Still here. Yet not here. Hovering. Thinking. Holding vigil. But for what? And was it just her imagination or was the room receding slightly?

As the office landscape faded to a foggy grey, small white lights appeared, pulsing gently, surrounding her like a miniature, sparsely populated galaxy. She felt easeful. And something else, something more.

Loved. That was it. With a small shock, she realized that she was suspended in love, supported by love. But it was a love she barely recognized. Love without limits, without conditions or demands, love that knew everything but judged nothing, love that…

It's time to go, Dana.

Despite its gentle monotone, the voice startled her. Slowly, almost imperceptibly, she felt herself being drawn away.

Time to go, the voice repeated, even more gently this time.

The lights moved in closer, grew sharper and more delineated. Panic fought its way through the dreamy haze.

"But what about Isabel?" she protested.

There was a slight pause.

She will grieve, and heal. And you will never be far from her.

Dana hesitated. Must speak. But it took so much effort even to shape a thought.

"My friends. My relatives. What about them?"

They, too, will grieve and go on.

Quieter now. "My clients?"

They will understand.

Then suddenly and surprisingly, a small sharp wave of anger surged within her. "And the one who did this to me?"

Another pause.

There is perfect justice. Finally. In the end.

Dana let herself surrender to the warm billows that surrounded her. The room was just a few fuzzy outlines now, small and growing smaller. She heard a sigh, and realized that it came from her.

Time to go.

Time to go.

She gazed like a child at the beings that encircled her, their features blurred by light.

Time to go.

CHAPTER 1

Friday – November 15

Elvis gazed at me from the kitchen wall and swiveled his hips as the minute hand crept toward a glitter-encrusted number two. Nine-ten. Meaning I had twenty minutes before Bixie arrived to sweep me off to my appointment with destiny.

Although I would have vastly preferred Elvis in his red sport coat or even that snug little hand-tailored denim jacket he wore in *Love Me Tender*, I do like the clock—gold lamé and all. It was a gift from my neighbors David and Paul, who can't seem to resist an opportunity to add kitsch to the world. Not that they'd ever clutter up their own impeccably decorated McMansion with anything so campy.

With the sigh of a martyr, I turned to my email. This morning's batch contained an account notice from a bank I'd never heard of, an urgent message from Robert Redford, a discount offer from Lands End and a holiday shopping reminder from L.L. Bean.

Lifting my finger from the delete key, I studied the headers that remained and opened the first few messages. There was a gentle nudge from a new client asking when she could she expect to see copy for a sales flyer. A local nonprofit had sent a list of topics for their next e-newsletter. The marketing director of an engineering firm in Romulus wanted to discuss a series of press releases. I groaned. Press releases are on a par with sewing buttons or scrubbing floors. And if Detroit suburbs were body parts, Romulus would be an armpit—or worse.

I moved the cursor down the grid. Six more messages to go.

To open or not to open?

My hand hovered above the keyboard then slid over to grab the handle of my coffee mug. I sipped, put the mug down, reached over and picked up a tower of overstuffed manila folders that had been defying gravity. Carefully, I divided them into two piles and aligned each pile precisely with the edge of the kitchen table. Then I arranged my two favorite pens to make them perfectly parallel to the folders.

I was just straightening the phone, making sure it was also parallel to the folders and the edge of the table, when the mass of black fur on the kitchen chair next to mine shifted slightly. Lifting his head with regal grace, Albert the MagnifiCat fixed me with a gold-green stare.

I leaned forward. "Don't look at me that way."

Albert uncoiled his twenty-pound frame and gave a luxuriant yawn.

"I know what you're thinking. Well, I can't help it."

Returning my stare, Al blinked slowly and deliberately, like some ancient sage. Exactly the way he did seven years ago when Terry brought him home, a two-pound orphan, all eyes and paws.

Terry had stopped at the Humane Society after work, on a whim he said. When the volunteer on duty happened to mention that black cats were always the last to be adopted, Terry naturally headed for the cage filled with midnight-colored kittens.

Of all the creatures in that particular litter, it was Albert who had stepped forward, put his head next to the bars and began his famous purr.

Sold.

Terry told me all this when he got home, certificate of adoption in one hand, vaccination schedule in the other. "Wait till you see him, Karin, he's got an incredible soul."

Which is something Terry would know, having one himself.

Terry.

Terrence Joseph Hartley.

Six foot two, sandy haired, blue-eyed, a young forty-five with the body of a runner. By training an urban planner, by choice my husband, by happenstance the best and kindest and wisest and funniest and most beautiful man I'd ever met.

Who could have known that, one bright bitterly cold January day, he would collapse at the office. That his lanky frame would be found on the conference room floor. And that three hours later, he would be dead from an aneurism.

Memory dragged me back along a well-worn road. Terry's co-workers had tracked me down at a meeting in a distant Detroit suburb. I broke all speed records getting to St. Joseph Mercy Hospital on Ann Arbor's east side and finally found my way through the labyrinth of corridors to his bedside.

But by that time, Terry was less than an hour away from death. All I could do was hold his hand, send up incoherent prayers to a God who seemed to be out for the day and murmur over and over, "I love you. Please don't leave me."

He did leave, though. And I wanted to go with him, wanted to vacate my body right then and there in that pastel, chrome-plated hospital room. But sometime during my vigil I was certain I heard Terry's voice telling me that if I really loved him, I would find a way to go on.

Ignoring all the pulsing, humming, whirring equipment, I carefully pushed aside tubes and wires and tucked myself around him in that narrow hospital bed. For what seemed like a long time I stroked his forehead and whispered over and over, "I'll find you again. Someday. Somehow. I promise."

That was ten months ago. Ten months, two days, seventeen hours and twenty-some minutes.

During that time, I somehow managed to hold myself together. I'd even reached a point where a sympathetic hug or kind word no longer sent me off in a tempest of tears. People assumed I was getting over it. Friends spoke about closure.

Closure. As if grief didn't last a lifetime. As if half my soul hadn't been ripped out of my body.

It's true I didn't look quite so brittle these days. The prison camp bruises under my eyes had retrenched. The glassy look was gone. But the emptiness and grief were always there, a fraction of an inch below the surface.

Dropping to my knees, I buried my face in Albert's warm, furry side. A few seconds later, I could feel his sandpaper tongue on my scalp.

After a minute, I lifted my face and blinked to clear the last tears. According to Elvis, it was five minutes to Bixie and counting. I propelled myself into the downstairs powder room and splashed cold water on my face. Then, without thinking, I cleaned the sink, patted the soap dry with a paper towel and ran a damp sponge over the floor tiles.

I was sitting at my laptop again when Bixie arrived. She rang the doorbell once and walked in. Her contralto echoed through the downstairs, "Hey Karin, it's me. You ready?" I never could understand why she bothered with the bell.

As usual, Bixie was a vision, from her white-blonde hair to her white pseudo ostrich leather boots. At the moment, those politically correct boots were leaking mud-veined water from last night's rain onto my otherwise spotless oak floor.

With no regard whatever for the baleful look I was giving her, she bent over to plant a kiss on the top of Albert's head, filled a mug with coffee and sat down in the chair opposite me.

After all these years—twenty and counting since she first walked into the Ann Arbor ad agency where I'd been working as a junior copywriter—Bixie still leaves me a little breathless. She tends to have that effect on people. Think Rossetti: statuesque women with ivory skin, smoky eyes, cascading hair, and a cool, androgynous energy.

Just for the record, "Bixie" is derived from a foreshortening of Beatrice, pronounced in the Italian manner. I suppose being named after Dante's beloved isn't all that bad, really, when you consider that Bixie's father was a professor of classical and medieval studies who spent as little time as possible in the current century.

He insisted on giving his two children their first names, leaving the middle names to his wife. So, really, Bixie—Beatrice, that is—could just as easily have been a Persephone. Or an Antigone. Or a Heloise. Or an Isolde. It positively staggers the imagination.

Bixie gave the sugar bowl a look of withering contempt. I walked over to the cupboard, fished out an aged jar of honey and placed it in front of her. I stirred my own cup of coffee, cold now, and kept my eyes on the table.

"You know," I hesitated, "I'm not sure this is such a good idea."

Bixie stopped digging out the crystallized honey and trained her Liz-Taylor-violet eyes on me. "Karin Niemi," she thundered. "What do you mean not a good idea? We've talked about this for hours and you agreed that it was time to do something."

"Yeah, I know..."

"I'm feeling stuck, you said. I'm frozen in place. I don't know how to move ahead. I don't..."

"Okay, okay." I lifted my hands in a give-up position. "I'm just not sure about this psychic counseling business. I mean, what if it backfires? What if I end up feeling more confused?" Or more miserable. More lost. More alone.

Bixie took a deep, loud, long-suffering breath and let it out. Then, with what she probably thought passed for patience, she went on. "This is an extraordinarily gifted therapist we're talking about." I rolled my eyes. "She has degrees from the U of M and Cornell. And you've seen for yourself how intelligent and down-to-earth she is."

"And spooky," I added, remembering Bixie's summer solstice party where I'd met the much-acclaimed therapist. "I mean, what am I supposed to think when a woman I've known for all of five minutes hauls me into a corner, leans in close and tells me she knows how deeply wounded I've been by my grief but that I'm running away from life and oh, by the way, my obsessive-compulsive housekeeping is just a failed attempt to impose some kind of order, to make myself believe I'm in control?" I could feel my face heating up as I relived the encounter.

Bixie winced ever so slightly. "Well sometimes she gets these flashes about people she's just met. And when the people seem to be worth the effort, she tells them what she's seeing. She told me once it's a kind of debt she owes the universe."

I took a swallow of cold coffee and wished I hadn't. "Great. So she blurts out my darkest secrets to a crowd of partygoers and the universe is somehow repaid."

"Karin, she was very discreet and you know it. She didn't blurt out anything. I wouldn't have known about it if you hadn't told me."

Bixie lowered her voice, leaned forward and let her eyes soften. I hate it when she does that, goes all gooey and compassionate and heartfelt. "Besides, you need to start somewhere. This is about healing. It's time. You know that."

I looked down at Albert, who had made himself at home on Bixie's lap. His chin was level with the tabletop and he was giving me The Stare. Then I looked up at Bixie.

Double whammy.

"Oh, alright. I'll go. But you're not coming with me."

Bixie shifted to the low singsong voice she uses with difficult children and benighted adults who buy their groceries at Meijers. "I've told you. Dana's been having computer problems, so I volunteered to help her out. Yesterday I backed up her files on a flash drive and installed the latest versions of her software."

Like most graphic designers, Bixie is a whiz with computers. Myself, I've never met a piece of software I liked or a download I trusted.

"I only have a few upgrades to go," Bixie continued, scratching Albert's big head absentmindedly. "Then I need to format the system so she can find her way around." She sipped her coffee. "It just so happens I'm free this morning. So this is the perfect time for me to finish up. I can be working upstairs while you're downstairs."

The challenge hung in the air. I opened my mouth and shut it again without saying a word. Who knows, maybe there was something to this psychic stuff after all. Maybe Dana Lewis could help me. At the very least, it would be a welcome distraction from brochures and ads and web sites.

"Okay, fine." I pushed myself away from the table. "I'll drive."

Score one for the fruitcake contingent.

CHAPTER 2

Friday – November 15

I think of Bixie and myself as the Mutt and Jeff of the fashion world. Or as Bixie might say, the yin and yang.

She's one of those women who looks as if she just walked out of a *Vogue* photo shoot, no matter what rag she happens to be wearing. I, on the other hand, belong in one of those cozy British mysteries. You know, the ones with a body in the library, a cunning village cop, a squirrelly parson and, tucked away in one of the nearby cottages, a tall, well-meaning woman who wears sensible but outdated tweeds. That would be me.

Bixie slid into her white quilted jacket—the one that makes her look like a blonde Mandarin—and rearranged a gauzy red scarf around her neck. On my way to the front closet, I glanced out at the snow-dotted landscape and remembered Terry's name for this early phase of winter. The dead season, he called it.

With a sigh, I struggled into my old grey pea coat and tucked in the scarf Aunt Ilsa had knit for me years back. My Lake Superior scarf, made with every imaginable shade of blue. Next, I pulled on ankle boots and, as an afterthought, dug a pair of leather gloves out of a basket on the closet shelf.

As someone who grew up in Michigan's upper peninsula, also known as True North, I've learned to never underestimate winter, even early winter. Where I come from, kids trick-or-treat in the snow and by the first week of November people have brushed the spider webs off their shovels, waxed their cross-country skis, tuned up their snowmobiles and stocked up on beer and bourbon.

I double-checked Albert's bowls to make sure he wouldn't waste away in the next hour or two. Then I glanced out the window at a few feeble snowflakes suspended in the grey morning air, harbingers of things to come.

Halfway out the front door, I called over my shoulder to Bixie who was still putzing around in the kitchen with Albert. "Ready to roll. Unless you'd prefer that we reschedule."

By the time I'd taken a few breaths of chilly air and turned around, key in hand, Bixie had manifested at my side. It's a trick of hers, seeming to materialize out of nowhere like some kind of apparition.

In deference to Bixie, I had parked my 1999 Malibu—Amelia by name—on the street to leave my tiny driveway free for her arthritic white Toyota Celica, age uncertain. From the top of the steps, I waved at Paul Mandotti, my next-door neighbor, who had come to a full stop in front of the house and was apparently waiting for us.

In his right hand, Paul held a leash occupied on the other end by a liquid-eyed beagle named Lew. That's Lew as in Lew Archer, the hard-boiled, heart-of-gold detective who punched and wisecracked his way through the novels of Ross McDonald. Murder mysteries were a mutual passion of Paul's and mine, and certainly the only guilty pleasure we were ever likely to share.

In his left hand, Paul held a copy of that morning's *Detroit News*. "Karin. Bixie. Have you *seen* this abomination?" Paul tends to speak in italics and, when the occasion calls for it, capital letters. He waved the paper in front of our faces in an agitated flutter. Under a corner banner that touted full coverage of the mid-term elections on page two, a fat boldface headline read: Bailey Nabs Senate Seat, Declares Mandate in GOP Upset.

"Mandate! *MAN*date no less. What moxie." Paul's voice moved up and down the register as if he were singing an aria. "This crypto-fascist right-wing nobody steals an election and wins, if you can call it that, by the smallest margin of any Michigan senator in more than a century, and he refers to it as a landslide. My God, what *are* they putting in that man's *break*fast cereal?"

Paul was a vision this morning in a pumpkin-colored leather jacket—he would have called it terra cotta—with bronze-colored buckles running up and down the front. For the hundredth time, and with a noticeable pang of envy, I found myself wondering where he got his clothes. Not that it would matter. Even if we haunted the same tony boutiques in the same chic suburbs of metro Detroit, even if I could afford it, I'd manage to find whatever dark turtlenecks and understated slacks they had and end up looking exactly as I always do.

Paul's face was now turning the same approximate color as his jacket. Lew, recognizing a grade-A hissy fit when he saw one, had plunked down on the sidewalk, head on paws, to wait out the fury with sad-eyed patience.

I bent down to comfort Lew, who returned the favor by licking my hand, my wrist, my nose and any other part of me he could reach.

Paul moaned. "Oh God. Six years. Six endless years of bad policy and crazy-making lies. I mean, think of the damage an idiot like that could do in six years. And the man was at least fifteen points behind in every poll. There's no way he could have won. Not in a fair election. Good grief. We might as well be living in China or Pakistan or one of those other hopeless places where officials are preordained."

As Paul raved, I glanced up and down the street, taking in the blue and white Kendall for Senate signs that decorated almost every lawn. The one notable exception being Mr. Benson, an ex-Marine five houses up who hosted the only pro-Bailey yard sign in the neighborhood and who was now balancing on a ladder, merrily draping Christmas lights around the pillars that flanked his wide front porch. Mr. Benson always likes to get a jump on the holiday season.

Catching my eye, Bixie winched up her eyebrows, hoisted her left wrist and pointed to her watch. I took my cue and stood up.

"Look, I'd love to stay and talk, but Bixie and I have an appointment," I said. "Now take some deep breaths before you have a stroke or something. The Democrats can't afford to lose a single voter." Paul moved his mouth into something that could have been a smile or a pout.

"Oh, alright." He breathed in and exhaled with a huffing sound. "If you *promise* to come by for tea this afternoon. I've given myself the day

9

off and David's away on a business trip in Las Vegas. Or maybe it's Los Altos." Paul, of course, knew exactly where David was.

"Well…"

"The word you're searching for is yes," Paul folded his newspaper and Lew began to look hopeful that the parade would start up again. "I'll look for you around three-thirty. And I'll have some fresh scones."

I weakened visibly. Most people know Paul as a four-star furniture designer and owner of a trendy home décor shop. Only a chosen few know that he also bakes like an angel.

Bixie was giving me her version of the evil eye. "Alright," I agreed. "Throw in a few of your German chocolate brownies, and it's a deal."

Paul pursed his lips and did a quick scan of my five-foot-nine-and-a-half frame. "I simply don't understand how you manage to eat like a pig without putting on a pound." He shrugged and winked at Bixie. "Ah well, some girls have all the luck." He tucked the offending newspaper under his arm, let himself be pulled along for a few yards by Lew and, without turning, gave us a wave.

Bixie and I stood side by side as dog and man strutted down the block. I sighed. "Too bad we can't stay for a few more minutes. I love watching him bait Mr. Benson."

CHAPTER 3

Friday – November 15

I live on Ann Arbor's Old West Side, sixteen square blocks of funky clapboard houses painted every color you can imagine and some you can't, plus a brick manse here and there, an occasional stucco-covered ark circa 1920, a couple of kit houses from the bygone Sears and Roebuck era, and a few Queen Anne whatnot's. All of them are enhanced by unbearably quaint cul-de-sacs, cottage gardens, front porches to die for, and some of the most potholed streets in the county.

As the first section of the city to be settled in the late nineteenth century, the Old West Side is under the vigilant eye of the Ann Arbor Historic Preservation Commission. Which means that nothing ever changes, not a door frame, not a kitchen window, nothing, at least not without bloodying a few high-minded bureaucrats in the process.

I guided Amelia along the narrow pavement, zigzagging around parked cars. As we crawled past a three-story Victorian in pale lavender with ivory trim and purply black shutters, I decided Terry was right when he used to say that, sometimes, progress means keeping things exactly as they are.

Dodging potholes, I headed toward the downtown area. At the Miller-First Street light, I looked over at Bixie. "So where are we heading?" Truth was, I had a pretty good idea, but I wanted her to stop messing with my radio settings.

"Arbor Woods." She fiddled with the buttons as she spoke. "Twelve-ten Leicester Drive." She pronounced it "Lester," the way a Brit would.

11

Evidently Dana was doing very well for herself. Arbor Woods is an enclave of handsome, sprawling, luxuriantly landscaped houses populated by senior faculty, deans, doctors, dentists, lawyers, real estate all-stars, the occasional CEO, and a smattering of well-to-do townies, occupations unknown, whose Ann Arbor roots go back for generations. While it may not have the glitz of the new high-ticket developments, it has something even better: understated affluence and quiet, self-assured class. In fact, Arbor Woods reeks with class.

Running red lights is a favorite motorsport of Ann Arbor drivers. So when the traffic light flicked green, I waited and began the mandatory three-second count. Right on cue, a glossy green Subaru Forester sped across our path. I tapped the horn in half-hearted protest and turned east on Huron, part of a major artery that loops through the city, changing its name along the way.

As we got closer to central campus, pedestrians—I like to think of them as the city's sacred cows—stepped out boldly in front of traffic. A small herd of undergraduates dressed identically in jeans and dark hoodies ambled by as if traffic lights were a mere suggestion.

I swerved to avoid a thirty-something decked out in grubby chinos, a Red Sox baseball cap, running shoes that had covered too many miles and a designer dress coat that was probably cashmere. Adjusting the leather briefcase slung over his shoulder, he lowered his iPhone just long enough to give me a drop-dead look.

A few more harrowing encounters brought us to tree lined, hilly, if-you-have-to-ask-how-much-you-can't-afford-it Geddes Avenue. "Okay," I announced, "from here on you'll have to play Girl Guide."

"Take Geddes to Belvedere, go two blocks, then left on Leicester and you're there. It's a three-story Tudor, second house on the right." Bixie still hadn't found the radio station of her dreams.

By the time Amelia glided around the final corner, with prompts from Bixie, my stomach was volcanic and my mind was completely preoccupied with the hour to come. So once I'd made the final left turn, it took me a couple of extra seconds to take in the scene and slam on the brakes. Just in time to avoid careening into one of two navy blue squad cars, property of the Ann Arbor Police, that were parked crosswise in the street to create an impromptu barricade.

An ambulance, another squad car and an assortment of dark sedans took up all available parking along the far side of the street, directly in front of a handsome white and brown Tudor house. Mouth open, eyes wide, I leaned forward on the steering wheel for a better look.

"Oh my God." It was a raspy croak and it came from Bixie, who was straining against her seatbelt, gripping the dashboard with two white-knuckled hands. "What's going on?" She turned to me, face as pale as her jacket, and began fumbling with the seatbelt buckle. Her voice was high and hysterical. "Turn off the engine, Karin. Now. We've got to make sure Dana's alright."

Locking eyes with Bixie, I pitched my voice calm and low. "Just wait a minute. We can't park here." I glanced at a uniformed cop about five yards away who was looking back at me with more than a little interest. "Not without getting arrested or questioned or something. Hang on."

I did a three-point turn in a driveway and rounded the corner, back the way we'd come. I was still in the process of parking when Bixie clawed open the passenger door and bolted toward the tangle of cars and uniforms.

By the time I caught up with her, she was standing in a cluster of people—a mix of genuinely concerned neighbors and the usual assortment of ghouls and gawkers—just a few feet from a length of yellow tape that bordered the lawn in front of Dana's house. On the other side of the tape was a man wearing a dark blue uniform and an uncomfortable expression. About fifteen feet away, one of his colleagues was videotaping the crowd.

I took in the scene. Police cars. Crime tape. Ambulance attendants. A red light revolving slowly and unnecessarily on top of a black four-door sedan. I'll be damned, I thought. It was like walking into an Ed McBain novel.

As I made my way over to Bixie, I could hear the guard-cop in conversation with a tall, thin man dressed in beige chinos and what was probably a Harris Tweed jacket. The man was punching the air with his unlit pipe, emphasizing every point as he droned on—"right to know"… "lived in this neighborhood for years"… "file a complaint." Finally, he stopped to take a breath.

"Sorry, sir." The cop held out his arms as if to keep the crowd from moving closer even though no one was stirring. He couldn't have been more than twenty-five or so, good looking in a moody Mediterranean sort of way. His attention was riveted on the tweedy neighbor. "There's nothing we can tell you now. You're wasting your time here." He upped his voice a few decibels. "I'd advise you all to go home. There's nothing to see, nothing you can do."

As he scanned the crowd, his eyes happened to land on Bixie, who had worked her way up to the tape. I saw his Adam's apple bob as he did a double take in spite of all those months in the police academy.

"Please," the intensity of her voice matched her tear-streaked face. "I've got to know what happened. The woman who lives in that house is a good friend of mine."

Officer Mediterranean swallowed hard but his training held. "Sorry, ma'am. The facts will all come out in due time. However, if you are a friend, I'll need your name, address and phone number. Same for her." He nodded at me, then looked around at the crowd. "Same for all of you folks. I'll want your names, addresses, phone numbers."

He let his eyes brush over Bixie's face once more and pulled out a small notebook and pen, a little more eagerly than he might have done otherwise. We gave him the information he needed. Then I put my hand on Bixie's shoulder. "He's right. There's nothing we can do here. We should go."

"No."

"Your friend is right, ma'am," Officer Mediterranean broke in. "We can get on with our work a lot better if you'd leave." He swung his head around and raised his voice. "That goes for all of you, as soon as we have your personal information."

I leaned closer to Bixie. She was hugging herself, probably to stop the tremors that were becoming more noticeable by the second.

"Listen," I whispered. "I know how you feel, I really do. But right now I'm going to take you back to your house."

"No."

"Make you some tea…"

"I said no."

"… fix us both something to eat."

14

"What part of the word NO don't you understand?"

"… And a little later we'll call Andrew. He might be able to tell us what happened."

For an instant, Bixie froze. Then she looked at me like a sleepwalker who'd just come to. "Andrew," she repeated.

I put my hand on her back.

"Right. Andrew. As in your brother. The cop."

Bixie gave a slow, zombie-like nod. "Andrew. Good idea."

With one last anguished look at the house, she let me guide her back to the car.

CHAPTER 4

Friday – November 15

The ride to Bixie's house seemed interminable even though she lives in Burns Park, less than a mile and a half from what I now thought of as *the crime scene.* Because suddenly Dana's house wasn't a home anymore. It wasn't a destination for friends and family and clients. It wasn't a refuge after a long, hard-fought day.

I wondered how long it would be, how many paper-booted, latex-gloved forensic specialists it would take before the house began to surrender its essence. And how long it would take—afterwards—to remove the taint.

But above all, I wondered what had happened to Dana Lewis. Given all the uniforms we'd seen, not to mention the grim faces of the other official types milling around the site, I could only assume the worst. For now, though, I refused to let myself think about Dana's fate. Instead, I focused all my attention on driving.

Friday traffic was even more nerve-jangling than usual because of the upcoming home game. The Goodyear blimp floated overhead, a sure sign that the Michigan Wolverines were playing tomorrow in the Big House, the U of M's legendary stadium.

Knots of bicycles, cars, trucks, delivery vans, passive-aggressive pedestrians and SUV's—or, as Terry preferred to call them, FUV's—cluttered up every corner and tangled traffic at every light. Meanwhile, Bixie rocked back and forth as much as her seat belt would allow, clasped and unclasped her fingers, and kept up a steady, nerve-wracking monologue. Sometimes it sounded like a chant: We've got to find out what happened We've got to find out what happened What in God's name could it be We've got to find out what happened.

I hate it when people fall apart.

Taken together, Bixie and the traffic should have been more than enough to occupy my attention. But despite a deep, stomach-gnawing fear for Dana and a concern for Bixie that was edging into panic, I couldn't ignore the bumper stickers around me. It's a silly longstanding habit, a compulsion really. Asking me not to read a bumper sticker is like asking a wine connoisseur not to sample a bottle of Chateau Neuf de Pape. The best of today's lot was a brazen message slapped on a big-ass Silverado that announced: *Liberals are great. FOR TARGET PRACTICE. Member NRA.*

It was a relief when the familiar Mission style bungalow came into view. "Almost there," I said stupidly, out of a need to be saying something, as if my voice could somehow break Bixie out of her shock and grief.

I pulled up and parked, admiring as always the solid lines of the house, the slate blue siding, the elegant wrought iron fence. The front yard had long ago been given over to a flower garden and now the space was dotted with mummified roses, brown stalks of indeterminate origin and a few woebegone chrysanthemums.

The house actually belongs to Bixie's parents, who retired to North Carolina a few years back. Loving her hugely and worrying incessantly about the future of their talented, gorgeous but unmarried daughter, they decided that she should live in the family home. It's a good arrangement, especially since her brother has no objections and no interest whatever in uprooting his family from their oversized ranch house on five acres in one of the semi-rural western townships.

In terms of affluence, Burns Park is maybe half a notch down from Arbor Woods. The houses are a little smaller and clustered closer together, with more of a first-generation-Ann-Arbor feel to the neighborhood. But basically it's the same mix of comfortable, solid citizens. Some of whom were no doubt watching as I helped Bixie out of the car and through the front door.

The house seemed to have a tonic effect on her. Even before her jacket was off, she asked me to fetch a bottle of Rescue Remedy from the kitchen counter, along with a glass of water. As the daughter of a hospital administrator, I've always harbored doubts about alternative medicines and nothing will ever persuade me to give up my trusty Tylenol or my cherished collection of allergy meds. But in the days and weeks following Terry's death, when Bixie had encouraged me to forego the heavy-duty sedatives and try her remedies instead, I became a convert.

While the teapot heated, I moved back and forth in the big sunny kitchen, glad to be busy since I had no idea of what to say or do. I know women are supposed to possess an innate talent for nurturing but I tend to shut down in the face of tragedy. It probably has a lot to do with all those second-generation reindeer herders I grew up with. In our house, strong emotions were frowned upon.

By the time I'd loaded an oversized wooden tray with a pot of herbal tea, two mugs, plates of cheese and tomato sandwiches—heavy on the mayo—plenty of napkins and some unsalted potato chips excavated from one of the cupboards, Bixie had recovered somewhat. Enough to start thinking about next steps.

As I came in with the tray, she announced, "We need to start calling the local hospitals."

I handed her a cup. "You can try," I told her. "But if," I paused, "if there's a crime involved, no one's going to tell you anything."

I took a cautious sip of tea and let it sit in my mouth for a few seconds. Not bad, although coffee would have been infinitely better.

Staring off into the distance, Bixie lifted her cup as if to drink, then stopped. "She's dead, Karin. I just know she is."

The cup began to quake. I reached out to steady her hand. "We don't know that. Right now all we can do is wait."

"I'm going to call Andrew."

"Fine. But he may not know anything either. And if he does, he won't tell you."

Almost absentmindedly, Bixie took a sip of tea. "Maybe not," she said, in a stronger voice than I'd heard in a while. "But at least I can make contact. He's met Dana, you know, several times. And he knows we're close. Besides, I've got to do something."

While I tackled one of the sandwiches, Bixie dialed her brother. After nearly a minute on hold, she left a message. Her hand was still on the receiver when she had a follow-up thought. "Omigosh. Isabel. I've got to call her right now..."

Isabel. I ransacked my memory. According to Bixie's gossipy ramblings, that would be Dana's semi-estranged daughter.

I walked over to the bookshelves that doubled as an entertainment console and tuned in the local NPR affiliate broadcasting from Eastern Michigan University. WEMU was always one of the first with late-breaking local news. Besides which, they play jazz. Real jazz, not the counterfeit stuff you hear in elevators and franchise restaurants. And they play it twenty-four hours a day. Bliss.

My timing was impeccable. The piercing sweet sounds of Miles Davis' trumpet led me through the opening bars of *Round Midnight*. I let the music wash over me for maybe half a minute, then walked back to the couch.

"Now if anything happens, we'll be the first to know." I waved the plate of sandwiches in front of Bixie. "How about giving one of these a try?"

Her eyebrows moved up and the corners of her mouth moved down. I nudged the plate closer. This was worse than trying to get my twelve-year-old nephew—Nathan the Impossible—to down his green vegetables. Gingerly, as if the tray were radioactive, Bixie picked up a sandwich and moved it in the general direction of her mouth. I cast my eyes heavenward before attacking the potato chips.

Of course I knew this meal was only a delaying tactic. As I trundled back to the kitchen with the wreckage of our lunch, I looked at the wall clock. Just after one. It was going to be a long afternoon. And wasn't there something I'd promised to do later, besides meeting a few client deadlines?

Of course. Paul. I reached for the kitchen phone and dialed his number, dreading the little scene that was certain to ensue.

When Paul picked up, I lowered my voice, just in case the radio didn't provide enough cover. He started in with his usual diva-done-wrong routine, but once he actually started listening to my story, his whole attitude shifted.

"Oh my God, do you think she's *dead*?" It was the same tone of voice he used when the lives of his favorite soap opera characters got particularly juicy.

"It's possible." I said slowly. "But in any case, I can't leave Bixie by herself."

"You poor things. What a shock." There was more envy than sympathy in his voice. "Tell you what. Since I've already made the scones, I'll just bring them over along with some second-flush Darjeeling. It's the least I can do for Bixie in her time of trial."

Time of trial? Good grief, I thought, he must be reading Wilkie Collins again.

"No, really, Paul. There's no need to go to all that trouble." To make all that trouble.

Too late. "No trouble, pet. It's all settled. I'll be over there around three-thirty. In the meantime, be brave. Hugs to Bixie."

My next sentence was directed to the dial tone. I put the phone down.

Great, I thought. Just what the afternoon didn't need. More drama.

CHAPTER 5

Friday – November 15

Say what you will about his emotional pyrotechnics, Paul does set a lovely tea table. He was just pouring out second cups and apologizing yet again for having brought his everyday china when the doorbell rang and Andrew blew into the room like a gust of cold air. That ring-once-and-enter routine seemed to be a family trait.

Before he'd taken two steps into the living room, Bixie flew off the couch and wrapped him in a hug. I could just make out the words "I'm so glad you're here" spoken into Andrew's sport coat.

From where I sat, his face was unreadable. But then it usually is.

"Hey, Bix. What's up?" He put his arms around her.

I stood up and walked over to them. Andrew worked his right hand free to shake mine. "Karin. Good to see you."

Andrew is tall enough that, even in two-inch heels, I had to look up slightly to meet his eyes. Pale grey, those eyes. Falcon grey, with that flinty, take-no-prisoners look that some women find so sexy but which I knew was just the gaze of a wary cop, the legacy of twenty-plus years on the Ann Arbor police force. He nodded past me at Paul, who smiled sweetly and wiggled the fingers of his right hand in greeting.

As I took in the brother-sister tableau, I decided that if Andrew Murray were allowed to have a bumper sticker on his unmarked police car, it would be very small. So small you'd have to get extremely close to read it. And when you did, you would find the words: *Mind Your Own Damn Business.*

While he and Bixie exchanged a few sentences, I gave Andrew a quick once-over. At least he was easy on the eyes. Today, he was wearing charcoal grey slacks, black merino wool turtleneck, and a salt-and-pepper tweed jacket that bulged out slightly around his holster. I've always suspected his fellow officers razz him about his GQ wardrobe—the pricey suits and elegant sport coats, the silk ties and immaculately tailored shirts.

Of course, it probably helps that his wife comes from money, as they say up north. Back in the 1950s, Helen O'Dell's father had the bright idea of starting a plumbing franchise. Who could have known he'd die a multi-multi-millionaire?

I let my thoughts linger for a few moments on the estimable Helen. Cloud-like blonde hair, acrylic nails, just enough Botox to cheat the calendar by ten years or so. Perfect housekeeper, perfect hostess, perfect all-American cook, perfect stay-at-home soccer mom. Organizer of PTO fundraisers, purveyor of cookies and lemon bars to church bake sales. The kind of woman it would be easy but dangerous to underestimate. Because lurking behind those beautifully made-up blue eyes, I knew from a few brief encounters, was a hard, calculating intelligence. And something else, something Bixie always referred to as Helen's whim of iron.

When I came back to earth, Andrew was seated beside Bixie on the couch, arching one eyebrow at the gold-rimmed tea set and asking if there was a decent drink in the house. That was my cue, since I'm the main contributor to Bixie's liquor cabinet. It's not generosity so much as self-interest. Herbal tea and a watery Chablis just don't cut it for me.

"Scotch on the rocks?" I asked, moving toward the kitchen.

Andrew leaned back on the leather cushions. "Perfect. And then my baby sister can tell me about that urgent message the desk sergeant handed me an hour ago."

Bixie bit her lower lip, fighting back tears, maybe, or vivid memories of the morning. Then she launched into her story. By the time she hit her stride, I was handing Andrew a glass that held two inches of single malt scotch and three ice cubes.

Five minutes later, Bixie ended with "I can't stand this not knowing and I figured you'd be able to find out what happened, if you didn't know already." She looked at her brother expectantly, fully aware that he wasn't at liberty to breathe a word of police business to us civilians.

Andrew took a long final swallow, leaned forward, clasped the glass in both hands and rattled the ice cubes in a noisy circle. He let his eyes travel from Bixie to me to Paul, who was literally on the edge of his seat twitching with anticipation. Like a storybook rabbit, I thought.

"Bixie, you know the rules." It was a good strong start. Unfortunately, he made the mistake of looking into those big violet-blue eyes, the same eyes that must have led him astray so many times during their childhood.

He paused. Stared at the carpet for a few seconds. Let out a long sigh of resignation.

"Alright. This much and no more. But only because Dana is such a close friend of yours. And none of this goes any further. You do not breathe a single word to anyone until it makes the local news. Not to anyone. Is that clear?"

He waited for a nod from his sister before aiming his grey gaze at Paul and me. "Is that clear?" he repeated. We bobbed our heads. He held us for a few seconds longer with his stare as if to seal the agreement, then went on.

"Right. So a nine-one-one call came through this morning, about eight-thirty. The next door neighbor, who is also a good friend of Dana's and looks after the house when she's away, had dropped by on her way to work to return something. Dana's car was in the driveway, some lights were on inside, but no one answered the doorbell. It was too early for her to be in session with a patient. And, according to the neighbor's report, Dana had been out of sorts lately, nervous, anxious, maybe not well."

Bixie gave a thoughtful nod, as if comparing her own impressions. Andrew continued. "Neighbor got worried. Let herself in with the cleverly hidden key that evidently half the population of Ann Arbor knew about. And found Dana Lewis dead in her office."

As Bixie let out a wailing sound, her brother gave each of us a quick, intense look. "Trust me, you don't want the details." The wail morphed into a sob and his sister pressed a balled-up fist against her mouth.

"Suicide is remotely possible," he continued in his remorseless cop way. "But, of course, every suspicious death is treated as a homicide.

23

And that's all I can tell you right now." He put a hand on Bixie's shoulder. "Sorry, Bix. I know how much she meant to you."

I went over to Bixie, who was struggling to speak through her tears. "Suicide?" she sobbed. "How can you even think that? Dana would never have committed suicide. Never."

Andrew shrugged. "Who can say for sure?" As always, any comfort he offered was likely to be cold around the edges. "But if it was murder, seeing as how she was a shrink and a controversial one at that, there won't be any shortage of suspects."

The glance he leveled at his sister and me seemed just a trifle uneasy. A small shockwave rippled through my mind as I held the weeping, clinging Bixie and attempted a few clumsy pats on the back.

First rule of policing: suspect everyone. In this case, that would be family, neighbors, clients. Including new clients, I reminded myself. Who were maybe on their way to their first appointment.

And of course friends.

I shifted Bixie's weight slightly and moved my head so that I could look directly into Andrew's face. He returned my gaze with surprising force, as if daring me to step over some invisible line. The grey eyes had iced over.

Still holding his gaze, I patted the back of Bixie's head.

"It's going to be alright," I whispered. "Everything's going to be alright."

CHAPTER 6

Friday – November 15

By the time I said my reluctant but relieved good-byes, it was after six and twilight had given way to a clear, cobalt-colored sky. The air had a bite to it and I pulled up the edges of my scarf to chin level.

A few stars strong enough to challenge Ann Arbor's light pollution hung suspended in the empty branches of a white oak that claimed a corner of the front yard. Another massive oak, standing like a sentinel next to Amelia, had captured the waning moon in its branches.

I thought of how, in summer, oaks and maples and beeches and shag bark hickories and the odd chestnut form leafy archways on almost every street. And how, by late August, most of the central city is covered by a dense canopy of green.

I moon gazed for a few more seconds, then shut my eyes and took in a long, slow, shaky breath. As I did, words suddenly popped out of nowhere:

> *Stars over snow--*
> *And in the west a planet swinging below a star.*
> *Look for a beautiful thing and you will find it.*
> *It is not far--*
> *It never will be far.* *

---

* *Night* by Sara Teasdale (1884-1933)

Amazing. There was Sara Teasdale, back after all these years. I'd memorized that poem when I was a kid. The words had become a mantra for me, something I'd repeat when I felt scared or sad or angry or hopeless in that secret, soul-deep way children have. By college, the poem had disappeared from memory, edged out by modern authors and biology and less noble pursuits. But here it was again.

I love it when my wayward mind tosses out something beautiful and totally unexpected, like a wave casting up shells on a beach. Although I have to wonder if these odd tidbits aren't taking up space that should be allocated to more useful items. Phone numbers. Dates. Names.

But that, as my friend Evan would point out, is reductionist thinking. The brain, despite propaganda to the contrary, is not a computer. Not a mechanism. Not a filing system. It is an organic, living, evolving entity. As a philosopher-turned-computer scientist, Evan—I liked to think— had the right credentials to make those pronouncements.

Of course, not everyone agrees. Looking up at the moon again, I remembered a hotshot neuroscientist I once interviewed who, with the help of earnest colleagues and eager graduate students, was mapping the brain, cell by cell. I can still see the printout on his office wall tracking their work in progress. It looked like a city map seen through the eyes of an abstract-impressionist painter. Fascinating but sinister.

The brain mapper cheerfully assured me that one day, sooner rather than later, they would be able to pinpoint the source of every human emotion, every impulse, every action. Love. Hate. Envy. Altruism. Faith.

Look for a beautiful thing and you will find it…

Opening the car door, I flashed on a freeze frame image of my eight-year-old self. Serious and shy. Too tall to be confident and too smart to be popular. Curled up in a lumpy old armchair and burrowing into yet another book for solace. I remembered the deep comfort Sara's words had given me and decided that I would never surrender that memory for a few micrometers of free brain space, wherever they happened to be.

That settled, I wedged myself in behind the wheel, leaned back against the headrest and arched until I heard my spine pop gently. Then I drummed on the steering wheel as I pondered my next move.

True to form, Andrew had taken charge of the situation. Bixie had vetoed his first plan—that she spend the night with Helen and her offspring in the hinterlands. I could understand Bixie's foot-dragging response to the prospect of an enforced pajama party in the leafy suburbs of Chelsea. The idea of sharing a house, even for one night, with two surly teenagers, a neurotic cocker spaniel, a wall-sized plasma TV that didn't seem to have an off button, assorted hyperactive cell phones and a Martha Stewart clone was definitely not my idea of a good time.

As it turned out, Bixie was able to escape everything but the sister-in-law. She finally gave in when Andrew insisted that Helen would be insulted if she weren't allowed to help and that he himself would be extremely upset. Emphasis on extremely.

Sure enough, once he dialed home and explained the situation, Helen promised to be at Bixie's within the hour. From across the room, I could hear her voice chirping on the receiver. Knowing her, she probably kept a packed bag under the bed, like some celebrity journalist always ready for the next assignment.

I probably should have forced myself to think about why Helen grated on me so much. I mean, it's not as if I coveted anything she was. Or anything she had.

Or did I? My fingers stopped their drumming in mid-tap. Nope. Better not go there.

Instead, I grinned into the dark, recalling Andrew's face when Paul had volunteered to spend the night. Fluttering across the room to Bixie's side, Paul had squeezed her shoulder and pressed his cheek against hers.

"She *really* shouldn't be alone tonight, you know. And Karin must be utterly *exhausted* after such an absolutely *brutal* day," he rolled his eyes. "Especially given all she's *been* through in the last year." Ouch. "So I'll just run home, throw a few things into my little kit bag and be back in a jiff." At that moment, I'm sure I saw a spasm ripple along the edge of Andrew's clenched jaw.

Certain he was winning the day, Paul looked soulfully at Bixie. "I think a soufflé is just the thing for dinner, don't you, hon? Followed by a cup of herbal tea and a long hot bath. Then bed for you. And," he looked around the living room with the eye of a born opportunist, "I'll just make myself comfortable down here with a good book and a blanket."

He paused for a second. "Oh, and of course I'll bring Lew with me. At times like this, it's comforting to have a guard dog around."

Guard dog? Well, there was a remote possibility Lew could overpower someone with his slobbery kisses.

Paul was clearly warming up to his new role as night nurse. And Bixie, having given up the vain hope that she'd be allowed to spend the night by herself, seemed okay with the notion of Paul as babysitter. But of course she'd forgotten about her brother. Taking his usual I-am-a-rock stance, Andrew announced that he would stay with his sister until Helen arrived. For a brief instant, I had an image of Andrew and Helen as a WWF tag team decked out in leotards, capes and tattoos.

Within a few minutes, I was being gently but firmly hustled out of the house, having elicited a solemn promise from Bixie to call immediately if any news broke or if she needed to talk. Paul began repacking his tea things in a quiet huff but interrupted his power pout just long enough to say that he'd catch up with me later.

So here I was, free for the rest of the evening and glad of it. But feeling anxious and antsy, too revved up to sit still, too tired to move, as if all my nerve endings were exposed to the open air.

Knowing there was no way I could face the cheerful, aggressive football crowds that were by now filling every restaurant and café in the city, I headed home, steering Amelia through bumper-to-bumper traffic, being especially careful to avoid the clusters of students who were chattering, shouting and staggering their way to and from house parties.

Stopping for a red light on Washtenaw, I lowered my window to let the cold night air wash over my face and heard a chorus of belligerent young voices chanting "GoBlueGoBlueGoBlueGoBlue" as if challenging some invisible rivals.

A group of six or seven aging alumni sauntered past me in the crosswalk. Talking loudly, their silver hair glinting in the streetlights, they were dressed in look-alike maize and blue jackets, sweaters and baseball caps, all emblazoned with the familiar block M. One of the males of the group glanced over at me and gave a thumbs-up sign. I offered a limp wave in return.

Launched from who knows where, a crumpled beer can traced a low trajectory and sailed past my windshield. As I always say, there's nothing like a college town in the fall.

CHAPTER 7

Friday – November 15

When I got home about twenty minutes later, the light on the living room phone was blinking. I'd picked up half a dozen messages earlier in the afternoon. Since then, three more calls had come in. I pulled off my jacket, unwound Aunt Ilsa's scarf, punched the play button harder than necessary and turned up the volume.

From the hall closet, I heard a familiar bear hug of a voice. "Hey, Karin, it's Evan." I stopped to listen, hanger in hand.

I've always thought of Evan Bernstein as an extra, unexpected wedding present. "Part of the total package," as Terry used to say, since he and Evan had been like brothers since their undergraduate days at Oberlin. They went their separate ways for graduate school, Evan heading to Princeton and Terry opting for the U of Wisconsin at Madison. But through some benign twist of fate, they both landed in Ann Arbor.

These days, Evan was happily ensconced in the university as an associate professor of computer science. Well, maybe happily is an exaggeration. To hear him tell it, the Computer Engineering Institute is a nest of vipers—conniving, backbiting strategists who make Machiavelli look like a rank amateur. He always insists that the reason his colleagues are so vicious and the battles are so brutal is because the stakes are so low. But he loves having time for research and he's a natural-born teacher. "Chained to my job," he likes to say. Although, given the fact that he's tenured, it's more like golden handcuffs.

Evan's voice boomed out. "I'm calling at, oh, it must be four-thirty or so. Of course, to those of us laboring in the groves of academe, time is relative. Anyway, just wanted to remind you that we're expecting you for Thanksgiving. Call us. Or if not, Maura or I will call you in the next day or two to firm up the details."

Since Terry's death, Evan and Maura had more or less adopted me. I'd always loved spending time with them, but this past year I'd avoided their company. Evan and Maura were the kind of couple who seemed to complete each other in some magical way. They were so connected, so deeply in love that, as kind and generous and concerned as they were, the contrast between what they had and what I'd lost was just too painful. So I had become—in Maura's words—Our Lady of Perpetual Excuses.

I cranked up the volume and headed into the kitchen. Burrowing in the freezer, with Albert rubbing up against my legs, I heard the singsong Finnish accent of Aunt Ilsa, my father's sister. His favorite sister, my favorite aunt.

Amazing how the sound of her voice always transports me back up north. True north, that is. Over the improbable five-mile span of the Mackinac Bridge. Past the haphazard small towns, driftwood-littered beaches and deep forests that line Lake Superior. I could see and smell the woods even now, a heady, tangy scent of birch and tamarack, juniper and white pine and, in the summer, wild blueberries.

As always, my answering machine seemed to take Aunt Ilsa by surprise. "Oh dear." Pause. "I was hoping you'd be home by now." Pause. "Karin, you know how I hate these machines." Longer pause. "Well, I suppose I better leave a message." Sound of Aune Ilsa clearing her throat. "I called to see how you're doing." Pause. "Uncle Jalo and I are fine. But the weather's getting pretty ugly up here already. We've got about twelve inches of snow with more on the way."

Her voice faded as she angled her head back to converse briefly with Uncle Jalo who was no doubt holding vigil in front of the television set. "That's about right, isn't it, Jalo? Twelve inches?" Pause while Uncle Jalo mumbled something I couldn't make out. "Well, you know what I always say. There are two seasons up north. Eleven months of winter and one month of tough sledding."

Aunt Ilsa paused to let the tired old joke soak in. "Anyway, much as we'd love to see you over the holiday, I don't want you to even think about driving up here. Maybe at Christmas you can fly up, hey? We'll talk about it. Give us a call sometime. And let me know if you want me to send you more cardamom rolls." Pause. "Bye now."

Cardamom rolls. The very thought of those sticky, sweet, buttery, fragrant confections was enough to make me swoon. Every few months, Aunt Ilsa would send care packages filled with Finnish breads, all neatly labeled and wrapped in aluminum foil, exactly as she'd done when I was in college. It was her form of grief counseling.

A fat tear formed in my left eye. With a sharp pang of homesickness, I drifted away. Northward.

By the time I returned to the here and now, the house was silent. I'd missed the last message. Leaving the freezer door open, I stalked into the living room, jabbed the replay button and fast-forwarded to number three.

"Hi, Karin. It's Margaret. I thought you were working at home today. You said you had a meeting-free day."

Too bad it also wasn't also death-free.

"In any case, sorry I missed you. I'm calling to see if we can move our Tuesday lunch back an hour or so. The staff meeting is likely to run late. Bill is on the warpath about that sermon I gave last Sunday." A chuckle rippled through her voice. "Rumor is, there's going to be hell to pay. So to speak. Anyway, how about if we meet at Oscar's at one o'clock? That will still leave time for a quick browse at Aunt Agatha's."

When she wasn't poring over the latest tomes on theology, Margaret Crawford shared my hopeless addiction to mysteries. She could never pass up an opportunity to check out the crowded, dim stacks of Ann Arbor's only bookstore devoted exclusively to detective fiction. "Let me know if that'll work for you. Oh, and if Bill is as mad as I think he is, you'd better say a prayer for me."

I went back to forage in the kitchen. Excavating boxes of frozen spinach, frozen strawberries and frozen sirloin, I finally spotted what I was looking for: a nearly full bottle of aquavit. I pulled it out by its dark blue glass neck.

Aquavit is a Scandinavian fetish, a thick clear liqueur best when frozen. The first sip tastes like a cross between gin and Listerine. By the second sip, you've forgotten about the taste and you're concentrating on the warm glow that extends from your mouth to your stomach. By the third swallow, you're a convert. Or a goner.

Having poured a jigger into a sherry class, I glanced down at Albert, who had seated himself next to my right ankle and was watching me with mild curiosity. I raised my glass in salute. "Al, you wouldn't believe the day I've had."

As I related the happenings of the past eight hours, I pulled items out of the refrigerator: herring in sour cream, a pristine wedge of sharp cheddar, the remains of a green salad, a loaf of rye bread from Zingerman's Bakehouse. I dropped two slices of bread in the toaster, spread the rest of dinner out on the kitchen table, popped Bill Evans and his trio into the CD player and took another sip of aquavit.

Back in his customary kitchen chair, Al studied the contents of the tabletop and cocked his head. I shrugged. "You know what they say, Al. Under stress, we all revert to type."

For the next half hour, I was lost in an orgy of tastes and memories. Every bite took me back to the drafty old kitchen of our house in Marquette. Once again, I was sitting on a cold vinyl chair. The one held together with duct tape following a rowdy episode with my Uncle Eino whose favorite pastime, next to smelt fishing, was downing boilermakers. Once again, Eino was hard at it, moving with piston-like precision between shot glass and beer schooner. Once again my father sat next to him, drinking Pabst Blue Ribbon and sneaking me a contraband sip now and then.

By the time I'd washed the dishes, tidied up the kitchen, fed Albert and locked the doors, the sense of tragedy had receded. But when I curled up in my favorite oversized leather armchair with Albert perched on one of the wide arms, the day came rushing back at me.

I switched the audio system from CD to radio just in time to hear a top-of-the-hour news report on WEMU. Dana Lewis was the lead story. The police were treating is as a suspicious death. Pursuing leads. Awaiting results from the forensics lab in Lansing. In other words, nothing yet. No indication of the how. Or why. Or who.

The announcer moved on to the latest flashpoint in the mid-term elections. A few enraged Democratic congressmen were challenging what they insisted were fast-and-loose vote tallies across the state.

According to the newscaster, election officials were being investigated for illegally locking out citizens and reporters during the official ballot count. There were rumblings about the mile-wide disparity between exit polls and election results statewide. There was a hue and cry from public interest groups about vote suppression, too few election sites and the lack of voting machines in poor districts, not to mention the voter intimidation squads. Even more troubling, though, were the irregularities being reported in districts that used the new paperless, trackless electronic voting machines.

Electronic voting machines. The phrase acted like a tripwire for my memory.

I suddenly recalled a scandal that had blossomed and faded in late summer when an email was leaked from Grunwald Industries. Headquartered in the nearby suburb of Livonia, Grunwald billed itself as the country's leading manufacturer of electronic voting machines. If my memory was firing on all cylinders, the place was run by two brothers and a sister—or was it two sisters and a brother?—who were all big-time GOP donors.

At the time, there was a flurry of news reports that had fascinated me. A disgruntled, or maybe conscience-stricken, staffer had leaked some cyber documents casting serious doubt on the company's claims that their technology was hack-proof. Not long after, a highly placed company official with one martini too many under his endangered-species belt had promised the audience at a Detroit fundraiser that Grunwald Industries would deliver the Midwest for the Republican Party, starting with Michigan.

After the usual defensive work by the company's PR machine—comments taken out of context, unwarranted attacks by the liberal media—followed up with a few faint-hearted investigations by politicos and journalists, the tempest died down and then seemed to disappear. I thought briefly about William Bailey's unexpected victory over the state's long-time Democratic senator, Joseph Kendall.

Then I snapped off the radio, let myself collapse in the chair again and began considering the odds that Ann Arbor's finest would be stopping by a for a little chat in the next few days. Right now, it was in the category of sure thing. After all, I *was* in Dana's appointment book. Although, not being an actual client, I'd be comfortably low on the list of likely suspects.

Sitting crosswise in the chair, one foot tapping empty air, I could feel the agitation rise in waves, giving me a full-body case of the jitters. Suddenly, out of nowhere, I remembered Bixie's tried and true remedy for stress.

I took a long, slow breath. Held it for a few seconds. Exhaled.

It felt good. I inhaled again.

Stars over snow.

Exhaled.

And in the west a planet, swinging below a star.

Inhaled.

Look for a beautiful thing and you will find it.

Exhaled.

It is not far. It never will be far.

CHAPTER 8

I hate dreams and I hate dreaming. I hate sifting through all the murky, mushy symbolism for a meaning or a message. Most of all, though, I hate the hangover—that ghostly way dreams have of clinging to you, insinuating themselves into your daylight hours, infecting an otherwise decent day.

In my dream, I was in a ratty, ramshackle maze of a building. If the Mad Hatter ever designed a hotel, this would be it. I was walking down endless corridors so narrow that I could touch opposite walls. Rotting floorboards groaned under my weight. As I trudged through the dim brown haze, shadowy tenants cracked open their doors and targeted me with malevolent one-eyed stares.

I had just arrived at a T-shaped passage when I caught the first whiff of smoke. That's when Dana Lewis appeared at my side. Wearing bifocals and a kindly look, carrying a cup of tea and swathed in a shapeless bathrobe, she bore no resemblance whatever to the elegant, perfectly turned out woman I'd met at Bixie's party. I almost grinned in spite of my peril.

Against a backdrop of screams and cries of "Fire," Dana gestured for me to follow her. I hesitated. She leaned close and spoke in a stagy whisper: "It's best this place is destroyed. Follow me. I know the way."

The way to what, I wondered.

Out of desperation, I trailed behind her stocky figure, pursued by a column of smoke that curled grey fingers around my back, my legs, my hair. The hot air was clotted with soot. Every breath was an effort, then an agony. Fears scuttled through my mind like the frenzied cockroaches that poured out, black streams of them, from cracked walls and rotten moldings.

Despite her bulky bathrobe and that ridiculous cup of tea, Dana was racing ahead at breakneck pace, seemingly oblivious to the heat and smoke.

I forced myself to move faster.

Faster.

Faster still.

Just behind me, a massive beam crashed to the floor. Dodging a storm of sparks and flames, I stumbled. And woke in a tangle of sheets and blankets, panting, terrified, drenched in sweat.

Heart thundering, lungs heaving, I lay in the damp pile of linens for a few seconds, getting my bearings, not quite trusting the familiar surroundings. From his favorite perch in the window well, Albert swiveled his head around in slow motion and gave me a placid, pitying look.

"What? Cats never have bad dreams?" Still breathing hard, I turned my face to the ceiling. "Lucky you."

Kicking away the tangle of bedclothes, I swung myself into a sitting position on the edge of the mattress and covered my eyes. After maybe thirty seconds, I parted two fingers to check the time.

Seven forty-three. Not exactly the crack of dawn, but respectably early for a Saturday. And I had plenty to do.

I lowered my hands and looked at the ceiling. "Dana," my voice was raspy from sleep and allergies and leftover terror. I cleared my throat and tried again. "Dana. Rest in peace. Angels attend you."

Now what was the phrase Bixie always used? "Go to your highest good." Then I added a wish of my own. "And please leave me alone."

Not bothering with slippers or robe, I stripped the bed, tearing off comforter, blanket, sheets and yanking off pillowcases with so much force that Albert made a beeline for the door. With brute force and awkwardness I wadded the entire mess into a huge pile, then hauled my precarious burden downstairs and into the laundry room.

Once the washing machine was chugging away in a sudsy cycle, I walked back through the downstairs to the hall closet, pulled out Terry's favorite cardigan and wrapped it around myself. I rubbed the collar against my cheek and the cabled wool gave up a faint aroma of soap and sweat and aftershave.

On the way back to the kitchen, I glanced out the dining room windows. A neon blue BMW in the driveway next door told me that David was back from Los-who-knows-where, which meant that Paul would be too preoccupied with domesticities to put in an appearance today. Things were looking up.

After two cups of high-octane French roast, heavy on the cream, and three pieces of buttered toast bending under the weight of Aunt Ilsa's thimbleberry jam, my expectations for the day were improving. By the time I stepped out of the shower, I was feeling human again and looking forward to a solid day of work. After all, I couldn't be following Dana Lewis around blind corners in my subconscious if I was pounding away at a computer keyboard.

I slid open a kitchen drawer and pulled out the small antique dagger that doubled as a letter opener. It was one of Terry's finds, discovered in some dusty junk shop or other. Normally I hate knives. Even relatively harmless paring knives make the hairs on the back of my neck stand up, always have. But this one was different. It felt familiar and comfortable. The silver handle—carved in the shape of a serpentine dragon—fit neatly in my hand.

For just a second, I felt a small, sharp sting of regret. Antique hunting was a passion of Terry's I never shared. Now I was left wishing I'd tried just a little harder, spent just a little more time prowling around those dingy, dusty shops he loved so much.

Well, as my mother used to say, without action to repair it, regret is a pointless exercise in self indulgence.

I picked up yesterday's mail from the kitchen counter where I'd left it the night before and fanned it out, leafing through an assortment of flyers and bills. I looked again. Mostly bills. Not a single check.

Damn.

I thought of the other, older bills in my office upstairs, neatly stacked and held together with a giant binder clip. A day of uninterrupted work was looking better and better.

After tossing the junk mail, I went upstairs, sat down at the computer, checked my master job list, summoned my muse and opened a manila file folder. By ten thirty, I had hit my stride. The sentences were flowing sweetly and effortlessly, as if I were taking dictation.

That's when Bixie called. I pulled over the plate of cookies that's always nearby when I'm working, picked one up and bit into it.

"So," I mumbled, "how did you manage to extricate yourself from the lovely Helen? And so soon? Wait. Don't tell me." I took another bite. "She had to leave because she's teaching a seminar this morning on how to bake the perfect tuna casserole. Or one hundred household uses for old toothbrushes."

I can be such a bitch sometimes.

"You don't know the half of it," Bixie fumed. "Would you believe I found her ironing my pillowcases this morning? By the time I got up, she had already reorganized the entire linen closet and I swear she was about to tackle my underwear drawer next."

"The linen closet." I chewed thoughtfully. "You mean the one you try not to open too often because stuff is always falling out?" Physicists seem to agree that the world is destined to fall into entropy. Bixie does what she can to help it along.

"Never mind. That's not the point. Besides, that isn't what I'm calling about."

"No, of course not." I sat up a little straighter, suddenly remembering the horrors of—was it only yesterday? "How are you?"

"Awful. But Isabel Lewis is a lot worse. I just got off the phone with her." I bit into another cookie—Fig Newton, one of my favorites—and settled in for a good long listen.

"The police tracked her down early yesterday afternoon at her office. You know she's on faculty at the U of M's Center for Visual Arts, right? Anyway, she says they told her that Dana had apparently died of poisoning and that they won't know what it was exactly until the lab results come back. And she thinks they probably wouldn't tell her anyway, even if they did know. Naturally, they've taken just about everything in the house. For analysis. Food, meds, herbs, bottled water, everything."

Bixie interrupted herself and I heard a swallowing sound. Probably something disgusting but fortifying.

"So," she went on, "they asked her all kinds of questions about Dana's state of mind. Had she seemed depressed lately. Was she distant or preoccupied. Did she appear to be troubled, that sort of thing. But Isabel said the worst of it was that they seemed to think she had something to do with her mother's death."

I choked on cookie crumbs and had to thump my chest a few times before I could speak. "No way," I gasped. "Isabel must be overreacting. Anyway, the police suspect everyone. Not trusting people is their job."

"Well," Bixie back-stepped. "They didn't actually accuse her. But they do think Isabel was probably the last person to see her mother alive."

My brain was leaping ahead. "But in a poisoning case, that wouldn't matter. It's beside the point. I mean, unless someone gave Dana an injection or somehow forced her to swallow something, and that's highly improbable, it's much likelier and much easier to just slip poison into a bottle of aspirin or liquor or leave behind some toxic chocolates or deli meat. That way, the murderer can be miles away when the person has a sudden hankering for a pain killer or a chocolate cream or a sandwich."

I heard a series of loud sniffs from the other end of the line. "Sorry, Bix. I know how much Dana meant to you. It's just that..."

Bixie gave one loud final sniff. "They're suspicious because Isabel and Dana had a knock-down-drag-out fight on Thursday night. Isabel says she stormed out of the house. Big scene. The neighbors couldn't have missed it."

"But was that unusual?" I remembered hearing stories about the tempestuous mother-daughter relationship that existed between Dana and her only child.

"No," Dixie admitted. "They argued constantly. But the fact that she and her mother fought all the time doesn't help Dana's case a whole lot. Does it, Miss Detective-Novel-A-Day?"

"No," I answered slowly, drawing the word out to several syllables. "But there are plenty of dysfunctional families around and very few of them solve their grievances by killing their nearest and dearest."

Bixie sighed. "Look. Isabel really needs some advice and support right now. So I promised we'd meet her at her place this afternoon."

"We," I repeated. "As in you and me?"

"Right."

I let a whiney tone creep into my voice. "But she won't want a stranger around at a time like this. I wouldn't." Memories came tiptoeing back, images of my own misery following Terry's death. "I didn't."

"But she *will* want you around because I've told her that you're incredibly smart and calm and logical. Besides which, you've read hundreds of detective novels."

There was a brief silence. Bixie let her voice drop. "And because I told her that I'd trust you with my life."

Damn the woman. Blast and damn her. Must be those t'ai chi courses she's always taking. That business about keeping the opponent off balance. It appeared that I was going to be spending some time with Isabel Lewis. Even so, I couldn't resist one more small protest.

"Okay. But does it have to be today? I've got a ton of work. Also, in case you hadn't noticed, we're in the middle of a football Saturday."

"No problem." Bixie was all business now. "The kickoff is at twelve-thirty. The game is being televised, so that's good for four hours at a minimum. I'll pick you up at one-thirty. We can be at Isabel's by two o'clock, and you'll be back home, safe and sound, by three-thirty at the latest."

"Well..."

For the second time in two days, I found myself deep in conversation with a dial tone.

CHAPTER 9

Saturday – November 16

The alarm clock went off promptly at noon, reminding me that I had no intention of missing lunch. By that time, I'd polished off a sales brochure and was working on a list of names for a new starter-castle housing development that, judging from the photos on my desk, must have been designed by a committee of Disney executives.

After feeding Albert, I stared blankly into the refrigerator. I picked up a package of smoked turkey but it didn't have much appeal. I put it back and plucked a can of soup from the cupboard. For dessert, I popped an allergy pill and washed it down, virtuously, with a glass of soymilk.

Half an hour to go. What did one wear to meet an artist? I looked down at my faded blue jeans and favorite t-shirt, a long-sleeved lavender job flecked with colorful splotches and featuring an artsy typeface that read "Marquette 2002 Art on the Rocks."

In Ann Arbor, you're generally considered well dressed if your shoes match. Even so, I could surely do better than this.

Upstairs, with Albert watching me from the bed like some kind of emissary from Mr. Blackwell's Worst-Dressed List, I finally settled on a tweedy turtleneck in shades of orange and coppery brown that, Paul has assured me, sets off my hair beautifully. Then I wiggled into a pair of dark brown slacks and ferreted around for some matching socks.

On my way out the bedroom, I did a U-turn, retraced my steps and began rummaging around in my jewelry case. Finally I found what I was looking for: a tiny gold cross that I'd had since kindergarten. I worked the clasp, let the cross fall under the sweater next to my skin and held my hand over it for a few seconds.

Standing in front of the bathroom mirror, an open make-up bag propped on the vanity, I tried to see myself objectively and, as usual, gave up. I pulled a comb through my hair which, after a radical post-funeral haircut, now resembles an auburn colored dust mop, short in back, long in front.

Then I picked up the make-up bag and got to work. Heaven help me, I've never felt ready for prime time without at least some camouflage. Even in my pseudo-hippie days, I was always the one sporting eye shadow and blusher beneath the regulation bandana.

Bixie arrived just before one-thirty, as promised, and insisted on taking her car. She said it would be calming for her to drive. Myself, I never use the words "calm" and "Bixie's driving" in the same sentence.

Offering up a small prayer, I lowered myself into her Toyota. At least it smelled good. I sniffed. The aromatherapy of the moment seemed to be lemon. With just a hint of grapefruit.

Bixie noticed me checking out the fragrance. "Citrus," she said. "Good for repelling bacteria and viruses." A silver dream catcher hung from the rearview mirror and watery sunshine glinted on a small chunk of amethyst caught in the metal web.

Out of deference to me, Bixie had shifted all the junk that usually rides in front onto the back seat where it had joined a couple of library books, some magazines, several day's worth of unopened mail, half a dozen Whole Foods grocery bags, an open box of protein bars, a pair of running shoes that had seen better days, and what looked like a dog leash. Also a hammer.

Squirming to find a comfortable spot, I cinched my seat belt as tightly as it would go. Through some inexplicable and mysterious process, when Bixie gets behind the wheel of a car, she's transformed from a meditating, vegetable-eating, peace-loving New Age goddess into a slightly crazed female road jockey who could easily compete in the Baja 1000 and win.

Today she was running true to form. We lurched forward and in the next few minutes managed to hit every pothole decorating the neighborhood streets. At a four-way stop, I grabbed the door handle to steady myself as we swerved around a double-parked Cooper Mini, nearly sideswiping an oncoming car in the process.

Bixie refuses to converse while she drives so, to distract myself, I scanned the traffic for bumper stickers. There was the usual crop of political protests. A modest black-and-white number reading: *Kendall for Senator.* A bold, oversized blue-and-white bumper hog declaring: *When Deceit Is Universal, Telling the Truth is a Revolutionary Act.*

Then as we careened along Plymouth Road, I spotted the prize of the day pasted on a metallic purple PT Cruiser:

> *Aunt Em --*
> *Hate you. Hate Kansas. Keep the Dog. -- Dorothy*

By the time I returned from the land of ruby slippers and Glinda the Good Witch, we were just north of the look-alike malls, franchise restaurants, interchangeable hotels and high-rise office complexes that line Plymouth Road. Bixie turned left and, narrowly missing an oncoming truck, wove through neighborhoods that had a settled feel and a comfortably affluent look. In this part of town, you find a lot of brick and cedar siding, plenty of big shade trees and at least one FUV in most of the driveways.

After a few minutes, the Toyota came to a shuddering halt in front of a sprawling ranch in redwood and glass. The house had two identical wings that flared out from the front door at a slight angle. It was an audacious standout in a neighborhood of well-behaved Dutch Colonials but, I supposed, just right for an artist.

At the top of the steps, Bixie reached out to press the doorbell. In place of the usual wreath or brass doorknocker, a handsome African mask stared back at us. Before Bixie's finger had released the bell, the door opened, a hand reached out to grab her wrist and I heard a husky female voice say, "Bixie, thanks so much for coming."

The woman who owned the hand and the voice was short by my standards and heavyset, with a contemporary looking shag, sky-high cheekbones and large eyes in a shade of coffee brown that matched her hair almost perfectly. Today the eyes were red and swollen, set over bruise-colored patches. They turned my way and widened in mild confusion.

Bixie broke the silence. "Isabel, this is my friend Karin Niemi. You remember. I told you she'd be coming with me today."

Isabel blinked. "Oh, of course." I took the large, slightly calloused hand she extended. It was hot and dry. "Thanks for coming." She gave a weak attempt at a smile. "I seem to need all the help I can get these days. Come in."

Isabel turned and led us through the hallway that bisected the house. The eggplant-colored walls were punctuated by crisp black-and-white photographs of nudes, landscapes, buildings, all taken at dramatic angles. Recessed lighting created small spotlights, adding to the sense of being in a small upscale art gallery. As we moved toward the back of the house, I caught glimpses of other rooms—a book-lined study to my left, a dining room on my right and, straight ahead, the living room.

It was definitely a room worth seeing.

On the far wall, floor-to-ceiling windows and sliding glass doors looked out on a multi-tiered redwood deck. A brick patio in the middle of the yard was dominated by an abstract sculpture of a huge bird about to take flight. Further back, a copse of birch trees, unusual for this latitude, glowed against the dull November landscape. I felt as if I'd walked into a tree house for grownups. Very privileged grownups.

We headed toward a fieldstone fireplace on the left side of the room. Next to it, two mocha-colored leather couches faced each other across one of the biggest coffee tables I'd ever seen—a slab of glass set on an S-shaped pedestal of burnished silver metal.

Isabel gestured to us. "Sit down, please. Can I offer you anything? Tea? Coffee? Wine?"

Bixie's "Nothing for me, thanks," was drowned out by my "Coffee would be great." Bixie shot me a frown that I chose to ignore.

As our hostess headed for the kitchen, I lowered myself onto one of the cloudlike couches and wondered where Isabel Lewis got her money. I decided she must be a wildly successful photographer because there was no way she could afford all this on an art professor's salary.

By the time Isabel returned carrying a red lacquerware tray laden with cups and glasses, I had worked my way through a bevy of other scenarios. Filthy rich husband. Indulgent boyfriend. Brilliant investment advisor. Real estate deals. Trust fund.

As Isabel handed Bixie a tall tumbler, the tremor in her hand was strong enough to land a small splotch of water on the coffee table. Ignoring it, she offered me a pottery cup filled with steaming, fragrant coffee and picked up a matching mug for herself. I poured a dollop of cream into my cup, looked around the room appreciatively and stated the obvious.

"Beautiful house."

My comment seemed to draw Isabel back from some distant place. She looked up from the cup she was holding in both hands and almost smiled. "Thanks. It's the one good thing I was able to salvage from my marriage."

She took a small sip. "Frank, my husband—ex-husband—and I worked for five years, renovating every square inch of this place. It was the center of our lives really. I love this house." Her red-rimmed eyes scanned the room for a few seconds. "Now if I can just figure out a way to keep it."

"There's a problem?"

She nodded. "Frank wants to cash out. Sell the house and get a small place of his own. For months now, I've been frantic, trying to find enough money to pay him for his half, so I won't have to put the house on the market. Parting with this place would break my heart."

As if hearing my unasked question, she went on. "My mother was absolutely enraged when Frank and I split up. You have no idea. Out of character for her, really. She was usually so calm and wise, in a crazy-making sort of way. You know, the angrier I got, the calmer she got, which made me escalate even more."

Isabel gave a ragged sigh and gazed out at the yard, her eyes shiny with tears on the brink of spilling over. "Mom loved Frank, really loved him. Sometimes I was almost envious. She insisted that he was perfect for me. She was always saying I never gave Frank a chance, never really committed to the marriage. When I told her I was filing for a divorce, she was so incredibly pissed off that she told me not to expect a dime from her. She said that if I was self-destructive enough to give up a man like Frank, someone who was destined for me, I should also be prepared to give up the house. Which really belonged to the marriage." Her voice faded. "Not to me."

She took in a long, deliberate breath. "My mother is—was—a very generous person. So it was an incredible shock. I just couldn't believe she'd…"

Isabel's cup came down with a small crash on the tray in front of her. She sat there, fisted hands on her knees, tears rolling down her face, making no effort to stifle the hiccoughs and sobs. In a heartbeat, Bixie was by Isabel's side, patting her back and mumbling the usual soothing lies: "It's alright. It's okay. Everything will be fine."

Watching them, I couldn't keep my mind from straying into treasonous territory.

Isabel needed money. Dana had money. But to punish her daughter, she refused to part with it. At least in this lifetime.

Isabel loved the house. Passionately. Maybe even obsessively.

I lowered my eyes.

So the question was: could she possibly love it enough to kill for it?

CHAPTER 10

Ridiculous, I thought, shaking my head to dislodge the possibility that Isabel Lewis would—could—have murdered her mother.

Absolutely ridiculous, I told myself again. Then I made a mental edit, changing *absolutely* to *probably*.

While Isabel's emotional storm raged on, I drank my coffee and wished to heaven I knew how to teleport. Finally, when tears had given way to sniffles and ragged breaths, Bixie released her friend's shoulder and retrieved her abandoned glass of water. After a couple of sips, she glanced briefly at me, then back at Isabel. "So," she said in the gentlest voice I'd ever heard her use, "tell us about the police."

Isabel focused wet eyes on her coffee cup as if it were a crystal ball. She picked up the cup, for something to do, and it shook slightly as if troubled by a tiny earthquake.

"I've already told you what happened," she began.

"But it would be helpful for me to hear it again," Bixie explained. "And Karin knows nothing about what went on between you and the police yesterday."

"Right." Isabel squared her shoulders and stared straight ahead, summoning memories. She took a deep breath and began. "A couple of plain clothes detective-types turned up at my office just a little after noon. Fortunately, I wasn't seeing any students at that particular moment."

She paused and went glassy-eyed for a few seconds, as if watching an internal video. "Funny how I could tell they were police. Just from looking at them. I keep wondering what it was—their posture, or their haircuts, or their attitudes, or what my mother would call their energy fields." She thought for a moment, then went on.

"They showed me their badges and said they had some bad news for me. When I heard those words, it was like having a pair of ice cold hands squeeze my heart. They told me about my mother." Isabel took a short, sharp breath and I willed her not to break down again. "They said it was a suspicious death. Possibly suicide."

Isabel put down her coffee cup and clenched her large hands until the they gleamed like bone. "Before I could even think, I blurted out that suicide was impossible. I told them it was ridiculous. My mother would never kill herself. But they didn't seem to react much to anything I said. One of them was taking down everything in a little notebook. They started asking me all kinds of questions. Was she depressed? Had she been acting strangely?"

Isabel let out a short sound that didn't quite make it as a laugh. "Of course, with my mother, the question should have been: when *hadn't* she acted strangely? I mean, normal for a psychic is hardly normal for the rest of us." She looked at me. "Is it?" Ignoring a tear that appeared at the outside corner of one eye, she pulled her arms close to her body and clutched opposite elbows with her hands.

"I think they were doing a good cop-bad cop number. One of them kept asking me if I'd prefer to talk later. But the other one kept saying he had just one more question. It was all very polite but I still felt like some kind of bacteria they were studying under a microscope."

Bixie nudged her back on track, still in that odd gentle voice. "So what else did they want to know?"

"All kinds of things. About her schedule. Her clients. What kind of therapist was she. Did she have any enemies, anyone who hated her, had a grudge. Did she work every day. Where did she keep her appointment book. They kept going back to that one. And did she take any prescription drugs. They also wanted to know where I'd been all morning, and when was the last time I'd seen her."

Isabel gave me a hurt look, as if I were a surrogate for the two detectives. "But that was obviously a trick question, because after I told them I'd been to the house the night before, the one with the notebook said yes, that jived with what one of the neighbors said about seeing us—my mother and me—in the front yard the night before, having a blow-up." Isabel pulled her elbows tighter and rocked back and forth slightly.

"When did all this happen?" I asked.

"I went there around six o'clock. Left directly from my office, in fact. We always tried to have dinner together once a week, unless things between us were really bad. Also, I wanted to pick up some old family photos for a project I'm working on."

She stopped rocking and turned to Bixie. "Mixed media. Photographs and found objects. I was planning a new series, something completely different from anything I'd done before. Maybe call it something like Familial Fractures."

Isabel looked my way again. "I didn't tell my mother anything about the project, of course, knowing it would just upset her. But she always picked up on things. Undercurrents. Often, not always but often, she could sense what you were up to, what you were thinking or at least the general direction. In this case, she somehow knew that the project wasn't going to be all that flattering to her or to us as a family because she said something like, 'Why can't you just let go of the past? Why can't you allow yourself to heal?' And before I knew it, we were having the same old argument again."

Her eyes took on a bleak look. "Only this time, I totally lost it."

"So you argued," Bixie chimed in. "That wasn't so unusual."

"Right," Isabel nodded and brushed at her wet cheeks. "Except it wasn't just an argument. I blew a gasket." She shook her head at the memory of it.

"It was probably a lot of things," she went on. "An accumulation. My tenure review is just eight months away, so I'm under a lot of pressure to produce. And then there's the financial problems. Knowing I'll probably have to put this house on the market. And all the messy leftover stuff with Frank, phone calls and recriminations and..."

Her voice trailed off. "Anyway, I just snapped. It was almost like watching a film of myself. There I was, screaming, bringing up all kinds of old grievances. Telling her what it was like to grow up with a freak for a mother."

Isabel's voice broke again, shifting into a near sob, but she caught herself. Bixie floated across the couch to close the space between them and draped an arm across her friend's back.

I decided to add my two cents' worth. "But some families are just very emotional." I thought of my own ice-shrouded family, where scenes never occurred, hurts were never aired and anger always turned to cold, forbidding silence.

Isabel looked up from the safe harbor of Bixie's protective arm. "You don't understand. This fight was different. It was as if I were dumping thirty-five years of anger all at once. In fact, we did a very white trash thing. Or I did. I took it outside. I stormed off toward the car, and my mother followed me. She kept trying to be reasonable."

"And?" I prompted.

"And it was like throwing oil on a fire. I refused to play her let's-calm-down game. I kept shouting. I didn't care who heard. Honestly, I must have been temporarily out of my mind."

I groped for something comforting to say. "So you made a scene."

"A scene? That's like calling D-Day a minor skirmish. Actually, though, the worst part was right at the end. Just before I got in the car, I turned to her."

Isabel stopped, pressed her lips together. "You turned to her," I prompted. "And…"

"I turned to her and said something I'd never said before. And I said it at the top of my lungs."

Another pause.

Isabel's eyes took on an anguished look.

"What I said was, 'Sometimes, I wish you were dead.'"

CHAPTER 11

Saturday – November 16

By the time Bixie and I had talked Isabel into a calmer state of mind, promised to be in touch soon and pulled out of her smooth, wide driveway, it was nearly four o'clock. Bixie drove with an urgency that only those who share their hometowns with major sporting events could understand.

As the landscape rolled by, I flashed back to one gruesome Football Saturday years ago when I stupidly set out to run errands half an hour before kickoff. Four blocks from the stadium, I was forced to stop the car and turn off the engine as hundreds of students swarmed through the intersection like giant two-legged fire ants on a rampage. After fifteen minutes that felt like forever, I was able to inch my way home. It was six months before I could bring myself to drive again on a Saturday.

Bixie's rule of silence prevailed during the entire drive back to my house. But once we'd parked and the engine had given its peculiar little death rattle, she began speculating about Isabel's plight. She was outraged that the police would dare to cast their suspicious eyes on Dana's daughter.

Inside the house, still talking, she unzipped her jacket and plunked down on the couch. While she ranted, I peeled off my pea coat and wiggled each of the buttons. One of them was loose.

"Be realistic, Bix," I spoke into the temporary silence. "You can't really blame the police for starting with the most obvious suspect."

Bixie rose to the challenge in a righteous, common-sense-be-damned tone of voice. "But why should Isabel be the prime suspect? You heard what Andrew told us. When you factor in colleagues and clients, it's a big field. There's no shortage of possible murderers to choose from."

Quelling an urge to run upstairs and retrieve my sewing kit, I rebuttoned the coat on a hanger, picked off a few stray hairs, made a space in the closet and closed the door carefully. "They have to start somewhere and unfortunately..."

"I know what you're going to say," Bixie began, then reached over to pet Albert who was sprawled along the top of the couch. Bixie gave his head a few lingering strokes before picking up her thought again. "You're going to remind me that some ridiculously high percentage of murders are committed by people related to the victim."

"Exactly." I lowered myself into Terry's favorite chair, a big Shaker-style rocker.

Bixie let her fingers burrow gently into Albert's fur. He closed his eyes in cat bliss. "Well, what are we going to do?"

"Do?"

"Yes. Do. About Isabel."

I pushed back the chair, lifted my feet, and let the rocker's momentum carry me forward. "I'm not sure there's anything for us *to* do at this point. The police know their job. They're going to cast a wide net. Once they've looked through Dana's patient records, they'll be talking to a lot of people." I paused. "Including you and me."

Bixie's eyes widened, as if the idea of being interrogated by the police was completely unexpected and utterly outrageous. Before she could say a word, I pursued a random thought. "What was it Isabel said about Dana's appointment book?"

"What?" Bixie rested her hand on Albert's broad back. "I don't remember her mentioning anything about the appointment book."

"Something about the police wanting to know where her mother kept it." I stopped the chair in mid-rock. "You were over there a lot. Where *did* she keep it?"

Bixie stroked the sweet spot under Albert's chin. "Usually on the desk in her study. Or sometimes the kitchen table. It was always out in plain sight, so I'm sure the police found it."

"Maybe." I rocked for a few seconds. "And then again, maybe not." I tipped the chair back as far as it would go. "Not if whoever murdered Dana found it first."

Bixie stopped stroking Albert and sat upright, eyes wide.

"Yes, alright." I hated admitting it. "I think your instincts are good on this one. Dana didn't kill herself."

I steepled my hands, Sherlock Holmes style. "From everything I know about her, it would make no sense. I mean here's a woman in the prime of her life. Loves her work. Successful. Lots of friends and admirers. Maybe a few bad-tempered colleagues suffering from terminal jealousy, but so what? Sure, she has some problems with her daughter but given her personal philosophy, or theology or cosmology or whatever you want to call it, she'd certainly want time to heal that relationship before leaving the planet."

I leaned my head against the slatted backrest and thought for a moment. "So, to return to my original question. Why would the police keep plying Isabel with questions about the appointment book? Obviously, my dear Watson, because the murderer took it. Probably with the intention of destroying it."

I stopped rocking and began thinking out loud. "Of course, there are always her patient records. But if Dana is like most people, she was probably behind in her paperwork, so the files weren't up to date. And it would slow things down considerably if the police had to pore over all those folders and try to figure out who she saw, when and for what."

The burr of the telephone cut through a very thoughtful silence. I caught it on the third ring, then wished I hadn't when I heard the plummy voice of Allegra Stevens, shrill with outrage.

"Karin, it's about time. I've been trying to reach you all afternoon. I left three messages. I was so desperate, I even tried your cell, although we all know what a fool's errand that is."

Allegra is one of those people who bring out my dark side. It probably has something to do with the fact that she's managed to elevate narcissism to an art form. That, and her lady of the manor tone.

On the plus side, it's pitifully easy to tip her over. I slipped into the most placating voice I could muster. "Sorry, Allegra, but I've been going dark lately." I glanced over at Bixie, who rolled her eyes.

As expected, there was a small silence. A dedicated style-chaser like Allegra would never be able to resist the lure of a new trend.

"Going where?"

"Dark, Allegra. Going dark. You know. The serenity factor? No one wants to be accessible 24/7 anymore." Bixie shook her head.

"Well…" I could almost see Allegra's brain flipping through a mental card file, cross-checking articles in *Vanity Fair, Cosmo,* her favorite high-style blog. Deciding it was safer to change the subject. "Actually, I just wanted to be sure we're still on for tonight."

"Tonight," I repeated. Tonight? Oh my God, tonight. "Naturally. It's been on my calendar for ages."

"Good. You know I hate going out alone."

"I've been looking forward to it all week."

"Wonderful. Parking is going to be a bitch, so let's give ourselves plenty of time. I'll pick you up around seven fifteen." There was a double click on the line. "Uh-oh. I've got to take that call."

So much for going dark.

As I hung up, Bixie arched one of her perfect eyebrows. "Hmmmm. I seem to remember you saying, not all that long ago, that Allegra Stevens had the morals of a rattlesnake in heat. And that you were determined to avoid her at all costs."

"Did I say that?" I sank onto the couch next to Bixie and Albert and scooped up a handful of cashews from a dish on the coffee table. "Sounds like I need to work on my Christian charity."

I chomped on a few nuts. "Well, it's true. She does have the morals of a rattlesnake. But…" I stuffed in a few more nuts. "She also happens to have an extra ticket to the Latin Jazz Summit tonight. Which has been sold out for weeks."

Bixie picked through the cashews as if she were looking for some perfect, Platonic example of nuthood. "Really? So why are you escorting the one and only Allegra to Hill Auditorium? Where's Bruce?"

"Not Bruce," I corrected her. "Girard."

"Girard?" She stopped sorting the nuts. "You mean she's on husband number four now? When did that happen? Why didn't someone tell me?"

"Technically speaking, she's finishing up divorce number three and being consoled by prospect number four. Who just happens to be in

New York for the weekend, supposedly working out some business deal that would make even The Donald salivate."

We both sat back on the couch and chewed our cashews in silence, thinking our thoughts. Mine veered toward the sinister allure of my date for the evening.

Allegra Stevens is a reasonably successful novelist of the potboiler-romance genre, sort of a Jacqueline Suzanne for the twenty-first century. Her books simmer with just enough sex and scandals, perversions and peccadilloes—heavily seasoned with four-letter words and four-star venues—to have earned her minor celebrity status and a hefty income.

They have also made her a constant predator, ever on the trail of fresh gossip to feed her plot lines. Which is why I generally steer clear.

"Look," I said. "I know the woman is an emotional cannibal. All novelists are and she's worse than most. But it's going to be an amazing concert."

"Well," Bixie picked out one last, flawless cashew for the road. "If you've got a hot date with Allegra, you're going to need every second between now and then to get ready."

She stood up and began zipping her jacket. "Just keep your head down and say as little as possible. And remember. If you hear a loud sucking sound, it's probably Allegra feeding on someone's vital juices."

"You exaggerate. Besides," I went on, "I'm just background to her foreground. The minute we set foot in Hill, she'll run into a dozen or so friends and I won't see her till the second encore."

I stopped talking when I realized that Bixie was gazing over my left shoulder at nothing in particular. I'd seen that faraway look of hers before and it never boded well.

"So what are you doing tonight?" I asked.

She floated back from wherever she'd been and looked at me in a hazy way. "Hmm? Sorry. What did you say?"

"Tonight. What are your plans for tonight?"

She gave a smile that told me absolutely nothing. "Oh, I've got a hot date with a computer. Doing a little lost and found work. Kind of a treasure hunt."

"Poor you."

Bixie pulled on her gloves. "Oh, I don't know. You never can tell where these things might lead."

A trickle of anxiety began seeping upward from the general vicinity of my stomach. "What aren't you telling me?"

"Nothing important." Her eyes tried for innocent and just missed. She kept smiling that irritating smile, gave my shoulder a pat, then opened the front door and started down the sidewalk. Just before pulling away from the curb, she rolled down the passenger-side window and yelled in a cheerful voice, "If I find what I'm looking for, you'll be the first to know."

The car rumbled to life and swerved away. I stood in the doorway and watched a line of thin blue smoke spuming from the tailpipe. Then I glanced down at Albert, sitting sphinx-like next to my left foot.

"Tell me, Al," I said. "Bixie says I'll be the first to know. So why does that sound more like a threat than a consolation?"

CHAPTER 12

Saturday – November 16

The three women clustered around Allegra Stevens gave little gasps of ghoulish delight. Ghoulish because the topic had shifted from when-did-you-get-back-from-Maui? and where-did-you-get-that-wonderful-coat? to the much more titillating did-Dana-Lewis-commit-suicide-or-was-she-murdered?

Having introduced the topic, Allegra was presenting her arguments in favor of murder.

Until I heard the M word, I'd been happily absent, mentally if not physically, content to admire the twenty-seven-million-dollar renovation that had brought Hill Auditorium back to its original 1914 glory. Terry and I both loved the building and I was sorry he wasn't around to see the long overdue facelift it had finally received.

I'd been amusing myself by scanning a nearby plaque that listed the luminaries who had appeared at Hill over the last century, starting with Caruso and Jenny Lind. I'd gotten as far as Vladimir Horowitz when Allegra's voice slithered into my consciousness.

Murder, she said.

On the remote possibility that one of her three so-called friends actually knew something about the crime, or about Dana's past, I pulled my gaze back from the soaring, gloriously gilded ceiling and focused it on my companions.

The trio had latched on to us almost as soon as we'd entered the building—no small feat considering the dense, elbow-to-elbow

57

crowd that was constantly shuffling through the foyer like a loud, living kaleidoscope. Although Allegra had attempted some quick introductions, they were lost in the din. It didn't matter, really, since I tend to forget names almost as soon as I hear them. Instead, during the chirpy conversation that followed, I entertained myself by renaming the three women: Red Blonde, Platinum Blonde and Brown Blonde.

Red Blonde had just a trace of a southern accent and a voluptuous figure that threatened to overflow her beautifully tailored clothes— purple fitted jacket over a skirt in the same shade.

Platinum Blonde was a borderline anorexic who made me think of Edgar Allen Poe's heroines. It must have been the filmy, multi-layered grey dress she was wearing. She kept swaying back and forth in her tight, towering black boots, which sent the layers of material swirling and gave the impression that she was disappearing into a fog bank.

The one who intrigued me most, though, was Brown Blonde, who seemed out of place with her shake-and-go haircut, minimal makeup, plain black boiled wool jacket, pearl earrings and sensible shoes.

By mutual consent, we had moved to a nook at the very end of the long hall, next to bathrooms and cloakrooms, where the commotion of the crowd was dampened to a roaring white noise. Allegra was holding forth, serenely confident that every word she uttered would captivate her audience.

In this instance, she was right. Three pairs of eyes were riveted on her pale, perfect, oval face. I tuned in just in time to hear her declare, "The whole idea of suicide is absurd. Maybe it's a police tactic of some kind, to confuse the murderer. But no one who knew Dana Lewis could possibly believe that she'd kill herself."

Her pronouncement caused a big reaction in Red Blonde, whose smooth, plump face had become more agitated with every sentence. Toying with the jeweled buttons on her jacket, she made her voice louder than it needed to be.

"But you can never predict that sort of thing." The accent was Deep South now and I noticed that one of her buttons was literally hanging by a thread. "You know better than anyone that under the right circumstances, human beings are capable of anything. Anything at all."

For a millisecond, Allegra looked as she'd been stung by an especially nasty insect. Then the pearly veneer was back in place.

"Don't be silly, Dorey. The woman loved what she did. And she was incredibly successful at it. She practically had a cult following among the local yuppies." Allegra let her eyes droop to half-mast. "Although what they saw in her rather quaint outlook, I can't imagine."

Amazing, I thought, how Dana managed to incite envy in just about everyone, even the hopelessly self-satisfied.

Allegra continued. "As far as I know, she was disgustingly healthy. And besides, suicide was against everything Dana believed in. She was always going on about personal transformation and the power of change and redemption and how it was possible to find delight in every moment, no matter what was going on in your life, and what was that phrase she always used? Ah yes. Honoring the dharma."

That earned her four blank looks. She gave an impatient little wave of one heavily ringed hand as if to disperse our collective ignorance.

"The dailyness of life. That's how she explained it. How our time on earth was sacred and how we had a responsibility to be our best selves in every role we played. You know. The best daughter. The best wife. The best sister. The best friend. The best teacher. The best whatever."

How, I wondered, did Allegra know all this? Was she writing the woman's biography, for God's sake? Surely she wasn't a client of Dana's. But of course she did have a knack for getting people to say more than they intended, and usually more than they should, even in casual conversations.

Allegra paused for a second, glanced away and then back at her listeners again. "And actually, to give the woman her due, she gave every indication of believing all that claptrap." A cat-like smile.

"Which brings me back to my point," she continued. "Dana Lewis would never have taken her own life. Besides," the cat smile got broader and she made a point of looking directly at Red Blonde, "if you can believe half the rumors you hear, Dana wasn't totally immersed in her work. She also managed to get her fair share of earthly delights. Which would have given her even more reasons for sticking around. But I guess you'd know all about that, wouldn't you, Dorey?"

That jibe drew some interesting reactions. Platinum Blonde gave an ugly one-sided smirk. Brown Blonde looked as if someone had farted during a Junior League meeting. And while Dorey wasn't exactly spluttering, her eyes bulged in a froggy way and her cheeks had turned an alarming shade of red.

Before she could rise to the bait, and possibly derail the conversation, I turned to her. "So you knew Dana Lewis?"

As if surprised that I had the gift of speech or would trespass on their conversation, the blondes stared at me in silence. For a moment, no one said a word. Then Red Blonde responded. "Just socially. I used to see her now and then at fundraisers, banquets, club meetings. Occasionally, I'd run into her at parties, that sort of thing."

Allegra lifted her eyebrows eloquently and gave one last dig. "And of course, George knew her quite well." She turned to me. "George is Dorey's husband."

Ah, so that was it. But would the other-worldly Dana Lewis have indulged in adulterous affairs? Or was Allegra simply throwing out lines with blind malice, to see what she might hook? I'd have to ask Paul about that. There wasn't a shred of local gossip that escaped his notice.

In the meantime, before things could get any uglier, I turned to Platinum Blonde. "So you must have known her as well?"

"Me?" She gave a hip-twitch that fluttered the layers of her skirt, lifted a bony arm and began rubbing her chin with the pale lacquered fingernails of one hand. "Very casually. Only to say hello to." Seems like no one wanted to admit a close acquaintance with the dear departed Dana.

Allegra angled her head back and tried to look surprised.

"But, Vickie, I'm sure I saw you at lunch with Dana just a couple of weeks ago. I know it was you. And I certainly recognized Dana. You were at that new Thai restaurant on Eisenhower. It's such a dim, dark, out-of-the-way little place that I looked twice to be sure it was you two. I remember thinking at the time what an odd choice it was, since you hate spicy food so much."

That comment earned her a deadly look, which she met with yet another feline smile. I was tempted to ask Allegra what she'd been doing at that dim, dark, out-of-the-way little place. Instead, I looked at each of them in turn. "So I must be the only one here who never actually met Dana Lewis," I lied. "What was she like?"

It was Brown Blonde who answered. "Dana was a very unusual woman." She nodded, as if verifying her own memories. "She always seemed to have so much going on under the surface, if you know what I mean." My turn to nod. "Personally, I never would have sought out her, uh, services myself. She was just too far out for me. But I liked her. Her methods were unorthodox, but I think she really did want to help people."

The moment was spoiled—or maybe saved—by three chimes warning us that the performance was about to begin. Amidst a flurry of insincere let's-have-lunch-soon's and be-sure-to-give-me-a-call's, our happy little group disbanded and the three blondes trundled off in search of their seats and their significant others.

Allegra and I threaded our way through the crowd. As we settled into our narrow velvet seats, I twisted around to arrange my coat and found myself staring at Allegra's profile. The lavish gold and rose and teal of the auditorium formed a perfect backdrop for her delicate features. Like beauty calling to beauty, I thought.

At the same time, and although it gave me a serious case of the Lutheran guilts, it was impossible to look at that lovely, symmetrical face without thinking of a beautiful but deadly flower. Something exotic. A poisonous lily, notoriously hardy, that releases its toxic perfume in the deepest, darkest, most secret passages of the night. The scent would reek of decay and...

Feeling my eyes on her, Allegra turned to face me. "Penny for your thoughts."

The house lights dimmed. I whispered. "Nothing. I wasn't thinking of anything."

Allegra leaned close and spoke low in my ear. "I promise not to be offended. Tell me." No response. "You know I'll keep nagging until you do."

The audience was in that magical hushed state of expectancy that always makes me feel as if time has been suspended. Almost against my will, and certainly against my better judgment, I answered in a slow cadence, as if every whispered word were being dragged out of me.

"All right. I was just thinking...I was thinking that you must have a portrait of yourself in your attic. And I was wondering what it looked like by now."

At that moment, the spotlights came up, the audience fell silent, a door opened and the performers strode onto the stage, accompanied by the sound of Allegra's delighted giggle.

CHAPTER 13

"You think I had a reason for wanting Dana Lewis dead. Is that it?" Allegra looked at me over the rim of her oversized martini glass. Her voice was several degrees colder than her drink.

I played with my wine glass while servers decked out in identical black outfits glided among tiny glass-topped tables. On a dais in one corner, a jazz quartet struggled to make itself heard over the crowd noises. A sleek mahogany bar across the room was barely visible through a thick haze of smoke.

As cigar stench wafted through the room, I coughed and wished that I'd had the presence of mind to bring along my stash of allergy pills. Stalling for time, I took a sip and grimaced at the tinny aftertaste. Then I directed a glare at the yuppies-in-training who lined the bar three deep, drinking, laughing and lighting up with abandon.

How the hell, I wondered, did this place ever get permission from Ann Arbor's sanctimonious city council to open a cigar bar? And how the hell did I allow myself to be persuaded to come to this polluted nightspot? I took another cautious sip.

The answer as to how I got there, of course, was obvious: guilt and curiosity, heavy on the guilt. After my Dorian Grey remark, an act of contrition seemed to be in order. So when Allegra suggested a drink, I only made her ask twice before agreeing.

I coughed again. Then, having run out of ploys, I looked into Allegra's ice green eyes. Except to purse her lips slightly, she hadn't moved a muscle and her accusation still hung in the air, mingling with the blue smoke.

I held up my glass between us like a flimsy shield. "All I said was, based on the way you talked about her, you must have known Dana very well. So what's the problem?"

With surgical precision, Allegra impaled one of three jumbo green olives on a tiny metal spear. "Considering that the lady is dead, under highly suspicious circumstances, I can't imagine why your veiled accusation would bother me. Why the fixation on Dana anyway?" Before I could dredge up an excuse, she went on. "Oh, it doesn't matter. We can play your little game."

She nibbled her olive. "So, how well did I know Dana? It's a small town, sweetie. We knew each other to say hello. We turned up at the same events, the same fundraisers and parties." Where had I heard that before? "Not to speak ill of the dead..." She paused and took a fortifying sip. "But I have to admit I found her earnest goodness just a little wearing. And all that endless Twilight Zone business. Voices and guides and dharma and karma and whatnot. I mean, obviously it worked for her. By all accounts the woman was positively raking in the money. But how tedious."

Allegra let her eyes wander over the crowd. Finally, spotting a familiar face, she smiled in a beguiling way, lifted her glass and blew a kiss. "In any case, I certainly didn't know her nearly as well as good old George Goldsmith."

Trying not to appear too eager, I asked, "Are you sure they had an affair? Or was it just one of those nasty rumors?"

Allegra rolled her eyes. "If by that you mean, did I follow them to a generic motel in some Detroit backwater and listen in on their steamy interludes from the room next door, the answer is no. I did not." She shook her hair and I watched, fascinated, as it swayed like a heavy curtain and then fell back into place, framing her face with not a single strand out of place. I thought of my own unruly mop and fought back an impulse to rush into the women's bathroom, comb in hand.

"But I have my sources," Allegra continued, still scanning the crowd with searchlight eyes. "From what I hear, that particular passion burned itself out months ago. Still, I suppose there could have been some warm embers left over, just waiting to reignite. The thing is, Dorey never got over the fact that she was the last to know. Or the fact that George could have been so smitten with, well, such an odd woman. Dorey was devastated."

Allegra helped herself to another sip of high-octane vodka. "I mean, here was her safe, predictable spouse—the man is an associate dean of engineering, for God's sake." As if that made him less likely to stray, I thought. "No problems for twenty-five years. And then…" She gave an eloquent shrug.

I took another pull of the red stuff in my glass. It seemed to be improving. "So do you think Dorey was angry enough and humiliated enough to murder Dana?"

Allegra finished her martini in one long swallow, put down the glass, patted her mouth carefully with a large white linen napkin and gave me a don't-be-such-a-Pollyanna look. "Maybe on a daytime soap. But, really…"

She lifted her empty glass to signal our waiter. Then she turned to face me. "I would still love to know why you're so interested in the fate of Ann Arbor's celebrity psychic."

"Just making conversation."

The waiter picked the glass out of her hand as he passed and Allegra rewarded him with a tight little smile. "Karin, have I ever told you you're a lousy liar?"

"Once or twice."

Allegra rested her lovely face on one hand. "Actually, I had every reason for wanting Dana Lewis to remain in the best of health. I'm using her as the basis for a character in my latest book. So I'd been trying to spend time with her. Lunch. Coffee. That sort of thing." She made what was probably a frown, but without any telltale wrinkles I couldn't be sure. "Although I must say, she was very good at avoiding me." An arch little smile took over from the frown. "Even better than you."

Finally, I thought. The connection. "You could have made an appointment with her as a client, approached it that way."

Allegra accepted her fresh martini from the waiter's tray with a queenly flourish. Placed it carefully and deliberately on the table as if it were a work of art. Took an equally careful, deliberate drink. Used her napkin. Ten, maybe twenty seconds went by—a small eternity for someone who constantly fills up every free space with chatter.

"Really, Karin. What a ridiculous idea. Of course not. Talk about carrying research to the extreme. Why would I ever put myself in the position of being Dana's client, for God's sake? Exposing myself to all that New Age voodoo?" She picked up her drink again and gazed at a spot over my left shoulder.

I picked up a full glass of wine that had, somehow, magically appeared and used it to hide my smug little smile. Gotcha, I thought. You did make an appointment with Dana, didn't you? And maybe it got out of hand.

My imagination rolled on. Maybe, just maybe, you lost some of your famous control. Maybe that dowdy little freak learned things about you. Ugly things. Inconvenient things. God knows there must be a lot of those.

At that moment, Allegra waved. The wave turned into a come-hither signal. I twisted around in my seat. From six or seven tables away, a tall sandy-haired man began weaving his way through the crowd toward our table.

Allegra turned to me briefly, eyes glinting. "It's Jeffrey Beaumont. Girard's lawyer."

I pulled myself out of a brown study and tried to get my bearings. The wine was tasting much better. They must have cracked open a new case. "Jeff did you say?"

"Not Jeff. Jeffrey." She leaned closer, clearly relishing the prospect of a little table time with the man. "I wonder what he's doing here without his fiancée. I always imagined it would take a surgical procedure to separate those two."

Ten seconds later, Jeffrey-not-Jeff was upon us. As he and Allegra clasped hands and did their schmoozing routine, I studied our guest. Late thirties, early forties. Lean. Lanky. Very fit looking under the elegant drape of his dark brown jacket and even darker silk t-shirt. Hair carefully spiked and moussed. Blue eyes, with a face saved from prettiness by some interesting wrinkles and a slightly outsized nose and mouth. On a good day, he could pass for Kevin Costner's younger brother. And he oozed that Peter Pan quality so irresistible to women who should know better.

After the initial gushing had died down and introductions were made, Allegra patted the chair next to hers. "Well..." Jeffrey-not-Jeff gave me a look intended to melt any objections. "If I'm not interrupting?"

I moved my mouth into a smile and let it freeze there. "Please. Join us." I took another drink. This stuff was improving wonderfully. Or maybe the cigar smoke was adding a certain *je ne sais quoi* to the bouquet.

Jeffrey-not-Jeff turned back to Allegra. What ensued was a conversation that was quintessential Ann Arbor.

Naturally, Jeffrey-not-Jeff's law practice was thriving. Naturally, he was just back from D.C. where, naturally, one of his clients had snagged an invitation to a Beltway insider cocktail party. The lovely Suzanne, his affianced, was—naturally—visiting friends in Hilton Head on her way back from—naturally—a public policy conference in Mexico City. She'd just been granted tenure at the U, so they planned to celebrate with a week in Paris. Naturally.

Noticing that my glass was empty—they really were pouring with a light hand tonight—I flagged down a waiter and nodded when he asked quietly if I'd like another. It was shaping up to be a long night.

I was two sips into my fresh glass when Jeffrey-not-Jeff turned his hundred watt smile on me. Disarming as hell when he was dealing with clients, no doubt. Maybe he could teach me how to light up like that.

Allegra, sensing that it might be time to share the spotlight just a teensy bit, turned to me as well. "You've been awfully quiet, Karin."

I took another sip—not a bad vintage at all—and smiled. "I've just been thinking," I said. Only it sounded more like "I've jush bin thanking."

They both looked at me expectantly.

"Aren't we all just frigging extraordinary? I mean, every one of us?" I swept my arm in a wide arc, grazing a waiter. "All of us Ann Arbor types. Aren't we just wonderful?"

I leaned forward. "I have a question for you, Jeffrey-not-Jeff." He smiled, a little patronizingly I thought. Allegra's smile was more of the cat-and-mouse variety. "I need to know. It's very important." As I paused, I noticed that the room seemed to be spinning.

I gripped the stem of my wine glass and leaned in toward the table. Jeffrey did the same. "Jeffrey. Not Jeff." I spoke in an earnest whisper. "Do you spell your name with a G?"

To his everlasting credit, the guy burst out laughing. Which I resented, since it made him harder to dislike. Allegra crossed her arms over her fabulously expensive little black dress. "Karin, I do believe you're drunk. How lovely."

I straightened my spine. "Am not," I replied with what I hoped was dignity. Just to prove that my social skills were fully intact, I turned to Jeffrey's still smiling face and searched for the perfect conversational gambit. Something subtle and sophisticated. Something that would prove I was in full command of the situation.

"So," I began. It came out as "Sho."

I tried again.

"So." Better. "Tell me, Jeffrey with a G. Who do you think murdered Dana Lewis?"

CHAPTER 14

Sunday – November 17

When I got back from church the next morning, Lew was sitting on the top step of the small side porch, his nose mashed against the sliding glass door that led into the kitchen. Albert, I knew from long experience, was on the other side of the glass, pressing one of his giant front paws against the damp black snout that was so near and yet so far. It was a greeting those two had worked out years ago when Al was still a kitten and Lew was a bounding puppy with a gift for slipping his leash, and it never failed to charm me.

Somewhat less charming was the sight of Paul, forehead pressed against the glass, holding a platter swathed in aluminum foil. A bribe no doubt. When they heard Amelia turn into the driveway, both man and dog swung their heads in my direction.

Normally I would have welcomed a nice gossipy chat with Paul over big mugs of tea and whatever was tucked away on that platter. But on the way home from church, I'd mapped out a perfect day for myself—and it didn't include nosey neighbors.

Amazingly enough, I had beaten back the worst of my well-deserved hangover with Tylenol, chased down with bottomless cups of coffee and an hour of old-time religion. Having purged myself, somewhat, of my toxic evening with Allegra, I was going to toss a coin.

Heads, I'd take myself into the basement and spend an hour or so in Terry's workout room. Tails, I'd slip into my favorite trekkers and hike over to the Fourth Avenue Food Co-op. I'd buy a bag of guilt-free groceries and do some therapeutic cooking. Maybe make my famous artichoke and pasta casserole. Or a big pot of soup. I'd tally my time sheets for the past week. Prepare some invoices. Relieve my burning desire to dust and vacuum and put my little world to rights. Then I'd raid my DVD collection. One of the *Thin Man* episodes. Or, better yet, *Laura*. Yes, this was definitely a *Laura* kind of day.

It was a delicious prospect. Delicious and—I glanced over at Paul and Lew—probably doomed.

Paul's "Oh there you are" was loud enough and musical enough to land him a spot with the local Gilbert and Sullivan Society. He seemed aggressively cheerful, considering the time of day.

I opened the car door, gathered up my purse and church bulletin, and waved. Maybe he wouldn't stay long. Right. And maybe the Pope would decide to enroll at Oral Roberts University.

At the top of the steps, I bent down to pat Lew's silky head and looked up at Paul. "Now what could possibly be important enough to tear you away from your café au lait and *New York Times* at eleven a.m. on a Sunday morning?"

"Oh, I've been up for ages," he waved airily with his free hand. "And this seemed like a good time to catch up on things."

"Things?" I echoed, pawing through my purse for the house key.

Paul threw a suspicious look over his shoulder as if expecting to find Mr. Benson or some other nefarious type spying on us from the boxwood hedge. "*You* know." His left eyebrow danced up and down. "The episode on Friday. And I couldn't help but notice that you and Bixie took off for destination unknown yesterday, so of course I assumed..." He let the sentence dribble away.

I nodded at the mysterious platter. "What have you got there?"

He gave a complacent little smile. "Oh, just some salmon salad sandwiches I threw together this morning." Salmon salad. My absolute favorite. "I thought we should have something to sustain us while we were catching up."

There's nothing like a plate of salmon salad sandwiches for breaking down my defenses, especially after a breakfast of V-8 juice and black coffee. I put my key in the lock. "Well, come on in. You too, Lew."

While Paul took off his jacket, I filled the teakettle. Lew bounced off in search of Albert the MagnifiCat. In every relationship, they say, one loves more than the other and Lew was never coy about his passion. I dug out my stash of organic dog biscuits and went in search of my four-legged guest.

I found him sitting on the hassock next to Al's official world-watching site in the bay window. As usual, Lew was gazing up with doggy adoration at my prize feline. And as usual, his only reward was an occasional condescending glance.

Lew gently snapped the biscuit out of my fingers. I looked over at the sloped, sculptural curve of Albert's back.

"And you," I said. "Would it kill you to be nice once in a while?" Al dismissed the idea with a lordly twitch of his tail.

Back in the kitchen, Paul was setting out plates and silverware. "Where's David?" I asked. "Isn't he going to be joining us?" I thought for a moment about David's quiet, solid, steadying presence and marveled yet again at the fact that opposites really do attract.

Paul ran his interior designer eyes over the kitchen, making a few mental adjustments here and there. "David's at home. When I told him I was coming over, he said that maybe after all you'd been through lately— although honestly, Karin, I didn't give him any of the details, you know, the stuff Andrew told us, none of it. I swear on my mother's grave."

Paul's mother, of course, was very much alive and living the good life in Bloomfield Hills with husband number two, or possibly three.

"Well anyway, he said that after all you'd been through, you might want some time to yourself and we should wait for an invitation. Not force ourselves on you." He pulled off the foil to reveal a perfect pyramid of sandwiches, creamy salmon and slivered chives nestled between slices of white and pumpernickel. "Honestly," he shook his head. "Wait for an invitation. Can you believe that?"

I pulled out a chair, sat down and tried to keep the irony out of my voice. "An invitation. What a wild idea."

Paul tried to snap open his paper napkin, gave up the effort and pulled it apart. He reached toward the platter, then stopped himself.

"You're not planning on saying grace are you? I mean, this is just a snack."

I cupped my hands around the plate, sent up a thank-you and picked up the top sandwich on the pyramid. "What I don't understand is why a well-brought-up Methodist like you would have a problem with something as simple as saying grace."

"*Lapsed* Methodist." Paul examined the sandwiches carefully and picked out a plump one near the bottom. "Oh, it just seems so Jerry Falwell."

I took a bite and closed my eyes in brief ecstasy before rising to the occasion. "You know, someone once said that anti-Christianity is the anti-Semitism of liberals."

Paul snorted. I nibbled at my sandwich and went on.

"If I were to say 'All gays are the same' or 'All Latinos are the same,' you'd go ballistic. But you have no problem believing that all Christians are patriarchal, intolerant, short-haired, stiff-spined, finger-pointing, knee-jerk, radical-right…" I fumbled for a finish and finally found it. "Bullies." I paused and took a quick bite. "Did I miss anything?"

Paul wiped his mouth in two dainty sweeps. "Nope. I think that covers it nicely."

"But that's ridiculous. There are dozens of different denominations. Some you and I have never even heard of." I held up my hand to stop his next comment. "And okay, yes, the Christian Right can be a problem. But there are also millions of Christian progressives. So how can you generalize?"

Paul stared at his sandwich before taking another bite. "Because we don't hear from those other Christians, do we? When the Right speaks, they speak for all of you."

I opened my mouth to protest, but he rushed in ahead of me. "So maybe it's time the rest of you came out of the closet, hmmm?" He took a sip of beer and gave a wicked grin. "Now that's something I could definitely help you with."

CHAPTER 15

Sunday – November 17

I was just about to aim a snappy retort across the table when the front door opened, followed by the brrrrring of the doorbell, followed in turn by a joyous bark and the scrabbling of Lew's claws as he danced around on the hardwood floors.

It never rains but it pours. "In the kitchen," I called.

Bixie strutted into the room, cheeks flushed, eyes glowing. Not at all the gloomy, grieving face I'd been expecting.

Paul studied her over his Heineken. "What's up with you, girlfriend? Have you fallen in love without telling us?"

Bixie yanked open the snaps of her violet-colored jean jacket and thumped down on the chair between Paul and me. "Better than that." She grinned and pushed a tangle of hair away from her beaming face.

Paul placed his schooner delicately on a coaster. "Well spill it, hon. We're all ears."

Bixie helped herself to my glass and took a long gulp. Whatever was on her mind, it was important enough to cause temporary amnesia. Bixie hates beer. She grabbed a napkin and wiped her mouth, removing a foam moustache but leaving the grin in place.

"You'll never guess, so I'll tell you…" she began. Then she leaned back against the chair and took a slower, smaller tug at the beer.

She glanced my way. "Remember I told you I'd been updating Dana's system software for her?" I nodded. "Well, at the time I didn't really pay attention to her files. Just concentrated on backing them up as quickly as possible. And then, of course, after everything that happened..."

She cleared her throat, blinked hard once, paused for five seconds, then went on. "After all that's happened in the last couple of days, I completely forgot about the whole computer thing."

"Ye-e-es?" Paul's patience—never in abundant supply—was wearing thin.

"So last night, I dug the flash drive out of my briefcase, the one I used to back up Dana's files."

"And?" Paul prompted.

"And I found some interesting things. I discovered, for instance, that Dana was very organized. Amazing, really, when you consider that she didn't seem to spend all that much time in the so-called real world."

Bixie paused for effect. "She kept records on all sorts of things. Dreams. Ideas for articles and essays. Notes to herself. And..." She reached inside her jacket, retrieved a small multicolored silk bag, pried open the drawstrings and pulled out a shiny red thumb drive. "I also happened to find a calendar of her appointments for the past year."

I started to speak and realized that my mouth was already open. "Her appointment book? Oh my God. That's what the police asked Isabel about." I grabbed for the drive a second too late. Bixie held it just beyond my reach, smiling.

"That needs to go to the police," I said. "This minute." I leaned further across the table and Bixie lifted the drive over her head, leaving me half-sitting, half-standing and totally indignant.

"Quit kidding around, Bix. That is evidence and as long as you have it in your possession, it is *withheld* evidence. And that makes you..." I fumbled for words. "An accessory after the fact. Or something. That thing should be in police custody. Now."

Paul, who was taking in the fracas with wide-eyed glee, kept sipping steadily at his beer. Bixie rolled her eyes. "Karin. Think. The police searched that place top to bottom. So of course they have her laptop."

She stared intently at the flash drive in her hand. "This isn't for the police," she unleashed a dazzler of a smile, "this is for us."

"For us?" Paul and I sounded like a Greek chorus.

"Of course."

I exchanged a look of bug-eyed wonder with Paul. "Bixie, there's absolutely no reason for us to have a copy of Dana's schedule."

"Oh but there is." Bixie flicked her eyes back and forth between Paul and me like an observer at a tennis match. She moved in closer and placed her elbows on the table. "By sheer bad luck and ugly coincidence, Isabel Lewis has presented the police with motive, opportunity and—depending on the poison that was used—maybe even means. Given that they've got a made-to-order murderer in hand, just how hard do you suppose they're going to look for another likely suspect?"

Paul lowered his beer. "Is that a rhetorical question?"

"Of course not," I snapped, then turned back to Bixie. "Look, we're not in Mexico or Romania. Or Alabama or Texas, for that matter. This is Ann Arbor. Michigan. You know. One of those places where the rule of law supposedly prevails. And if Isabel is innocent, the police might make her life miserable for a few weeks, but beyond that she has nothing to worry about."

Bixie and Paul flashed me cynical looks.

"Well, okay. She *probably* has nothing to worry about. But that's not the point. The fact is, there's nothing we can do about it."

In the very loud silence that followed, I noticed that Lew and Albert had settled themselves in the kitchen and were sitting side by side. A small ripple of anxiety moved up my spine.

I looked at Bixie. "Please tell me you're not suggesting that we start some kind of half-assed investigation of our own. Because that would be insane."

Bixie couldn't seem to keep away from the beer. She put down the glass and smacked her lips. This conversation was taking on a surreal tone. "I don't agree," she took another quick sip. "I mean, why can't we ask a few questions here and there, turn over some rocks the police might have missed? What's the problem? Maybe we can—what's the phrase?—open up a new line of investigation, isn't that what they call it?"

I glanced pleadingly at Paul and got a blank look in return. Forcing myself to speak slowly and calmly, I went on. "Have you been watching reruns of *Murder She Wrote*?" Bixie gave a very un-Bixie-like snort. "The phrase 'amateur detective' is an oxymoron."

"I don't believe what I'm hearing," Bixie huffed at me in a chilly voice that matched mine almost perfectly. "Your shelves are filled with books about ordinary people who solve crimes."

I grabbed a fistful of my hair and tugged gently. "Yes. You're right. And there's a name for those books. They're called fiction. Let me repeat that. Fiction. Fick-Shun. As opposed to non-fick-shun. And fortunately, most people understand the difference."

Nothing. I sighed and tried again.

"Okay. Let me get this straight. You're proposing that we look through Dana's appointment schedule, which is privileged information and which probably contains dozens maybe even hundreds of names, that we pick out a few at random, then start bumbling around, lurking in parked cars, knocking at doors, whatever, trying to get strangers to answer questions that might incriminate them in a murder investigation. Have I got that right?"

Bixie lifted her eyes from the crumpled napkin she'd been toying with during my outburst. "Not quite. What I'm suggesting is that we look over Dana's schedule for the past few months, see if we recognize any of the names, pick out the most likely suspects and then figure out a believable ploy for approaching them—one that won't raise any suspicions."

She held up the flash drive. "What I'm suggesting is that we make a small effort to prove Isabel's innocence."

I sighed in exasperation. Paul still hadn't said a word.

"A believable ploy," I repeated, fighting off the distinct feeling that I was losing ground. "And what exactly would that be?"

"Well, Ann Arbor is a small town in a lot of ways. If Dana was seeing patients who were, shall we say, metaphysically inclined, chances are pretty good that I've met them somewhere or other. Paul," she nodded in his direction, "knows every yupster and stylista from here to Southfield. And you know a ton of people from your work. Plus, as a freelance writer, you've got the perfect cover."

"I beg your pardon?"

"Don't be so dense, Karin. You've got ideal credentials for this kind of work. You can call up almost anybody on Dana's client list and say you're writing an article about something or other and you want to interview them. They'll feel flattered. People love that sort of thing."

I made an involuntary sound, a kind of outraged squeak. "Oh that's a great idea. And what about the small matter of my professional reputation?"

Before Bixie could frame an answer she might regret, Paul spoke up. "Well, I suppose if I saw someone I knew on Dana's schedule, I could give them a call. Invite them to the shop. Tell them I've got a new piece they simply have to see." He had obviously stopped listening to me a few minutes earlier. "And once I got them talking, I could shift the conversation to Dana. I mean, what could be more natural than slipping into some juicy gossip about a local murder?"

Looking incredibly pleased with himself, he gave Bixie a radiant smile. "And besides, what harm could it do to just look through the names?"

In an instant, the two of them were heading for the stairs. Without bothering to slow down or turn around, Bixie called out over her shoulder, "Karin, you don't mind if we use your computer, do you?"

By the time I got to my feet, they were clattering up the steps with Albert and Lew in pursuit. Why did I suddenly feel as if I were trapped in an episode of *Spanky and Our Gang?*

I moved in the direction of the stairs. "Not without me, you don't."

CHAPTER 16

Sunday – November 17

"H. Ackerman." Paul let out a long, drawn-out squeal. "H as in *Helena*? I don't believe it." He tapped an immaculately filed nail against the screen of my Mac. I glanced down at my hands and made a mental note to excavate the manicure set Aunt Ilsa had given me last Christmas.

"She's a corporate lawyer," he mused. "Very Birmingham. Very button-down. You know, one of those women who probably wore pinstripe diapers as a baby and dressed her Barbie in power suits." He rubbed his chin. "What on earth could have driven her to consult with Dana Lewis," his finger traced a ragged line across the calendar grid, "every other Tuesday?"

His finger moved to another section. "Oh my God. This is a *gold* mine. It's like a *Who's Who* of Ann Arbor." He pointed to a name on the screen. "J. Whittaker. Our very own city councilman. Oh, and check out the following Thursday. G. Bronsky."

"Ann Arbor's answer to Rupert Murdoch," I added, not wanting to be totally sidelined in this name game.

Paul continued as if I hadn't said a word. "And—oh don't tell me—M. Madigan. That can't *possibly* be Michael. I *refuse* to believe it. He's *such* a blowhard. A total egoist. I can't imagine him asking anyone's advice on *anything*. It must be Mercedes. And look at all those appointments."

He threw his voice over towards Bixie. "Once a week. Isn't that kind of intense, considering the work Dana did? I mean, shouldn't there be some time between sessions for processing or integration or whatever it's called?"

"Depends," Bixie spoke to the computer screen. She moved the scroll bar down slightly. "If someone is in crisis, they might need a lot of work in a short period of time. Oh, look. Charles Chang, the Qi Gong master. I wonder what he and Dana were getting together about."

Paul, being blessed with a one-track mind, was still back on the Madigans. "So what could possibly push Mercedes into the arms of Dana Lewis, so to speak?"

I shifted my eyes away from the screen toward Paul's profile. "Mercedes? You made that up."

"*Pas du tout*, my dear," Paul countered. "Mercedes Madigan is the dutiful but druggy wife of Michael, cosmetic surgeon, semi-professional golfer and raging Republican. They have two children, Mariah and Mark, who—if they belonged to parents with less money and influence—would probably be in some juvey lock-up by now. Oh, and I seem to remember a poodle. Nasty beast. Name of Mandy, I think."

Bixie was still poring over the names on the screen. We were now in October, having worked our way through the prior nine months. The names and notes filled nearly two pages of my legal pad.

I looked down at my scrawls. Each entry had a series of hash marks next to it, indicating the number of times that person had consulted with Dana. On the far left, I'd noted the date of the first appointment.

At Bixie's insistence or, as she preferred to call it, intuition, we focused mainly on the last few months. Her idea was that if Dana had managed to piss off or scare someone badly enough to turn them into a murderer, it must have happened fairly recently. She reasoned—and Paul and I agreed with her—that if our psychic friend knew something that made her dangerous, the fearful party would act quickly to shut her up.

We had also limited ourselves to clients whose names cropped up regularly in the schedule—at least twice a month. I stopped to count and gave a quiet little sigh. Thirty-six. Too many.

What had slowed us down was Dana's idiosyncratic shorthand—the way she'd sometimes use a first name followed by an initial. Sometimes initials only. Occasionally just nicknames. One in particular fascinated me. Chaz. That was all. Just Chaz.

The first time it appeared was in late September. I'd noticed a couple of entries earlier in the month for C. Anderson. Chaz Anderson? For some reason, the name kept tickling my brain.

Bixie pushed away from the screen, hunched her shoulders and then lowered them. I heard a small clicking sound as she rolled her head in slow circles. She fired a question at Paul. "How do you know so much about all these people anyway?"

"You said it yourself, hon." Paul began massaging her shoulders. "I design furniture for them. I sell them chotschkies at exorbitant prices. Now and then, I can even be persuaded to help them pick out paint colors and window treatments. That puts me in the same league as bartenders and beauticians. You'd be amazed at the things I hear. Of course, God knows I'd never kiss and tell."

As Paul continued working out the knots in her neck, Bixie scrolled to November and December. We did a quick scan without spotting any new names. Except for mine.

"Okay." Bixie's voice took on the tones of a field commander. "So who have we got?" She wheeled the desk chair over to my left side and Paul pulled up a hassock on my right.

I spread my hands out over the first page. "You do realize how flakey this is, don't you? I mean, it's just as likely that Dana was killed by a crackpot cousin who thought he might inherit something, or a colleague who was insanely jealous, or a neighbor who'd been nursing a grudge for years, or... Well, we could be talking about a very long list here."

Bixie pulled the notepad out from under my hands. "Fine. Crazy relatives and feuding neighbors and nasty colleagues. So we leave them to the police. Aren't those their specialties? I told you from the start, this is about us making sure nothing is overlooked."

Fortunately, the phone chose that moment to ring. Margaret's voice had never sounded quite so welcome or so sane. "Hey Karin, I missed you at church this morning. Bill posted me at the rear entry. What are you up to?"

I stared at Bixie and Paul, who were huddled over the legal pad. Paul was pointing at names and murmuring. Bixie was drawing circles and mysterious X's and writing tiny notes in the margins.

"No good. But I'll tell you all about it in a minute. Hold on."

After giving Paul strict orders to hang up the phone when I picked up downstairs—and having to endure his pouty "Well *really*!"—I hurried down to the living room.

As I lifted the receiver, a memory bolt hit home. "Oh, jeez, Margaret," I said into the receiver, "I just realized I never returned your call from Friday. Sorry." There was a satisfying click as Paul surrendered the upstairs extension.

"Consider yourself forgiven. Now tell me. What's going on?"

"You heard about Dana Lewis, right?"

"Of course, who hasn't? What a terrible thing." Margaret's voice was quiet and sad. "The police seem to think it's murder, at least that's what this morning's paper said."

I picked up my story again. "Well, she and Bixie were very close. Truth is, Bixie and I arrived at Dana's house just a couple of hours after... after the fact." I heard a sharp intake of breath. "You know how Bixie always has to be helping. She just can't leave anything alone, especially when friends are involved. Well, this time she's cast herself in the role of Nancy Drew. She and Paul have been here for the past two hours, working out a crazy scheme."

After swearing Margaret to secrecy, I explained. To be fair, I mentioned the heavy load of suspicion that had fallen on Isabel. "So that's it. Bixie seems to be fixated on the idea that we're going to find something the police have overlooked. Or are likely to overlook. And we'll find ourselves a murderer."

Out of the corner of my eye, I caught a small movement. The living room curtains were billowing slightly, like someone taking shallow, shivery breaths. I watched the rhythmic motion for a few seconds. Probably some fluke in the heating vent, I decided.

Margaret was silent. Then she stunned me by saying, "Well, I suppose Bixie could be right. In any case, there's no harm in giving it a try." Into the silence that followed, she added, "Is there?"

How can people I like be so dense?

"Oh no, there's no harm at all." My voice came out angrier than I'd intended. "Not unless you consider the fact that we're likely to muddy up the investigation. Or the fact that one of these poor sods might have the good sense to complain to the police. At the very least, we'll probably make raging fools out of ourselves. Break a few laws here and there. And, of course, we'll be operating under false pretenses, since I'm supposed to be writing articles that require interviews with some of these people."

"Well, that part doesn't have to be a lie exactly, does it? Not if you tell them you're *thinking* about writing an article, doing some preliminary research."

I could feel my blood pressure crawling into the danger zone. "Not a lie? It sounds to me like you're doing a fandango on the head of a pin."

She chuckled. "Of course. What do you think they teach us in seminary?" Her tone changed. "Listen, I've got to run. I'll see you Tuesday at one, right?"

I grunted.

"In the meantime, do something for me, would you?" She paused for a second. "Spend a little time thinking about how much Terry loved life. That's something I really admired about him—how he'd make the most of every moment, every event. He was always up for an adventure, and he used to find fun in the oddest places."

I tried to stifle a loud sniff.

"Terry was married to you, Karin. Really and truly and profoundly married. But he was also married to life. And you know, I think that's our job here as human beings. To be wedded to life. Even if it seems pointless or scary or—what was the word you used? Crazy." Margaret paused. "You still there?"

I found my voice again, but the words came out in a croak, "Did anyone ever tell you that you're preachy?"

Margaret gave her trademark chuckle. "One last thing and then I'll stop with the sermons. Remember that poem you like so well, the one by Wallace Stevens? The one that starts..."

"The houses are haunted by white nightgowns," I jumped in. "None of them are green or purple with green rings, or green with yellow rings. People are not going to dream of baboons and periwinkles…"*

"That's the one," Margaret interrupted. "It ends with a great line about an old drunk sailor, asleep in his boots, catching tigers in red weather."

"Right," I said, surprised that she remembered so much of the poem.

"So I have a question for you."

I waited.

"What color is your nightgown these days, Karin?"

---

* *Disillusionment of Ten O'Clock* by Wallace Stevens, © Alfred A. Knopf, Inc.

CHAPTER 17

Monday – November 18

Washington Street starts out in the cozy neighborhoods of the old West Side, heads due east and dead-ends on the U of M central campus just across from the soaring glass walls of the Power Center for the Performing Arts. Along the way, it crosses Main Street and plays host to a dozen or so coffee bars, restaurants, brew pubs, and boutiques. Paul's shop, Chez Vous, was sandwiched between a Hungarian eatery and a sassy little hair salon.

As I opened the door, a series of irritating bell-like chimes went off. One day very soon, I vowed, I would find a way to disconnect that vile contraption.

Paul was behind the counter sorting through fabric swatches on a large metal ring. Audrey, his doe-eyed assistant, was in the back of the long, narrow showroom, moving like a ballerina among racks of hand-knotted rugs and displays of oversized brass and copper vases. Along one wall, a model living room featured several of Paul's pieces including a to-die-for rocker and a metro chic couch.

Against my better judgment, I'd agreed to be on hand when Mercedes showed up for her appointment to see Paul's new creations, along with his latest shipment of geegaws and whatnots for the well-dressed home. Introductions would be made. One thing would lead to another and I would charm her into being interviewed for an article. Or not.

At three o'clock, Bixie and I were heading out to corral another unsuspecting suspect, Charles Chang, this time for a phantom article on energy healers and alternative medicine. Then of course there would be the inevitable debriefing with Bixie and Paul, whom I'd begun thinking of as Nancy and Bess.

Tuesday's schedule was equally crazy: a list of back-to-back encounters with people hapless enough to be included on our homemade list of suspects. Floating in the middle, like a lonely island of sanity, was my lunch with Margaret.

The upshot was, if I didn't sleep, eat or go to the bathroom for a couple of days, I stood a decent chance of doing Bixie's bidding without missing any deadlines or ticking off any clients. *Paying* clients, I reminded myself.

Entering Paul's shop, I offered up a short, fervent and probably futile prayer: please, God, don't let the police ever find out about this.

Paul glared at me over the rim of his reading glasses. "You're late. It's one minute to two."

I closed the door. Loudly. "That's because the half-life of a parking spot in this town is seven seconds. I had to park over on William and Ashley and hike the rest of the way."

He stared pointedly at the steaming cup of latte in my left hand. "I see you had enough time to stray into Starbucks."

"You bet. I had to fortify myself for this..." I glanced toward the back at Audrey and lowered my voice. "For this farce."

At the exact moment Paul opened his mouth, the bells over the entryway gave another cascade of sound. The woman who opened the door was five foot six or thereabouts and too thin to be merely svelte. Her heavily moussed blonde hair had been pulled back into a high ponytail, leaving behind a thick fringe of bangs.

She paused in the doorway, one hand on the knob, as if to find her balance or get her bearings. Her sleek, carmel-colored leather pantsuit screamed Prada and, even at a distance of twenty feet, I caught whiffs of Chanel Number Five.

A few seconds ticked by. Standing there in the doorway, motionless, she reminded me of an incredibly bad movie I'd seen years ago about high-style department store mannequins that came to life at night.

Keeping a toothy smile firmly in place, Paul pitched his voice so low it was barely audible and spoke without moving his lips. "Looks as if someone is having a bad day. Could be good for us though." That weird little trick of his always reminds me of the third-rate ventriloquists who overpopulated kid shows a generation ago. Creepy.

Paul moved out from the behind the counter, both hands extended. "Mercedes. *Wonderful* to see you, darling. It's been *too* long." He air-kissed her on both cheeks. "You're the second good thing that's happened to me this afternoon." Holding her elbow, he steered his prey gently towards me. "Karin here was the first. She surprised me by just popping in."

With fingers that shook slightly, Mercedes eased off her sunglasses to reveal a pair of dilated pupils. The opiate eyes made her smile look even more artificial.

"Karin," Paul draped a hand over my shoulder as he spoke, "Mercedes Madigan is one of my favorite customers. She dropped by this afternoon to take a look at some of my new tables, the ones I was telling you about."

He turned up his smile full-force. "Mercedes, Karin Niemi is a dear friend of mine. She's a freelance writer who works on all sorts of fascinating projects. You've probably seen some of her work."

That little introduction earned him a slightly puzzled look from Mercedes, who stretched her smile a little wider and tighter. The long, bony and well-tended hand she offered me was hot and moist. "How nice. What sort of things do you write?"

Standing next to her, Paul did a Groucho Marx with his eyebrows. I knew this particular look very well. In Paul-speak, it translates roughly into, *Well what in God's name are you waiting for? Say something intelligent.*

I tried to oblige. "I work on ad campaigns, brochures, annual reports, web sites, e-newsletters, the occasional video script. And, lately, quite a few magazine articles."

"Ah. How interesting," Mercedes said the words almost as if she meant them. Her face had the perpetually surprised look of the heavily Botoxed.

Paul took that as his cue. "That's right. You were just telling me about that, weren't you dear?" He turned to Mercedes. "Karin is working on an article about local Republican women. Prominent Republican women. You know the sort of thing. Their lives. Their values."

"Really?" If Mercedes could have wrinkled her forehead, she would have. Instead, she let her long fingers flutter aimlessly. "But isn't it a little soon after the election for that? I mean, right now a lot of people, Democrats I mean, are so…" Her eyes moved back and forth like a pendulum as she searched out the right word. "Upset. Even a lot of Republicans I know are incredibly angry. Almost as if we'd lost the election. And of course, no one can seem to talk about anything *but* the election."

She sighed and went on. "It just doesn't seem like the best timing." Her voice faded, as if she despaired of ever making me understand.

Well, well, I thought, behind those belladonna eyes was a functioning brain. So Mercedes wasn't going to be a complete pushover. There was some small comfort in that.

"You make a good point," I said, deliberately ignoring Paul's rolling eyes, "but I haven't really worked out the story angle yet. And you have to remember that magazines require a lot of lead time. Usually, a piece written in November or December won't appear in print until March or April. Maybe even later."

I took a breath before diving back in. "Anyway, right now I'm just casting around for women who'd be willing to be interviewed."

Paul put his hand on Mercedes' shoulder. "Darling, you'd be perfect."

She gave Paul and me a deer-in-the-headlights look. "Me?" She held her hands up, as if to ward off the evil eye. "Oh I really don't think so…" Her eyes flicked around the store, probably in search of the nearest exit. I had a slightly sick feeling, as if I'd laid a trap for a puppy or hooked a goldfish out of its bowl.

"So you and your husband are Republicans?" Stupid question, but the only one I could think of.

"What an understatement," Paul answered for her. "Honestly, Karin. Sometimes I think you live under a rock. The Madigans are *prominent* Republicans." Mercedes' panicky look faded and a slight flush bloomed beneath the expensive make-up. "Mercedes' husband, Michael, is co-chair of the Washtenaw County Republican Delegation—I got that title right didn't I, dear? It's called a delegation? And didn't I hear recently that he's also involved with the Young Republican group on campus?"

"Well, yes…"

"And didn't you two host a major fundraiser about a month ago for Bailey's senate campaign?" The man was astounding. How did he keep up with all this social to-ing and fro-ing?

Merdeces nodded. "As a matter of fact, we did."

Paul grinned knowingly. "There's even a juicy rumor circulating that Michael has his eyes on the state party chairmanship. Or something bigger."

Mercedes managed a brittle smile. "Really, Paul. You're amazing."

Paul grabbed her left hand in a girlfriend sort of way. "Darling, Michael would absolutely love for you to get some press. He'd be thrilled. And he'd probably be very disappointed if he knew you'd let this opportunity pass you by."

Mercedes' smile disappeared as fast as a freak snowfall in June. "With Michael, you never know, really." She looked straight ahead and then, seeing nothing or maybe too much, pulled herself back. "Although it's true he's always complaining about how biased the local media is and how conservatives in this town never get a fair hearing."

Mercedes had that mannequin look again, as if she were withdrawing into a plasticine shell. With a determined glint in his eyes, Paul edged behind me, grabbed my arms with a little more force than necessary and began his version of damage control.

"Unfortunately, Karin has another appointment this afternoon and needs to run." He put his cheek close to mine. "You did say two-thirty, didn't you, hon? But I'd hate to lose this lovely momentum. Karin, why don't you leave one of your business cards with us?"

I gave him the darkest look I dared under the circumstances, shook my arms free and began rummaging around my bag while he continued his chatter. "Mercedes and I will take a look at those tables of mine. Then we'll have a little chat over some latte." He darted a look at Mercedes. "I've got a wonderful new machine, almost like having a live-in barista. I just know that, between us, we'll figure out how to approach Michael. He's going to love this."

As I handed over a card, the word *Judas* kept flitting through my mind. I looked into Mercedes' wary, hyperthyroid eyes.

"Great," I said, hating myself as I spoke. "I can't wait."

CHAPTER 18

Monday – November 18

It took me a while to locate Charles Chang's understated brick ranch. It was set on a wide tree-lined avenue of nearly identical houses, a legacy from the GI Bill.

In this neighborhood, the Chang home was notable mainly for what it lacked. No flimsy carport. No jerry-rigged front porch. Nothing to distinguish it but a smooth patch of lawn, a scrupulously clean front walk and, hanging in the standard-issue picture window, a bright red banner with Chinese calligraphy running down the center.

Far more interesting was the driveway, which contained one of the most amazing objects I had ever beheld. At one time, it must have been a normal looking car. Now it was a rusted-out contraption sporting four wheels and two hubcaps, a steering wheel wrapped in fake leopard fur and—plastered over a cotton-candy-pink finish—the most remarkable collection of bumper stickers I'd ever seen.

As if pulled by an invisible force, I got out of Amelia and walked a slow circle around the little pink marvel, savoring every word:

> *Ankh if you love Isis.*
> *Voting is a witch's rite.*
> *Wiccan-mobile.*
> *My Karma, My Car.*
> *Pagan and Proud.*

There was a stunning little number in Gothic typeface that read, *Come the Rapture, we'll have the Earth to ourselves.* Pasted next to the driver's side-view mirror was my personal favorite: *Don't make me release the flying monkeys.*

I was still gaping when Bixie drove up. She marched over in long, purposeful strides. With her platinum hair, cardinal red wool jacket and black skirt flapping in the breeze, she reminded me of a large exotic bird blown off course.

"Tell me again what I'm supposed to be writing about," I said, without taking my eyes off the car. "I want to be sure I'm telling the right lies."

Bixie moved closer and pitched her voice to a loud whisper which, considering that we were standing outdoors in a brisk wind, seemed a bit melodramatic. "You're writing about alternative healers in the community. Fascinating locals doing fascinating things. You know."

I did indeed know. Ann Arbor is one of those places where you can run into a rocket scientist at the deli counter or stand behind a neurosurgeon at the dry cleaners. In this town, you can't spit without hitting a Somebody.

Bixie continued in the same stage whisper. "So you've heard from me that Charles is a qi gong practitioner."

I raised my eyebrows and felt wrinkles clustering on my forehead.

"*Qi,*" she repeated, pronouncing it *chee.* "Meaning life force. *Gong.* Meaning to direct or move. *Qi gong.* Consciously directing the life force for purposes of healing." My wrinkles turned into furrows.

Bixie patted my arm. "Just follow my lead. And try not to fall asleep, okay?"

Before I could protest, the front door opened and a short, bulky woman filled the doorway. Six inches of Indian print skirt hung below the uneven hemline of her black wool coat and, as she moved, one hand adjusted a blue and black paisley shawl. With the other hand, she fluffed out her shoulder-length hair. Also black. From where I stood, it had the telltale lifeless look of cheap hair dye.

Behind her, I caught a flicker of movement. As the woman made her way down the front steps, the movement turned into a slender man with close-cropped dark hair and a calm, composed face that any serious poker player would envy.

Standing on the top step, Charles Chang bowed in our direction and allowed his mouth to form the faintest suggestion of a smile. By that time, the frizzy-haired woman had arrived at her car and was fumbling around under the shawl, searching for her keys—or maybe her broom. Feeling my eyes on her, she lifted her head and trained a glacial blue gaze on me.

What does one say to a witch?

"Great bumper stickers," I offered.

The ice blue eyes got a little icier.

"Really," I added for emphasis. Without saying a word, she jerked open the car door just as Bixie grabbed my sleeve and began towing me toward the house.

With a small, elegant movement, Charles stepped aside. After Bixie had made introductions, he gestured toward a soft-looking grey couch. "Please make yourselves comfortable. I was just about to brew some tea." He walked across room and into a miniscule kitchen with Bixie at his heels. I sat down and took in my surroundings.

It was the biggest little room I'd ever seen. Half-walls and graceful columns separated the living area from the dining space and kitchen, creating the illusion of three good-sized spaces. Except for the red silk banner in the window, the only other wall decoration was a large Chinese-style landscape done in pale washes of grey and green. The low granite-topped table in front of the couch held a pile of books, a pen, a notebook and a modest bouquet of carnations, all red, in a plain glass vase. One corner of the room was occupied by a large armoire in dark wood, carved with intricate figures of gods and demons and just large enough to hold a television set.

The entire scene had a strangely calming effect. Lulled by the indistinct murmurs coming from the kitchen, I rested my head against the back of the couch. The room was scented with something. I looked around for burning incense and was just about to take another deep whiff when Charles looked up from the tray he was carrying and gave that barely-there smile of his.

91

"Ma huang," he said as if reading my mind. "A traditional Chinese herb. Astringent. Healing." He looked at me. "And, some say, very relaxing."

All of his movements, even something as simple as putting down a tea tray, were graceful and deliberate. He arranged himself on a hard wooden chair facing the couch, filled a teacup and then poured it back into the pot. "Old Chinese custom," he said without lifting his eyes. "The first cup goes back, to be strengthened."

When we all had full cups in hand, Charles spoke again. "Bixie tells me you're writing an article on local healers."

Somehow I couldn't make myself tell this man an out-and-out lie. "*Thinking* about writing at this point. Doing some background research." I smothered a yawn and took a long sip of tea, hoping it might fend off the drowsiness that was creeping through my body.

Holding his cup lightly in both hands, Charles inclined his head in a slight bow. "I am deeply honored." Was it just my incipient paranoia, or did I detect an edge of sarcasm?

"So. Qi gong," I began, giving my head a hard shake. "What is it exactly? And how does it work?"

Charles lowered his cup. "I like to tell people it works by magic. That's because, even after all these years, I look at what it does and I think, this cannot be."

His eyes seemed to be smiling although the rest of his face was still and utterly without emotion. "Here is a force that heals wounds and mends bones, a force that draws out infection, without harm, without side effects. This defies reality."

He took a sip of tea, then placed his cup carefully on the tray. "Fortunately, recent experiments seem to indicate that it has to do with the manipulation of electromagnetic fields. Much more comforting for us modern types, don't you agree?"

He paused, took a deep breath that seemed to start in his abdomen, lifted his hands slightly and lowered them until they pointed toward me in a gentle arc. Suddenly, a small circle of heat bloomed in the center of my chest. With every shift of his hands, the heat pulsed.

Bixie let her right hand rest lightly on her own chest, as if she were feeling the same pulsing glow. Her voice broke through my slightly panicked amazement. "Karin told me that she wanted to interview some really outstanding alternative healers. Naturally, you came to mind. Of course, I also recommended Dana. But then…" Her voice faltered.

My turn. "Did you know Dana well?"

Charles moved his hands as if he were pulling down a thick invisible substance from the ether. "I admired Dana very much. She was a gifted healer. But her talents could be very draining."

The glow in the center of my chest seemed to expand. "From time to time, she came to me for a treatment. Other times, we simply drank tea together."

I waited a few minutes, then tried again. "It's wonderful that you and Dana got along so well. Especially since I've heard that some of her other colleagues suffered from serious cases of professional jealousy. In fact, I understand that the police are looking at some of them as possible suspects."

I regretted my words almost instantly. After eight or ten minutes of silence, during which he seemed totally intent on moving invisible flows of energy into me, Charles spoke. "Dana was my friend. I will miss her greatly."

In one abrupt movement, he pushed his chair back and placed his hands on his knees. "What time is it, please?"

Bixie lifted her watch hand. "Not quite three-thirty."

"Ah. Then at the risk of being discourteous, I must ask you to leave. I have to be at the U of M hospital in half an hour."

As we said our thank you's and filed out the door, I felt a small electrical surge as Charles touched my shoulder. "If you like, I will be happy to discuss qi gong with you in greater detail." Before I could offer my guilty gratitude, he continued. "But I have found that it always pays to exercise caution when entering unknown realms."

I turned to stare at him. "Are you saying this research of mine might be dangerous?"

For a second, he looked exactly like the small Buddha head that topped his bookcase. "No. I am citing an old Chinese proverb. 'Every act has unintended consequences.'"

Despite a very dry mouth, I managed to reply. "Is that really a Chinese proverb? Or did you make it up?"

He bowed from the neck. "You are quite correct. It was something Dana was fond of saying. But I apologize. Lies for any purpose are inexcusable—are they not?"

The glowing circle in the middle of my chest faded slowly as Charles closed the door with a soft click.

"You mean he zapped you with some kind of energy?"

As he spoke, Paul reached over to nab another gingersnap from a plate on the kitchen counter. He had dropped by—briefly, he promised—on his way to Tae Kwon Do or whatever martial art it was that had captured his attention these days. His white cropped pants looked slightly ridiculous under the leather bomber jacket and cashmere scarf.

"He didn't zap me exactly." Why was I sounding so waspish? "It was more like…" I reached for a cookie. "Like he flowed energy into me."

Paul gave me a round-eyed look and dipped his cookie absentmindedly into my coffee cup. "If you say so. But I don't see what motive he could possibly have for killing Dana."

"Who knows?" I refilled my cup, surprised at how irritated this conversation was making me feel. "Maybe Dana knew something about him. About his past. Maybe the qi accidentally backfired or he misjudged his own powers or something and accidentally killed a patient."

Paul scrunched his face in disbelief. "I'm not buying it. Now, Mercedes on the other hand…"

I looked up at Elvis—a minute past six—and raised a hand to hush Paul. Then I clicked on the kitchen radio to catch the local news on the hour. Same-old-same-old. The police were still pursuing leads in the Lewis case.

Paul was polishing off his third gingersnap when the announcer switched to the growing controversy over state election fraud. Once again, the focus was Grunwald Industries. A group calling itself Michigan Democrats for Fair Elections supposedly had evidence of software tampering in the company's paperless electronic voting machines. After denouncing Grunwald's refusal to release their software code for public examination, the accusers were in turn denounced by the company's perky-voiced spokeswoman.

I turned down the volume control.

Paul broke off a small chunk of his cookie and handed it to Albert. Then he zipped up his jacket and turned toward the sliding glass door. "Gotta go."

"Before you take off, just one thing."

He half turned. "Sure. What?"

"Why do you take all these Kung Fu courses year after year?"

Paul looked down at his wide-legged white cotton pants. "Well, it's not because I like the houseboy look. Actually, I assumed you figured it out ages ago." He winked. "It's a great place to meet men."

Another wink as he slid open the door.

"You really ought to try it, hon."

CHAPTER 19

Detective Sergeant Moses B. Caldwell wasn't what I expected. But then I really didn't know what to expect when Ann Arbor's finest showed up on my doorstep.

I had set the alarm for five-thirty, hoping to log a couple of hours at the computer before Bixie and I set out on our next wild goose chase. This morning we were scheduled to meet with Samantha Berger, a registered nurse and lukewarm acquaintance of Bixie's who had made regular appearances on Dana's schedule.

By seven, I was exercised, fed, showered, dressed and sitting in my tiny upstairs office. By eight-forty-five, I was deep in the zone. When the doorbell buzzed, I jolted upright and spoiled the sentence I was working on with a line of dddddddddddddddd's. Limiting myself to just one "damn" out of deference to Albert, who was sprawled Odalisque-style on the desk, I grabbed my empty coffee cup, raced downstairs and opened the door.

The man waiting for me on the other side was just under six feet. Despite the fat lazy snowflakes that had been drifting down for hours, his heavy grey trench coat had been left unbuttoned to reveal a tan wool sport coat and a brown shirt just a shade darker than his skin.

He was standing in profile, scoping out the neighborhood. Mr. Benson had chosen this particular time for a morning constitutional and was staring at the man with equal parts curiosity and hostility. When

I lifted my coffee cup in salute, he flushed, snapped his head front and center, squared his shoulders and continued his morning patrol.

The man turned my way.

"Ms. Niemi?"

He didn't serve up any smiles but at least his voice was polite. At my nod, he reached into an inner pocket, pulled out a little black wallet with his badge and ID. *Detective Sergeant Moses B. Caldwell, Ann Arbor Police Department.*

"Is this a good time for us to talk?" It wasn't really a question and we both knew it. "There are a few things I'd like to ask you about Dana Lewis."

"Well, I've got a busy day ahead of me..." I opened the door wider. "But I can spare half an hour or so."

Like a bulky shadow, Moses Caldwell followed me into the living room and commandeered the oversized Windsor chair—leaving me a choice of squishy couch or equally squishy armchair, both of which would put me about four inches closer to the floor than he was.

I put on my best hostess voice. "Before we start, would you like a cup of coffee?"

The bottomless brown eyes looked at me with no expression whatever. "Sure. Sugar no cream. Thanks."

Five minutes later, I was carrying a tray crowded with mugs, cream, sugar, coffee pot and a plate of oatmeal cookies when the phone rang. I stopped in my tracks for a second, considered the distance to the living room and decided to let the answering machine pick up.

Pity that Dana Lewis wasn't around just then to warn me I was making a very big mistake. Three rings later, as I lowered my burden onto the coffee table, Bixie's voice seemed to fill every available space.

They say that timing is everything but somehow Bixie never got that memo. Ever since I've known her, she's shown a remarkable knack for being in the wrong place at the wrong time—as, for example, our foray to Dana's house on that fateful Friday morning—and for saying the wrong thing to the wrong person.

At least she's consistent.

"Karin, did you catch the local news a few minutes ago?" Her words tumbled out. "A U of M computer engineering student committed suicide. At least they're calling it suicide. He jumped off the parking structure at Miller and Ashley."

I didn't move a muscle, just stood where I was, bent over, holding onto the tray handles, waiting for the other shoe to drop. "His name," she slowed down to make sure I heard every syllable, "was Charles Anderson. C. Anderson. Sound familiar?"

Damn damn damn damn.

I considered reaching across Detective Sergeant Moses B. Caldwell to pick up the phone, but his eyes were locked on mine with a don't-even-think-about-it look.

I sent out a thought wave: *Stop. Now.* But Bixie's voice flowed on. "He was the one who had so many appointments with Dana during September."

As I straightened up, I realized my fingers were numb from clutching the tray so tightly. Bixie kept going. "Evidently he went by the name of Chaz." Brief pause. "So obviously, this changes everything. I'm going to call Isabel and find out if she knows anything about this guy. And I think we should cancel our interview with Samantha. Suddenly, she's looking much less like a murder suspect."

Uncurling my fingers with great difficulty and trying to keep my face composed, I sat on the couch and fussed with the coffee things as Bixie began wrapping up her endless—and, from the look on the detective-sergeant's face, disastrous—message.

"Anyway, we need to restrategize. So I'll call you after I talk to Isabel. Do me a favor would you? If you leave the house, take your cell phone with you. And turn it on." The click of the receiver was followed by a loud, long silence.

I kept my eyes glued to the coffee cups, poured, added some cream to mine, began stirring. And kept stirring, not daring to lift my eyes.

Moses Caldwell was the first to speak. "Restrategize? Suspects?"

"Yeah, well," I stirred my coffee furiously. "Unusual word choices."

He pulled out a small notebook and uncapped his pen. "Let's start at the beginning, shall we?"

Twenty-five minutes later, the detective sergeant had a Cliff's Notes version of my life story and the truth, more or less, about what Bixie and I had been up to. I'd left Paul out of it, seeing no reason to drag him into the melée.

Caldwell looked up from his notebook and tapped his pen against his knee. "Let's recap." He flipped back five or six pages and began reading. "According to what you've told me, your friend Bixie Murray convinced you to consult with Dana Lewis, who she's known for years, to help you through your grief over the loss of your husband."

His voice was so matter-of-fact, it gave his words all the drama of a laundry list. Yet every syllable seemed ominous

"Against your better judgment," he punctuated the phrase by glancing up at me. "Against your better judgment, you scheduled an appointment with Ms. Lewis and, purely by coincidence, you and Ms. Murray arrived at the victim's home not long after her death." He looked up again and went off script. "That fits with our records anyway."

Back to the notes.

"Ms. Murray was extremely upset and insisted from the start that Ms. Lewis must have been murdered. She also believed that the police would botch the investigation and convict the wrong person." The Detective Sergeant frowned. "Most likely Dana Lewis' daughter, Isabel. With that as her argument, she convinced you to help her launch her own investigation to make sure that justice would be done."

My turn for some throat clearing. "When you put it like that, it sounds ridiculous. Doesn't it?"

The take-no-prisoners look stayed firmly in place. "So who have you interviewed so far?"

"No one," I lied and realized I'd spoken too quickly. "We were going to start today."

"Ms. Niemi," he went on in a weary, fed-up voice. My shoulders inched upward, as if to ward off a blow. "I couldn't help but notice that you have a sizable collection of detective novels."

He leaned toward me to give his words more force. "Well I have news for you. In the real world, it doesn't work that way. Little old ladies and bookstore owners and bored housewives don't solve crimes. Even hotshot reporters rarely solve crimes. Private detectives don't either, not usually. The police solve crimes." He snapped his notebook shut. "When they're allowed to do their job, that is."

He let that sink in before going on. "Has it occurred to you that if there's a murderer out there—and we're pretty sure there is—then that person is scared and dangerous and probably feeling pretty reckless right now? So you and your little friend are not only compromising an official investigation, you're also endangering your own lives."

Had it ever crossed my mind? My little friend? The anger that had been simmering just under the surface—anger at Bixie, at myself and, most especially, at Detective Sergeant Caldwell—threatened to erupt. Only the fact that his face was now looking very much like an Easter Island monolith persuaded me to swallow my words.

"The last thing we need is a couple of gung-ho amateurs screwing up our investigation." I felt a burst of heat along my cheeks. "I better not hear from anyone that you two have been continuing with your so-called inquiries. Because if I do, you will find yourself in deep, deep trouble."

"But..." I murmured.

"Obstructing justice," he cut me off. "Impeding an investigation. Interfering with a witness. Those are serious charges. And I'm sure I could find a few more." He slipped his notebook into an inside jacket pocket. "Leave it to the police, Ms. Niemi."

I swallowed hard. Twice. While I was exercising my throat muscles, Detective Sergeant Caldwell stood up and reached behind him for his coat. I followed him to the door. As he stopped to do up some buttons, I gripped the doorknob, trying to collect some shreds of dignity, my hand clammy against the cold metal.

From one of his many pockets, he drew out a business card and handed it to me. "If you hear anything that pertains to this case, anything at all, call me. Immediately. Is that clear?"

I took the card and listened to the faint sound of my teeth grinding. "Very clear."

He stepped over the threshold, then turned around and nodded. "Thanks for the coffee."

I watched him trudge through the snow, kicking a messy path on his way to the black Crown Victoria that waited for him at the curb. Back inside, I pressed my forehead against the door. Then temporarily forgetting the basic laws of physics, I lifted one moccasin-clad foot, gave the door a much harder kick than I'd intended and let out a "Goddamnit" that propelled Albert halfway up the steps.

After limping into the living room, I plunked down next to the phone and, massaging my wounded toes with one hand, used the other hand to yank the phone out of its cradle.

I jabbed out Bixie's number and nearly slammed the receiver back down when her recording kicked in. By the time she reached the "please leave a message" part, I was ready to explode.

"Just wanted to let you know I had a visitor this morning." My voice vibrated with rage. "Detective Sergeant Moses Caldwell. He happened to be here when you left your message. In fact, he and I spent a fair amount of time discussing it. Oh, and I thought you should also know that as of," I looked at my watch, "nine fifty-eight this morning, you and I are officially and permanently off the case. I have been utterly humiliated. Not to mention threatened. Sort of." I let out an exasperated breath. "I can't believe I let you talk me into this."

I slammed down the phone with a surge of righteousness. So that was that. Adventure over. Case closed.

Albert, who had returned during my outburst, was sitting in the middle of the room, completely immobile, staring up into the empty air with a rapt expression. I watched him as I struggled to get my breathing under control.

He didn't move except to cock his head, the way he did when he was listening to someone. A human-type someone.

Suddenly, a chill ran down my spine. For one crazy second, I could have sworn there was another presence in the room.

As I massaged my throbbing foot, I thought about how Dana had continued to plague my dreams. To the point that I'd started sleeping in the big leather armchair downstairs.

And lately, as if that weren't bad enough, at odd moments I'd catch sight of something out of the corner of my eye. A fleeting, flickering, dark, shadowy something that was roughly the size of a human being. But when I turned to look at it straight on, whatever it was disappeared.

And now with Charles—Chaz—Anderson dead…

As Albert watched whatever or whoever he was watching, I found myself wondering.

Was I being haunted?

And if so, by one ghost? Or two?

CHAPTER 20

Tuesday – November 19

Every town has a dark little secret—something you won't find on the chamber of commerce web site. Ann Arbor is no exception. Walk down almost any street, step into almost any restaurant, browse in almost any shop, and within a few minutes you'll discover it for yourself.

The city has an Attitude problem.

The Attitude made local headlines a few years back when two earnest undergraduates from somewhere in the heartland launched a "Smile Ann Arbor" campaign to counteract the town's frosty atmosphere. It failed miserably, of course. Not from any active opposition. It just fizzled out, like a lit match hitting a wintry puddle.

I remembered all this as I sat in Oscar's, waiting for Margaret to appear. In that self-consciously cool place, every patron gets a hefty serving of Ann Arbor Attitude along with the daily special.

My server was a case in point.

Just this side of twenty, she looked out at the world from under heavy lids caked with soot-grey eye shadow. Her short hair, the color of orange juice, had been moussed into angry little porcupine tufts. The metal stud in one nostril was set off by a silver ring that pierced her lower lip. She wore a form-fitting black T-shirt that read *Ann Arbor: 17 Square Miles Surrounded by Reality*. A tattoo in the shape of a chain adorned the three-inch border of bare skin between her shirt and her low-slung dusty black pants.

Hip cocked, gaze riveted on the table directly behind mine, she asked in a voice of exquisite boredom if I wanted anything to drink while I waited. Just to keep things exciting, I asked for water with a slice of lemon.

She shifted her eyes briefly in my general direction and decided I dressed too much like her mother to merit anything but disdain. The smoky gaze returned to distant vistas. "That's all?"

"For now."

She shrugged. "You got it." And away she glided, never once lifting her feet.

On a low room divider next to my table, an oversized goldfish bowl—normally filled with multicolored condoms and little cards advertising an AIDS hotline—had been stuffed with straggly looking bamboo plants. I studied my fellow diners. Among the usual assortment of geeky young men with laptops, intense young women with laptops and middle-aged business types, laptops optional, was a long table of older women laughing raucously and wearing red hats. There were also a few highly visible out-of-towners—mostly females in designer jeans, stiletto heels, overabundant jewelry and sky-high hair.

Given the atmospherics, you might wonder why anyone would subject themselves to Oscar's. The answer is simple. For the incredible food, of course. I picked up one of the oversized menus and had just begun salivating when I caught sight of Margaret.

As she squeezed her plump frame between the tables, calling out cheerful apologies and beaming good will at one and all, I decided—not for the first time—that Margaret was probably some kind of saint. Not a major league saint. Maybe not even a minor league saint. But a farm team saint. Practical. Down to earth. Quietly effective. I decided it was a shame that Lutherans couldn't be canonized.

By the time she slotted herself into the chair opposite mine, she had single-handedly transformed the atmosphere of the place from sulky chic to half-hearted cheerfulness. She'd also managed to buoy up my own spirits, all without saying a word. Margaret is like that.

"Been waiting long?" she asked, peeling off layers. A shapeless navy blue jacket. A raspberry colored scarf that should have been living in a

Salvation Army bin. Lumpy gloves, hand knitted in rainbow-colored yarn and beginning to unravel.

"Just long enough to make a new friend."

"That's nice." Margaret is oblivious to sarcasm. She also frowns on gossip, except in her weaker moments.

By mutual consent, she and I have an order-first, talk-later policy. We pored over our menus and when the server finally showed up, a few degrees warmer thanks to Margaret's sunny presence, we were ready. With a little sigh that was second cousin to a whimper, Margaret ordered the Vegetable Delight Salad, dressing on the side. I opted for a goat cheese and asparagus omelet with extra bread.

Margaret sighed again and took a sip of water. "And I suppose you'll have dessert, too, won't you?" She already knew the answer. "Do you have any idea of how lucky you are to be blessed with that cock-eyed metabolism of yours?"

Time to change the subject. "So, have you been properly chastised for spouting heresy from the pulpit?"

Margaret, elbows on the table, cupped her face in her hands. "It hardly qualifies as heresy. Bill asked me to preach on the first commandment. *I am the Lord your God. You shall have no other gods before me.* So that's what I did. I just offered a new perspective. Opened the door to let in some fresh air."

"Fresh air?" I laughed out loud. "More like gale force winds. I was there, remember? Your main point was that…wait a sec, I want to get this right…was that anything we allow to stand between us and a direct, personal experience of the living God, anything at all, including the Bible, qualifies as idolatry. You know, a few hundred years ago, that kind of talk would have earned you a one-way ticket to the stake." I took a pull at my water. "Actually, it probably still does in parts of Mississippi."

As usual, Margaret remained unruffled. "I made it very clear that, depending on how it's used, the Bible can either be a powerful guide for spirituality or a stumbling block." She shrugged.

"If it's any consolation, I don't think I've ever seen the congregation so…uh… attentive during a sermon." Aghast and appalled was more like it. I leaned across the table. "It was brilliant, Margaret. Really. But you must have known the effect it was going to have."

"Well, you know what I always say. The job of a pastor is to comfort the afflicted..."

We finished the sentence together: "And afflict the comfortable."

I went on. "Even so, I'm surprised Bill didn't put you on probation, or whatever it is senior pastors do to renegade junior pastors."

"Let's just say that this junior pastor is going to be on a very short leash from now on. Bill has *requested*," she made little quotation signs with her fingers, "that I submit all my sermons to him by Friday morning to avert any further incidents." There was no rancor in her voice. No poor-me overtones. Not even the merest hint of a whine.

Before we could take the conversation any further, our food arrived and we pounced on our plates. Jousting with Moses B. Caldwell had given me a voracious appetite, or maybe it was the fact that I'd decided to drain off some tension by walking the mile and a half to Oscar's.

A muffled set of chimes sounded from the depths of my purse. Margaret looked startled. "Is that your cell?"

"I believe so," I managed to answer between bites.

"You have your cell with you? And it's ringing?"

I stopped chewing to listen. "It appears to be."

"Amazing. Are you going to answer it?"

The chimes stopped.

"No."

Ever the diplomat, Margaret refocused on her salad. After a few more bites, she let her fork hover in mid-air. "So how are things going in the world of Nancy Drew? Detected anything interesting lately?"

For a few seconds, I was back in my living room, more scared than I wanted to admit but more resentful than scared, meekly submitting to the expert bullying of Moses B. Caldwell.

I put down my fork and gave her a blow-by-blow of my disastrous encounter with the detective sergeant. She took in every word, nodding now and then, munching thoughtfully on her organic lettuce. When I'd finished, she cocked her head, looked at me with guileless green eyes and asked, "So what are you going to do?"

I cut myself a wedge of egg, scooped up the creamy stream of cheese that drizzled out and topped it all with a bite-size piece of asparagus. "What do you *think* I'm going to do? What would any sane person do?

Back off, of course. I always thought it was a terrible idea anyway—trying to out-police the police."

We chewed in silence for a minute. Finally, I gave in. "Okay. What do you think I should do?"

Margaret smiled sweetly. "Whatever you feel compelled to do. Whatever your conscience calls you to do." She speared a crouton. "What do you think Dana Lewis would want you to do?"

That caught me off guard. "I thought you were going to ask what Terry would want me to do."

Margaret grinned like an elf. "That was next."

CHAPTER 21

Tuesday – November 19

Margaret pushed a stray piece of radicchio around her plate. "Look, I can't advise you but…"

I never heard the rest of her thought because, at that moment, a giant decked out in a Detroit Tigers' warm-up jacket and leather cowboy hat stepped up to our table and bellowed her name. Margaret looked up at him with genuine pleasure and took the hand he extended. "George Morrison. Great to see you." Then, craning her neck, she spoke to a tiny woman standing behind him, nearly eclipsed by his bulk. "And Janis. What brings you two here?"

George looked around, spotted a free chair, dragged it noisily across the floor and plunked himself down in it. Smiling broadly at his companion, he pointed at another empty chair. "Grab a seat, hon."

While all this was going on, Margaret made introductions. George engulfed my hand in one warm paw and, with the other, began rummaging through the scruffy canvas briefcase on his lap. "We just got out of a meeting at Democratic campaign headquarters. A group of us have decided to organize a series of public protests over the vote stealing."

Margaret and I exchanged glances. Meanwhile, George found what he'd been searching for and pulled out a brochure. The cover was dominated by the words: *Voting Rights*. Only *Rights* had an X through it and had been replaced by the word *Wrongs*. Beneath it was the message: *Election Fraud in Michigan and What You Can Do About It.*

He handed one to me, found another one for Margaret, and then asked in an outsized voice, "Have you been keeping up with this crap in the news? It's unbelievable. There's practically a new scandal breaking every hour."

Before Margaret could answer and before I could change the subject, he grabbed the brochure from my hand, opened it to a long list of bullet points and tapped the page. "Just take a look."

George waved the brochure like a small flag. "First, there's the Secretary of State, who also happens to be honorary co-chair of the Bailey for Senate campaign. Can you say conflict of interest?"

He gave the trifold a sharp slap as if, somehow, he could transfer his rage directly to the Secretary of State. "But I have to hand it to him, that sonofabitch didn't miss a single dirty trick."

The brochure quaked in George's grasp. "Weeks before the election, he started rejecting voter registration applications based on paper weight." Sensing my lukewarm interest, he inched his face closer to mine. "The weight of the paper." He let out a noisy stream of air through his nose. "Even though the forms that were being submitted by voters were the same ones, on the same paper, that had been used legally for years." George wagged his head back and forth like a distraught lion.

"Then the Republicans picked out some thirty-five thousand voters, most of them minorities, for intimidation. Some were threatened, some were given the wrong date for the election, some were told to go to the wrong polling places." He took another chop at the brochure, which was beginning to buckle under his attacks.

"That wasn't bad enough. They also got on the phone to several thousand people. Some had been convicted of misdemeanors, some had recently been released from prison, some were waiting for trial, but every one of them could have voted legally. Only the folks at the phone bank told them that if they showed up at the polls, they'd be arrested. Nice."

Another whack at the brochure.

"Meanwhile, the Secretary of State was doing everything he could to restrict provisional ballots. Plus, thousands of people who had requested absentee ballots never got them on time." I winced as the brochure endured yet another mighty whap.

"And those assholes were just warming up." His eyes gripped mine and refused to let go. He moved his finger down the list. "The Secretary of State is responsible for allocating voting machines. So naturally, the wards with the most voting machines also happened to be the wards that polled heavily Republican. And the wards with the fewest and oldest machines tended to be pro-Democrat."

I should have been more interested and under normal circumstances I would have been. But at that moment all I could think of was my morning fiasco and Oscar's dessert menu. Margaret was gazing with rapt attention at George's large, angry face.

He droned on. "In heavily Democratic precincts, thousands of voters had to wait outside in the rain for up to eight hours. A lot of them never even made it into the polls. Meanwhile, in the richer, whiter suburbs, voters were breezing in and out."

His baritone bounced off the tin ceiling and hard enameled walls. Across the room, several patrons grinned and gave a thumbs-up sign. One young woman glared at us and pulled her laptop closer.

I stifled a sigh. George paused for a quick breath. "And how about those mysterious electronic voting machines? Almost every one of them manufactured by Michigan's own Grunwald Industries—otherwise known as Bailey Backers, Inc."

He entered my air space again and brought his eyes level with mine. "Do you know what professional computer hackers call them? The machines that is, not the company?" I shook my head. "Black Boxes. Push and Pray Technology. And why?" I shrugged. "Because you never know what happens to your vote."

He grabbed a hunk of his hair and bellowed. "My God, you want anomalies? You want high crimes and misdemeanors?"

At that moment, all I wanted was a piece of Oscar's Death by Chocolate Cake and a cup of coffee. Even so, I tried to look interested.

"In one county alone, more than ten thousand votes were lost due to unexplained, untraceable glitches in the machines. And those are just the ones we know about. Statewide, more than fifty-three thousand ballots were spoiled by computer error and were never inspected. Never will be."

He shook the brochure which by now was in a state of collapse.

"Hundreds of people who tried to vote for Kendall—possibly more, but we won't know that till all the official complaints are in—reported that the machines flipped their votes into the Bailey column. And some precincts showed a lot more votes than there were voters. In one case, after the voting had stopped, poll workers say that the tally suddenly jumped by five thousand votes in favor of Bailey. No idea where they came from."

George let out a gust of air and started in again. "Oh, and did I mention that last month *Popular Science* ran an article on the election debacle that was likely to result from electronic voting machines? And this month, *Popular Mechanics* featured a piece on how easy it is to rig electronic voting machines."

After a quick swig from my water glass, George was ready for the next round. Fortunately, Janis chose that moment to intervene by placing one small hand lightly on the arm that held the brochure. She closed her other hand gently over the fingers that were doing the paper whapping.

"Hon, that's enough. They can read all about it for themselves. Later."

"But I haven't gotten to the irregularities in the vote counting yet."

Janis persisted. "We really should go. I've got to get back to work."

Looking as if someone had slapped him hard, George handed me the battered brochure. Then his face lit up. "Hey. Why don't you two come to the election celebration on Friday night? Seven thirty at the Grotto."

Margaret hesitated. "A celebration? What exactly is there to celebrate?"

Giving George a series of shoulder pats as if he were a large, well-trained St. Bernard, Janis answered in a soft voice. "Well, we managed to elect two key Congressional representatives. Southeastern Michigan came out strong for Kendall. And as usual, the Upper Peninsula was rock solid Democratic. So Michigan is still pretty much a blue state."

Margaret voiced her approval. "I hadn't looked at it that way."

George perked up. "So you'll come?"

"Maybe," Margaret answered. "But it will have to be an early night for me. I've got a funeral Saturday morning. What about you, Karin?"

The morning had left me in no mood for celebrating anything. Besides which, the Grotto—essentially a series of catacombs carved out of raw earth, a sort of glorified Michigan basement—triggers my latent claustrophobia. Thirty seconds in those clammy, rock-lined rooms and I start hyperventilating.

"Thanks, but I've got plans for Friday night."

As George and Janis said their good-by's, my cell phone went off again. That made three times in the past hour. Margaret squinted hard at me, until finally courtesy gave way to curiosity and she asked, "Do you have any idea who's been calling you?"

"I have a feeling it's probably Bixie."

"And?"

"And I'm not ready to talk to her. But I want to be able to tell her that I did what she asked. I turned on my phone and took it with me."

To her credit, Margaret said not a word. No homily. No finger wagging. The bill arrived, and as she ferreted around for bills and change in her exhausted-looking wallet, she apologized. "Bill asked me to take over one of his committee meetings this afternoon. Penance, I suppose. So I'll have to pass on Miss Marple's."

She began rewrapping herself in her shabby layers. Then she reached into her jacket pocket and pulled out a crushed scrap of paper. "Here's something I came across the other day. You might find it helpful." She smiled and shrugged. "Or not."

I ironed out the paper with my hands and looked at the four lines of type. "It's from the Book of Thomas," she explained. "Part of the Gnostic gospels. A new translation."

I read the words out loud:

> *If you bring forth what is within you,*
> *What is within you will save you.*
> *But if you do not bring forth what is within you,*
> *What is within you will destroy you.*

I looked up at Margaret. Her face was surrounded by what appeared to be a cherry-red halo but was actually a very large beret.

"Gee thanks," I said, knowing my sarcasm was wasted on her. "This makes everything crystal clear."

From *The Gnostic Gospels* by Elaine Pagels (Random House, Inc.), © 1979 Elaine Pagels

CHAPTER 22

Tuesday – November 19

I used to think of myself as a decisive person, a competent person, a hard-to-tip-over person. Terry's death forced me to realize how much of that confidence was actually the result of all the endless conferring and easy chatter that take place in a good marriage—all the by-the-way's and what-do-you-think's and how-about's.

Big decisions, small decisions, major dilemmas, stupid little no-brainers. Whatever it was, Terry and I talked about it and worked through it, together.

Together.

Only now there was no together.

As I gripped the edge of the wobbly café table, my throat began to burn with the peculiar aching heat that comes from unshed tears. I stared down at my coffee cup and empty dessert plate, willing myself not to cry.

Time to trot out my mantra.

I am the Queen of England. The Queen of England. The Queen of England.

I pictured Elizabeth in the glare of the cameras at Princess Di's funeral, ramrod spine, dignified and dry faced, while so many around her surrendered to wayward sniffles and outright sobs.

I am the Queen of England. Nothing can make me cry. I am the Queen of England. No one must ever see me cry.

Sounds crazy, I know, but it never fails. Sitting there in Oscar's, I lengthened my neck and stared regally as the last of the lunchtime crowd collapsed their laptops, buttoned their trendy coats and headed back to their offices. Then I called for my bill and joined the parade.

As I walked home, I tried to sort out all the facts and feelings that swirled through my head. But it was hopeless, like trying to organize a waterfall. I was deluged with images, fragments of conversation, flash-frozen scenes, faces. Mainly faces.

Dana. Isabel. Bixie. Paul. Andrew. Allegra. The Blondes. Charles Chang. Mercedes Madigan. Moses B. Caldwell. And now the mysterious—and dead—Charles Anderson. Chaz.

No good. I mentally blotted out the faces. Words, I reminded myself. Stick to words. That's what you do best.

I tried again.

Dana Lewis, by all accounts an extraordinary woman, is murdered. A tragedy, yes. But just one tragedy in a world of tragedies. Every day, nearly four thousand children die from starvation and disease. So why should it matter so very much when a well-heeled, middle-aged psychic is killed in an affluent Midwestern town? And more to the point, what makes that particular tragedy my responsibility? Because Bixie insists that it is? That it should be? Everyone knows Bixie is wound way too tightly. Why should I let myself be pulled into her personal craziness? Where does one draw the line between friendship and folly? More important, why did I feel so guilty about letting Bixie down? Or, stranger still, about letting Dana Lewis down?

Every shred of common sense is telling me to chuck it, to go back to my normal, safe, empty life. But is it common sense, really, or am I deceiving myself? When does common sense become a smoke screen for personal convenience? Or, worse, for personal cowardice? Was it cowardice that was driving me? Or an instinct for survival? When does danger become acceptable? When does defiance become the better path? When does craziness slip over the boundary into valor? How do we know when it's time to throw off our blankets and furs, stand up and dance around the campfire? Whoa. Now there's a thought worthy of Bixie.

Leave it to the police. I've been told to leave it to the police. Told *by* the police. But it's not as if the police never make mistakes, never follow the wrong leads. I mean, what if I did nothing and Isabel was wrongly convicted of murdering her mother?

Of course, there's always the possibility that she actually did murder her mother. And either way, what will my blundering accomplish? I mean, really, what have we got? Some names in an appointment book. A lot of guesswork.

And then there's Saint Margaret and all that business about being wedded to life. What is that supposed to mean anyway? Why can't people leave me alone? I just want to be left alone. Well, no, that's not entirely true. It's just that...

"You okay, lady?"

A gravelly male voice jolted me out of my fugue state. The man who owned the voice was dressed in a dust-colored parka, a grimy watch cap with a University of Michigan insignia and faded red corduroy slacks crisscrossed with mud stains. The grocery cart he was pushing overflowed with plastic bags of every size. He cleared his throat, spat out a wad of mucous, wiped his mouth with the back of his hand and repeated the question: "You okay?"

I came to a sudden halt a couple of feet from his cart. "Yeah, I'm fine, thanks." My voice was strained, embarrassed and, I had to admit, unconvincing. "I was just trying to figure something out."

The man grabbed a bag that had worked itself loose, stuffed it back into place and gave me an uneasy look. I reached into my coat pocket and fumbled out a few singles, part of my street stash for chance encounters with Salvation Army bell ringers, veterans selling poppies and homeless people begging change.

"Thanks for bringing me back to reality." I held out the money. "Here. Maybe you'd like a cup of coffee. Or something."

What is it about street people, I wondered, that makes me so uncomfortable? Is it some old primal fear tickling my reptilian brain? A genetically imprinted aversion? A suspicion that if I acknowledge them, they'll somehow have a claim on me? Or is it the terror of being contaminated by their suffering and failure?

He accepted the money without comment but kept his worried eyes on my face.

"I'm fine," I repeated, more for my benefit than his.

"If you say so." As he restarted his one-man caravan, I stepped onto the snow-covered grass to give him room to maneuver. He trudged along for a few steps, then swung his head back toward me. "You take care now or you gonna wind up like me."

I raised my hand. "Okay. Thanks again."

Great, I thought. Now this stupid situation has me talking to myself. I stood absolutely still, took a couple of breaths and sent out a silent call to Terry. Or maybe I was just sending an SOS into the cosmos, aiming for any vagrant angel who happened to be nearby. Whatever I was doing, the words came out in a rush. I whispered rapid-fire, barely moving my lips.

"Hey, it's me. Down here. I seem to be in the damnedest mess."

Blinking back tears, I started walking slowly without breaking my concentration.

"I don't know what to do. I don't know what I'm *supposed* to do. I'm lost and I'm tired and I'm confused. Help me. Please. If you can."

I kept repeating those last three thoughts over and over, keeping time with my steps.

Help me. Please. If you can.

Help me. Please. If you can

By the time my front door was in sight, I felt calmer. All the churning thoughts had been replaced by a cool, clean, empty silence. But that was the problem. Silence, when what I needed was an answer.

I let myself into the house, closed the door, sat on my favorite step—third from the bottom—and looked upward. "Hey, I could use a little inspiration."

I waited. Five seconds. Ten. Fifteen. Twenty.

Nothing.

I grunted as I tugged at my left boot, which refused to separate itself from one of the thick wool socks I'd pulled out of Terry's drawer that morning. Albert arranged himself on the lowest step to supervise.

At that instant, two words flitted through my mind.

Benny Goodman.

I stopped yanking on my boot.

Benny Goodman? Oh wonderful. Maybe I should nab a grocery cart now rather than later, save some time. Put everything into plastic bags and away I go, off in my own little world. Benny Goodman. I shook my head.

And then it came to me. Benny Goodman. Of course. Benny Goodman.

The Carnegie Hall concert of 1938.

One boot on, one off, I hobbled over to the bookshelves that housed my CD collection and located the G's. I pulled out the disk I wanted, plunked it into the player, checked the selections on the play list and pushed the forward button until I got to the right number.

Momentary silence, then scratchy applause followed by Benny Goodman's high, slightly nasal voice introducing the next tune: *Sing, Sing, Sing.*

There's some dispute among music history buffs as to what really happened that night. A few so-called experts will tell you that the Carnegie Hall concert was a knockout success from the first. Others—lots of them—will disagree and point out that the performance was curiously lackluster, plagued by technical problems and Goodman's own nervousness.

The band was certainly out of its element. They were in a hallowed venue normally reserved for Bach, Brahms and Beethoven. There had been a public furor over whether or not a popular orchestra should even be allowed to tread the sacred floorboards of that stage. The tension was palpable. And the band couldn't quite break through.

Oh they played well enough, in a careful, controlled sort of way. Not taking chances. Not jumping off any cliffs, creatively speaking. And to be fair, they never struck a false note. Goodman, after all, was a meticulous performer and a notoriously tough taskmaster.

If you look at the jumpy black-and-white footage from that event and study the faces of the audience, you can see curiosity and expectation gradually give way to disappointment as one tepid number follows another. You can almost read the question in their eyes: So *this* is the king of swing?

The minutes passed. Goodman and his crew plodded on, tune after tune.

Then something amazing happened.

The band launched themselves into *Sing, Sing, Sing*—one of their signature pieces. Finally, there was a break in the orchestration for the drum solo.

And Gene Krupa was ready. More than ready.

He must have been yearning, itching, panting for that moment in the spotlight. Was he feeling panicky by then? Embarrassed for himself and his fellow band members? Pissed off?

Didn't matter. All that mattered was what he did.

Gene Krupa did what no one else could do that night. He let loose. He shattered the nice-nice atmosphere. He broke through. He was like a wild man, but a wild man with an incredible talent.

He changed everything.

Some music critics say he gave the performance of his life that night. During that brazen, ballsy solo of his, Krupa reminded every musician on stage of what they were about.

And when they came back in, they were swinging.

The audience not only heard it, they felt it. They smiled. They swayed. They clapped. They laughed. They gave each other nudges and knowing glances. They danced in the aisles.

I stood there, listening, moving to the wild beat of that long-dead drummer, tears running down my face. Finally, when the last perfect note had died away and the last moment of raspy applause had signaled the end of the record, I had my answer.

I knew what I was going to do.

As I pushed the off button and scrubbed away the tears that were drying on my cheeks, Albert nuzzled my leg. I stooped down to scratch his head. "Thanks, Al. I think I've figured it out. This whole thing still seems crazy to me but what the hell? Moses B. Caldwell can go sit on his badge. I'm going to give it my best."

CHAPTER 23

Tuesday – November 19

Of course, *saying* is one thing. *Doing* is another. My swagger faded fast. And having made my decision, I naturally delayed the inevitable for as long as possible.

I slowly removed my other boot. Rearranged all my winter footwear on the mat next to the front door. Put away my coat, scarf, gloves, hat. Wiped up the mud and melted snow that pooled on the tiles. Brushed my teeth. Splashed cold water on my face. Poured myself a glass of milk I didn't want. Ran a sponge over the perfectly clean kitchen counter. Watered a plant.

Only when I had exhausted all possible diversions and distractions did I sit myself down next to the living room phone. The little screen flashed a "9" at me. And that was in addition to the three or more messages that were probably waiting for me on my cell.

Gene Krupa, I reminded myself. Then I pushed the play button.

There were three messages from Bixie, each longer and more apologetic than the last. There was one from Paul, conveyed in a dramatic semi-whisper, explaining that he'd just spoken with Bixie and wanted to know where we went from here. One from Maura, double-checking the Thanksgiving menu and wondering did I plan to make my usual salad and Finnish bread. Three from clients, two wanting to schedule meetings and one ready to review the latest batch of copy for their web site.

The final message took me completely by surprise.

Mercedes Madigan had let the machine run for a few seconds before starting. Her voice was so breathy and low, I had to strain to catch all the words.

"Yes. Hi. This is Mercedes. Madigan. We met yesterday. At Paul's shop? I've been thinking about what you said, about the article you're writing? I haven't had a chance to talk with my husband yet, but I think it might be, that is, if you're still interested, I'd be willing to talk with you. I… I'm not promising anything. I'd want to know more about your slant on the article. But we could meet at my house, say tomorrow sometime? If you're free? Maybe you could bring some examples of things you've written. And we can chat." She left a number where I could reach her.

Suddenly, I began to have second thoughts about my new resolve. Chattering fears, uncertainties, doubts and better-nots were growing slowly in my mind, like a mob gradually working up its energy.

I squared my shoulders and looked down at the message pad filled with notes and phone numbers.

I started dialing.

First, Bixie. There was no answer. Just as well. I waited for the beep. "It's me. Considering all that's happened today, I think we should all meet at Paul's house. Seven o'clock." Neutral territory seemed best. "Right now I'm going to call Paul. I'll let you know if there's a problem. Otherwise, I'll see you tonight."

Next, Paul. Who was extremely upset when I refused to give him any details about my morning tête-à-tête but who mellowed considerably when I proposed a get-together at his place. "Seven is perfect," he chimed. "See you then, hon. Although I still think it's perfectly *rotten* of you not to tell me what's going on. I don't see why I should be left out of the…"

Maura was out. I left a message. Yes, of course, I would show up with my salad, my bread and whatever else she might need to complete the feast. Was it possible that Thanksgiving was just a little more than a week away? The clients, I decided, could wait for half an hour or so, until I was in a more businesslike frame of mind. I dialed the number Mercedes had whispered and after two rings, a brisk female voice announced that I had reached the Madigan residence.

"Hi, this is Karin Niemi. Returning a call from Mercedes." Nice touch, I thought. Mercedes rather than Mrs. Madigan. Makes it sound as if we were old buddies—or biddies—on the same social circuit.

After a minute or so, Mercedes was on the line. Her husky voice sounded nervous and slightly out of breath, but also excited. I imagined a kid who'd been left home alone for an evening and was just about to break one of her parents' cardinal rules.

Would tomorrow at four o'clock work? It would. Then she'd expect me at four. With samples. And we could see where things went from there. Oh, and did I have her address? It was twenty-five Sylvan Lane. In Oakbridge Estates. Did I know where that was? Yes, of course. After all the public Stürm und Drang, the windy editorials, the endless tug of war between city council members and the notorious Detroit developer with deep, deep pockets and ruthless lawyers, everyone in town knew where the latest millionaire's enclave was located.

One more call to make. I dialed a university number. After three rings, Evan's voice boomed out. "Hey, Karin. What's up?"

I always forget about caller ID.

"Evan. I need you to do something for me."

"Sure thing. Name it." You've got to love a guy who doesn't hesitate for even a nanosecond when granting an unspecified favor.

"I need you to find out everything you can about Charles Anderson. Also known as Chaz Anderson. He's… That is, he was a computer engineering student. Until early this morning."

Evan let out an energetic groan. "Oh no. Not you too. The department has been crawling with police all day. Asking questions. Confiscating records and equipment. Writing in those neat little notebooks of theirs. Do you think the police department hands them out, by the way? Or does everyone have to buy their own? I've always wondered about that."

"Evan, could you focus please? Chaz Anderson. Information. It's important."

Big sigh. "Why? What's going on? You writing an article for the paper or something?"

"It's complicated. I'll explain it all once you've got something for me. Promise."

"Once I've got something for you? Like what?"

"Anything. Everything. His resumé, for a start. I know for a fact that every engineering student is required to keep a current CV on file."

"Yeah, okay. I can probably pull a copy for you. What else do you want to know?"

"Like I said, anything. What classes he took. His grades. Who mentored him. Clubs he was involved in. People he hung around with. His career plans. What he was like. Where he came from."

"Really. Is that all? Sure there's nothing else you'd like to know? His shoe size maybe? His favorite color? The last time he had a wet dream?" Evan paused for a short impatient breath. "You know, Karin, a lot of the stuff you want to know is privileged information. At least his transcripts are."

"Oh come on," I wheedled. "Just keep your ears open. Please. The entire department is probably talking about nothing else right now. All you have to do is station yourself in some strategic spot, like the department secretary's office, and keep your ears open. Trust me. The facts will be thick on the ground."

Evan let out an exasperated groan, but I knew he was weakening. "Okay. I'll see what I can do. And when do you want me to deliver all this information?"

"How about tomorrow morning? Around eleven o'clock. Your office."

Yet another sigh. The man had an endless supply. "You don't ask for much, do you? Alright. I'll try. But I'm not promising anything."

"Thanks, Evan. You're a mensch."

"Tell me something I don't know."

The moment I hung up, a wave of anxiety splashed over me full-force. Still gripping the phone, I said out loud to no one in particular, "What in God's name am I doing?"

An answering thought came floating through the room, cool as a breeze, and lodged gently in my agitated brain.

Gene Krupa, it whispered. Gene Krupa.

CHAPTER 24

Tuesday – November 19

As if cued by an invisible stagehand, the phone rang just as I was letting myself out the front door. I glanced at the hallway clock. Seven p.m.

Bixie had arrived at Paul's ten minutes earlier. I knew this from the sound of her engine as she pulled into the driveway. Her car's signature ping-rattle-wheeze was unmistakable, like the opening bars of a very bad theme song.

Now that I'd steeled myself for this little gathering, I had no intention of being waylaid by a phone call. I reached for the door handle but then, on a sudden impulse, wheeled around and trotted over to the machine.

"Karin." At the sound of Andrew's voice, my stomach gave a flutter, exactly the way it did years back whenever my beautiful, bastardly high school boyfriend would take pity on me and call.

"Andrew. What a surprise." Odd, how all of a sudden I was slightly short of breath. "What's up?"

"We need to talk about Bixie."

"Bixie? What about her?"

"Come off it, Karin. It's been a helluva long day. You know exactly what I'm talking about. She's got some crazy idea that she's going to solve the Dana Lewis murder. And if that's not bad enough, now I hear she's messing around in the Charles Anderson case. And that you've been aiding and abetting."

Thank you, Moses B. Caldwell.

"Look," he went on, "Bixie's heading into serious trouble if she doesn't back off. Serious. This is not some goddamn TV series. This is the real deal. Judges. Lawyers. Criminal charges. The whole nine yards."

My temper began to uncoil. "I've already been beaten up once today. As you probably know. So what do you want from me?"

Andrew ratcheted down his voice a couple of notches. "Sorry. I'm worried, okay? Bixie won't listen to me. Ever. But you're her best friend. You've gotta get her to back off."

On Andrew's end, the hive-like buzz grew louder. I heard someone call out, "Hey, Murray, let's get a move on." Andrew yelled back, "Okay, I'll be right there." More buzzing, then back to me. "I can't talk now. Do me a favor. Meet me at Jansens's, nine o'clock, for a drink."

"Nine o'clock?" By then, the only drink I was usually contemplating was a cup of cocoa, in bed, with Albert at my side and a book propped up on my knees.

"Yeah, I know it's kinda late. But I can't get away till then."

"I thought you were on the day shift."

He gave a short bark that could have been a laugh. "Are you kidding? With two suspicious deaths? Most of us are pulling double shifts. Besides which, I've been assigned to the Charles Anderson case."

Ah, the good news just kept on coming.

"So how about it? Jansen's? I promise not to keep you long."

Before I could think, I heard myself say, "Alright. Nine o'clock. Jansen's."

David answered the doorbell with a lopsided smile. "Karin, good to see you." He air-kissed my right cheek. "Your fellow PI's are waiting for you in the living room."

He was wearing grey sweatpants and a long-sleeve black tee. Ever the gentleman, he held out his hands for my coat.

I had to ask. "So, will you be sitting in on our meeting?"

David made a face as he draped my jacket and scarf over his arm and smoothed out the folds. "Are you kidding? The less I know about this, the less I'll be able to tell the District Attorney when the time comes."

He headed toward the closet, chuckling and shaking his head. I blew out a long breath and walked down the short hall into the living room.

Paul changes his décor as often as most people change their sheets. The last time I'd paid a visit—about two weeks ago—the place was decked out in minimalist furniture in shades of ivory, aqua and spring green. His current motifs were running to deep reds and burnished golds.

I looked around in mild amazement at the transformation. A large persimmon-colored couch, smothered in hand-woven pillows, was flanked by two wing chairs in camel-colored leather. The walls were painted a dark tan, although in the golden glow of the various lamps, it was hard to be certain about colors. On the mantel—oak, Mission style—primitive-looking carved animals capered amidst pots of cascading ivy.

In one corner of the vast couch, completing the picture, was Bixie. Tonight she was wearing jeans with a white blouse, a dark green velvet vest and the defiant look of a teenager who'd been caught sneaking into the house after curfew.

Before she could make up her mind to speak, Paul jumped in.

"Karin. Sit down. Have a drink." He handed me a short-stemmed cordial glass filled to the brim with sherry. "And now tell us *exactly* what happened this morning. *All* of it. We're *dying* to hear." From the grim look on Bixie's face, I judged that dying was just about the right word.

Holding the glass carefully, I sank into one of the leather chairs and gave a short and only slightly exaggerated recap of my disastrous encounter with Detective Sergeant Caldwell. When I was through, Paul let out a groan. Eyes wide, hand pressed against one cheek, he put down his glass.

"So that's it. Case closed." He leaned back into the couch, pushed out his lower lip and crossed his arms. "Crap. And just when I was *zeroing* in on some suspects. I know for a fact, based on some very reliable gossip, that James Whitaker and George Brodsky both had recent dealings with Dana Lewis they'd rather *never* came to light."

I thought about Dorey Goldsmith. And Allegra. "It's a big club."

Bixie looked at me in silence and continued stroking Lew's head, which seemed to be permanently affixed to her lap. She combed his ears gently through her fingers.

I waited a few seconds before making my announcement.

"The fact is, I'm not ready to quit. I'm certainly not going to let Detective Sergeant Moses B. Caldwell tell me what I can and cannot do." I was sounding a lot braver than I felt. "I think we should keep going." Paul's face lit up and I pointed a warning finger at him. "Provided we don't go charging around like..."

"Bulls in a police station?" Paul offered. He picked up his glass and swirled it in small circles. Knowing how much he hates sherry, I could only assume that he chose the stuff because it meshed with his color scheme so nicely. "So what do you suggest?"

I took a sip. Sticky. Warm. Rich. "I think we should pursue the Charles Anderson connection. I mean, look at the facts. Young. Male. Computer geek. All of which tells us he's not likely to go running to any touchy-feely therapist. So the fact that this kid turns up in Dana's office, and not just once but repeatedly, week after week, that seems very suspicious to me. Or at least damn curious. I for one would like to know what was going on."

I could almost see the cogs moving in Paul's brain. "So you think he may have killed Dana, then killed himself?"

"That's one possibility, I suppose." Another sip of sherry and a glance at the still-silent Bixie. "But there are others. Maybe Chaz killed himself out of desperation when he learned that Dana was dead." Just one more sip. "Maybe he was clinically depressed. Maybe he'd become totally dependent on her and went over the edge when she died." That seemed a bit far-fetched but what the heck, we were just brainstorming. "Or maybe," I couldn't seem to stop, "he was mentally unhinged and somehow thought the blame for her murder would fall on him, so he panicked."

"Or," Bixie stretched the word into two long, slow syllables, "maybe he didn't kill himself at all. Maybe he was murdered. By the same person who killed Dana."

Paul put down his glass. "So how do we find out more about the mysterious Charles Anderson, who may or may not have killed Dana, and who may or may not have committed suicide?"

"I've got Evan Bernstein checking around in the Computer Sci department. We're meeting tomorrow around eleven."

"I've got something even better," Bixie broke in. She had shed her bad-kid look and her face had that glittery, excited glow again, the one that always makes me nervous.

Since I refused to give her the satisfaction of begging her to continue, we waited in silence until Paul had the good grace to ask: "Something better? Like what?"

"Like Charles Anderson's former girlfriend. Willing to talk."

Trumped. I gave in. "His ex-girlfriend? How'd you manage that?"

Bixie shifted Lew's head gently and leaned forward. "It turns out that she's a student of Isabel's, or was. In fact, Isabel has been her unofficial mentor for the last couple of years. From what I hear, they're pretty close. And when Chaz, Charles, started acting really odd a while back, to the point that he was scaring the girlfriend—I think her name is Rocky or Ricki or something like that—she went to Isabel. And Isabel suggested that she, the girlfriend or maybe ex-girlfriend by then, I don't know for sure, should try to get Chaz lined up for a session or two with Dana."

Paul mulled over that revelation with a skeptical look on his face. "But I thought Dana hated her mother."

Bixie waved her long fingers back and forth. "An exaggeration. Besides which, no matter what the weather was like between them, Isabel had a lot of respect for her mother's ability as a therapist. Anyway, we'll know all the details soon enough because I've got an appointment..." She looked at me. "Because *we've* got an appointment to talk with Rocky or Ricki tomorrow at ten o'clock in Isabel's office."

While I took that in, Paul raised his glass and gave a Cheshire Cat smile. "I can't wait to hear what this Ricki person thinks about how Chaz died, and why."

Bixie pressed her hands together and her whole body seemed to vibrate. "I can't wait to hear what she thinks about Chaz and Dana."

As for me, I thought, I can't wait to hear what lies I'm going to conjure up to convince Andrew we won't be giving the Ann Arbor Homicide Division any more competition.

CHAPTER 25

Tuesday – November 19

Jansen's parking lot is a long rectangle, gravel or mud depending on the weather. On this particular night it was a slick, cold mud. As I trekked to the front door, a fine cold rain shimmered in misty halos around the streetlights and worked its way into my scalp.

A Lincoln Town Car prowled between the tight rows of vehicles in search of an open slot. A bumper sticker glowed fluorescent in the gloom: *Vote Democrat? I'd Rather Eat Glass.*

In the remote reaches of the Upper Peninsula, Jansen's would be known as a supper club. Here, it was just a glorified bar and grill, a time machine for people who could still remember when Ann Arbor was a sleepy college town. In Jansen's, the lights are always dim, the waitresses are always locals, beer comes in cans, the bar is littered with martini glasses, steaks are the size of turkey platters, and tofu is considered an alien life form.

I was studying the bar when I heard my name called and saw Andrew emerge from one of the shadowy booths lining the far wall. I walked toward him feeling like a fifteen-year-old girl trapped in the body of a middle-aged woman.

"Hey, Karin." He reached out to shake my hand. "Thanks for coming."

"Sure." I looked around at the loud, lively crowd hoisting drinks and shoveling in food. "Honestly, though, I don't know what you expect to accomplish." I shrugged off my wet coat before Andrew could do the gentlemanly thing and help me out of it.

"You know as well as I do that your sister is a force of nature. If she wants to do something, she does it. Period." I sank into the comfort of dark green plush and tried not to sigh too loudly.

Andrew sat down opposite me, pulled his glass of beer a little closer and looked up at our waitress, a no-nonsense size sixteen with a rhinestone-studded cross lodged firmly in her cleavage. Holding a tray at her side, she gave me a quick professional smile. "What can I get you, hon?"

"Club soda please," I answered automatically. Then I thought about the cold rain, the miserable day I'd had, the miserable day that was probably waiting for me tomorrow and, after a two-second battle with my evil twin, I surrendered to the dark side. "And a large order of french fries with mayo."

She turned to Andrew who had covered his mouth in a hopeless effort to stop laughing. "What about you, Andy? Another?" Without removing his hand, he nodded. She bustled away.

Just for something to do, I moved my coaster around in little circles. "What's so funny...Andy?"

He lowered his hand and shook his head. "How the hell do you do it? Every woman I know is living on rabbit food and still putting on weight. You eat like a Suma wrestler and..." He left the sentence unfinished. "As my father would say, life is inherently unfair."

How many times have I had to suffer through this same stupid conversation? "What's not fair is the way people feel free to comment on my eating habits and my body." I sat back against the thick plush, feeling like a sulky kid.

Andrew let his eyes wander from my face down to my waist and back up again. "Well, you can't blame them. It's a very nice body."

At that moment, completely unaware of her perfect timing, the waitress returned with our drinks. By the time my fries arrived, I'd reclaimed enough of my composure to look across the table and say, "So. Bixie."

"Right." Andrew sipped at his beer. "What are we going to do about her?"

"Well, aside from locking her in the house or slipping sedatives into her rice milk, there isn't much that either of us *can* do."

"Karin, I wasn't kidding earlier. If she keeps screwing around in this investigation, there's going to be hell to pay. She could face charges." He took another swig. "And so could you."

I chewed slowly, savoring the fried potato and mayonnaise taste as long as I could before chasing it down with a sip of club soda. "But why? It's not as if we're withholding evidence." Not much anyway. "We're just poking around. Wasting our time. The only thing that's suffered so far is my billable hours." I bit into another fry. "So what's the problem?"

Andrew's voice whipped at me like a blast of hail. "She doesn't know what the fuck she's doing and neither do you. That's the problem."

For a second or two I felt as if I'd been flash-frozen. Then my temper rekindled. "Did you ever stop to think how much your sister cared about Dana Lewis? She adored that woman. They were friends for—what?— fifteen years? And suddenly Dana is murdered. And along with the grief, Bixie has to deal with the anxiety that Dana's daughter—also her friend—might be blamed for the murder. Plus of course, you don't tell her a thing about what's going on."

Another sharp blast of disapproval hit me from across the table.

"Okay," I admitted in a quieter voice, "you *can't* tell her. On one level, she understands that. But she's frustrated, Andrew. And worried. She sees injustice taking place in slow motion. And so, being Bixie, she doesn't just sit around and wring her hands, which is what most of us would do. Which is what I'd certainly prefer to do. She rushes in. And also being Bixie, she drags her friends along."

From above the clenched hands that supported his chin, Andrew raised one eyebrow. I kept going. "You need to cut her some slack."

He rolled his eyes. "No really," I continued. "You know she's not going to hold anything back from you." More eye rolling. "Alright, let me put it this way. If by some miracle she stumbles onto something important, I won't *let* her hold anything back. It would be irresponsible. And much as I hate to admit that Detective Sergeant Caldwell could be right about anything, it could also be dangerous."

Andrew's face seemed to unclench. "Now we're getting somewhere." He finished the last swig of beer and swiped his mouth with a paper napkin. "Maybe we can do a deal."

My own mouth suddenly felt dry. "What kind of deal?"

"Simple. First, you do everything you can to slow my sister down. Get her off track." He tapped the edge of his beer coaster lightly on the tabletop. "Second, you and Bixie...well, forget about Bixie. You agree to share any information you uncover."

"And what do I get in return?"

"In return?" He seemed genuinely surprised by the question. "Well, you don't have the police on your ass, for the time being anyway. We don't file any charges. Unless we're provoked."

I picked up my half-empty tumbler of soda and looked at him over the rim. "That's not a deal. That's an ultimatum."

I have to admit that I really love the way Andrew laughs, even when he's laughing at me. "Okay, counselor," he grinned. "What are your terms?"

I took a breath. He wasn't going to like this. "You tell me what you can about the cases. Both of them."

Andrew's forehead puckered and I knew I had only a few seconds to convince him. "Look, I'm not asking you to do anything unethical." Not too unethical anyway. "I'm just asking you to tell me a little—just a little—about what's going on. Anything that will reassure Bixie. Without compromising the investigation."

"What sorts of things are we talking about here?'

"Basics. The kind of stuff you're going to feed to the media eventually anyway. Like how did Dana die?" No point in letting him know I knew about the poison from Isabel. "And are there people besides Isabel on your suspect list?" He threw me a major frown. "I'm not asking for names." Although that would be nice. "Just the general direction of the case."

"So you can reassure my sister." He tapped the coaster a few times. "Without really telling her anything, because we both know what a blabbermouth she is."

"That's not true."

"Yes it is and you know it."

Andrew stared off into space for a minute or so, still tapping the coaster absentmindedly. Finally, he seemed to come to a decision. "Okay. Listen up. I'm going to tell you a few things. Even though I don't know why you think you need to know them." His voice got lower and colder. "This is in absolute confidence."

He took my silence for consent.

"Dana Lewis was poisoned by atropine."

The gears in my brain started grinding. "Atropine? Isn't that the main ingredient in eye drops?" I thought for a few seconds. "And in prescription meds for severe diarrhea?"

"Very good. Also for bronchospasms, nerve gas attacks, mushroom poisoning and a few other things I can't remember. Actually, it's been used for centuries—mostly as a poison, occasionally as a medicine."

"Right." I was remembering more now, pulling up buried factoids from mystery novel plots. "In fact, some forensic experts have described it as the perfect murder weapon. Readily available. Hard to trace. Of course, there are problems with it, mainly..."

"Has anyone ever told you that you read too much?" Andrew shook his head in a God-save-me-from-amateurs kind of way. "So, to continue. Atropine was found in a bottle of something called Rescue Remedy, but the heaviest concentration was in a jar of some herbal swill she kept in the refrigerator. The dose was fairly large. Even so, it might not have killed her if her heart had been in better shape. According to the coroner, turns out she had a defect. Mitral something or other."

"Mitral valve prolapse," I said and thought of Dana, alone, dying of atropine poisoning. Then I thought of my own bottle of Rescue Remedy, sitting primly on the bedside table. I knew I'd never be able to touch the stuff again.

"As to suspects, well, we should probably start handing out numbers. Kind of like Zingerman's deli counter." He pushed his empty glass around the table, left, right, up, down.

He glanced up at me. "I'm not saying Isabel Lewis is off the hook. It's way too early for that. But I can tell you she's got a lot of company." He shoved the glass to the middle of the table. "That'll have to do for now."

"But what about Charles Anderson?"

"What about him?"

"Well, we know from Dana's schedule that he was a patient of hers. So what was he seeing her about?"

Andrew looked at me too long for comfort. "Investigations are underway. Let's just leave it at that."

"Okay, but..."

"No buts. Right now, you concentrate on keeping my sister under control—or at least keep her from breaking the law. Anything you find out, you call me." He scrawled his cell phone number on the back of a card and handed it to me. I added it to the growing collection in my purse.

I watched as Andrew pulled out a twenty-dollar bill and tossed it on the table. I had to give it one more try. "You sure there's nothing more you can tell me?"

Andrew looked at his watch, one of those ugly do-everything models with buttons, bells and buzzers. "Yeah. I can tell you it's time for us to go." In one seamless movement, he swept up his jacket, grabbed mine off its hook and held it out to me. "Come on. I'll follow you to your house."

My eyes widened. "My house?"

"Yup. It's a cop's version of escorting a lady home. Make sure all that club soda doesn't impair your driving."

"You really don't..."

"But I'm going to anyway. Besides it's on my way to the station. End of."

As I turned left out of the still-full parking lot, Andrew's car shadowed me into the slanting November rain. After so many months of living alone, being alone, traveling alone, it felt strange—but also strangely comforting—to have those friendly headlights behind me.

Like having a brother around, I told myself firmly.

Andrew waited at the curb while I walked up the front steps. As I opened the door, he called out, "G'night, Karin. Don't forget our deal."

He tapped his horn and pulled away. Under the glow of the porch light, I turned and watched him drive down the dark, deserted street.

Albert swiveled out from the partly open door and rubbed against my calf. I looked down into his wide golden eyes.

"Nothing to worry about, Al. I've just been borrowing Bixie's brother." I watched the tail lights disappear around a turn. "You know. Bixie's very married, drop-dead-gorgeous brother. That one."

Albert let out a long mew.

"Right. Just what every girl needs."

CHAPTER 26

By nine forty-five, I was standing at the entrance to the Center for Visual Arts, a nearly windowless brick building with all the charm of an auto parts factory. After ten minutes of wandering through dismal cinderblock corridors, I found Isabel's office. My knock interrupted a low murmur of conversation. At Isabel's "Come in," I pushed the door open.

The front half of the office was occupied by a large worktable and six straight-backed chairs. Bookshelves and lateral files hugged the walls, creating a space that was either cozy or claustrophobic, depending on your point of view.

Further back, framed against three tall windows, Isabel sat behind a battered oak desk surrounded by precarious columns of files and papers. Four small chairs had been placed in a semi-circle around the desk. Bixie sat at Isabel's left. Opposite her, two young women huddled close together, their shoulders nearly touching. While I arranged myself on the vacant seat next to Bixie, Isabel made introductions.

She nodded to the young woman nearest her and I found myself looking into a face straight out of a fairytale. Flawless ivory skin, cobalt blue eyes, delicate nose, cupid mouth, short ruffled blonde hair. If I were in charge of casting for *Sleeping Beauty*, this kid would get the lead, no question.

"Karin, this is Rochelle Christiansen. Also known as Ricki. Ricki, this is Karin Niemi." The fairy princess gave me a "Hi" along with a guarded look.

Isabel moved her gaze to Ricki's right. "And this is her friend Imani O'Brien." The friend didn't waste any breath, just jerked her dreadlocks in my direction. Her skin was a glossy copper and her body seemed ready to burst out of its Indian print cotton blouse and faded jeans.

Isabel was decked out in black and white, with the white provided mainly by the detailing on a pair of black, hand-tooled boots. She spoke as if she were chairing a committee meeting. "First, I want thank you all for coming here today." She nodded at the princess. "You especially, Ricki. I know how hard this is for you."

At that moment, Isabel's strong, sculpted face seemed to crack and I caught a glimpse of the fear and grief beneath the surface. After a full stop that lasted maybe five seconds, she pulled herself together. "So," she turned to Bixie, "how shall we begin?"

It was Imani who answered. Her tones were acid. "First, tell me. Why is Ricki talking to you two when she's already gone over everything with the police?"

Reasonable question. But for some reason, Bixie was too startled to speak, so I jumped in. "We're doing this," I explained, "because we think there's a possibility that the deaths of Chaz and Dana Lewis are connected. And because we're concerned that in the case of Dana, the police," I tried not to look at Isabel, "are focusing on the wrong suspects."

Imani crossed her arms and let out a small but unmistakable snort. "But you're not private detectives. What can you do?"

"Maybe we can find out the truth or some piece of it." I looked into those hot brown eyes. "And since Bixie's brother is on the police force, there's a chance the authorities will pay attention if we do."

"Does her brother know you're doing this?"

"Yes, he does" I shot back, imagining Andrew ready to burst a blood vessel. Bixie blinked. Imani leaned back in her chair and re-crossed her arms.

Clenching a soggy tissue in one fist, Ricki brought her blue eyes back into focus. Her voice was thick and congested. "What do you want to know?"

I leaned forward. "Anything you can tell us about Chaz. I know it must be hard, losing a friend to suicide…"

"You don't know it was suicide," she threw the words at me.

"Sorry," I back-stepped. "You're right. That's one of the things we want to find out. But first we need a better sense of who he was, how he spent his time, who his friends were."

Ricki stifled a sob with a throat-bruising gulp. "He didn't have friends."

Bixie and I glanced at each other. "But he must have," I said gently.

Teary-eyed, tissues poised under her nose, Ricki shook her head. "Not Chaz. Oh, he knew people. There were guys he partied with, hung out with once in a while. But he didn't have any real friends. No one he trusted. He never got close to anyone. Never had a roommate. And he and I…" she took a trembling breath.

I stepped back in. "How did you two meet?"

Ricki looked down at her hands which were busy shredding tissues, wadding them into moist little pellets and then patting the whole mess back together as if it were potter's clay. "I met Chaz about a year ago, at the start of fall term. At a house party."

Memory made her eyes glaze over. "My first thought was, what an ass. He was so arrogant." There was that word again. "But he was hard to ignore. Smart. Funny in a sarcastic way. And it didn't hurt that he was a ringer for Brad Pitt." She gave a smile that faded almost before it began. "We had a few drinks and after a while I started thinking, why not?"

"You started seeing each other."

"We hooked up. Yeah."

"What can you tell us about his background?"

Ricki ran one hand through her tousled blonde hair. "Not a whole lot. He grew up in Grosse Pointe. His dad is some kind of lawyer and his mother is a teacher. I met her once when she came to campus for a visit. But she was alone. Chaz and his father didn't get along. At all." She kept her eyes fixed straight ahead of her, like a sleepwalker.

"So he was in computer engineering," I said.

"Yeah," Ricki nodded. "He was incredibly intense about academics. Arrogant really." There was that word again. "He was totally committed to the idea of being, like, a superstar. You know, the next Steve Jobs. It was what he lived for. It sort of took over."

"What do you mean took over?"

"I mean," Ricki looked around the room for inspiration. "I mean, this is the University of Michigan, right? So it's totally competitive. For everyone. But the computer engineering department is the worst. They have these incredible egos. And it's all so personal with them. Chaz was always talking about how important it was to prove how good he was." She held the wad of tissues under her nose for a few seconds.

"Is that so wrong?" I wondered out loud.

"Yeah, if that's all there is." Another bleak look. "It reached a point when I finally got it that he didn't really like people. He just used them. He could turn on the charm when he wanted something. Which he usually did. But it was always about winning. And he could be such a bastard sometimes." She gulped, swallowing hot tears and hard memories. "One day it just came to head. We were talking, and he said something really obnoxious about one of his classmates. And I stared at him and thought, this guy is so not what I want. Why am I with him?"

"So you broke up?"

Ricki shook her head. "It's more like we both backed off. School was getting really intense for me. And Chaz was incredibly busy. Sometimes, he'd spend the entire night in that stupid building, working. It reached a point where we hardly ever saw each other."

"Did he belong to any clubs? Professional groups?" I asked.

Ricki shook her head. Imani touched her arm lightly. "Don't forget about the Young Republicans."

The Young Republicans? Where had I heard that phrase recently?

"He joined the Young Republicans?" Bixie croaked.

Ricki shrugged. "I don't know if he actually joined. But he hung out with them, went to meetings."

"Why?" I asked.

"Connections." She ran a hand through her hair. "I told you, he had this idea of himself as the next big thing in the cyber world. He'd see people graduate and go off and become programmers for cell phone companies or something and he always thought that was pathetic. He wanted way more than that."

"So when did you finally break up?"

Ricki looked at Isabel as if weighing whether their friendship deserved all this effort. "It was January of last year." A long breath. "By then we were just friends. If you can call it that. Chaz had been acting weird for a while. Really weird, even for him. Then he called one day and said we had to stop seeing each other. He wouldn't go into it, just kept saying he couldn't see me anymore. That it was better this way."

"So that was it."

"Sort of." Ricki bit her lips and scrunched her beautiful eyes into a mass of temporary wrinkles. "It was just that, well, he was so not himself. It was like he was scared. Excited but scared. I was kind of worried. So I made him promise to stay in touch—at least text me every now and then."

"And did he?"

"Not really." She lifted one shoulder and let it drop. "Not unless he wanted a favor. Once in a while, he'd ask me to store things for him. Old computer equipment, notebooks, stuff like that. And maybe once a week I'd get a message saying something lame like 'still here.' Until last spring anyway. Then everything stopped. He wouldn't pick up my calls, wouldn't text, ignored my emails."

"Why?"

"I don't know." She shook her head. "But I was so pissed, I didn't even try to make contact over the summer. I was working in Ann Arbor. I heard he had an internship with some company. In Plymouth, I think. Griswold or Grunner, something like that. Anyway, I didn't hear from him. And then when I saw him at the end of August, I just, like, couldn't believe it."

"You arranged to meet?"

Ricki gave an exasperated sigh, reached down, picked up a bottle of water next to her chair and unscrewed the cap. "No, I told you, he cut me off." She took a sip. "I ran into him at the Commons."

"And?" Bixie asked. Bent forward in her chair, chin in her hands, she looked like a large child listening to a bedtime story.

"He was, like, totally coming apart. He'd lost weight. He had these dark circles under his eyes. He was in a complete panic. It was like watching a rubber band about to break. I told him he should see a doctor. That's when he blew up, knocked everything off the table, told me to mind my own fucking business." Her eyes roamed the room, like a prisoner looking for a way out of an interrogation cell.

"But you got him to see Dana? How'd you manage that?'

"Well," Ricki locked eyes with Isabel. "I couldn't stop thinking about him. So not long after, I was talking to Isabel and I told her about Chaz. Just saying how worried I was. How he was falling apart. And she said she knew this incredible therapist, who happened to be her mother."

Another look at Isabel, this time tinged with guilt. Or was my imagination doing overtime?

"So we sort of worked out a strategy. I kept leaving voice mails, texting, telling him about this amazing therapist I knew, and that the sessions would be completely confidential, and what could it hurt just to check her out. He ignored me." She took another tug at the water bottle.

"But I kept at him." She looked intently at the bottle of water and shrugged. "I don't know why. Maybe I felt guilty or something. For ignoring him all summer." She took a sip. "Anyway, he finally called and left a message saying he'd seen her. That's it. No details. I figured he was lying just to get me off his case."

"Well," I leaned back in my chair, "he did see Dana. But I can understand why you'd have a hard time believing it. I do, too."

Isabel picked up a pen and began drawing angular shapes in the margins of a departmental memo. "Don't underestimate my mother."

Bixie reached over and put her hand on top of Isabel's. "It's true," she said. "Dana was phenomenal. She could get right inside of your life. Your thoughts and fears. And somehow you just knew she could help you out of whatever mess you were in. That's probably what Chaz was tuning into."

She reached across the desk, liberated a handful of tissues and blew her nose. Watching Bixie wipe away tears, I suddenly felt cheated by fate, genuinely sorry that Dana and I hadn't been able to keep our appointment.

I turned back to Ricki, who by now had a small mountain of used tissues on her lap. "So Chaz called you," I said.

"Just that once. Then nothing. I was incredibly busy and I didn't hear a word from him. So I assumed he was okay." Her voice broke. "Oh God," she wailed, "why didn't I call him?"

Imani put an arm around her friend and gave me a fiery look, which she shared with Bixie. "That's enough. For whatever it is you think you're doing."

Bixie nodded at me. I got out of my chair and knelt next to Ricki.

"Thanks," I said. "And I'm so sorry. I know what it's like to lose someone you care about." But, I thought, at least I loved the person I lost. In your case, it's probably more about guilt than grief. And that's harder.

I stood up, reached into the pocket of my blazer and pulled out a business card. "If you want to talk, for any reason, give me a call. Anytime." I put the card on her knee.

I wanted to rest a comforting hand on that blonde head. Instead, I gathered up my things. At the door, I looked back at Ricki. "You did what you could," I told her. "You did as much as Chaz would let you do. And if Dana were here," I paused, thinking to myself that she probably was, "she'd tell you that he isn't really gone."

I thought of the flickering shadows darting around my bungalow.

"In fact," I added, "he's probably a lot closer than you think."

CHAPTER 27

Was Chaz really such a loner as Ricki seemed to think? Was it possible? I had to believe there was a high school buddy, a coach, a teacher, an uncle, a cousin, a classmate, a somebody somewhere who could shed light on his apparent breakdown over the summer. And what about Ricki? Had she forgotten some potentially important detail, a text message, an email, a throwaway remark that might tell us more?

I checked my watch. Ten forty-five. Barely enough time to pick up my messages, make a few calls and get over to Evan's office.

As I wriggled into my coat, I thought about life. My life. The one with deadlines and invoices and bills. Unbeknownst to clients, I'd placed several projects on hold. I shook my head. This wasn't like me at all.

Outside, a malicious wind ripped along the concrete canyon, bending small trees and sending up dust devils from raw-looking construction sites. By the time I reached the brick fortress that houses the computer engineering department, my face was stinging from the cold.

I hurried through the lobby, a collection of brushed steel tubes and hard plastic surfaces that made me wonder if the interior designer had been trapped in a hard drive. Fighting back an urge to look for hidden cameras, I stepped into the elevator, pushed seven and, when the doors slid open, walked into a hallway lined with computer cast-offs.

Hearing voices behind Evan's office door, I headed down the hall to the student lounge. Two young men sharing a battered couch glanced up briefly, then went back to their laptops and cell phones. My shoes stuck to whatever was on the floor as I made my way over to a small round table piled high with tired-looking plastic containers of M&M's, trail mix, popcorn and breakfast cereals. I pushed the plastic tubs aside to make room for my phone and a small notebook.

By the time Evan discovered me, I had finished rescheduling a meeting and was in the process of moving back a couple of project deadlines. "Just for a few days," I explained in a nasal voice. "Until I'm feeling better." When pressed, I can do a very credible imitation of someone suffering from the flu. I gave one last wheezy cough and hung up.

"Karin, haven't I warned you about telling lies? You'll go to hell." Evan's baritone wrapped itself around me like a warm blanket.

I turned off the phone and stood up. "I thought Jews didn't believe in hell."

Evan enclosed me in a bear hug. "For you I'll make an exception."

When we got to his large corner office, he swept a pile of books and journals off a desk chair and wheeled it over to me. "Sit. Be comfortable. Would you like a snack?"

I thought of the smeary plastic containers in the student lounge. "No thanks."

Peering over the top of his glasses in fine professorial style, Evan shuffled through a stack of papers on his desk. "Now to the business at hand. Charles Anderson."

I sat up straighter. "Should I take notes or do you plan to part with those documents you're holding?"

"I'll have you know that the papers which I now clutch so tightly were obtained at great personal and professional risk to myself. But, yes, you can take them with you."

"So what did you find out… at great personal and professional risk to yourself?"

Evan shuffled the papers, scanned them, pursed his lips. "This kid was a real piece of work, God rest his soul." He looked up at me. "But first I'll tell you what I heard when I dipped into the faculty gossip well. You were right about the graduate secretary's office, by the way."

Evan riffled through the sheets, found one he liked and put it on top of the pile. "Anyway, according to the people who taught him,

Chaz Anderson was a real wünderkind even by U of M standards. He whipped through all the entry level courses. Straight A's. I talked with Sharon Dubcek, who knows everything there is to know about computer security, and she said the kid seemed to have a natural gift for hacking."

"Hacking. As in breaking into databases and infecting software."

"Right, among other things." I could see that Evan was trying hard not to roll his eyes or groan out loud, as he often did, at my gross ignorance of all things technological. "To continue. Although Mr. Anderson was unquestionably brilliant—as good as some of our grad students—he was also immensely unpopular."

"Professor Bernstein?" A head pushed its way into the office, followed by a female body in T-shirt and jeans. Two very pretty, very large green eyes glowed with hero worship. "Oh, sorry. I didn't know you were busy."

"Hey, Maria," Evan's voice was completely neutral. "I'm in a meeting right now. Come back at," he pecked at his keyboard and a five-day calendar popped up on the screen, "about two o'clock and we'll discuss the latest chapter of your dissertation. I have a couple of ideas."

Maria ducked her head slightly. "Sure thing. See you then." Any woman would have noticed the disappointment in her voice. But like so many of his species, Evan tends to be emotionally tone-deaf.

"Now then, where was I?" he rubbed his chin. "Oh yeah. Unpopular. Seems that Chaz Anderson was a real prima donna. Knew just how good he was and wanted the rest of the world to know it, too. Perpetual showoff. A royal pain in the ass. At least according to his academic advisor and three of his teachers."

"Is that so unusual in this department?"

Evan took off his glasses and rubbed the bridge of his nose. "Was it unusual? Not at all. We see it all the time. True, most of the students that come through here buy into the idea of teamwork and group projects. Mainly because they're practical and they know we're trying to prepare them for real companies and real jobs with real colleagues. But a lot of times, we get kids like Chaz who are too smart for their own good. It's usually graduate students though."

Evan slid his glasses back on and ran a hand through his ever-wayward hair. "We've got one guy here, for example, a phenomenal talent who's two years into his Ph.D. He lives here. Literally. I've heard that he has an apartment somewhere. But the notion that he leaves the building is only a rumor."

I thought of the slummy student lounge and the hallways strewn with old equipment and office furniture. "How sad. Kind of like an updated version of *Bartleby the Scrivener.* Only in this case, the guy is actually working."

Evan nudged his glasses down and looked at me over the rims. "Did I mention that literary allusions are neither allowed nor welcomed in this department?" He leaned back in his chair and clasped his hands behind his head.

"Help me understand, Evan. What drives these kids? The prima donnas. Is it money? Ambition? A craving for fame? Charles Anderson's former girlfriend seemed to think that was part of his motivation. She said he wanted to be the next Steve Jobs."

Evan focused his gaze on the ceiling for maybe ten seconds before answering. "I'd have to say that in most cases, money has very little to do with it. There are a few who have their eyes on the prize and are going after the big-buck jobs. But for the most part, it's about ego."

He leaned back in his chair and stretched.

"Yeah," he went on, "if I had to pick the one Greek myth that best describes our students, it would be Narcissus. Or maybe Icarus. A lot of them are totally wrapped up in themselves. They want to prove that they can out-program, out-think, out-create and out-hack anybody—including the faculty." He gave an oversized grin. "Especially the faculty. Sounds as if Charles Anderson belonged in that category."

"Speaking of which." The grin faded slowly. "Back to the recently departed Charles." He handed me a small stack of papers. "As you can see, he was a superb student. I managed to get copies of his transcripts." Another sheet of paper came over the desk. "And here's his CV. You'll notice that he belonged to a couple of professional clubs on campus. But that's about it."

I scanned the resume and then stopped abruptly. "Hey, look at this. For the past two summers, he was an intern at Grunwald Industries. The electronic voting machine company."

"Among other things," Evan corrected me. "They also manufacture safes and vaults. And I think they just added a line of home security systems."

"Yeah. But they happen to be very much in the news right now—and not because of their home security systems."

I stared at the CV for a while, musing about the boy who had written it, letting myself wonder what he'd been thinking at the time, what his hopes were, what angles he was playing, how he'd feel if he could see us poring over his words, trying to find clues to his death.

I let my brain buzz for a minute. "So what would someone like Charles actually do as a summer intern at Grunwald?"

Evan gave a mighty shrug. "If I had to guess, I'd say that he probably worked under one of the systems analysts. His title would be something like system administrator. Most likely he'd be assigned to troubleshoot, solve minor problems, do routine inspections of employee computers, install software upgrades, patches, that sort of thing. Basically, he'd be responsible for maintaining the code."

"The code?"

"Karin, please tell me you're just playing at being simple." He stared at me. "No. Alright. I'm referring to the Windows operating system that forms the basis for all of Grunwald's software—you know, the system used by all of its programmers."

"Seriously?" I asked. "Are you telling me that the software used for electronic voting machines is the same software used on desktop computers around the world? The same software that's always getting infected?"

Evan nodded. My mind was whirring away like an overheated piece of machinery. "That's incredible. What level of access would he have?'

Another shrug. "Again, I can't say for sure. But it would have been pretty low-level stuff he was doing. Why? Where are you going with this?"

"I'm not sure. Just trying to get a sense of all the possibilities." I put the papers down and gripped the edge of Evan's desk.

"Think about it. This kid committed suicide. Maybe. Or maybe he was murdered. So what can these documents tell us? What could he have been doing that would have driven him to take his own life? Or, worse, driven someone else to do it for him?"

Evan's eyes popped open. "Murder? What are you talking about? The poor schlub jumped off a parking structure."

"I'm just theorizing."

Evan narrowed his eyes and lowered his voice into stern mode. "Karin, you still haven't told me why you want to know all this. I assume you're not writing the kid's obit. I also assume you haven't been hired to do a warm and fuzzy story on him for the local papers, because you've never been on good terms with local editors. And you're not the type to do an exposé on his sad little life and shop it around. So what's going on?"

I said not a word. Evan leaned on his desktop until he was half standing, half sitting. "Karin. Talk to me."

More silence.

"Wait a minute." He lowered himself back into his chair. "This involves Bixie somehow, doesn't it?" I could see him thinking, his eyes moving back and forth as if he were reading some text inside his brain. Suddenly, the nickel dropped. His eyes stopped moving and looked straight into mine.

"Oh no. Please tell me I'm wrong. Tell me your mind hasn't been rotted by all those detective novels. Tell me you're not doing what I think you're doing."

"And what is it you think I'm doing?"

"I think you're doing a Miss Marple."

Why, I wondered, did people always pick on poor old doddering Miss Marple? Why not Kinsey Millhone? Or V.I. Warshawsky? Or even Agatha Raisin? Or Sister Fidelma?

Evan's voice crashed in on my musings. "Karin. Explain. Now."

Well, I reasoned, he was a friend, a good one. He'd done me a favor, not the first. He probably deserved some answers. "Okay," I capitulated. "It's like this."

Ten minutes later, Professor Evan Bernstein was staring at me in tight-lipped silence. "This is insane. You've got to stop. Before you wind up in jail. Or worse. Do you have any idea how dangerous this is? Leave it to the police."

"But I am. I told you, I promised Caldwell and Bixie's brother that if I learned anything important, I'd let them know."

He put his head in his hands. "Karin, the police have all the information I've given you. And more. They were here all day, herds of them. They're still here. Trust me. If there's a lead to be found, they'll find it."

"How you can be sure of that?"

Evan stared at me through his fingers. "You're not going to give up this craziness are you?"

I shook my head.

"Terry always said you were pigheaded."

True. Although he usually said it with more affection than I was hearing in Evan's voice right now.

Evan went on. "Okay. There's just one thing you need to know."

"What's that?"

"If you keep playing Little Miss Detective and if there's a murderer on the loose, I'll understand completely if he kills you. In fact, I'll sympathize. Because I'm thinking along those lines myself right now."

"Right," I grinned. "Just one question."

"What's that?"

"Wanna go to lunch?"

Evan stared at me, glanced up at the wall clock and gave one of his hallmark sighs.

"Why not? Your treat." He pushed his chair back and stood up. "The way things are going, it'll probably be the last lunch you ever buy me."

CHAPTER 28

Wednesday – November 20

The late great Philip Marlowe, sweating and drinking and swatting at orchids in General Sternwood's overheated conservatory, couldn't have felt more out of place than I did in the living room of Mercedes and Michael Madigan.

The room was large enough to contain my entire downstairs with space left over for a cozy nook or two, and the soaring two-story ceiling made me feel insignificant. That feeling was helped along considerably by Mercedes' personal assistant, a well-put-together redhead with hard green eyes who introduced herself as Gail Gibson. Had we been in an English novel of fifty years ago, the estimable Ms. Gibson would have insisted that I use the servants' entrance and take my tea in the kitchen.

As it was, she served up a chilly smile, escorted me to the living room and kept up a constant flow of small talk, all the while appraising my clothes, briefcase and battered portfolio as if they were items at an estate sale. Finally, satisfied that I wouldn't attempt to lift the family silver, Ms. Gibson excused herself and disappeared through the hand-carved double doors.

Sinking into a mauve-colored leather couch that triggered fantasies of quicksand, I was reminded of the opening lines from one of Humphrey Bogart's minor films. Wrapped in a rumpled trench coat, shoulders hunched against a rain of Biblical proportions, Bogart stands just outside the circle of mourners at a graveside ceremony and stares at an effigy of Ava Gardner, the Barefoot Contessa. Then in his smoky, never-to-be-repeated voice, he declares: *Life occasionally behaves as if it had seen too many bad movies.*

After passing muster at the guardhouse, I'd parked in the Madigan's circular drive between a late model silver Volvo and a gleaming black Porsche. To my middle-class eyes, the three story grey brick box with Doric columns and drawbridge-sized front door looked like a small country club or a tony little hotel.

Now, as I rubbed my sweaty palms together and stared down a large white poodle occupying the other end of the couch, I patted the right hand pocket of my blazer, just to make sure I hadn't forgotten my new, incredibly small, ridiculously expensive, voice-activated digital recorder. By law, of course, I'm obliged to ask for permission before recording a conversation. And I always do. But on this particular day, I planned to make an exception to that rule, which accounted in part for the sweaty palms.

I was studying the fieldstone fireplace at the opposite end of the room, wondering if they ever used it for roasting oxen, when Mercedes walked in. Except for the fact that she'd exchanged her leather pantsuit, probably Prada, for a knit pantsuit, probably Tahari, she looked exactly the same. Her eyes still had that faraway look, her blonde-right-down-to-the-roots hair was still moussed to perfection, and her skin still had the airbrushed sheen you'd expect from someone married to a hotshot plastic surgeon

After some polite conversation, we settled down to look at portfolio pieces. Mercedes seemed dazzled by all the brochures, flyers, ad slicks and magazines. She spread them out on the vast coffee table, touched them and turned them over as if they were items in a department store display. After maybe ten minutes, she put down a slick four-color tabloid and announced that she was ready to do the interview.

I opened my briefcase and took out a fresh notepad and pen. But before I could lob a single question, Mercedes asked one of her own in an unexpectedly businesslike voice.

"I *will* have a chance to see this article before it goes to print, won't I? I want to be able to edit my quotes and make sure all the facts are right."

Since there would never be an article, I could offer her a "yes of course" without telling an outright lie. That made for a nice change.

Knowing it would take her a while to relax into the interview process, I began with routine biographical questions. By the time we'd finished with her childhood (Indianapolis), her family (two brothers, banker father, stay-at-home mother), high school highlights (cheerleading squad, theater club, photographer for the school paper), college (University of Indiana), academic major (business administration), sorority (Delta Gamma), and first job (executive assistant at the hospital where she met Michael), she was almost loquacious.

Gradually, we worked our way through the early years of her marriage and the family's move to Ann Arbor. "Then Michael got a wonderful job offer from St. Joe's," she made her smile brighter. "So we said good-bye to all our friends and family in Indianapolis. And fifteen years later, here we are." She paused for a few seconds, then blinked a couple of times and gazed around the living room as if it were an alien landscape.

I'll say this for her—she stayed on message. Her answers were smooth and practiced, polished no doubt from past interviews and endless social events.

But every interview, like every conversation, has a superscript and a subscript, the words we hear and the words we infer. In Mercedes' case, the subscript threatened to overwhelm her upbeat, predictable, well-rehearsed answers. There was the successful, overscheduled husband who, she noted in a desperately bright voice, was rarely home these days. There were the children who, she confided, had always been "a handful." There were the committee meetings and luncheons and social clubs and Republican fundraisers and the fuzzy plans to get a graduate degree in something, someday, maybe.

Listening to her, I let myself imagine the daily doses of boredom, the slightly bitchy friends, the tennis lessons and manicures and teas for good causes, the thankless soccer-mom mornings and afternoons, the unappreciative and undisciplined kids, the evenings alone, the hours spent wondering whether her husband's endless committee meetings were really meetings with committees. Maybe I was embroidering a bit. But all was not well within the Madigan household. I'd bet my iMac on it.

I felt a pang of something like pity. As if guessing my thoughts, Mercedes abruptly straightened her spine and gave me a made-for-the-media smile. "I'm very grateful to have such a full and rich life." She looked at me, half defiant, half expectant.

"Yes. Of course." I nodded in agreement. At least she got the rich part right.

"I've been blessed with a wonderful family." I nodded again. "And there's nothing I wouldn't do for them."

Her smile didn't budge, but neither did it reach her eyes. "Nothing I wouldn't do to protect them."

Another, smaller nod from me.

"Nothing." The smile was gone now.

There was an awkward pause. I was beginning to feel distinctly creeped-out and would have loved nothing better than to walk out those double doors, push the erase button on my hand-dandy digital recorder, locate a very large scotch and pretend this whole afternoon had never happened.

Instead, I consoled myself with the fact that we were finally approaching my holy grail: people and politics. Fortunately, Mercedes was a congenital name-dropper. When I hinted that she and Michael must have a wide acquaintance, she promptly rattled off a list of semi-celebrities in the metro Detroit area. Including the Grunwald family.

Bingo.

The Grunwalds?" I asked.

"That's right. Sharon and I have been friends for years." Sharon. I filed that away for future reference.

I smiled. "Interesting. Then you must have known Dana Lewis as well."

Her blonde head gave a sudden jerk, like a horse that smells smoke. "What makes you say that?"

Time for my innocent face. "Oh, it's just that in a lot of ways Ann Arbor is a small town. I assume everyone knew Dana Lewis. Or knew of her. Also, what with all the press coverage surrounding her death, I guess she's just on my mind these days."

Mercedes kept her wary look in place. "You're right. Ann Arbor can seem like a small town. And I did know her. Slightly. But then, we know so many people." Her right hand shook slightly as it reached for a glass of ice water. "Actually, Michael doesn't approve of therapists. He says psychology is a pseudo-science. And even for a therapist, Dana was...unusual."

Before Mercedes could freeze up on me, I changed the subject. "So tell me how you and Michael came to be so active in the Republican Party."

Her face relaxed. "Michael is much more articulate on that subject than I am. But we both believe in the core conservative values. Always have."

"Such as?" I prompted.

"Well, such as small government. A strong national defense. A focus on the family. Also you have to understand, the Republicans in this county are a close-knit group. We got involved almost as soon as we moved here. And really, from there on, it was just a natural progression for someone like Michael."

"A born leader," I murmured. "He must be terribly busy, though, what with his work and all his commitments to the local GOP."

"Oh yes," Mercedes gave a weak giggle. "I'm always complaining that I have to make an appointment if I want to see him."

I lowered my eyes. "Yet he somehow manages to find time to serve as an advisor to the UM chapter of the Young Republicans. Tell me about that."

At that moment, the leaded crystal glass Mercedes was holding slipped out of her thin fingers and toppled in my direction. Within seconds, icy mineral water was blossoming across the front of my slacks.

We both jumped up. Mercedes flapped a linen napkin in the general direction of my waist while I tried to keep the fabric from touching my skin.

"Oh I'm so sorry," she squealed.

"It's okay," I lied. "I just need a bathroom," I pulled at my slacks, "and a hair dryer."

"Yes of course. Down the hall, third door on your right. The hair dryer should be on the counter."

The hall, as she called it, was as wide as my driveway and decorated with Bombay chests and prim little chairs. I was closing in on my destination when a door opened and a teenage girl stepped out.

According to Paul, this would be Mariah. She was dressed in a purple sports bra and white yoga pants cut low enough to reveal a jeweled navel ring. Her thick blonde hair was caught up in a ponytail, and if the cross-shaped pendant she wore was really made of diamonds—and not zircons as it would be for most mortals—it could easily have paid all the bills stacked on my desk and then some.

The girl lowered her cell phone a fraction of an inch and gave me a once-over, stopping for an extra second or two to take in my stained crotch. Then, in a voice that managed to blend contempt and boredom, she asked, "Where did *you* come from?"

I tried out a smile. "The living room. Where did you come from?"

After a few frigid seconds, she moved the phone back into position and sauntered past me. "What? Oh, nobody. Just one of my mother's dorky friends." She smirked. "With a serious bladder problem."

Resisting an urge to kick her taut little behind, I walked into the bathroom and immediately did a slow pirouette. The raised whirlpool tub was sized just right for bathing baby elephants. There was a marble-lined shower for two. A sleek toilet and bidet. The twin sinks were in the shape of heavy glass bowls and, when I ran a hand under the gold-plated taps, water gushed out automatically. The inset medicine cabinets must have spanned six or seven feet.

After debating with myself for a few seconds, I offered silent apologies to Aunt Ilsa and my dear departed mother, then pressed the catches on the cabinets one by one. The first door revealed an array of expensive cosmetics. As did the second one, with the addition of various deodorants and male shaving gear.

I got lucky with door number three. Two of the shelves were crowded with over-the-counter meds, rows of orange and blue prescription containers, and at least half a dozen bottles of what could have been eye drops. I glanced at the unpronounceable drug names and tried to commit them to memory, then gave up. Without pen and notebook, I'm hopeless.

For one crazy second, I considered dropping a few bottles into my jacket pockets. But the way my luck was running lately, I'd forget about them, bend over and find myself in a highly compromising situation. Instead, I blasted my slacks with the hair dryer until they were more or less back to normal. Then I used the facilities, played with the taps for a while and let myself out.

As I cracked the bathroom door open, an angry male voice wafted down the hallway from the direction of the living room.

"Just what the hell do you think you're doing?" it boomed through the half-open doors.

Walking slowly and thinking fast, I made my way down the hall as I listened to Mercedes' attempts at an apology. "I just thought…" she began.

"Well, that's usually where our problems start, isn't it?"

A mumbled reply. Then a fresh bellow. "Are you out of your mind? Agreeing to an interview at a time like this? What have you been telling that bitch?"

As I stood in the partly open doorway waiting for Mercedes' answer and wondering what to do next, Ms. Gibson appeared at my side. At that same moment, sensing our presence, Michael Madigan spun around and I found myself staring at a large blonde man, big as a linebacker, with a florid complexion, wide-set blue eyes, a chiseled nose lightly mapped with broken capillaries, a slight cleft in the chin and remarkably few wrinkles.

Before he could say a word, Ms. Gibson whispered "Wait here, please," then stepped over the threshold and quietly but firmly closed the doors behind her.

Through the heavy wood, I could hear bits of a three-way conversation.

"What did she want to know?"

"I didn't tell her…"

"I suppose we'd better assume…"

"Mr. M, may I suggest…?"

A rapid-fire pulse throbbed in my temples. After what seemed like a minor eternity, Ms. Gibson opened one of the doors slightly and slipped through. She was carrying my pea coat, portfolio, briefcase and purse.

"I'm sorry, Ms. Niemi. There's been a misunderstanding. I'm afraid you'll have to leave."

Fine with me. I was more than ready to shake off the dust of the House of Usher. Hot faced and quaking, I took my things and walked behind Ms. Gibson's trim black-clad figure.

She opened the front door. "Good-bye, Ms. Niemi." Her voice was crisp and unflustered, as if she did this sort of thing every day.

"Please thank Mercedes for me. I hope I haven't..."

"Yes, of course. Good-bye."

I didn't stop until I was past the guardhouse and back on the service road. Then I pulled over and rested my forehead on the steering wheel. Feeling myself tremble against the plastic rim, I thought of F. Scott Fitzgerald's famous line: *The rich are different from you and me.*

Right you are, Scott, I murmured. They are. And until now, I had no idea of just how different.

CHAPTER 29

Wednesday – November 20

Never underestimate the reviving power of pastries. Particularly the double-chocolate-cherry-cappuccino moon cakes produced in tiny but delicious quantities by the Small Planet Bakery.

In the few years since it opened for business, the bakery has become an Old West Side landmark. I pulled into the tiny parking lot behind a pock-marked white Ford station wagon. Between the patches of rust, someone had used black paint to hand-letter their manifesto to the world:

> *No more blood for oil.*
> *Thou shalt not kill.*
> *Bailey will pay come Judgment Day!!*
> *Of course it hurts. You're being screwed by an elephant.*

Small Planet is run by a group of young hippies, the kind of folks who help give Ann Arbor its reputation as the Berkeley of the Midwest. As the door chimes tinkled behind me, a young woman wearing a gold bandana, a man's undershirt and a sweet smile stepped up to the counter. While I pointed, she filled a crisp white bakery bag with three moon cakes, two cranberry scones, one peanut butter-chocolate chip cookie and an organic dog biscuit.

When Paul discovered me half an hour later, I was sitting at the kitchen table with a cup of fresh-brewed coffee, a pitcher of cream, a pile of napkins, a silver fork and the last of my mother's favorite dessert plates piled high with pastries. Pop-eyed at the spectacle, he opened the sliding glass door slowly, never taking his eyes off me and the plate.

"Moon cakes. And an *overdose* at that." He shook his head in a knowing way. "Just how bad was your interview with Mercedes?"

Without answering, I reached for a cake but he was too quick for me. I found myself grasping air and looking up at the dessert plate, now poised above his head.

"*Not* before dinner. I don't care *how* bad it was."

"Paul." I used my don't-screw-with-me voice. "Put. Them. Down. Now."

He gave me a stern look, then relented and began lowering the plate slowly. "At least come over and have a bowl of chicken soup. I made it last night. I'll even pop a loaf of Jeff Renner's bread in the oven."

The soup by itself was incredibly tempting. But the bread pushed it over the edge. Jeff Renner claims to make the best French bread this side of Paris, and he does not exaggerate.

"With beer?"

Paul shrugged. "Why not?" He put the plate down at the other end of the table. "So we'll just leave these right here."

I cast a suspicious look over at Albert who was licking his right paw with far too much nonchalance. "Don't even think about it, Al," I warned. He stopped in mid-lick, the tip of his pink tongue protruding slightly, then blinked and, with an offended air, picked up where he'd left off.

While I got my pea coat and purse, Paul putzed around the kitchen. Ten minutes later, I was seated at a well-scrubbed pine table with a napkin on my lap. Cloth, of course. As we ate, I told my sad tale. In fact, I described the entire sequence of bizarre encounters—from Ricki and Evan to Mercedes, Mariah, Mandy and Michael.

Except for an occasional "Oh my God," "No way" and "You poor baby," Paul kept quiet. When I was through, he pushed away his soup plate, put his elbows on the table and cupped his chin.

"Well, of course, it's common knowledge that the Madigan marriage was not made in heaven." He sighed. "It's a pity you weren't able to keep pushing on the subject of Dana, though. Mercedes was bound to spill sooner or later. Of course, we already know she was seeing Dana on a regular basis. And given her history, she had plenty of issues to work on."

He drummed his fingers on the table. "Normally, I'd say it's not even worth thinking about. But Michael's reaction makes me suspect there's something more to it."

I halted my spoon in mid-air. "What do you mean? It's obvious, isn't it? Michael blew up because he didn't want his wife—his unstable wife—talking to a journalist." I emptied the contents of my spoon. "Or in my case, a pseudo-journalist."

I fed myself another mouthful. "It's perfectly understandable. Would you want Mercedes representing you in an interview? Chatting up a storm?" I put myself in Michael's place for a microsecond. Mercedes talking to the press. Scary thought.

"Yeah, yeah, yeah," Paul chanted. "The fact that he disapproved, that I understand. The fact that he was pissed, that I understand. But it's the *magnitude* of his response. *That's* what makes me suspicious. I mean, the man could have handled the situation in ten different ways, most of them pretty low key. But instead he went ballistic."

Paul took a swallow of his pilsner. "You've got to remember, this guy is on boards, committees, he co-chairs fund drives, he sponsors golf outings for good causes, if you consider the Republican Party a good cause. And believe me, he's not in the habit of blowing up in public."

Paul twirled his glass and thought some more. "He always comes across as charming, in a very guys-R-us kind of way. You know. Big smile. Slap on the back. Plenty of small talk. Even if he can't stand the sight of you. You never know what he's really thinking or feeling. In fact, based on the few times I've met him, I wasn't even sure he *had* feelings."

A mini-flashback hit and I saw myself cowering in the vast hallway again. "Trust me, he's got feelings. Loud ones."

I helped myself to another piece of buttered bread, took a bite and smothered a moan. "So maybe he's been under a lot of stress lately. God knows it was a nasty election and he was probably at the center of it—at least in southeastern Michigan."

Paul tapped the beer glass gently against his mouth while he thought. "That still doesn't account for the huge gaffe he made today." He leaned toward me. "You don't get it, Karin. This guy is an expert at public relations. He doesn't want anyone to think badly of him—not even anonymous hacks."

Ignoring my gasp of outrage, Paul went on. "The problem is, we're working at such a *huge* disadvantage here. I mean, the police know all sorts of things we don't. By now they've talked with all of Dana's neighbors. So they know that Mercedes was seeing Dana on a regular basis. And they probably know if she went alone or not."

"Alone? Why wouldn't she go alone?"

Paul gave me one of his how-can-you-be-so-dense looks. "Because depending on the day of the week and the drugs at hand, Mercedes Madigan can be very fragile. And that's putting it kindly. She likes to have people around her, for support. People like Gail Gibson, for instance, who is more keeper than personal assistant. Which brings us to an interesting possibility. Did Mercedes take a friend along when she went to see Dana? And if so, who?"

He put the glass back on the table, centering it on a coaster. "Even more interesting, is it possible that Michael went with her, dropped her off, picked her up? Maybe even waited for her? Thus giving him easy access to Dana's entire house."

Somehow, I couldn't picture Michael Madigan as a doting husband. "You're making a lot of assumptions."

"That's because all we *have* is assumptions."

"Okay, then how about doing some assuming about Chaz Anderson?"

Paul shook his head and began gathering up the wreckage of our dinner. "No. Not enough to go on there. Better to focus on what and who we know."

My turn for head shaking. Somehow I was certain that the key to the murders—or the murder and suicide—revolved around Chaz Anderson. "Well, you know what a real detective would do at this point." I dangled the bait.

Paul looked up from the sink and gave me a wry look. "By real detective, I suppose you mean someone like Travis McGee or Jim Chee?"

"Of course." I picked up my purse. "A real detective would write down everything she knew about the case. Or at least the names of suspects. And then she'd try to made some sense out of it." I dug out my business card case and a pen. "And that's exactly what we're going to do now."

For the next twenty minutes, Paul and I brainstormed, argued and scribbled names on the back of my business cards. When we were through, we had two neat little rows of suspects—one for Dana Lewis and one for Charles Anderson. The Dana Lewis side was crowded with names. On the Chaz Anderson side, there were just two: Isabel Lewis and Michael Madigan, with a question mark after Michael's name.

Paul shook his head in a fussy way and pointed to a series of three cards, clustered near Allegra's name. "White-Blonde, Red-Blonde and Brown-Blonde. What's that about?"

"They're friends of Allegra's. Although, when it comes to Allegra, maybe 'friend' is too strong a word." I told him briefly about my encounter with the trio in Hill Auditorium.

He poked at the cards. "This isn't telling us anything. How about if we try the old motive, means and opportunity approach?"

I shook my head. "Won't work. At least not with Dana. The means were available to anyone who suffered from eye problems or gut problems or lung problems or who could lie convincingly to their doctor about symptoms and get the necessary prescription. Or happened to be a doctor themselves." I began lining up the edges of the cards.

"The opportunity thing might help a little," I continued, "except that the poison could have been planted just about anytime. Also, Dana knew a lot of people and more than a few of them seemed to have a grudge against her. So we have more motive than we can possibly handle."

It was almost enough to make me feel some sympathy for Andrew Murray and Moses B. Caldwell. Almost.

I took my hands out from under my chin and placed them next to the mass of cards. "What we're looking for is points of intersection. People who knew both Dana and Chaz." I pulled out two sets of cards with identical names and slapped them down near Paul. "Isabel Lewis. And Michael Madigan. Maybe. Depending on the Young Republican connection."

Paul nodded and stared at the two names. "But there must be more. We just don't know who they are." He gave a disgusted look and began collecting all the cards into two neat little stacks. "That's the real problem. We don't have enough information to build a case against anyone." He tapped the cards to even all the edges. "So our next step is?"

I gave that some thought. I desperately wanted to check out Grunwald Industries and their summer intern program. But how?

I could try the I'm-writing-an-article ploy with the Grunwalds but I wouldn't get far without a solid reference. And after today's fiasco, I certainly wouldn't dare use Mercedes' name. Not being a real reporter, I couldn't call the HR department for background on Chaz Anderson. And for reasons political and otherwise, Grunwald was probably inundated with reporters these days and turning them away in droves.

I could say I was doing a project for the UM Engineering Center. But it would be pitifully easy for them to check. And did I really want to risk alienating a client for the sake of this wild goose chase?

I tapped my fingers on the table. "The next step is for me to do more prying and poking around. I think I'll start with the Young Republicans and some of their mentors. Then I'll check out Grunwald Industries. Somehow."

Lew, still groggy from a long nap, padded up to the table and planted his front paws on my lap. For a few minutes, I stroked his head and tried to avoid getting my face washed in the process.

Finally Paul broke the silence. "When you look at it objectively, this whole idea of chasing down a murderer is pretty crazy, isn't it?"

"It is." I gave a nod and stood up. "Thanks for dinner. It was delicious, as usual. And you probably saved me from glycemic shock." I gave Lew one more pat on the head and began walking toward the front hall closet. "Time for me to head home."

As he handed me my coat, Paul opened his mouth to speak but then changed his mind. Forcing me to ask: "Anything wrong?"

He crossed his arms and watched me pull on my jacket. "Not really. It's just that…" He consulted with himself and tried again. "I was just wondering if you've noticed anything unusual going on at your place lately."

"Unusual." I slung my purse over one shoulder. "As in celebrity poker tournaments? Tupperware parties? What did you have in mind?"

He pursed his lips, swung his eyes left and right, and seemed to come to a decision. "I ask because while I was standing in your kitchen earlier, there seemed to be some kind of…and I know how crazy this sounds…but it was some shadow thing hovering around the room."

He gave me a look that managed to be both embarrassed and defensive. "I can't describe it any better than that. A flickering sort of shadow that I saw out of the corner of my eye. And whenever I tried to focus on it…"

"It disappeared." I patted his arm. "Yes, I know. Don't worry. I see it all the time. Spooky, isn't it? I'm pretty sure it's Dana Lewis."

Paul hugged himself tighter with his crossed arms. "No, I don't think so. It seemed… My impression was that this…thing…this…"

"Spirit? Ghost?"

"This thing," he repeated firmly, "was young and probably male. It just had that kind of energy."

He slapped a hand over his eyes. "Oh I can't believe I said that. No, God, please. Don't let me turn into a granola head."

The warm comfortable feeling in my stomach was suddenly replaced by a churning queasiness. "Male? Are you sure?"

"No, of course I'm not sure," Paul snapped. "I just know that there was something in your kitchen, or someone, and it seemed like, or felt like, a young man. Or what had been a young man."

The unspoken words hung in the air between us.

Like a young man.

And not just any young man.

A very particular young man.

A recently deceased young man by the name of Chaz Anderson.

CHAPTER 30

The call from Michael Madigan's office came through at ten a.m., just as I was working out a cover story for the HR director at Grunwald Industries. I was still debating the wisdom of taking the Engineering Institute's name in vain. Risky as it was, the idea was sounding better all the time.

It had been a productive morning but a long one. After some crack-of-dawn web research followed by a few phone calls at a decent hour, I tracked down the current president of the Young Republicans, a confident sounding kid named Steve Browning. Once I explained that I was writing an article on Chaz Anderson for the *Grosse Pointe Telegraph*, he was happy to cooperate. I knew I was taking a chance, using the name of a real newspaper. But given the fact that the Millennials practically live online, it seemed safer to cite an actual paper rather than risk being outed by a three-second Google search.

"So you're on staff at the paper?" Steve asked.

"No, I'm a stringer, this is a freelance assignment."

"Huh. Must be a tough way to make a living."

Smart kid. "Well at least I'm never bored. Now, about Charles Anderson..."

According to Steve, Chaz turned up at YR get-togethers when it suited him. In a voice that betrayed only the mildest disapproval, he explained that Chaz was a regular at social events and networking sessions, especially when adult mentors and corporate advisors were on hand. He'd generally make himself scarce for work sessions, telephone marathons and get-out-the-vote canvasses in local neighborhoods.

"Was he particularly close to anyone in the organization?" I wanted to know. "Maybe one of the advisors, someone who might be willing to talk with me, share some anecdotes?"

After thinking for a few seconds, Steve gave me two names: Ben Popoulous and Harry Stewart. He spelled both for me and offered phone numbers. I scribbled it all down, then sat back in my chair. So that was it? A dead end?

Hope revived when he had an afterthought. "Oh, and you might try Michael Madigan. He and Chaz seemed to hit it off. And I heard that Chaz helped Mrs. Madigan do some social media promos for her charity events. Michael is probably too busy to talk, but give him a call anyway. You never know."

Oh you are so right, I thought as I jotted down Michael's office phone number below the other two. You never know. After saying my thank you's and ringing off, I gave myself a minute or two to gloat. Then I looked at the set of three names and decided to start with Ben Popoulous to see what clues he might give me about Michael's role in the organization. Something I certainly wasn't likely to learn from Michael himself.

I was in luck. The crisp female voice that answered—"Popoulous Enterprises, Mr. Popoulous' office"—listened patiently. I was careful to drop Steve's name and mention the Young Republicans. She surprised me by offering to see when Mr. Popoulous might be available.

After a minute or so, she was back on the line with another surprise. Mr. Popoulous could meet with me briefly at two this afternoon. Would that work? It would.

"Good. Then he'll expect you at two. At the Mediterranean Isles Restaurant on Washtenaw. Just ask for him at the reception desk."

Hot damn. I gave Albert a wink and got one of his inscrutable old-man-on-the-mountain stares in return. Basking in the glow of my success, I scrawled out some questions for Mr. Popoulous. Then, since I was obviously on a roll, I decided to tackle Grunwald Industries.

I was deep in thought when the phone rang. To my relief, it wasn't the female voice from Popoulous Enterprises calling to cancel my impromptu meeting with her boss. It was another female voice, this one all syrupy and slow, the kind that makes me want to blurt out something rude.

Instead, I turned up my impulse control and simply said yes when she asked if I was Karin Niemi. Would I please hold for Dr. Michael Madigan? Oh yes. Absolutely.

Within five seconds, Madigan himself was on the phone. He sounded so calm and pleasant, I could scarcely believe it was the same man I'd heard roaring at his wife the day before.

The good doctor wanted to apologize for yesterday's unfortunate incident. He forced out a chuckle that sounded almost painful. "I'm afraid you caught our family at a bad time, Ms. Niemi."

Like any good therapist, I didn't say a word.

"What with my work schedule these days plus the election, we've all been under tremendous pressure. One of my practice partners retired and I've had to pick up most of his patients..." Realizing that he was beginning to ramble, he let the rest of the sentence drift away.

More silence on my end. I was beginning to enjoy this.

"Anyway, I feel a need to apologize to you. In person." Paul was right. This guy really did have an instinct for PR. I could almost feel myself begin to melt.

"Is there any chance you could stop by my office this afternoon for a few minutes?"

"Really, there's no need..." I began.

"Oh but there is. Please. Humor me. How about one o'clock? I'm in the Huron Professional Building. I really need to do this, to make amends, try to set things right." More like spin control than amends, I thought. Still, I was impressed.

"Well, if you insist..."

"I do."

I relented. By then, my curiosity was running rampant and nothing short of the apocalypse could have kept me away. "Okay then. One o'clock, your office."

After a stunned minute or two, I reached for the phone again. As I began dialing Bixie's number, I noticed a fuzzy grey blob under the Windsor rocker. Could it possibly be? I nearly dropped the receiver.

A dust bunny? In my house? Impossible. Albert walked up to the offending object for a closer look and blinked twice.

"You're right, Al. I'm losing it. I hardly know myself these days."

In her burgundy blazer, tight black jeans and stiletto-heel boots, Bixie created a major stir in Michael Madigan's immaculate waiting room. Here was a woman clearly not in need of Dr. Madigan's ministrations. Everyone probably assumed she was a former patient, a walking testimonial, living proof of the man's skill with lasers and scalpels.

While everyone else was staring at Bixie, I fixed my attention on the five women in bright white lab coats behind the counter. They were various and sundry sizes—and probably ages as well—but they all bore an eerie similarity to each other.

For one thing, they were all blonde. The same blonde, a sort of sunshine yellow, soft-and-shiny, generic Hollywood blonde. But what riveted my attention was their faces. There were no bags, no lines, no dark circles, no crinkles, no liver spots, not even the slightest hint of a jowl or a sag. Just tight little smiles set in flawless complexions.

"Bixie," I whispered into the side of her face. "I think we've stumbled onto the Stepford Staff." For which I earned an elbow in the ribs.

As we approached the reception area, I could see that the blondes were in conference around the office copier. Spotting us, one of them broke free from the klatsch. "You have an appointment?" I gave her my name and she waved a manicured hand at one of the nearby seating areas. Then she hustled back to the copier and a mad buzz of whispers ensued. I seemed to be the breaking news of the day.

"You want me to go in with you?" Bixie asked. A tiny worry line fluttered across her forehead as she spoke. I found it curiously reassuring.

"No, of course not. I just needed moral support. Besides…"

At that moment, Michael Madigan walked into the waiting room. The largest and probably the most senior of the blondes whispered to him and pointed at me. He came over, hand extended. At his invitation, I followed him down a long hallway to a door with a brass nameplate. Inside, he motioned me into a remarkably comfortable chair and then sat on a corner of the desk, facing me.

He spread his hands out and gave me a warm smile. "Ms. Niemi, what can I say, except that I'm terribly sorry you got such an unfortunate impression of us yesterday."

Us? "Oh," I fumbled for something coherent to say. What does one say after witnessing a tantrum that tips into spouse abuse? "Really, as I told you on the phone, there's no need to apologize. You obviously hadn't been warned that I was coming. And," I finished weakly, "you'd be surprised at the number of people who really don't like journalists much."

He held up his right hand as if to deflect my forgiveness. "No. What I did was, well, simply not acceptable. I was completely out of line. And it wasn't you, really. As I mentioned, I've been under a lot of pressure, what with the election. You wouldn't believe the number of meetings and teleconferences and fundraisers it takes to get someone elected in this state. And that's in addition to the twelve-hour days I normally put in around here. I guess it all caught up with me."

I tried to look cool and in charge but the effect was spoiled by a triple-sneeze and a cough. I pulled out a wad of tissues.

"As a goodwill gesture, I want you to know that Mercedes and I will be happy to do an interview with you. At some future time. When things are a bit more settled." I sneezed again and looked around the soothing blue-and-grey office. Mold? Chemicals? I blew my nose.

Michael's smile began to fade and his eyes frosted over. "Of course, we'd want your assurance of professional discretion." Starting now, I assumed. "And we'd reserve the right to approve or veto anything you wrote. Is that agreeable?" He took my silence for a yes. It was probably a word he heard quite often.

"Good." He stood up and rubbed his hands together. "Why don't you give us a call in a couple of weeks then?" His smile was in place again, revealing two rows of perfect teeth. "I'm sure we can schedule something." Provided I didn't spread any of this around town in the meantime.

"Okay," I sniffled into a tissue. "I'll do that."

He paused to study me for a second. "Allergies?"

"Yeah," I tried to clear my throat.

He held up a large index finger. "Wait here. I'll be right back. I've got just the thing for you." Before I could stop him, he made a quick exit and returned a minute later with an orange pharmacy bottle, no label, containing maybe a dozen pills.

"And this is what exactly?" I asked.

"It's new, just on the market." He rattled off some long complicated Latin-sounding name that started with a B. "I take it myself and recommend it to patients who suffer from allergies. Great stuff."

He handed me the bottle. "Here. Take two of these and your problems will be over."

I shook the bottle and watched the pills rattle around. Paranoia loomed large in my soul and dark thoughts scuttled up to the surface.

My problems will be over? I looked at Michael Madigan's handsome, unreadable face. Or is it more likely, doctor, that if I take two of these, *your* problems will be over?

CHAPTER 31

According to my sketchy on-line research, Ben Popoulous was what used to be known as a big shot. In today's parlance, a player. He owned five successful restaurants, three in Ann Arbor, one in Royal Oak and one in Roseville, plus a half-interest in a Canadian hockey team. He was also a major philanthropist and his list of civic affiliations was too long to make me want to read the whole thing. He was active in the local Greek Orthodox church and, like Michael Madigan, was a prominent member of the Michigan Republican Party.

The hostess who greeted me was a striking brunette in her mid-twenties. Her form-fitting knit dress made me acutely aware of how dowdy I must look in my L.L. Bean turtleneck and generic slacks. She led me through the main seating area, past murals of Grecian ruins and seaside villages, up a flight of steps, down a short hallway, then knocked on a slightly open door before entering.

In my imagination, I'd sketched out a portrait of Ben Popoulous: florid, self-absorbed face, maybe a little cruel around the edges, topping a body that was running to fat but beautifully camouflaged in an expensive suit. Instead, I found myself in the presence of a minor Greek god, a man whose face belonged on a mosaic in the antiquities room of the British Museum. He stood up, smiled as I were an old friend and gave my hand a firm, warm squeeze.

The smile chilled down considerably as he turned to my escort. "Didn't you offer our guest anything to drink? To eat? What were you thinking?" Then another just-for-me smile. "These young people, sometimes they forget the basic courtesies. So what can I offer you, Miss—it's Niemi, isn't it? An espresso perhaps? With some baklava?"

I wavered. He pressed. "Made just this morning in our own kitchens. My mother's recipe."

I surrendered. "Sounds wonderful, thanks. Are you having anything?"

He patted his not very large stomach. "My doctor tell me I need to cut back on caffeine, sugar, fats, alcohol." He gave a Zorba the Greek shrug. "So I told him, alright. But at least leave me some wickedness." He laughed. It was a very nice sound. "Luckily, I still have a few vices he hasn't discovered." He winked.

Rich. Handsome. Charming. Civic-minded. Republican, of course. But then no one is perfect. I began to entertain fantasies. Maybe I could persuade him to adopt me.

As we chatted about nothing in particular, warming up for the interview, the chastised hostess returned with a tray containing fragrant coffee in a shiny metal pot, a tiny cup and saucer, a pitcher of cream and a plate of golden baklava gleaming with honey.

Satisfied that the courtesies, as he called them, had been attended to, Ben Popoulous turned down his smile slightly to indicate he was ready to get to work. "So what can I tell you about poor Charles Anderson?"

I gave myself a little shake and pulled out my notebook and pen. "Well, Mr. Popoulous…"

"Please. It's Ben."

"Okay." I smiled. "Ben." Good grief, I was positively smitten with the man. Somewhere in the back of my mind, I heard my Aunt Ilsa's voice telling me to shape up. "Right. Well, I'm interested in anything you can tell me about Chaz, Charles that is. What you remember about him. Any projects or activities he might have been involved in with the Young Republicans."

Ben played with the gold pen on his desk for a moment before framing an answer. When he spoke, I could hear the evasion in his words. "Yes, well, Charles struck me as being a very ambitious young man. Quite charming at times. Highly intelligent." He moved the pen around some more. "Of course, I never got to know him well."

"I understand you've been an advisor to the group for some years now. What does that involve exactly?"

He looked up at me, apparently relieved to be talking about something besides Chaz. "Just what you'd expect." He leaned back in his chair. "We help them choose their projects, organize, recruit new members, coordinate with Michigan Republican Party headquarters. We see that they get any resources they might need—phones, computers, office equipment, space, as well as access to voter databases, names of party members, addresses, phone numbers, that sort of thing. So, you might say we help with practical matters as well as strategy."

I warned myself to be very careful in phrasing the next question. "I would imagine," I spoke slowly and deliberately, "that, on occasion, an advisor might form a friendship of sorts with one of the members."

The pen came into play again as Ben phrased his own careful answer to my careful question. "I'd say that friendship is overstating it. Certainly, we try to be supportive. Sometimes we hold special events, receptions, parties, fundraisers, that sort of thing, at our homes. So, yes, we do get to know some of the kids—the more proactive, involved kids anyway. But close? No, I wouldn't say that."

"Was Charles one of those? Proactive? Involved? Putting himself forward?"

"As I said, I never really got to know him very well."

Now was the moment to push. "But what about the other advisors?" I made a pretense of checking my notes. "Michael Madigan for instance?"

Ben folded his hands and leaned forward slightly. "Michael is a very hard-working, very dedicated mentor. Has been for years."

"But," I persisted, "was he close to Chaz?"

"I really couldn't say. They worked on projects together occasionally. Fundraisers and social events mainly." He offered me another killer smile. "You'd really have to ask him yourself. Honestly, all I can tell you is what I've already told you—that Chaz was intelligent, quick, obviously a kid with a bright future ahead of him. He helped us out now and then with the computers. Brilliant he was. We're all very sorry to lose him." He lowered his eyes. "It's a tragedy."

"Did he ever seem depressed or desperate?"

"I told you," the voice was growing steelier by the second. "We weren't close." He cocked his head. "And really, what does my impression of his mental state have to do with an obituary for his hometown paper? I assume you'd want to focus on the positive."

Oops. "Sorry. Sometimes I get so involved in my subjects, I dig a little deeper than I need to," I offered my best smile. "It's a professional liability, I'm afraid." I consulted my notebook again for something to do, then looked up at Ben. "Sounds as if I should track down Michael Madigan. From what you've told me, he spent more time with Chaz."

The smile was purely a formality now. "Did I say that?" He looked pointedly as his Rolex. "Ah, I'm afraid I must get to my next appointment." He stood up and held out his hand. "Pleasure meeting you, my dear."

He bent slightly to press a buzzer on his desk, then straightened up. "Oh, one last thing. It's probably best not to bother Michael. He's a very busy man." He ran one hand through his silver mane of hair. I could hear the approach of high heels in the hallway. "And now Miss Melzian will see you out."

Curiouser and curiouser I thought, as I sat in the car regrouping. I couldn't decide whether Ben Popoulous was being naturally cautious or unnaturally protective of Michael Madigan. And I could have kicked myself for not managing to snarf up at least one of those pastries before I left. Too bad I couldn't ask for a doggy bag.

Just then my cell phone rang, an event that always gives me an adrenal jolt. It was on ring number four by the time I finally had it out of my purse and checked the caller ID. "Hey Andy. What's up?"

The slight pause told me I'd hit a small nerve. "Funny, that was exactly what I was going to ask you. How's it going?"

"Fine."

"Maybe I should be more specific," he growled. "What's been going on with you and Bixie and your so-called case?"

What to say? The truth had been working pretty well for me lately, so I decided to chance it one more time. I told him I'd spoken with Mercedes Madigan. "Just to keep Bixie happy," I assured him.

"Tell me you didn't do that."

"Look, they never suspected a thing, I mean they never guessed I wasn't kosher," I insisted. "In fact," this was the hard part, admitting failure, "in fact, I didn't even get much information. When Michael Madigan got home, he basically threw me out."

I waited for the inevitable burst of laughter. Instead, Andrew's voice was edgy and interested. "Tell me more."

So I did. Pretty much the whole thing, ending with my visit to Michael's office. And the bit about the pills.

Silence. Was he going to yell, I wondered. I hated yelling, never having had much experience with it as a child. To break the suspense, I jumped in with my big bold request.

"I know you're going to think this is paranoid, but I was just wondering if you could maybe have the pills analyzed for me. You know. Just in case."

"In case what?"

I fumed. "In case they're not allergy pills. In case they're go-to-sleep-and-never-wake-up-again pills."

He waited for a few seconds before speaking. "Do you have any idea how busy the path lab is these days?"

"No," I admitted.

"They have a huge backlog. Always do. And it's worse than ever right now, thanks to the current body count in our pleasant little community. But if I ask nicely, I might be able to talk them into analyzing those pills of yours within, say, two weeks or so."

"Really?"

"Drop them off at the station. At the front desk. Put the bottle in a sealed envelope with my name on it." I thought he was about to ring off, but suspicion was evidently a family trait. I heard a lot of it in his next question: "So what's your next step? And don't tell me that you're not thinking about a next step."

Tell him? Not tell him? "Grunwald Industries," I blurted out before I could check myself. "I thought I might try to get an interview with the HR department, see what they can tell me about their intern program since…"

"Since Chaz Anderson interned with them twice," Andrew finished the sentence for me. Until that last little slip of mine, he'd kept his temper under control, but I sensed that was about to change.

Anticipating an explosion, I held the phone a couple of inches away from my ear. Smart move, as it turned out.

"I have one word of advice for you, Karin. Don't. Do not, I repeat, do not contact anyone at Grunwald Industries. Do not even think about it." Did he ever stop for breath? "If I hear even the slightest, most unreliable rumor that you have approached Grunwald Industries, I swear I will charge you with something and make it stick, and believe me, given what you've been up to lately, it won't be hard."

Still shouting, he went on. "You do understand—don't you—that if you attempt to contact Grunwald Industries, I will find out about it?"

"If you say so." I pouted for a couple of seconds. "Tell me, does this fall under the category of 'serve'? Or 'protect'?"

"I'm not fucking around here, Karin. Stay out of Grunwald Industries. I mean it. In fact, stay out of the whole case." Slight pause to collect himself. Then, in a somewhat calmer voice: "Clear enough for you?"

"Perfectly."

"Good." Deep breath on his end of the line. "Don't forget to drop off those pills. I'll check in again with you. Soon."

I pressed the call-end button and let out a long, pent-up breath.

Over the past few days, I'd almost gotten used to the spirits or energies or manifestations or whatever it was that seemed to be haunting my little bungalow. But lately I had the distinct impression that I wasn't always alone outside of the house. Sometimes it felt like one or more ghostly guests were hanging around, keeping me company as I moved through the world. On the other hand, I reminded myself firmly, I didn't really believe in them—whatever they were.

Still, this was definitely and undeniably one of those not-alone moments. And if by some remote chance they were real, why not make the most the most of it? God knows I needed all the help I could get.

I spoke out loud to whoever might be listening, from this world or the next. "Well, you heard what he said."

I leaned against the headrest and looked out at the dusty, pollution-choked trees in the parking lot. The traffic along Washtenaw moved at a furious pace, almost as fast as the thoughts that were racing around in my poor fevered brain.

"Let's take a vote. What do you think I should do?"

CHAPTER 32

"Grunwald Industries, Human Resources Department. May I help you?"

My palms were hot and sticky, either from a fear of screwing up in the next few minutes or the dread of having Andrew find out what I'd done. Probably both. Before dialing the number, I'd rehearsed my shtick a couple of times. I took a quick breath and plunged in, trying to give my voice a professional gloss.

"Yes, this is Karin Niemi. I'm a freelance writer, working on a project for the U of M Engineering Institute. A brochure and web segment for their summer intern program. They suggested I call you folks to see if I could talk to, uh," I looked down at my notes, cribbed from the company web site, "to Keith Soderblum who I understand directs your intern program. They thought he might be able to give me some useful background information, maybe some quotes we could use." Not bad.

"The University of Michigan, did you say? Engineering?" I guessed she was writing as she spoke.

"That's right," I lied. Then I followed it up with a thought wave: You can take my word for it. No need to check with Engineering.

"I believe Mr. Soderblum is in his office right now. Can you hold while I try to reach him?"

"Of course." I wiped my palms on my sweater but succeeded only in picking up bits of lint and wool, so I moved on to my slacks instead. Maybe this wasn't such a great idea.

"Hello, Keith Soderblum speaking." The voice belonged to someone who was used to dealing with the public in general and media types in particular. Calm. Confident. No nonsense.

I repeated my cover story, verbatim.

"Well, we're always happy to help out U of M Engineering. They've been one of our top recruiting sources for years."

"Yes, I know." I hoped he couldn't hear how much I wanted this whole conversation to be over and done with.

"How's Tad by the way?" Tad as in Tad Weiczorek, the Institute's marketing director.

"The last time I talked to him, he was just fine." True enough, although that conversation had taken place some months ago. "So, Mr. Soderblum. I know how busy you must be, but I was hoping you could find time in your schedule for an interview. I apologize for the short notice. We're on a tight deadline."

As I spoke, I had to fight down a rising sense of panic. Strange. Because, except for the risk of pushing Andrew's rage button yet again and the threat of jail time which, surely, he wasn't serious about, and except for the fact that I was jeopardizing a relationship with an on-again-off-again client, except for all that I wasn't in any real danger. Yet weirdly enough, that's what it felt like.

Maybe, I decided, everyone was right. Maybe I've just read too many detective novels.

"Yes, well, let's see." I could hear a faint clicking sound as he moused and keyboarded. A pause. "It looks like I have some time next Tuesday morning, early." Drat. I couldn't wait that long. "Or," he stretched the word out, "I have a little time right now. So if you're ready to do this, we could chat for a few minutes."

I swallowed a knot in my throat and hoped Keith Soderblum hadn't heard the gulp. "Uh, sure, we can talk now." Frantically, I began jotting down key words, sketching out questions.

It was actually a good interview, as these things go. And a waste, really, when I considered that not one single word was going to make it into print or online. After we'd discussed the intern program in broad outlines, and after Keith had promised to send me PDF's of their latest brochures and posters for reference, and after he'd sung more hymns of praise to the U of M, I was ready to make my move.

"So," I asked, as casually as I could manage, "what sorts of things could a summer intern expect to be doing at Grunwald Industries? Let's say, for example, a student from computer engineering since that seems to be the biggest group you hire." It was a guess, of course.

"Well that depends on the student, the project manager and the needs of the department," Keith hedged, as any decent corporate spokesman should. "But generally, a computer engineering student would be assigned to basic maintenance. Trouble-shooting. Software upgrades." Exactly what Evan had said.

"Would they ever be involved," I took a flyer, "in software development, that sort of thing?"

"Almost never," Kevin assured me in his best corporate voice. "As you probably know, our work is very proprietary. And given the fact that we're involved in the security industry..."

"Actually, I was thinking more in terms of your electronic voting machines. Since they account for such a large portion of your business." Another guess that went uncorrected.

"Well, in that case, security is even more of a concern. So an intern could expect a great deal of close supervision and, at most, would be involved in helping to debug program segments. Generally, though, we tend to keep them on repairs, basic upgrade work and preventive maintenance. It gives us a chance to scope them out, test their skills, see how well they fit with our organization and how well they understand our systems."

"Of course," I agreed. "So they'd never be directly engaged in, say, helping to write source code for the machines or..."

The voice became clipped and distant. "No, definitely not. As I told you."

New direction. "I suppose that, during the course of the summer, a lot of the interns really meld with the organization, become part of the team."

"Absolutely. As I'm sure you know, many of our interns eventually receive offers of full-time employment and a large number of them choose to join our company. I think the actual rate of job offers is somewhere around forty or forty-five percent of the total pool, although I'm sure Tad can give you a more accurate number."

"I'm sure," I echoed. "You know, I was just thinking that the recent death of Charles Anderson—you know, the young man who killed himself here in Ann Arbor a few days ago—must have come as something of a shock, at least a minor one, to you folks."

For a few seconds it was very quiet on the other end of the line. Then Keith responded. "And why would that be?"

"Well," keep it light I told myself, "from what I've been reading, Charles interned with Grunwald for one summer. Or was it two? I can't recall."

"I really can't comment on that, Ms. Niemi. I'm sure his co-workers at the company were deeply saddened. But of course dozens of interns cycle through this company every summer."

As a fellow professional, I had to admire his agility. He went on. "And while the young man's death was certainly a tragedy, I doubt that there are many employees who were close to him or even remember him all that well." Which, of course, contradicted his earlier comment about close company ties among workers. Pause. "So, do you feel you have enough information?"

I looked down at my notes. "Oh yes," I assured him. "You've been more helpful than you know."

CHAPTER 33

Thursday- November 21

"But what do we really *know*?" Paul demanded as he loaded up a cracker with white cheddar and smoked turkey. He took a resounding bite and crumbs rained down on the kitchen table. Ignoring the paper napkin next to his plate, he pulled out a monogrammed handkerchief and dabbed at his lips. I grabbed the napkin and swept the crumbs into a neat little pile. Paul gave his mouth one final pat before adding, "I mean, what have we really got in terms of concrete facts?"

Bixie pulled a face. "Would you please not talk with your mouth full?" We were sitting in my kitchen, conferring about the case and staving off hunger pangs. At the moment, Bixie was making a big show of reading the ingredients on a package of sliced turkey. But even sulfites couldn't dim the glow she always gets when things become interesting—things in this case being our wild gropings in quest of whoever murdered Dana Lewis and, possibly, Chaz Anderson.

She put the package down and shoved it dismissively toward the middle of the table. "What we've got is quite a bit, thanks to Karin. We know, for instance, that..."

"Wait." I cleared a space on the table. "Let's do this right." I twisted around and found that I could just reach the kitchen notepad and pen.

Paul, who was intently building his second cheddar and turkey tower, waved the cheese knife in my direction. "Oh please, spare us. Do you have to play Kinsey Milhone?"

I turned to a fresh page. "For your information," I said smugly, "she tends to favor three-by-five cards." I wrote a large satisfying number one and circled it. Paul shrugged and kept eating.

I started writing. "Number one," I began, "we know that Dana was killed on Friday morning by poison. But because she was poisoned, we also know that timing wasn't crucial. We can assume that the murderer simply wanted her out of the way within a reasonable period of time. And wanted to be far away, with a comfortable alibi, when it happened."

Paul nudged a few stray crumbs from the corners of his mouth. "Number two, we know that Chaz was seeing Dana. And that he was getting better, or seemed calmer anyway. But we don't know what he was seeing her about."

Bixie crossed her arms. "Alright. Number three, we know that Chaz died late Monday or early Tuesday morning. Which, factoring out a huge coincidence, suggests that the two deaths are related."

Paul claimed the last piece of cheese before adding, "But we don't know how."

"Four," I said as I wrote. "A lot of people were not exactly members of the Dana Lewis Fan Club. The woman had more than a few enemies."

I moved to the next line and scrawled a number five. "We also know that Isabel was probably the last person to see her mother alive, that they had a huge fight in public view. And," I slid a quick glance over at Bixie, "we know that Dana had stopped all financial support to Isabel, thereby giving her a motive for murder since she's probably her mother's sole heir."

Bixie slammed down the Oreo she'd been contemplating. Chunks of cookie chipped off on impact, adding to the tabletop litter. "But it would make just as much sense for her to want Dana to live, in hopes that she'd relent." She broke what was left of the Oreo into three jagged black and white pieces. "Besides, Isabel is incapable of murder."

Paul stopped rummaging through the pantry and peered around the door. "No one is incapable of murder," he pronounced, then popped his head back behind the door.

"Alright," I said. "We also know some things about Chaz that could be significant." I wrote down a six. "We know that he was egoistic, brilliant with computers and had a ruthless streak."

"We know he was ambitious," Bixie added. "That he was a member, more or less, of the Young Republicans." She was shifting bits of fractured Oreo around as if they were puzzle pieces. "And that sometime last spring and continuing into the summer, the same period of time he was interning at Grunwald Industries, he had some kind of a crisis."

Paul spoke up from the depths of my refrigerator. "Which may or may not be related to his internship." He lifted up a plastic container of homemade Finnish yogurt, tilted it and watched the white goo slide around. "Good God, what is this? It looks like something left over from the last *Alien* sequel." Gingerly, he put it back and wiped his hands on his shirt.

"Okay," I leaned back and ruffled my hair. "So much for the victims." I drew a line on the page. "Now for the suspects."

Paul interrupted his search and turned toward us, eyes shining. "Wait, I've got it." He pulled a bag of Paul Newman pretzels out of the cupboard. "Ricki."

"What about her?" Bixie asked.

"Well, maybe Chaz had some major professional failure at Grunwald. Maybe he got fired or demoted or whatever happens to bad interns." Paul leaned against the countertop. "Maybe his ego was crushed, maybe he needed to put his world back together again. So he turns to Ricki. Only she spurns him."

Paul gazed at a point between Bixie and me where these dramatic scenes were being played out. "Being an over-the-top kind of kid, totally self involved and utterly desperate, it's too much for him. He can't take the rejection. He's devastated. Broken. So he climbs to the top of the parking structure and—."

Bixie made room in her lap for Albert, who jumped up, velveted his paws and began kneading her sweater. "Sorry, Paul," she shook her head. "But considering what we know about Chaz, you're way off base. The kid had an indestructible ego."

Paul lowered the cookie he was about to lob into his mouth and gave Bixie a withering look. "Well, there's always Allegra." He took a bite. "She says Dana was just a research project, fodder for her next novel. But maybe she was careless, got caught up in the therapist-client thing and let something slip. God knows that woman must have a whole kennel full of moral uglies."

Moral uglies. I could almost see the little beasts straining on their rhinestone leashes. "An outside possibility," I agreed. "And don't forget Dorey Goldsmith, the wife done wrong." I added a number for Dorey. "And Mercedes Madigan," another number, "who was seeing Dana but probably never met Chaz."

"Except," Bixie pointed out, "possibly at one of those Young Republican parties that Ben Popoulous told you about. Or maybe the Madigans hosted meetings now and then." She reached over to grab a handful of pretzels. "And let's not overlook Paul's favorite suspect, Michael Madigan. Who certainly knew Chaz. And who may have known Dana through his wife."

Paul's turn. "Although, given the state of their marriage, maybe not."

Time for me to mount by hobbyhorse. "And don't forget that the Madigans are on very intimate terms with the Grunwalds. Who hired Chaz as an intern for two summers." I leaned back in my chair and stretched. "Which brings us to the voting question."

Bixie shot me a puzzled look. Paul was more direct. "Oh please. You're not implying…" He sighed. "Look, hon. I'm supposed to be the drama queen in this group. So why don't you just leave the conspiracy theories to Oliver Stone?"

"I'm just saying…"

"I know what you're saying. And I'm perfectly willing to believe that the election was stolen. Again. But even if there was something illegal going on—and you yourself have told us that's highly unlikely, given that Chaz was just a lowly intern—it's way too big for us to handle. I mean, how could we begin to prove something like that?"

He gave me a vampy smile. "Besides, it's much more likely that Chaz stumbled into the juicy personal life of a Grunwald CEO."

Just to spite Paul, I wrote out in capital letters: VOTING MACHINE FRAUD? Then I studied the names and random facts, looking vainly for a pattern to emerge.

Paul pushed his chair back. "Now to the real question." Bixie and I looked up at him expectantly. "Should we try for table service at Zingerman's or order sandwiches to go?"

Table service won by a three-to-nothing vote. I was just pulling on my jacket when the phone rang. Having learned my lesson the hard way—thank you, Moses B. Caldwell—I rushed over and picked it up.

Margaret didn't waste any time getting to the point. "Exorcism?" Her voice was so loud I was sure Paul and Bixie could hear it in the next room. "You want to know if I can perform an exorcism for you?"

I hoisted the jacket over my left shoulder until my hand found its way through the wrist opening. "I guess you got my message."

"Yes, Karin. I got your message. So what are we talking about here? Projectile vomiting? Phantoms in the cupboards? Will your head be doing three-hundred-sixty-degree rotations the next time I see you?"

I glanced over at Paul and Bixie, who were standing in the foyer. They had stopped chatting and were looking my way. "Who is it?" Paul yelled out.

"Margaret," I yelled back, then lowered my voice. "Look, don't worry. It's not that big a deal. I'm on my way out right now. Can I call you later?"

"You'd *better* call me later." Even though she's five years younger I am, Margaret can sound like the Ultimate Jungian Mother when it serves her purposes. "In the meantime, I think I'll call Father Bart. I seem to remember some kind of ceremony in the Episcopalian Book of Common Prayer for putting spirits to rest." She paused briefly. "You are serious about this, right?"

A tiny disturbance in the air brushed past me, raising goose bumps on my neck and pushing a few stray hairs into my face. I shivered and clutched at my old grey jacket.

Did Paul feel the same thing, I wondered, not daring to turn my head and look at him. Had Bixie noticed? Worse yet, was there anything *to* notice? Or was all this just a product of grief run amok? Was I a borderline psychotic?

"Oh yeah," I said into the mouthpiece. "Yeah. I'm very serious about this."

CHAPTER 34

Friday – November 22

Remember that old cliché about the moment of death? How our entire life is supposed to pass before our eyes as we shuffle off this mortal coil?

It's not true.

I know this because, when two tons of steel came hurtling toward me on Friday afternoon, I thought about nothing at all. My mind was a complete blank, quick frozen in a mental whiteout.

I'd been standing at the corner of Miller and Main, waiting for the light to change. Behind me, I could hear bits of conversation. I was lost in my thoughts, but not so lost that I didn't notice the sleek, dark, late-model car about a block away. Not so lost that I didn't see the "walk" sign flick on. What I failed to notice was that the driver of the car hit the accelerator at about the same moment I stepped off the curb.

After that, it's just memory shards. A fast-moving mass of shiny black steel. A pale face behind the steering wheel. Oversized sunglasses. Dark jacket. Strands of blonde hair escaping from a black watch cap.

The one thing I do remember is being pulled back to safety at the very last moment, yanked so fast and hard that I heard my shoulder joint pop as I fell into the wobbly wall of bodies behind me. My rescuer was a sweet-looking, unassuming guy in his mid-thirties with a thatch of brown hair, forgettable features, nondescript clothes, the instincts of a guardian angel and the reflexes of an athlete.

For a minute or two, a crowd of onlookers clustered around me, clucking their tongues and patting my back, holding me up, clasping my cold hands, asking me again and again if I was alright. One faculty type with flyaway white hair shook his briefcase at the traffic and threatened to report the incident, something I was eager to avoid, having spent far too much time with the Ann Arbor Police already this week.

"No, please," I gasped. "Not necessary." That and the sight of my face, ghastly wan and pale, seemed to quell his enthusiasm.

Finally, after the last of my companions—a kind-faced grandmotherly type—was convinced I could manage on my own, I made my way slowly back to Amelia who was waiting for me a few blocks away in the same parking structure where Chaz had ended his life. Or had it ended for him.

Once I was safely tucked into the driver's seat and heard the reassuring click of the door locks, I let myself shake and listened to my teeth chatter as my thoughts ran wild.

The first thing that struck me, surprised me really, was how glad, how relieved, how grateful I was to be alive. How good it felt to be here on this crazy doomed planet pursuing my crazy doomed project.

For one wild moment, I felt disloyal to Terry, ashamed that I was still breathing, still living in this bag of skin and bones. After all, this opening into the nether realm had been my big chance, an opportunity to see my wonderful husband again, maybe forever, and I'd opted out.

Then I remembered what he'd told me on his deathbed. It wasn't my time. If I loved him, I would live on.

I fumbled around for the box of tissues in the back seat, pulled out a handful and blew my nose, hoping it might have the effect of clearing my brain as well as my sinuses. All it did was release an avalanche of troubling thoughts.

A car accident was a crime of opportunity. Not nearly as certain as death by gun or knife. Or poison. Or a fall from a high place. So if this wasn't an accident, was it just the first in a series of attempts on my life? But surely it must have been an accident.

It must have.

Until then, I'd been having a pretty good day. An extremely good day by my standards which, granted, haven't been very high for some time now.

The good feelings had started the night before with a late call-back to Margaret. Once she was convinced I didn't belong in the psych unit at UM Hospital, she was incredibly supportive in her take-charge, pastoral way. Turns out, after picking up my message, she'd spoken to her friend Father Bart from St. Timothy's and the Reverend Father had agreed to conduct a private service for the repose of souls.

"They don't call it an exorcism. It's more like a ritual for putting souls to rest," Margaret explained. "Father Bart is available late Saturday afternoon or Sunday evening," she added comfortingly. Problem is, I didn't feel comforted. Instead, I felt panicky at the thought of sending my ghostly companions on their way.

How pathetic is that, I thought. Was I so desperate for company that I couldn't bear to release Dana Lewis and Chaz Anderson and whatever other bits of ectoplasm had been stalking me for the past week? Or was it something else? A sense that I owed them something?

Yes. That was it. These two human beings, dead before their time, had chosen me to help them. And so, until the police solved these ugly crimes—and I knew it would be the police and not our bumbling little Westside Ann Arbor trio—until these ghostly presences were ready to go, I couldn't bring myself to *make* them go. Short of solving the crimes myself, I couldn't speed them on their way.

Rather than try to explain all this to Margaret, I simply thanked her and promised to call soon, once I'd cleared a space in my schedule. "Alright," she said doubtfully, drawing out the word. "But don't let it go too long."

Whether out of gratitude or boredom or some otherworldly sense of discretion, Dana and Chaz were remarkably quiet that night. I awoke to a cloudless early morning sky minus my usual bad dream hangover.

By eight-thirty, I had skimmed through last night's paper, returned a dozen or so emails, scheduled two meetings and had three checks processed and ready for deposit. By eight forty-five, I was nursing my third cup of coffee and listening to a defensive chief of police being interviewed by an aggressive radio reporter about the city's two unsolved deaths.

By nine a.m., coffee mug empty, I had mapped out my day. I'd go to the bank. Stop at the infamous parking structure where Chaz had died, poke around to get a feel for the place and see what I could see. I'd run some errands. Tackle that new web site project. And in the evening, I'd head into the catacombs for what I expected would be a brave but pathetic post-election party.

I dreaded the thought of those damp, rock-lined subterranean spaces. A Goth bar was not my natural habitat, especially when it was underground. But a nagging hunch, so strong it was almost like a voice in my head, made me willing to risk a bout of claustrophobia and some seriously boring conversation in order to learn anything I could about Republican dirty tricks in the last election.

Whatever Paul might believe to the contrary, it seemed obvious to me that Chaz Anderson's death was involved with Grunwald Industries. That could mean he discovered one of the Grunwald boys cross-dressing in the executive washroom. It could mean he stumbled on financial fraud à la Enron. But it was also possible that whatever got him killed involved those electronic voting machines that were making the company so much money and generating so much bad press along the way.

I'd just finished my bit of business at the bank when I nearly became road kill. And now here I was, quaking and cowering in my car, shivering from shock with the heater turned on high.

I summoned up a memory of Aunt Ilsa comforting my junior high school self after a soul-scarring debacle having to do with cheerleader tryouts. "Just keep your head high and hold on to your dignity," was her commonsense suggestion. She kissed my forehead firmly. "And remember, there's nothing that can happen to you, not today, not ever, that you and God together can't handle."

Nothing that God and I couldn't handle.

I squared my shoulders, checked my face in the rear view mirror, blew my nose one final time and got out of the car. Time to examine the crime scene, if that's what it was.

The parking structure in question is a towering cement block building, two buildings really, spanning nearly two city blocks and linked by a pedestrian overpass. I walked through the dim filtered light of the ground floor following signs that promised an elevator and—next to them—other, newer signs warning that the sixth floor was off limits, with access blocked by order of the Ann Arbor Police.

The elevator door was open. Out of sheer perversity, I stepped in and pushed the "6" button. Nothing. I pushed it again. And again. When I tried "5," the doors closed and the grimy little box lurched upward, depositing me next to a square-cut window. Set against the bleak grey cement walls, the aerial view of Ann Arbor looked like a painting.

Except for a few vehicles, the fifth level was completely empty. The place seemed to be holding its breath, as if waiting for something or someone. Before I could stop myself, classic movie clips of parking lot murders began running through my brain. From somewhere outside, I could hear tires squealing, then silence.

At that moment, the echo of my footsteps was eerie enough—and my errand creepy enough—to make me do something completely out of character. I pulled out my cell phone and dialed Bixie's number. The sound of her voice filled me with relief.

"Hey, Bix," I forced myself to sound cheerful. "How about a dose of moral support?"

"Karin? What's up?" I could almost hear her thoughts chasing each other around. "Where are you calling from? You *are* at home, aren't you?" Good guess, considering the near-virginal state of my cell phone. I thought of the five thousand unused minutes I'd accumulated and wondered if I could trade them in for a magazine subscription or a ticket to Key West.

"Actually, I'm in the Ashley Street parking structure." I jumped at the sound of horns blaring five floors below. "The Chaz Anderson parking structure."

"What are you doing there?" This in a somewhat amazed voice.

I stopped at the door to the stairwell, which was now sealed off by yellow crime tape and a metal sawhorse, one of those orange-and-white striped contraptions that normally inhabit highway construction zones. "Right now I'm contemplating whether to try to squeeze myself around a police barricade." I studied it for a moment. "Probably not."

Spotting another elevator, I walked over to it and stepped in. By the time I was outdoors again, I'd filled Bixie in on my recent brush with death.

"Karin, you need to go home. Now."

"Not until I've looked around the outside of this place." I lowered my head as I walked, letting my eyes scour the ground. The police had obviously finished their work because there was no yellow tape in evidence, nothing to fend off the inquisitive. Just assorted candy bar wrappers and a discarded paper cup.

"So tell me," Bixie demanded. "What do you see?"

I stopped and stared at a mark on the pavement, a disturbing dark-colored stain of no particular shape. There was something mesmerizing about it that made it hard to look away, what Bixie—or Dana—would probably call a resonance.

I kept my eyes fixed on the spot. "I think I see the last fading remnants of Chaz Anderson."

I heard a sharp intake of breath on the line. Then I looked up and took a quick jagged breath of my own. Oh no. It couldn't be.

I stared at the two male figures striding towards me in lockstep, their jackets flapping like flags in the brisk November breeze. The men had stopped talking and were looking my way. The taller one began moving faster on a direct intercept course. I braced myself.

"Unless I'm mistaken, I also see your brother." I looked at the dark, expressionless face of his companion. "And God help me, it looks as if he's got my favorite detective sergeant with him."

CHAPTER 35

Friday – November 22

"You're sure you didn't recognize the face? The getup? The car? Something?" Andrew's voice was loud enough that even the two nonchalant baristas broke off their conversation to stare at us.

"I told you," I forced my voice into a whisper. "Nothing." I stirred what was left of my coffee and kept my eyes focused on the scarred wooden tabletop.

Before I could exit the parking lot, Andrew had quickstepped me two blocks to a cafe. Since then, except for occasional interruptions from his pager and cell phone, he'd been asking questions nonstop and I'd been doing my best to dodge them.

Topic number one was my presence at the parking lot. What was I doing there? What was I looking for? When the dialogue began to deteriorate—was I moonlighting as a meter maid? or did I think the police didn't know how to do their goddamned job?—I derailed him by mentioning my close encounter with the afterlife.

Turns out Andrew was very interested in the car episode. Only now I was tired of the subject. In fact, I was tired. Period.

I glanced up at Andrew's face and instantly regretted it. "So Karin," his voice was as hard as flint, "do you have a death wish?"

"Obviously not," I shot back, trying to suppress my snarl impulse. "Otherwise I wouldn't be here, would I?"

I looked across the room and found myself envying the two plump grey-haired women who stood at the counter debating the merits of raspberry muffins versus sour cream coffee cake. Well, at least Andrew had rescued me from Detective Sergeant Caldwell. I shivered at the thought of sharing an interrogation room with that man.

"Here." Andrew ripped open a package of brown sugar crystals and dumped the contents in my coffee. A few grains escaped and rolled around the table. "You're probably still in shock. This'll help."

I pushed the cup away so hard that a few drops spattered his sleeve. "I don't need help," I growled and gave the cup another vicious shove in his direction. "Besides, sugar is toxic. I'm off the stuff."

He surprised me by smiling. Briefly. "You? That'll be the day." He gave his own coffee a stir and shook his head. "Anyway, at the rate you're going, it won't be sugar that kills you. There won't be time. Something or somebody else will get you first." He looked at me with such intensity that I recoiled a few inches.

I was still fumbling for some choice words to throw back at him when I heard a familiar female voice fluting my name from across the room. I hunched my shoulders, shut my eyes and wished myself into a parallel universe.

One thing about Allegra, her timing is impeccable. She always manages to turn up where she's least wanted and can do the most damage.

With an elegant wave, she made her way to our table. Swaying provocatively on her sky-high boots and unwrapping herself from a sapphire blue cloaky thing as she moved, black hair gleaming and swinging, smile so white it almost called for sunglasses, I had to admit she was stunning. To his credit, Andrew recovered quickly from his momentary testosterone-induced stupor.

Allegra drew off one slinky elbow-length leather glove and let her bare hand rest lightly on my shoulder. "Karin darling, what luck. I was going to call you today. You made quite a conquest the other night. I do believe that if Jeffrey weren't so hogtied to that fiancée of his, you would have heard from him by now." She gave a low chuckle. "And knowing Jeffrey, you still might."

Allegra unfurled a slow, serpentine smile as she slanted her eyes over at Andrew. She looked like a lioness picking out its lunch from a herd of zebra. Keeping her eyes riveted on him, she asked, "Well, aren't you going to introduce us?"

Andrew gave an irritating smirk. "Yes, Karin. Where are your manners? Introduce me to your friend."

Before I could say a word, Allegra flung her jewel-colored wrap onto one of the two empty chairs at our table and arranged herself in the other, managing to shift it about six inches closer to Andrew. As I made introductions, she slipped her hand in his. And kept it there. She was wearing a form-fitting emerald green cashmere sweater that didn't so much clothe her as caress her. The emerald ring on her engagement finger flashed cold and beautiful from within a circle of tiny diamonds.

Allegra cocked her head in my direction and fired her opening salvo. "So, darling, made any arrests yet?" Turning to Andrew, she spoke in a stage whisper, "Did she tell you? Our Karin has taken up a new line of work." Two-second pause for dramatic effect. "She's investigating the murder of Dana Lewis."

She moved her emerald green breasts closer to his coat sleeve. "And believe it or not, I'm one of her prime suspects. So exciting. Of course, being a rookie, I suppose she had to start somewhere."

Andrew leaned in. "Really? I had no idea. Karin likes to keep things from me." As if drawn by an irresistible force, Allegra moved her face closer to his. From where I sat, their noses were almost touching. With a wolfish smile, he went on. "Tell me. What could possibly put you at the top of Karin's suspect list? You look as if you might be capable of a lot of things but murder isn't the first one that comes to mind."

Allegra gave a delighted squeal. "Karin darling, where have you been keeping this wicked man? And how did you manage to snag him?"

I smiled. "Oh, I haven't snagged anyone. Darling. I leave that sort of thing to Andrew." I consulted my watch, pushed my chair back and reached for my pea coat, which looked unspeakably shabby next to Allegra's electrifying blue drapery. "You two obviously have a lot to talk about. And I need to be somewhere in half an hour." Anywhere at all.

Allegra let a contented smile play over her perfect lips. I wondered briefly what it felt like to kiss all that collagen. Maybe Andrew could tell me later. When he started to rise, I held out a restraining hand. "No, don't bother." I clutched my coat and purse. "I'll catch up with you later."

"Sure thing," he said. From where I stood, the look in those pale grey eyes was flashing danger, but Allegra no doubt misread it for something else entirely. Something hormonal. His fingers stroked the table near her hand.

Suddenly the fingers stopped moving and he turned to look at me full-face. "I'll call you. And Karin, remember what we talked about, okay? Behave yourself. And don't," he hesitated, "don't snag anything while I'm not looking. You know I hate surprises."

Allegra managed to look both jealous and proprietary, as if I were the uninvited stranger and she and Andrew were, well, whatever. I waved, turned and left them to it. Maybe she'd finally met her match. In any case, I realized I didn't care much one way or the other. At that moment, all I wanted was my favorite alpaca blanket, my favorite armchair, my favorite drink, and my favorite cat, in approximately that order. Followed by a deep, refreshing, ghost-free nap.

Fifteen minutes later, I had just stepped into my foyer and was about to close the front door behind me when suddenly it pushed back, sending me into a near sprawl. Grabbing at the banister to break my fall, I spun around. There, framed in the doorway, was Paul hugging two large white bags that bulged with mysterious shapes. He stepped into the foyer without being asked, bumped the door shut with one hip and chirped, "Cherry Ames reporting for duty."

With a wink, he put the bags down on the hallway steps and started sorting through the items near the top, checking to make sure he hadn't forgotten anything. All the while he chattered away, totally oblivious to my chilly silence.

It seems that, after the abrupt end to our phone call, Bixie sounded the alarm. In typical Bixie fashion, she had left messages for Paul at his home, his studio, his design shop, everywhere she could think of. "So here I am," he concluded. "On a mission of mercy."

Before I could stop him, he headed down the hallway toward the kitchen, followed at a sauntering pace by Albert who, despite his burning curiosity, managed to give the impression of regal indifference.

"Yes, Albert my love," Paul crooned over his shoulder. "Your instincts are spot on, as usual. I remembered to pick up your favorite cat treats on the way over here." He sniffed loudly. "I'm glad at least someone in this house is happy to see me and grateful for my concern."

"Well, don't forget Chaz and Dana," I yelled after him. "I'm sure they're both thrilled that you're here."

At that moment, the doorbell rang. As I reached for the knob, the door came rushing toward me. I threw a hand up just in time to cushion my face. Even so, the impact sent me reeling into the nearby wall. By the time I had steadied myself and could focus again, Bixie was standing next me, asking over and over if I was alright.

Of course I wasn't alright. How could I possibly be alright? And why did people always ask that stupid question anyway? After a few seconds, I realized she was trying to force me into the nearest living room chair. I was in just enough pain to slap at her hands.

Probing the back of my head gingerly, I turned to face her. "What kind of home training did you have anyway? What do you think doorbells are for? Why even bother to ring if you're just going to barge in?" I struggled for a few seconds to keep my balance. "Did anyone ever tell you that you're one dangerous woman?"

Bixie's violet-blue eyes suddenly got very shiny.

"Oh no you don't," I said, then added an "Ouch" as my fingers found a tender spot on the back of my skull. "Don't you dare start crying. If anyone here is going to cry, it'll be me."

"Oh stop picking on her, Karin." It was Cherry Ames himself, drawn out of the kitchen by the noise. Albert, I noticed, had plunked himself down next to Paul's left shin—his version of a ringside seat.

"I am so sorry," Bixie moaned. "But what were you doing there next to the door?"

"It's my house," I snapped at her. The three of them—Albert, Paul and Bixie—were standing in a line staring at me, which only increased my hostility. "Why shouldn't I be standing at the door? It's my door. I can stand there if I like. I can stand anywhere I want." I let out an exasperated sigh. "The real question is, what are you doing here?"

Without saying a word, Bixie stepped aside to give me an unimpeded view of the still-open front door. There on the front porch was my answer. Next to a small but alarmingly full suitcase were two Whole Foods grocery bags, also alarmingly full.

"No." It was the first word that came to mind. It sounded so good, I repeated it. "No." I looked at Bixie, then at her bags. "Tell me you're taking a road trip and just stopped in to say good-bye."

Paul patted Bixie's arm. "Ignore her, hon. It's the pain talking."

Heeding his advice, Bixie dove in. "After what happened today, not to mention that weirdness with Michael Madigan and his pills, I am not going to let you stay here by yourself."

The firmness in her tone was both intimidating and infuriating. She turned around, marched outside, brought back the grocery bags and handed them to Paul, went back out again, retrieved her suitcase and deposited it next to the stairs. Then she closed the door with a firm click.

As a finale, she pulled herself up to her full height, lifted her chin defiantly, steeled her eyes, shook her wild ringlets and, looking for all the world like a blonde Amazon, announced, "I'm not going anywhere. Until this is over and I know you're safe, you've got yourself a roommate." To reinforce the message, she crossed her arms.

With his "so there" smile firmly in place and his eyes all squinty, Paul looked as determined as Bixie. And from his position next to Paul, Albert seemed to be weighing in on their side, too.

I looked at each one of them. Then I turned and began trudging toward the kitchen in quest of the ice pack I always kept in the freezer.

"Use the small guest room," I called out in a tired voice, not even bothering to turn my head. "Dana and Chaz seem to like the other one. And I'm not sure there's room for all three of you in there."

CHAPTER 36

Friday – November 22

The receptionist at the Grotto was a Morticia Addams look-alike, from her pasty white makeup and limp black hair to her long-sleeved cobwebby gown. When she smiled, I half-expected to see vampire incisors curling over her lower lip. "The Washtenaw Democrats?" she repeated. "Furthest chamber in. Past the bar, take a left, keep walking till you see a big cement archway."

Great, I thought. It wasn't bad enough that the party was being held in a crypt. It had to be in the darkest, dankest, deepest corner of the place. It had to be in a frigging chamber, for God's sake. My voice wobbled as I thanked Morticia and my red sweaty palms told me the panic reaction was already setting in.

I took a couple of uneven breaths and headed for the bar. On the way, I nearly collided with a lesbian couple sporting shaved heads and decked out in identical nose rings, studded collars, black t-shirts, jeans and jackboots. They unglued their gaze just long enough to offer apologies, then reclasped hands and continued on in their love-struck way.

I was still looking at them thoughtfully when a hand grabbed my shoulder and a familiar voice intoned, "Isn't love grand?"

"Depends," I answered without turning around. When I got to the bar, I parked myself on one of the stools.

Paul perched himself next to me and grinned. "Surprised? You didn't really think Bixie and I would let you wander around on your own tonight, did you?"

I stared at him for maybe five seconds. "Surprised hardly begins to describe what I feel."

Fortunately, the bartender chose that moment to take our orders. He was young, with an over-muscled weightlifter body that no white shirt and black leather vest could disguise. I ordered a double scotch and Paul asked for a gin and tonic. For a minute or two, I stared into the vast expanse of mirror bolted onto the boulders that formed the back wall.

"So," I asked finally, "how did you get the evening shift? Did you and Bixie draw straws and you got the short one?"

Paul swiveled his stool around, leaned backwards against the bar and propped himself up on his elbows to watch the passing show. "Bixie is meeting Isabel at some campus lecture-and-movie thing tonight," he drawled, "as you know. So I volunteered to look after baby." He reached behind him for his drink, took a sip and let out a long satisfied aaaahhhh. "Now, if you promise to stop sulking, I'll tell you the latest dirt on your favorite cosmetic surgeon and his lovely wife."

"The Madigans?" I straightened up too fast. Scotch and ice cubes slopped over my wrist and made cold nasty patches on my newest pair of old jeans.

Paul gave a sly grin. "I thought that might get your attention."

I put the glass down on the bar, wiped my hands with a napkin, patted the wet spots on my thighs and turned so I could see Paul's face. "You have news? Why didn't you tell me back at the house?"

Paul let his eyes slide around the dim cavernous space. Black candles flickering on every table cast shadows that danced around the rock walls, making it impossible to forget we were underground. I wiped away a film of cold sweat from my forehead.

"Oh you poor baby," Paul said, patting my damp thigh. "I forgot about that phobia of yours. Well, take a deep breath or have another drink or something and I'll tell you what I heard today."

I obediently finished what was left of my scotch although it didn't seem to be doing any good. I nodded at the bartender and pointed at my glass. My breath was coming short and fast.

"Oh shit," Paul blurted out as he fumbled in the pocket of his tailored black denim jacket. "I nearly forgot." He fished out a small

197

Linda W. Fitzgerald

bottle of Rescue Remedy. "Bixie told me to give you this. She said you should put some in your drink."

Before I could stop him, he squeezed the dropper over my fresh scotch. I thought briefly of Dana, what it must have been like to die from poison. I wondered how long it took. How much she suffered. Then I lifted my drink in salute. "Here's to the lesser of two evils."

"And you call *me* a drama queen," Paul sighed and turned back toward the bar. "Okay, now for the good stuff." In preparation, he moved a napkin out of the way, shifted a bowl of nuts and shot a suspicious glance at two young women a few stools down from us, giggling over their glasses of white wine.

Then he took a deep breath. "Well, I was talking to Connie Pederson today. You know Connie, don't you? Professional wife. Sits on about a dozen nonprofit boards. Anyway, she's married to Carl Heikkola, the famous ambulance chaser. I heard he just took a huge case. Something to do with…"

"Paul. Please." I put a hand on his arm. "The Madigans."

Paul let out a humphing sound but the urge to gossip overwhelmed every other consideration. "According to Connie," he continued, "who was talking with Harold Kim, who works in…"

"Paul," I warned. "Cut to the chase."

"But this *is* the chase," he insisted. "Because Harold works in the office suite next door to Michael. Surely you remember the place? All those glass walls? Perfect for snooping on office neighbors?" I nodded. The offices in Michael Madigan's building were like elegant, angular fish bowls. "Well Harold said that the police have been making a lot of office visits to our boy lately. A lot."

Paul wiggled a few inches closer to me and lowered his voice slightly. "And that's not all. According to Harold's secretary, who's actually his sister-in-law and who hangs out with the women on Madigan's staff, Mercedes showed up at the office the other day. Something Michael evidently frowns upon." He fortified himself with a swig of gin and tonic. "And from what was overheard behind closed doors, she was extremely upset."

I could just see it. One or two of the Stepford girls—I bet they called themselves girls—conveniently dropping a handful of files just outside Michael's office door and taking a very long time to pick them up.

One more sip and Paul was ready to go again. "The police had evidently turned up at the Madigan house as well as the office. Because one of the secretaries swears she heard Mercedes say something like, 'They asked me all kinds of questions. What am I supposed to tell them?' Then, and this is the good part, Mercedes says 'What have you done?'"

The forgotten drink tipping dangerously in his hand, Paul paused for emphasis. "At that point, Michael supposedly threw it right back at her. Said he hadn't done a thing and what the hell was she talking about. Then he kept telling her she had to pull herself together. Anyway, according to eye witnesses, or ear witnesses anyway, they went back and forth arguing like two junkyard dogs for maybe twenty minutes. He kept trying to get her to quiet down. So they'd whisper for a while, and then there would be these outbursts. She—that's Harold's secretary—told Connie that the Madigan secretaries said Michael and Mercedes kept blaming each other. And Michael kept telling her this wasn't the time or place to discuss things. Finally, he marched her out of the office and put her in her car."

Paul came up briefly for air, righted his glass and took a quick slurp. "Then our Michael did the unthinkable. Cancelled a couple of late afternoon appointments, no explanation, and took off for destination unknown." He straightened up and beamed like a kid who'd just won a spelling bee. "So what do you think?"

After one and a half double scotches, my head was swimming with he-saids and she-saids and she-said-they-saids. I began to wonder if drinking was such a good idea after getting smacked on the head. Then again, it could be the Rescue Remedy taking effect. "I think I want to know more," I answered. "A lot more. And I wish there were a way to get Andrew to tell us what he knows about this."

The sudden chiming of my cell phone nearly tipped me off my stool. It was Paul who pulled the phone out of my jacket pocket and checked the display. "Andrew." He whistled. "And right after you said his name. How spooky is that?"

He flipped it open. "Hi, Andrew. It's Paul. But Karin is right here and I know she'd love to talk to you. Hold on a sec."

Teeth clenched, I put the phone to my ear. "Hey, Andrew. How's it going?"

"Let's just say I consider myself lucky to be alive. That bitch goddess was ready to swallow me whole."

"From where I sat, you were pretty well matched. So what did you learn from the lovely Allegra?" Paul, desperate to hear both ends of the conversation, pressed his cheek against mine. I aimed an elbow at his ribs and he put a couple of inches between us.

"First thing I learned is that you need a better class of friends. She is one scary broad. Second thing I learned is that you've been nosing around more than you should." Still leaning in close, Paul was struggling to hear every word and sipping at what was left of his gin.

"Speaking of nosing around," I said, "I hear you and your colleagues have been spending some quality time with the Madigans."

"Who told you that?"

"I have my sources. So what did you find out about the good doctor?"

"You don't really think I'd tell you..."

I put some pepper in my voice. "Well, considering he may have made an attempt on my life with those stupid pills of his, I think I have a right to know. He is your prime suspect now, isn't he? You are looking into his connection with the Young Republicans and Grunwald Industries?"

"Do I smell a conspiracy theory?"

"Andrew, connect the dots. Young Republicans. Old friends. Grunwald Industries. Summer internships. Election. Voting machines. Politics. Power. It's so obvious."

"Karin, the only thing that's obvious is that you are going to stop all this. You can do it voluntarily. Or I can stick your lovely ass in a nice warm cell for a few days. For your own good and my peace of mind."

Paul let out a little whoop, then slapped his hand over his mouth. "What the hell was that?" Andrew demanded. "Where are you?"

The abrupt change of subject disoriented me for a second. "I'm, uh, just having a drink with Paul." I held the phone away from me as far as my arm would reach. By then, the noise of the crowd had reached a steady roar. "You're breaking up Andrew. I can't hear a thing. I'll have to call you later. Bye."

I pushed the "end" button, then wrapped my hands around Paul's jacket collar and pulled his face next to mine.

"Do not say a word," I breathed, giving every word as much weight as I could. "Not one word. Not now. Not ever. Bixie never hears about this, do you understand?"

I could see the struggle in his eyes. "I mean it Paul."

Time for some heavy-duty emotional blackmail. "If you value our friendship, if you ever want to enjoy a Heineken in my kitchen again, if you ever want Lew to share a happy moment over organic dog biscuits in my living room, you will keep this to yourself."

I let go of his jacket and slipped the phone back in my pocket. "It's not important anyway. Just some minor issues with Andrew."

"Minor issues?" Paul rolled his eyes as he smoothed out the wrinkles I'd left on his jacket. "Yeah. Right."

Before he could say anything more, I grabbed his hand. There were things I needed to know about election fraud and electronic voting machines, and I knew just where to find the information. "Come with me."

Paul stood up, looking confused. "Where?"

I began to pull him along like a large earth-bound kite, threading my way through the dense crowd, bumping into bodies along the way. I could hear him mumbling sorry's and excuse-me's as we moved toward the back of the building.

Finally, Paul half-shouted over the din, "I asked you, where are we going?"

The cement archway leading to the farthest chamber was finally in sight. I could see George Morrison towering above the rest of the crowd. And if I wasn't mistaken, that was Margaret's red beret bobbing around next to his shoulder.

I picked up the pace and said loudly enough to be heard over the general chatter, "We're going to where we can get some answers."

"Answers?" Paul echoed from behind me. "But I don't even know what the questions are."

CHAPTER 37

Saturday – November 23

There are certain sounds one might reasonably expect to hear at sunrise on a drizzly, dreary Saturday in November. The tapping of bare branches against a windowpane. The chirruping of a squirrel. The early winter melody of cardinals and bluejays. These are all acceptable.

But a chainsaw?

My first guess was a gung-ho Detroit Edison tree removal team. My second guess was an idiot neighbor exercising his early Christmas present. Only as the brain fog began to lift did I realize that the offending noise was coming from the vicinity of my kitchen.

"Stop," I moaned into the pillow. The sound grew louder. I rolled onto my back, eyes still glued shut. "I said stop."

The touch of a large soft paw on my cheek forced me to open one eye. Albert, who had wedged himself between my shoulder and neck, bent down until our noses were nearly touching. With his right paw, he batted my cheek again, gently but firmly.

I opened my other eye, regretted it, rolled to the edge of the bed and swung myself into a sitting position. The room swayed for a few seconds, then righted itself. The chainsaw paused briefly before revving up again.

I pushed the hair out of my face and moved my feet around the floor in search of bedroom slippers. "Okay, okay," I reassured Albert. "I'll look into it. I don't have anything better to do anyway."

As I shuffled through the downstairs hall, bursts of noise battered at my aching scotch-soaked head. I paused in the archway. At first glance,

202

I thought I must have walked into someone else's kitchen. But the tall blonde in the Aztec-print bathrobe looked familiar, even if nothing else did.

My normally pristine counters and floors were littered with the carcasses of vegetables. Beets. Carrots. Celery. Lettuce leaves. Mangy-looking parsley. I counted five knives of various sizes and three cutting boards.

Bixie was standing next to the biggest damned juicer I'd ever seen, a huge contraption with a motor that could have powered a small plane. She was shoving chunks of vegetables into a little chute on top. A slow, steady stream of brackish red liquid was coming out another chute on the end. Most of it was dripping into a cup. The rest was pooling over the counter.

"What's going on here?" I shouted to make myself heard over the relentless whir of the motor.

Bixie turned to me with a beatific smile, switched off the juicer and held out a small glass of red muck. "I'm making us a special energy drink. It's a recipe I got from my nutritionist. She say's there's nothing better for cleansing the liver. Here, have some."

I placed both hands on my churning stomach. "My liver," I swallowed hard to keep from gagging, "doesn't want to be cleansed. My liver wants a cup of a coffee and a Danish." I swallowed again and tried to push down the queasy feeling making its way through my gut. "Or maybe we'll skip the Danish this morning." I looked hopefully at the stove. "Where's the coffee?"

Bixie's face managed to convey anger, pity and disgust all at the same time. Never one to give up, she grabbed my right hand and tried to press my fingers around the glass. "You need this," she insisted.

"No one needs this." I wrinkled my nose and held the glass by the rim with two fingers. "It looks like animal blood, for God's sake."

I put the offending concoction back on the counter. "If I drink it, I will vomit. Or die. Or both." Nudging Bixie aside, I reached into the cupboard and pulled out a bag of Free Trade French Roast and my favorite coffee grinder. "Now I'm going to show you what human beings—normal human beings—have for breakfast."

Bixie gave a shrug, picked up the discarded glass of vegetable juice, sat down at the kitchen table, located a few square inches not covered by pieces of the morning newspaper and proceeded to cleanse her liver. I resisted an ungracious urge to put the newspaper back together and arrange it neatly where it belonged—next to my placemat. Wherever that was.

Instead, I focused on making myself a much-needed cup of coffee, with extra cream and three sugars for added nutrition. Once I'd located my placemat under the business section of the paper, I made a space for my cup, sat down and started in on the coffee.

I was on my second cup before I trusted myself to speak "So." I cradled the cup between my hands and leaned toward my guest with a miniscule smile. "How long did you say you were staying?"

Bixie didn't even bother to look up from the paper. "I told you yesterday. I'm bunking in with you until all of this has blown over. Until whoever killed Dana is arrested and behind bars."

She looked up from the editorial page which, I couldn't help but notice, bore red splotches from where her foul juice had stained it. If only the paper towels didn't seem so far away right now. "You can expect to see my friendly face around here until I'm sure you're safe. Although," she added with a hurt-little-girl pout, "I honestly don't know why I should even care."

Until I'm safe, I thought and inventoried the kitchen once again. Safe, and most certainly insane. From where he sat in the doorway leading to the hall, Albert blinked at me in telepathic agreement. You're right, he seemed to be saying, a few days of this and we'll both be driven round the bend.

"Uh, tell me," I ventured, "did you happen to bring any other large appliances with you?"

Bixie put down the paper next to her empty juice glass and sighed. "Okay. I can leave you to your so-called breakfast and take a shower now. Or we can talk about what I learned from Isabel last night and what you discovered while you and Paul were out partying with the Washtenaw Democrats till dawn."

"It wasn't dawn exactly," I corrected her. "Although I was up until nearly three this morning doing some research." I thought about the stack of printouts on my desk upstairs. "You're looking at a woman who knows almost everything there is to know about electronic voting machines and election fraud."

Shoving the newspapers aside as best I could, I put my elbows on the table. "Were you aware that within this past year the software code for the Grunwald electronic voting machines was accidentally posted on the company's web site?" The newspaper crunched as I shifted forward. "And did you know that about six months ago, a couple of computer science professors from Cornell challenged their undergraduates to hack that code for extra credit? And nearly eighty-five percent of the students were able to do it, no problem?"

Bixie continued to comb her hair with her fingers, something she'd been doing the entire time I was talking. "Your point being?"

I put down my coffee cup with a clunk. "My point being that if some smart undergraduates from Cornell could hack the Grunwald code, so could a smart undergraduate from Michigan. Especially if he was on the premises. The Grunwald premises, I mean."

Bixie let head sink backward. "Oh, Karin. Why would Chaz do that? Why would he risk losing his job and possibly getting himself arrested? Why would he take such a huge chance?"

"Because," I spluttered. "To prove that he could. Or to make friends in high places. Or maybe both."

Bixie closed her eyes as if warding off a headache. "That doesn't make sense."

Without thinking, I began picking up the rumpled sheets of newspaper that littered the table and part of the floor. "Oh but it does," I insisted. "If you know anything about the mind of a geek with a gift for hacking, it makes perfect sense."

Bixie watched me wonderingly as I sorted the papers, slotting each section back into its correct order. "And I suppose you're on intimate terms with geeks?" she asked.

"No," I admitted. I patted the last errant section into place, tapped all the sides to make the pages even and folded the paper so that only the upper half of the front page was showing. Then I placed the whole thing in the center of the table. "But Evan is. And from what Ricki told us, we know that Chaz was a prime example of his species, an ego run amok. Also, don't forget, he hung around with the Young Republicans. Which means he also hung around with old Republicans. Who you must admit had a pretty big stake in the election."

She folded her hands on the now clear tabletop in a businesslike way. "So is it my turn now?"

Feeling like a deflated balloon, I drifted over to the stove for a third cup of coffee. On my way back, I nabbed a bag of slightly stale almond cookies from the pantry.

By the time I had dipped my way through half the cookies in the bag, Bixie had filled me in on Isabel. Not that there was a lot to tell. The police were still questioning her, finding excuses to drop by, keeping her off balance. They had also questioned her neighbors, the chair of the art department, various colleagues. Nothing I hadn't expected to hear.

The only real news was that Dana's body had finally been released from police custody and Isabel had decided on cremation now, followed by a memorial service at some undetermined future time. Presumably weeks or more likely months hence, when the turmoil of the murder investigation was but a memory.

Bixie stared at the crumpled bag next to my coffee cup. "I can't believe you ate all those cookies."

"Me either." I eyed the refrigerator and debated whether or not to break open the latest batch of Aunt Ilsa's cardamom rolls. They had arrived late on Friday afternoon, well packed and nestled in the sturdy arms of a FedEx delivery man. Deciding on a path of moderation, I got up and poured myself a large glass of soy milk.

"I'll have one of those," Bixie said. Then a light seemed to on behind her eyes and her mouth formed an elongated O. "I completely forgot. You got a whole slew of phone calls last night. Now where did I put the messages?" She stood up and trundled out of the kitchen, retying her robe as she went.

"The calls must have come in pretty late," I called out. "When did you get back from the lecture?"

"We didn't go to the lecture," she yelled back from the living room. I could hear her moving things around and wondered why she hadn't left the message pad where it always was. Where it should be. Next to the telephone. But of course that would have been too easy. "Isabel decided she didn't feel like going out after all. Too tired. So we wound up having a bottle of wine in the living room and talking for a couple of hours. Oh here they are."

Bixie returned to the kitchen with three or four small squares of paper fanned out in one hand. "Let's see. Your Aunt Ilsa called to say hello. What a sweet lady. She's going to send me the recipe for that braided bread she makes."

She pulled up the next little slip of paper. "Evan told me to tell you he called to make sure you were still alive and wondered if you planned to stay that way." A quizzical look crossed her face. "Oh, and Andrew called too."

The bewildered look morphed into suspicion. "He wanted to know where you were." Bixie leaned against the kitchen doorframe. "When I told him, he didn't sound happy at all."

I picked up my half-finished glass of soy milk. "When was the last time your brother sounded happy about anything?" I asked. "He's a cop. He doesn't do happy." I downed the remaining soy milk in a few gulps.

Bixie picked up the last note. "Allegra called and left a weird message. She said to tell you she owes you for Friday afternoon and will definitely repay the debt. What's that all about?" I shrugged. Bixie studied me for a few seconds. "She also said that she's leaving tickets for you and me to the Junior League Fashion Show. At the door. Heywood Hall. Two p.m. this afternoon."

I gave a whoop. "A fashion show?" I pictured my collection of turtlenecks and slacks. Then I pictured a room full of tanned, buff, manicured, massaged, face-lifted, lipo-suctioned, well-vacationed women swanking around in their latest designer whatnots.

"Obviously just a bad joke on Allegra's part," I chuckled. "Or maybe a snide reference to our wardrobe deficiencies."

Bixie straightened her shoulders and tossed back her head. "Speak for yourself," she said. "To continue, Allegra said that, considering your new career as an amateur detective, you'd definitely want to be there."

"Why? To check out the latest hemlines?" I grinned at Bixie and readjusted the newspaper, carefully lining it up with the top edge of my placemat.

"Noooooo," Bixie said, smiling in a superior sort of way and waving the message under her chin as if it were a tiny fan. "She thought you might want to check out Mercedes Madigan. Who happens to be co-chair of the event."

CHAPTER 38

Six hours later, Bixie and I stood in the mahogany-trimmed lobby of Heywood Hall. I'd been there once before, years back, for the annual Women's Club book sale. The place looked much the same. Velvet swags still framed the floor-to-ceiling windows. The walls were still painted in rich tones of plum and cypress green. The hushed hallways were still lined with oriental rugs. Portraits of matronly women still gazed down condescendingly from ornate gold frames.

I shifted from foot to foot as a perky redhead in a leopard-print dress checked our names against the list on her clipboard. "Oh yes, here you are," she smiled as she spoke. "Allegra's friends."

She made two neat little checkmarks on the appropriate lines and let her smile grow to dazzling proportions. "The ballroom is straight ahead. Enjoy." We joined the herd of well-dressed women who were migrating slowly down the long hallway.

The ballroom was glorious. Three chandeliers sparkled overhead, nearly overpowering the sunshine that spilled into the room from a wall of French doors flanking the courtyard garden. Dozens of white-draped café tables were piled with flowers, porcelain, goblets and ornate silver place settings. My stomach gave a lurch and the refrain of an old Mason Williams' song came to mind: *These are not my people.*

Picking up on my anxiety, Bixie linked her arm through mine and whispered, "Cheer up. This could be fun." She gave my arm a squeeze. "Besides which, you look terrific."

She herself was resplendent in a form-fitting jacket and skirt of brown bouclé flecked with gold. The towering heels of her pointy-toed brown alligator shoes—fake of course—sent her soaring into the stratosphere.

Thanks to Paul's expert ministrations, I was quite presentable in a high-necked green paisley velvet jacket, something I'd bought in a moment of weakness and never had the courage or occasion to wear. From the furthest reaches of the guestroom closet, he had also rescued my one good black skirt, untouched since Terry's funeral.

Although I vetoed the skirt at first, Paul had insisted that it needed to be worn again in a completely different setting. "Think of it as a wardrobe exorcism," he said with a knowing smile. Which made me wonder if he'd somehow overheard my phone conversation with Margaret. Or wormed the story out of her last night at the so-called celebration.

"Bixie. Karin." I caught a whiff of expensive perfume at the same moment that Allegra clamped her burgundy-enameled talons on our shoulders.

Bixie eased herself free from the long tapered fingers. Pretending not to notice the slight, Allegra waved at a large woman in a red pantsuit, then went on in a bright voice. "So glad you could come."

She moved closer and let her lips brush against my ear. "Think of it as my small contribution to your investigation. Besides which, I wanted to thank you for being so generous with Andrew yesterday. What a hunk." She gave an under-the-bed-sheets laugh. "I had no idea, Karin. You are one lucky woman."

Most people break out in a warning flush when they get dangerously angry. Bixie, on the other hand, goes all still and white, very Ice Queen. She did that now. "That hunk happens to be my brother," she said in a frozen voice.

Allegra put on one of those who-gives-a-damn smiles she does so well. "Yes, I did figure that out eventually, dear. Same last names and all."

I jumped in. "It didn't upset you that he's a cop?"

Allegra shrugged and adjusted the heavy silver and onyx necklace on display just above her collarbone. "Everyone has to earn a living."

Her eyes glinted. "And Andrew could take me into custody anytime. Especially if he promised to do a strip search."

By now, Bixie was looking like a death goddess in a Hindu epic. I caught her wrist and pointed at no one in particular. "Oh look. There's Corrine." I began hauling her toward the center of the ballroom. "She'll be hurt if we don't say hi. Catch up with you later, Allegra. Thanks for the tickets."

"Happy hunting," our benefactress called out after us in a voice loud enough to draw stares.

As we wandered among the tables, I caught sight of Dorey Goldstein. Brown-Blonde was with her and the two were deep in conversation. Even from a distance, Dorey looked worried. She was gesturing in an agitated way. In fact, everything about her looked agitated. I began steering Bixie in their direction.

As we sidled up to our quarry, Dorey and Brown-Blonde looked at us as if we'd just parachuted in which, in a sense, we had. I introduced myself and reminded them of where we'd met, then did the honors with Bixie. Despite their polite smiles, it was clear they were eager to get back to whatever it was they'd been discussing.

I decided to goose things along. "I remember that evening at Hill Auditorium very well."

"Oh really?" Dorey seemed surprised.

"Yes," I went on. "Mainly because we spent so much time talking about Dana Lewis. Allegra was certain that Dana had been murdered. So we ended up discussing who might have killed her. And why."

The effect was electrifying. Brown-Blonde froze in place and clutched her wine glass so tightly I was amazed the stem didn't shatter. She made a huge effort not to look at her friend, whose face had lost all color except for what it borrowed from Estée Lauder.

Dorey dabbed at her damp, shiny forehead with a cocktail napkin. "I'm afraid I don't recall any of it."

"Oh but you must," I insisted, keeping my smile in place. "Because Allegra talked at some length about what close friends Dana and your husband were. And so naturally I assumed that you…"

"I'm sorry," Dorey interrupted in a hoarse voice. "I really don't remember and in any case it seems ghoulish to talk about poor Dana."

She darted a glance at Brown-Blonde, who nodded ever so slightly. "You'll have to excuse us. We're on the planning committee and we need to check on a few details."

I watched them scurry away.

"Well," Bixie's voice was sarcastic, "that was very successful. You've managed to scare away one possible suspect. Shall we try for two?"

It took about five minutes of milling around before I spotted Mercedes. She was standing near the podium with several other women, her lips drawn into an all-purpose smile, her hyperthyroid eyes magnified behind a stylish pair of glasses. The black rectangular frames picked up the geometric pattern of her dress, black on red. The ubiquitous Ms. Gibson, quietly elegant in a navy pantsuit, was at her side.

I watched Mercedes as she stood there, making a brave effort to follow the conversation. Normally I don't waste pity on the super-rich, but in her case I decided to make an exception.

As we got closer, she jerked her head around and stared at me for a few long seconds. Finally, as my face registered, her eyes grew wide and her mouth opened. Sensing a change in atmospherics, Ms. Gibson turned and, with practiced discretion, laid a restraining hand on Mercedes' upper arm.

"Oh look, Mrs. M. It's Karin Niemi. The writer." Her voice had the same honeyed quality I remembered. She dismissed their companions with a smile and tightened her hold on Mercedes.

"How nice to see you again, Ms. Niemi." As she spoke, I wondered if she had a first name or if she had simply been Ms. Gibson from birth. "Perfect venue for a fashion show, don't you think?"

But Mercedes was having none of it.

"You," she managed to turn the word into an accusation. "You." Amazing how much loathing she packed into that one syllable. "How dare you go behind our backs like that? I thought we had an agreement. Michael made it absolutely clear what he expected and you agreed!"

"Behind your back?" I repeated, baffled.

Ms. Gibson switched to a two-handed grip and uttered another soothing "Mrs. M." But in a violent gesture that nearly toppled her companion, Mercedes pulled free and moved so close to me that I could feel the heat from her body. She pitched her voice to a loud hiss. "Yes, behind our backs. Sharon Grunwald called to tell me you'd been in touch with the company's human resource department. Asking questions about Charles Anderson. That poor boy who committed suicide."

So that was it. I should have used a fake name. Clearly, if I were going to continue in the deception business, I would have to master the fundamentals.

I marveled at the efficiency of the Madigan's social network. But why would my call trigger such alarm in Sharon Grunwald? And why alert the Madigans? She couldn't have known about my tenuous connection with Mercedes. Or could she? And if all these folks were so tight, then maybe, just maybe, the Madigans had also heard from their dear friend Ben Popoulous about my unseemly interest in the Chaz-Michael connection. Which could explain the explosion now underway.

Mercedes went on. "Why are you doing this? Why are you trying to make trouble? What do you want from us?" By now, the clusters of women nearest to us had halted their conversations and were openly eavesdropping.

I backed away a few steps. "Mrs. Madigan," I began and grabbed for the nearest cliché. "I'm sure there's been some kind of mistake." Somehow, that line sounded better when Lauren Bacall said it.

Mercedes' face glowed with rage. "The only mistake was letting you into our home. Trusting you. Believing all that bullshit about the article you were writing. You lying bitch."

She came at me then, moving so fast that I bumped into one of the nearby eavesdroppers in my attempt to avoid her. Before Ms. Gibson could restrain her, Mercedes pulled me close in a bruising grip.

"Leave me and my family alone." I could feel little pellets of spittle strike my face as she spoke. "If you don't, I promise we will make you regret that you ever walked through our door."

I could have told her that I regretted walking through her door the moment I sat down on her oversized couch next to her evil dog.

Ms. Gibson whispered something into Mercedes' ear. The only words I could make out were "Mr. M" and "very upset." Whatever else she said, it stopped Mercedes in her tracks.

Once her charge was under control, she turned to me. "You seem to have a knack for creating high drama wherever you go, Ms. Niemi.

Interesting technique for a journalist, I must say. Now you will excuse us, won't you?"

She steered Mercedes toward the exit, leaving us at the center of a circle of women, some openly hostile, some clearly disgusted, some amused, all desperately curious. At that moment, Allegra broke through the perimeter. I realized that this was the first and only time in my life I was genuinely glad to see her.

She positioned herself between Bixie and me and gave us a big, showy and completely fake double hug. "Poor Mercedes," she purred in a condescending tone. "It takes so little to set her off these days." She gave us each a wide-eyed look. "I'm so sorry she turned on you that way and for no reason at all. Please forgive her, won't you? And do stay for the rest of the show." She giggled. "Or should I say, for what remains of the show?"

As Allegra took center stage, Bixie and I melted in the crowd. Given our height and newfound notoriety, it wasn't easy. Fortunately, within a minute or two, a woman with a plummy voice took the podium and invited everyone to take their seats.

While a bevy of young servers in black slacks and white shirts fanned out through the room and began dispensing shrimp cocktails, I snagged a table near the door. As Bixie and I pulled out chairs, I studied our tablemates, three elderly women in pastel suits and over-controlled hair. They stared back at me with bright hard eyes and inscrutable little smiles. Like undersized vultures, I thought.

Bixie was quivering. "Now tell me. What was that all about?"

I arranged the napkin on my lap and found myself wishing that her voice had a remote control. Then I looked at the three muses sitting across the table and noticed that two of them were dialing up the volume on their hearing aids.

I stood up and retrieved my purse from the back of the chair. "Come on."

Bewildered, Bixie pushed back her chair. "Where are we going?"

I cast a farewell look at those chubby, succulent shrimp. Then I grabbed Bixie's arm.

"Somewhere a little less fashionable."

CHAPTER 39

Saturday – November 23 through Thursday – November 28

As usual, the Arbor Brew Pub was doing a brisk business. Students, faculty and townies crowded around the scarred bar, calling out their orders and quarterbacking the Big Ten game that played out on two oversized TV screens.

With their scruffy jeans and nondescript jackets, the bar patrons were almost indistinguishable. In contrast, the booths and tables in the adjoining room were occupied mainly by day trippers. Their neat, unstained khakis and fresh-out-of-the-box Lands End squall jackets marked them as tourists, as surely as if they'd been branded by hot irons when they crossed the city line. Which, I pondered as I stared into my scotch, might not be such a bad idea.

Bixie lifted her Chablis to the murky light and took a ladylike sip. "So what now, Sherlock?"

I grabbed some paper napkins and swabbed up a small puddle of booze that threatened to saturate my coaster. "Don't rub it in," I said. "Who could have guessed that the Madigans and the Grunwalds and even Ben Populous were all so tight?"

I took a generous swig of scotch and felt it blaze a warm trail down my esophagus. For a chaser, I downed a handful of bar pretzels. "I mean, it's like some kind of cabal." I chewed for a few seconds. "There's definitely something sinister going on."

Bixie took another sip and blotted her lips with a napkin, leaving a rosy mark on her napkin. "You're exaggerating," she assured me.

"Republicans are an endangered species in this county. It's only natural they'd stick together." She stared at my reflection in the bar mirror. "I just can't believe you lied to that HR guy at Grunwald. If your clients at Engineering ever find out…"

"Which they probably have by now," I interjected.

"Which they probably have by now," she agreed. "You are in big trouble."

"You think I don't know that?" I sighed and comforted myself with another handful of pretzels. "Once the Madigans get through with me, my pathetic little career will be in tatters."

Bixie chewed at a fingernail thoughtfully. "What do you think Mercedes meant when she said they'd make you regret you ever walked into their house? You don't suppose…" Worry lines corrugated her forehead and weighted down the corners of her mouth.

I waved her anxiety away. "No. I'm not going to find some hit man waiting for me in my kitchen at midnight." Probably not. Hopefully not. Although, with the nation's murder capital a mere forty miles away, anything was possible.

"Besides," I went on, "they won't have to kill me. By the time the Madigans finish dragging my name through the dirt, I'll be as good as dead. Professionally speaking, that is."

I let the scotch do its work again. "Destitution will follow in short order." I gazed into the bar mirror at my gloomy face. "I wonder if SafeHouse Center will let me stay at their shelter until I can change my name and find a new line of work. I did write their last fundraising brochure pro bono. So they owe me something."

Bixie gestured to the bartender and when he came by, smiling the way men always smile when they're around her, she said, "A cheese quesadilla for me, please. And for my friend, a chicken quesadilla. Large." She looked at my empty scotch glass. "You better bring an order of fries with that, too. Mayonnaise on the side."

By the time I finished eating, the world was a much kinder-looking place. Still, I wasn't underestimating the damage I'd done with my third-rate detective work. I felt embarrassed. What naiveté. What hubris. What colossal blundering.

As we paid up and piled into our coats, I took a silent oath. No more meddling with murder. No checking out crime scenes. No lying to suspects or anyone else for that matter. Except maybe Bixie when the occasion called for it. And Aunt Ilsa every now and then, if it was kinder than the truth. And Andrew. And my brother, of course.

Obviously, I'd have to work on the lying thing. But for sure, no more amateur gum-shoeing. No more confrontations with the police.

From this point forward, I would be a changed woman. Head down, shoulder to the wheel, hands on the computer keyboard. It was back to business for me, if there was any business. Somehow, I would weather whatever storm was heading my way.

And then what? The question hung in my mind, challenging me, taunting me as I buttoned my coat.

For the next six days, I was as good as my word. My nose was firmly glued to the grindstone. To my surprise, work went well. There was enough of it to keep me busy and keep the invoices flowing. And if the Madigans were slandering me around town, they were doing it quietly. Or in rarefied circles that didn't seem to intersect with my clients. Not yet, anyway.

In fact, life in my little bungalow got to be so boring, so predictable, so Girl-Scouty, that on Tuesday afternoon Bixie moved out—lock, stock and juicer. She did express some reservations about the move, mainly because she couldn't get past the idea that the Madigans, Michael in particular, intended me actual physical harm. But I finally managed to convince her that all would be well and that I was completely safe, especially with two ghosts still at large in the house.

Actually, that was the only drawback in my decision to stand down. Feeling angry and betrayed, I suppose, Dana and Chaz became much more active.

Small items began to disappear and then reappear elsewhere in the house or not at all. Pens, earrings, shoes, sticky-note reminders, pieces of mail, my favorite watch were all pilfered. Some of them turned up in odd places—the bathtub, the treadmill in the basement, the washing machine, even, in the case of my watch, Albert's litter box, something both Al and I took as a grave insult.

The little puffs of cold air got to be such a common occurrence that I hardly noticed them anymore.

Dana and Chaz also invaded my dreams again. Dana always appeared as herself, which was bad enough. But Chaz was often disguised as a crying baby or an abandoned child, which was far worse. Once again, Albert and I began spending our nights downstairs in the oversized leather chair.

The thing is, I couldn't really blame Dana and Chaz for being upset. But I did worry that my decision might have caused them to extend their stay indefinitely.

By Wednesday, I was feeling so haunted and hunted that I briefly considered phoning Margaret to schedule a spirit-removal session. Instead, I called Aunt Ilsa and Uncle Jalo, wished them a happy holiday and got caught up on the local gossip (juicy) and the local weather (snowy).

Then came Thursday.

Thanksgiving was sweet in a mildly dysfunctional sort of way. I was able to dodge a last-minute, guilt-induced dinner invitation from my brother, who lives about three hours away in Grand Rapids, the proud hometown of Amway and Gerald Ford. Instead, I spent a thoroughly pleasant day enjoying the exuberant, quarrelsome clash of cultures that inevitably took place whenever Evan's parents—in from Brooklyn for the holiday—crossed paths with Moira's Irish Catholic mother and assorted relations.

As an outsider, I was exempt from the good-natured arguments that seemed to spring up every minute. Because Moira's alcoholic and slightly lecherous Uncle Leo was spending the holiday with his new girlfriend in Orlando, I was spared his unwelcome attentions—definitely something to be thankful for. And despite their teenage angst, even Mackenzie and Phillip were in a tolerably good mood.

All in all, it was a day that would have warmed Mr. Fezziwig's Victorian heart. When I got home that night just after eight, I was feeling well fed and well loved. Although, I reminded myself, it was probably just a triptophan high, the result of excessive turkey intake.

As I put away the leftovers Moira had packed for me, I thought of all the things I had to be grateful for. It was a long list. And yet…

Something was missing. Something to ignite my energy and give shape to the day. Margaret would probably call it Spirit. Charles Chang would call it Chi. Whatever it was, I decided as I settled into the leather chair with Albert, it just wasn't there.

Half an hour later, I was walking behind Dana as she opened the front door to her house. From somewhere in her living room, a phone began ringing. But there was no phone in sight. As we searched, the ringing stopped and a man's voice boomed through the room. "Come on, Karin, pick up. I know you're there because I saw you drive up ages ago."

I opened my eyes and struggled to throw off the alpaca blanket that had become hopelessly entangled with my legs. The voice continued, "I would have called earlier, but we just got rid of Sam and Angela. You know how they tend to overstay their welcome." With the blanket still wrapped around my ankles, I stumbled across the room like someone in a gunnysack race and grabbed the receiver.

"Paul," I said in a groggy voice. "What's up?" I half-sat, half-fell on the couch and, with my free hand, began untangling the blanket. Albert, miffed at having his long winter's nap interrupted, settled himself on the arm of the couch and stared past me at the fireplace.

"Did I wake you?" he asked with not a shred of remorse. "You'll be glad I did when I tell you what I learned from the Harrises tonight."

Every Thanksgiving, Paul and David put on a gourmet feed for ten or twelve of the most interesting people they know, the ones most likely to come bearing scandal and gossip along with their hostess gifts. Even though I have a standing invitation, I've always felt more at home with the bumptious O'Hara-Bernstein clan.

"The Harrises?" I repeated, not being able to put faces to the name.

"Oh you wouldn't know them," Paul said. "He's an estate planner and she, well never mind, it doesn't matter. The point is that they're very tight with the Goldsteins. As in Dorey and her hubby. And they were both clearly shaken when they arrived this afternoon, nearly an hour and a half late I might add. I had to turn the turkey way down and pray that it wouldn't dry out. And of course I couldn't pry the wine bottle out of Jerry Zukowski's hot little fist, so he proceeded to get roaring drunk. Anyway, when they finally got here, they wouldn't say a word beyond the usual polite excuses. But after a drink or three, they spilled. And you'll never guess..."

I realized I could use a drink myself but settled for trying to fold the blanket with one hand. "So tell me."

Paul's voice was triumphant. "Evidently, Dorey tried to commit suicide."

I dropped the blanket. In that horrible instant, I felt as if I'd been flash-frozen to the phone.

"Suicide," I repeated. "Why? Did they tell you? Did she leave a note?"

"If they knew, they wouldn't say," Paul answered. "But it does look as if Dorey had something preying on her mind, doesn't it?"

Yes, I thought. Something like my barely veiled accusations at the fashion show. Maybe my comments had been the tipping point, had given her that last little nudge into desperation and despair. I felt sick and terrified at what I might have done.

"So what do you think?" I could feel Paul's energy over the phone line.

Without waiting for my answer, he continued. "Personally I think it's obvious that Dorey murdered Dana out of jealousy. Then, after her husband became grief-stricken, she had to face the fact that he loved Dana more than her. That would probably be enough to push some people over the edge." Paul's voice implied that he was not among them.

He circled back to his original question. "So what do you think?"

I clutched the blanket as if it were a teddy bear. Albert, sensing that something was amiss, had given up his sulk and parked himself next to me. I reached down and buried my fingers in his thick shiny fur.

"I think..." I stopped to steady my voice. "I think I should learn to keep my mouth shut. Starting last Saturday."

CHAPTER 40

Friday – November 29

I was just braking for the US-23 South exit, wondering if the sixteen-wheeler behind me could manage to get any closer, when my cell phone went off. Against my better judgment, I glanced at it. Andrew's number.

Pressing it to my ear, I called down curses on the engineers who had figured out how to make telephones work without wires. "Hello, Andrew," I said, packing resentment into every syllable.

"Karin, how goes it?" A bass voice rumbled in the background, then Andrew was on the line again. "Hold on a sec. Sure thing, Brad. Now where the hell did I put that file?"

A mud-splattered van bearing the words Baptist Bibleland Church Transport pulled out slowly from an entrance ramp just ahead. I veered into the passing lane between a Dodge pick-up and a Honda Accord. The Accord driver exercised his horn for several irritating seconds.

"Karin?" Andrew's voice reminded me I was holding a cell phone. "You there?"

"More or less. Until some Detroit driver puts me out of my misery anyway. What's up? Are you calling about that news report this morning? Must be a huge relief for the department to finally announce a break in the Dana Lewis case. Or did you just feel like bullying someone and my number happened to come up in your Rolodex?"

"Why are you always so goddamn defensive?" he asked. The Accord driver had finally given up tailgating me, found an opening, passed on the right and nearly cut me off when he swerved back into my lane. I glanced at the speedometer—which was quivering at eighty—and sent up a prayer, promising God that if She got me back to Ann Arbor safely, I would never stray beyond the city limits again.

"So," I said. "Are you guys trying to pin this on Dorey Goldstein? Or have you finally realized that I'm right and Michael Madigan is your boy? Actually, I'm glad you phoned because now you can tell me where Michael was on the night of Chaz Anderson's death."

Most people get their buzz from caffeine. For me, it's life-threatening traffic. My adrenal gland gets supercharged and, if anyone is unlucky enough to be close at hand, I chatter at them. The way I was chattering at Andrew now.

"I suppose you've confiscated the records of the rent-a-cop agency that guards the Madigan's cozy little compound? Of course you have. And there are videos from security cameras, aren't there? It's that kind of place. Tell you what. I'll bet you a lunch that Michael was out that night and that he returned to Fortress America sometime after the estimated time of death."

There was silence on the other end. I caught sight of the Ann Arbor exit sign and edged into the right lane. Finally Andrew spoke. "The guard goes off duty at nine p.m. After that, the system switches to key card access. And," his voice slowed, "according to the video from that night, Michael Madigan did return home late, or early, depending on your point of view."

"What did I tell you?" I crowed. Sometimes I think I'd rather be right than happy.

"But he has an ironclad alibi," Andrew countered. "He was at a dinner meeting with a group of friends who are all investors in some Miami real estate development. Then he spent a couple of hours at his office."

"How convenient." I steered Amelia onto the Main Street exit ramp. "But you only have his word that he went to the office."

"His word," Andrew agreed. "And the surveillance videos of the office parking lot. Oh, and the sworn statement of his secretary."

"Ah. His secretary." I thought of the blondes who inhabited Michael Madigan's reception area and wondered which one it was. "But murderers almost always have an alibi. Maybe he excused himself from the dinner meeting on the pretext of an important phone call he had to make. Or some family emergency. If he was downtown, he'd only need fifteen or twenty minutes. And what about the time lapse between when he left the office and when he got home?" Even as I spoke, I knew the police had checked and double-checked every one of those possibilities.

"We're way ahead of you," Andrew confirmed. "And unless they taught him to teleport in medical school, Michael Madigan did not murder that kid. In fact—here's a bone for you—we have no reason to believe Chaz Anderson's death was anything other than a suicide."

He let that revelation soak in for a second. "I'll give you a call next week to schedule that lunch. I'm thinking Gratzi's or maybe the Gandy Dancer. Oh, and just for the record. The thing about murderers always having alibis? It's a myth."

He hung up before I could say a word. I threw the phone so hard it bounced off the passenger seat and onto the floor.

As I navigated the familiar streets, I thought about Chaz Anderson. What must it have been like, I wondered, standing up there on the top floor of the parking deck in the eerie late-night silence, alone and scared, buffeted by chilly November winds? How long was he up there? What was he thinking? Did he go there planning to commit suicide? Or was he expecting to meet someone? Michael maybe? Or Ricki? For a confrontation? Or a confession? Or a strategy session?

I pulled into the driveway and parked, letting my mind wander. I could see Chaz looking at his watch, pacing, maybe pounding on one of the cars, kicking tires in frustration or fear. He waits. And waits. No one shows.

Or maybe someone does show. But the conversation goes wrong. There are recriminations. Pleas. Threats. Maybe whoever is with him pulls a gun. Chaz does the natural thing and starts backing away. One step. Another. Another. Each step taking him closer to the low balustrade, until…

The sound of violent pounding on the passenger-side window made me jump. "Karin, you alright in there?" Paul shouted.

Once my heart restarted, I struggled out of the car. "Don't," I began, heaving for air like a beached trout. "Don't ever sneak up on me like that again." I paused for breath. "Ever."

To my surprise, Paul looked contrite. "Sorry. But you were just sitting there, staring off into space. I thought you'd had a stroke."

"No," I said, letting the car support my weight. "A stroke is what I nearly had when you started pounding on the window. Now do me a favor. Hand me my purse and briefcase. And I think my cell phone is on the floor."

Paul collected the paraphernalia and walked around to my side of the car. "Here you go," he said, transferring the stuff to me. "Where've you been anyway?"

"Some of us are at the beck and call of clients whose offices are open the day after Thanksgiving," I told him.

I started toward the side door but Paul got ahead of me and pulled out his keys. After Terry's death, it had seemed like a good idea for Paul and David to have access to the house. Now, watching Paul open the sliding glass door and step into the kitchen, I wasn't so sure.

Paul made himself comfortable in one of the kitchen chairs while I piled my business-girl bits and pieces on the counter. I filled the teakettle and turned on one of the burners. "Was there something you wanted or is this just a social call?"

Paul shrugged out of his jacket. "I was on my way out to run an errand when I saw you parked in the driveway." He reached down to scratch Albert behind the ears. "Looking like you were ready for the EMT."

Albert purred, stretched and then curled himself under the kitchen table, equidistant between Paul and me. "Although now that I'm here, I did remember something I wanted to ask you."

"Which is?" I placed tea bags in two large mugs and found a plate for cookies.

"Which is," Paul continued, "have you happened to notice a Volvo hanging around the neighborhood lately? Silver? Smoked glass windows?"

I went over to stand beside the teakettle, ready for the whistle to go off. "Nope, can't say that I have. Why?"

Paul frowned. "It keeps turning up. Sometimes it's parked in front of Mr. Benson's house, sometimes directly across the street from you, sometimes at the end of the block."

I filled the cups with boiling water, put the teakettle back on the stove, located two teabag holders and was about to transfer the cups to the table when it suddenly dawned on me why Paul was fixated on the car.

"Wait a second. Don't tell me you're worried that someone is casing my house. Or yours." I shook my head in disbelief. "Really, Paul. You've got to rein in your imagination. A Volvo? A silver Volvo no less? Are you serious?" I removed the teabag from my cup. "Any self-respecting mystery reader knows that when someone is stalking someone else, they don't do it in a silver Volvo. They find the most nondescript car possible. Preferably black or dark blue. And second-hand."

Paul tossed his head the way he does when he's embarrassed and ticked off at the same time. He came over to the counter, rescued his tea which by now was brackish, deposited the tea bag carefully in one of the little porcelain dishes I'd put out and picked up the milk jug. "I'll need some of this," he said in a school-marmy voice.

I brought my cup over to the table and sat down. Paul was stirring milk into this tea with the intensity of a child. Funny how a little everyday gesture like that can shift everything. Looking at him, it was as if a tiny window in my heart opened and, through it, I saw a sweet man, a well-intentioned man who was genuinely concerned for a friend.

I reached across the table and put my hand on his. "Hey, thanks."

Paul looked up, startled but pleased. "For what?"

"For caring enough to nearly give me a heart attack. And for worrying about that silver Volvo."

Our eyes locked for a second and I pulled my hand away abruptly. I can't help it. It's a Finnish thing. "I really do appreciate your concern, but don't forget," I reminded him, "I'm off the case. Permanently."

"I don't believe that for a second," he said airily. He sipped at his tea, made a face and added more milk.

"No, really," I insisted. "You're looking at a reformed woman. I've turned in my amateur detective badge."

Paul's face collapsed. He looked so downcast that, against my better judgment, I told him about my conversation with Andrew.

He listened intently, raising an eyebrow here, giving a nod there. When I'd wrapped up my little story, he set his cup down on the table. "Oh if that parking deck could only talk."

My hand hovered above Albert, who had arranged himself on my lap for a serious petting session. "You mean that, even after what Andrew said, you still don't believe that Chaz committed suicide?"

Paul got up to make himself a fresh cup of tea. "I'm not sure. I just know that I wouldn't automatically believe Andrew. He could be wrong. Or deliberately leading you astray, putting you off the scent."

He sorted through the tea bags, found one that was worthy and lowered it into his cup. "I'm still interested in Dorey's suicide attempt and what that means." He poured boiling water into his cup and watched the teabag surface for a moment before sinking. "And I think we should be thinking in new categories. Such as, there were two murders. Maybe. So maybe we should be looking for two murderers. And if you ask me, Michael Madigan's alibi is just a little too airtight."

I felt a rush of excitement as my mind began flitting from possibility to possibility. Paul cocked his head in my direction. "Now don't tell me you're not interested."

Calling up an image of Dorey Goldstein's face, I took a breath, wrapped both hands around my teacup as if it were an anchor and said firmly, "Paul. I told you. I'm off the case."

And I was. Until the following day.

CHAPTER 41

The NPR interviewer was heating things up a bit. "But, congressman, the fact is that in nearly every historically Democratic precinct in the state of Michigan, electronic voting machines recorded an unprecedented number of congressional undervotes. In other words, citizens of your state presumably took the time to cast their ballots for city council or the local school board, but relatively few of them voted for senators or members of the House of Representatives. Surely these rather surprising facts demand a vigorous and immediate investigation. After all…"

Tuning out the radio for a moment, I dove headlong into the morning's first cup of coffee. Delicious. Perfect.

When the interviewer finally paused to draw breath, the esteemed congressman took over the microphone and threw around a few stock phrases, beginning with "sore losers" and "unfounded allegations."

Enough.

I turned off the radio. Picked up the entertainment section of the morning paper. Ruffled through a few pages. Put the paper down. Retrieved my coffee. Shuffled into the laundry room. Then, twenty seconds later, with a load of damp clothes kerchunking in the dryer, I refilled my coffee cup and began prowling through the downstairs.

I felt like a kid in the middle of summer vacation. Not the overscheduled summer vacations that children endure these days. The old-fashioned kind, filled with long, empty, identical, searingly hot days that stretched out like eternity. The kind of summer vacations when absolutely nothing appealed, not long pointless bike rides on baking streets that smelled of tar and hot grass, not bruising games of spud or dodge ball, not reading *Robin Hood* or *Little House on the Prairie* for the third time. I'm talking about the kind of summer vacations when kids sat on porch swings and drank sticky glasses of lemonade and blew on ripe dandelions and played endless games of Go Fish and Crazy Eights and yearned for something they couldn't describe and probably wouldn't have recognized even if they found it.

Nudging Albert aside, I made a space for myself in the big leather armchair and gazed at the telephone, willing it to ring. Even a call from Andrew would have been welcome at that moment.

Then it came to me. Jane Austen.

As I walked across the room to the "A" section of the downstairs library, I felt like a fist that was gradually unclenching. Maybe recovery was possible, I thought. Maybe there was hope for me. Maybe I'd survive my premature retirement from the ranks of amateur detectives.

Book in hand, I nestled into the chair and opened to chapter one.

"*The family of Dashwood had been long settled in Sussex. Their estate was large, and their residence was at Norland Park...*"

When the phone rang a little after eleven, it was as if a time machine had suddenly and brutally yanked me out of the eighteenth century and plunked me back down in this one.

"Karin?" The voice was young, female, hesitant. And vaguely familiar. "This is Ricki. Ricki Christiansen? We met last week in Isabel's office?"

I gave myself a couple of seconds to get past the mild shock of having Chaz Anderson's ex-sort-of-girlfriend on the other end of the line. "Of course. How are you, Ricki?"

"Alright I guess." Pause. "Well, actually, I've got a problem."

I felt a tingle in my spine. Steady and grown-up, I reminded myself. "What kind of problem?"

"I hope you don't mind me calling you. Especially on a Saturday."

"No, not at all. What's going on?"

Was that a tiny sigh of relief I heard on the other end of the line? "Like I said, I'm just not sure what to do. I mean, obviously, I suppose,

I should call the police. But I don't know. I thought since you were so concerned about Isabel and everything, I should maybe call you first."

"Sure. Tell me how I can help." And get to the point.

"Right. Well, it's like this. Remember how I told you that, even after we broke up, Chaz would show up at my apartment now and then and ask me to store some of his junk?"

"Yes, I remember that."

"Well, last night, really late, I was working on a painting for my senior exhibit and all of a sudden for no particular reason, except maybe I'd been thinking about Chaz so much lately, I suddenly remembered that last year near the end of winter term he came over with a laptop and asked me to store it for him in the basement."

"Right," I drew out the word to buy myself some time. "But if he was always dropping off stuff, what makes you think..."

"Because," Ricki interrupted, "it was new. Anyone could see that. When I pointed that out and asked him if he was sure he wanted to store it, he made a big deal about what a useless piece of garbage it was. I can't remember what he said exactly, something about hardware glitches. Which didn't make sense, because he was incredibly good at fixing things like that. He used to make money doing computer repairs for other students."

I realized I was holding my breath and forced myself to exhale slowly as Ricki went on.

"So he takes this laptop and we go into the basement and he puts it way in the back of my storage space. Way back. I mean, so far back he had to move a bunch of stuff to make room for it in the corner. It was," she stopped for a second, searching for words. "It was almost like he was trying to bury the thing. He put some ratty old rugs over it and then piled all kinds of stuff around it, old tennis rackets, luggage, things like that."

For some reason I wasn't yet sure of, my heart was pounding.

"The problem is," Ricki continued, "when the police asked me if I had anything that belonged to Chaz that could help their investigation, I honestly didn't remember that laptop. It's not as if I see it every time I go into my storage unit."

She hesitated. "I don't want to bother them if it's not important. I guess maybe I just don't want to have to deal with them again if I don't have to." Soft sigh. "What do you think I should do?"

Good self wrestled with bad self.

"I'll tell you what..." I was surprised at how confident I sounded. "First, I'm going to throw on some clothes, make a couple of phone calls and then I'll head over to your place."

"But...but what about the police?"

"I'll call them later," I said soothingly, knowing it might be a while before I kept that promise. "Look. This might be nothing at all. It probably *is* nothing at all. So before we bother the police, I think we should try to figure out what's going on with the laptop."

It took a few seconds for Ricki to decide. "I'm at three-two-five-oh Brockman, second floor," she said in a little girl voice.

I wrote down the address on the phone message pad.

"Great. I'll be there in half an hour or less. Then you and I will dig out that laptop and decide what we're going to do next. Okay?"

It took me about a minute to jump into a pair of jeans and a turtleneck. While I was pulling a comb through my hair, I left a message for Bixie, telling her to meet me at Ricki's and giving her the address. I debated about phoning Paul but—on the theory of too many cooks or, in Paul's case, too many prima donnas—I decided to pass.

Instead I dialed Evan's number and nearly yelped for joy when he came on the line. "Karin. You're still alive. What a pleasant surprise. What's up?"

"Evan, listen carefully," I began and then forged on, not giving him time to disagree or second-guess. "I need you to meet me at three-two-five-oh Brockman as soon as possible. Sooner. It's where Chaz Anderson's ex-girlfriend lives. You remember, I told you about her on Thanksgiving. You asked about the case and..."

"You mean now?"

I rolled my eyes. "You know, for a brilliant computer scientist, you can be a little dense sometimes. Yes, now."

"And you want me to do this because?" The suspicion in his voice was so thick you could have sliced it and spread it on a bagel.

"Because I think she may have stumbled on a very important clue having to do with Chaz Anderson's death—or maybe his murder. It's a computer. Something he left with her before he went off to his internship at Grunwald. I've got a feeling this is big. Although I suppose it could be nothing. But in any case, I need you to break into it."

"What the fuck are you up to?" Evan could bellow like a bull when provoked and right now he was clearly provoked. "Are you asking me to help you withhold evidence? In a possible murder investigation? You need to call the police. And if you don't, I will."

Panic welled up and lodged in my throat, making it hard to form my next sentences.

"I *will* call the police." I crossed the fingers of both hands. "As soon as I get over to Ricki's. But she's just a kid and she's been through a lot already." I laid it on thick, hoping that Evan's fatherly instincts would kick in. "I don't want to get her more deeply involved in the case unless it's absolutely necessary. She trusts me. I'm not going to betray her by calling the police."

"Since when is calling the police with new evidence that could bring her former boyfriend's killer to justice an act of betrayal?" His voice was heavy with sarcasm.

"Evan, look. You're my friend and I need your help." Shameless, absolutely shameless. "I will call the police, really I will. But after everything that's happened in the past two weeks, I have to do this. I have to know what's on that computer. And why Chaz hid it away in a dark corner of someone's basement. And I will do it. With or without your help."

Silence. I made my voice softer. "Please, Evan."

More silence. Then one of those trademark Evan sighs. "Just promise me this. If I wind up in jail, you'll help Maura look after the kids."

I couldn't keep from breaking out in a big grin.

"That won't be necessary," I assured him. "Because if you wind up in jail, I'll be in the next cell block. Women's wing."

CHAPTER 42

Saturday – November 30

"Holy shit."

Ricki, Bixie and I broke off our chatter and looked over at Evan, his bulky frame hunched around the glowing screen of a late-model laptop. The chair he was sitting on—a dilapidated armless wonder that probably did hard time in a dorm before finding its way to Ricki's apartment—looked incredibly uncomfortable and far too small for his two hundred-plus pounds.

But Evan didn't seem to notice either the chair or the rickety Ikea knick-knack table that held the computer. In fact, he didn't seem to notice anything at all but the flickering screen. His fingers flew over the keyboard as he opened file after file—a process punctuated only by an occasional "Holy shit."

At first, I doubted that he'd be able to break into the system, assuming that Chaz would have set up some brain-bending firewalls. But Evan explained that Chaz had used the Computer Science Department's own security protocols which, Evan pointed out with a chuckle, were extremely good in large part because he himself had helped design them.

Ricki was surprisingly cool and calm. She had been relieved to see me when I showed up ten minutes ahead of schedule. Surprised to see Bixie five minutes later. And only slightly taken aback when Evan arrived about five minutes after that, lugging a gigantic briefcase and a laptop carryall.

With Ricki acting as our guide, we dug out the laptop from her locked storage unit in the building's very large, very damp and very nasty basement, hauled it up two flights of steps and set up an ad hoc workstation on one of her so-called coffee tables.

While Ricki and Bixie made coffee, I sat next to Evan and, when I couldn't bear the suspense, asked what I hoped were intelligent questions.

"Interesting," he said, pointing a large index finger at the screen. "There are no servers mounted on this system."

"Which tells us what exactly?" I asked.

"Which tells us that this is a dumb terminal," Evan explained with more patience than usual. "From what I can see, this unit was never connected to the Internet. There are no browsers. No email programs. Nothing. So it appears that Chaz used this purely for work."

Something clicked in my brain. "I read somewhere that Carl Bernstein writes all of his books on a dumb terminal."

Evan kept typing as he spoke. "Wouldn't surprise me at all, considering the topics he's tackled and the enemies he's collected. It's the only way, really, to assure complete security and privacy if you're working on a computer."

His first "Holy shit" came when he opened a file labeled simply "Notes." Since then he'd been repeating that same phrase regularly, almost like a mantra, every minute or so for the past half hour.

After fifteen minutes, I drifted away to Ricki's mouse-colored couch, where she and Bixie were talking earnestly over their cups of instant coffee. After a while, Evan's "holy shits" became nothing more than white noise, like the ticking of a grandfather clock or the rumble of traffic, something Ricki, Bixie and I barely noticed as we debated when to call Andrew and what to tell him.

We had finally settled on a story and agreed that Bixie would call her brother within the next thirty minutes when Evan let out another "holy shit," this one louder than the rest.

He shook his large burly head, leaned away from the screen without taking his eyes off it and muttered, "Brilliant. Absolutely brilliant. I can't fucking believe this. What balls." Then, throwing his voice in our direction, he announced, "I think it's time to call Andrew."

I was at Evan's side in a flash, with Bixie and Ricki close behind me. "Not until you tell us what you found," I said. "In plain English, please. We deserve that much. Especially if the wrath of the Ann Arbor Police is going to descend on us."

Ricki gave me a stricken look that slashed temporary stress lines across her forehead. "I'm going to be in trouble with the police, aren't I?"

Bixie touched Ricki's shoulder lightly. "No you're not," she said.

I nodded. "You're in the clear on this one. If anyone's going to be in trouble, it'll be Bixie and me."

Evan gave me a wry look. "And?" he prodded.

"Alright. And you." I turned back to Ricki, who was gnawing on a fingernail, her blue eyes looking too large for her face.

Evan took a few gulps of his cold, oily-looking coffee, ran a hand through his hair until he looked a like an Albert Einstein tribute artist and then surprised me by saying, "Okay. You're right. You need to know this."

Forgetting her anxiety for the moment, Ricki pulled up a cracked leather hassock for herself and a small wooden chair for Bixie. When we were all seated, Evan studied the ceiling for a few seconds. Staring at his profile, I realized I hadn't noticed the new patch of grey at his temples or the webbed lines under his eyes.

Then it hit me—what a huge chance he was taking, being here, playing this dangerous game of mine. Breaking the law. Unless we handled this very carefully, his entire career could be jeopardized.

Suddenly, I wished I could have a re-do on the entire day. I should have never called him. What was I thinking? What would Terry say? How could I endanger his best friend this way? How could I be so selfish, so—what was it Evan had called me the other day?—so pig-headed?

Breaking out of his reverie, Evan lowered his head and looked at each one of us in turn. "Alright," he began. "You've all heard of the UNIX operating system, right? The first commercially successful, portable operating system in the world?"

We nodded.

"Okay, good. What you probably don't know is that UNIX was created in 1969 at Bell Labs by two genius programmers named Ken

Thompson and Dennis Ritchie. And some others as well, but Thompson and Ritchie primarily."

Evan sipped his cold coffee and his eyes took on that glazed sheen they get when he's living in what Moira refers to as Computerville. "Right," he went on. "What you have to realize is that UNIX, and the C programming language those two guys wrote along with it, changed everything. I mean everything. It became *the* programming system for business, industry, academe, Internet servers, you name it. To this day, it's still pretty much unchallenged."

Evan checked to make sure we were following his thoughts. "So you got the picture, right? UNIX is a big deal." We nodded again. I was starting to feel like a bobble-head doll.

"Back in 1983," Evan continued, "a professional group called the Turing Society decided to honor Ken Thompson and his partner with a major award. They invited Thompson to give a speech at the ceremony. Which he did. And he completely blew them away." Bixie, Ricki and I all leaned forward in our seats as if Evan were telling us a ghost story around a campfire.

"Thompson entitled his talk *Reflections on Trusting Trust*. And it sent shock waves through the entire computer programming world." Evan looked at each of us, one by one. "You have to understand that UNIX was the most trusted operating system of its kind. It was used by everybody in the business. Every programmer. We're talking very savvy, very smart people here."

Evan rubbed the back of his neck and stretched. "And Thompson stood up in front of these guys, calm as you please, and said he wanted to tell them about the cutest program he ever wrote. Those were his words. The cutest program he ever wrote." He shook his head and grinned, as if he and Ken Thompson were sharing a private joke.

"Then he dropped his bombshell. He confessed that he had inserted a bug into the UNIX system when he was creating it." If Evan noticed our puzzled expressions, he chose to ignore them. "What we call a Trojan Horse. In other words, he deliberately compromised the entire system. And he did it in a way that made it impossible for those incredibly smart programmers to detect."

Evan paused as if struck by the immensity of the act. "Do you realize how huge that was? Hundreds, maybe thousands of computer programmers are looking at this guy, this genius, at the podium. Their hero. Creator of the system they use every day. And he's telling them that he pre-hacked it. And they never knew it, because he inserted this Trojan Horse too far upstream, in the compiler."

"The what?" Bixie, looking as bewildered as I was, broke into Evan's story.

Realizing that he'd lost us, Evan fumbled around in his briefcase, pulled out a notebook, began sketching a diagram and then thought better of it. He let the notebook rest on his lap. "Never mind. You don't need to know. The point is that because he inserted this bug way upstream in the programming process, it could never be detected and would go on replicating itself indefinitely. Which meant that Thompson could theoretically access any UNIX-based system in the world, using his own password."

"Fascinating," I said. "But why are you telling us all this? What does it have to do with Chaz Anderson?"

Evan tossed the notebook on the floor. "I'm telling you this because this laptop contains a detailed file on Thompson, all kinds of materials including the complete text of the Turing speech."

He rubbed his forehead with both hands as if to ward off a headache.

"Chaz also stored voluminous notes about the Grunwald operating system. Plus a copy of the code they use for their electronic voting machines, which is actually nothing more than commodity software tarted up. And in his notes," Evan slowed down, as if he couldn't quite bring himself to finish the thought, "in his notes, Chaz outlines in detail how it would be possible to apply Thompson's tactics to Grunwald's software."

Except for Ricki's soft "oh my God," there was complete silence for maybe ten seconds.

Evan leaned forward and stared at me intently. "Do you realize how brilliant this is?"

"Well, I..."

"I'm telling you this kid figured out that he could go about his dreary, daily little duties, adding software patches, doing routine maintenance at Grunwald, and while he was doing it, while he was working on these systems in a very public, apparently innocuous way, he could hack the software. And it would never be noticed. Because he was working way upstream, where no one would think to look for a hack. Just like his hero Thompson."

Evan sat back in his chair and the joints creaked in protest. "The question is," he mused, "was all this just an intellectual exercise? Or did he actually slip new, self-replicating code into the Grunwald system? If he did, he could reprogram a huge number of voting machines used in the last election. Particularly in the Midwest, since those states account for the lion's share of Grunwald's market." He paused and two lines appeared between his eyes. "And of course, since Michigan and Ohio both had hotly contested senatorial races…" He let the sentence peter out.

"My God," Bixie said, almost in a trance state. "Rigging an election. What are the police going to do when they find out?" She let the question drift away.

Evan crossed his arms and allowed himself the luxury of a smug smile. "So, Karin. What do you have to say about all this?"

I looked past him and out the window at the bare tree branches that tapped lightly on the windowpanes, at the errant rays of sunshine slanting between heavy grey snow clouds, at the traffic crawling by on Packard. Everything had a slow, surreal quality.

"What can anyone possibly say?" I blinked and swallowed hard. "Except…holy shit."

CHAPTER 43

Saturday – November 30

Bixie refused to call Andrew, insisting that her brother was less likely to be pissed if he didn't know she was involved, at least not right away. Evan was still hard at work at the laptop. I wasn't craven enough to ask Ricki to do the deed. And as I kept reminding myself, this was my mess.

So, tensing my shoulders in anticipation, I began dialing Andrew's direct number, which I now knew by heart.

Bixie looked up from the dog-eared little address book she keeps in her purse. "I was just finding Andrew's work number for you," she said in tones sharp enough to filet a trout. "But evidently you don't need it."

She shut the tiny book with a snap and I could feel her radar revving up. "Half the time you can't even remember *my* number. Since when have you two gotten so close?"

"Since we launched this little case of ours and your brother decided I was a public menace." I pressed the last digit and waited for the ring tone, hoping to God he wouldn't pick up so I could leave a nice, safe message instead.

"Murray here." His voice was all business.

Damn.

"Hey, Andrew. It's Karin. I've, uh, got something for you. Something you're going to want to see."

He didn't say much as I explained what was happening at Ricki's, just listened intently and asked an occasional question. When I finally wound down my tale with "...so I figured you'd want to get over here sooner rather than later," he blew out a gust of air and let it float on the silence for a few seconds.

"Well, I would tell you not to touch anything but it's obviously too late for that." I couldn't decide if he sounded angry or resigned or both. Probably both. "Okay. Whatever it is you've been doing with that computer, stop. I'm going to round up one of our tech guys. We'll be there in five minutes."

He was wrong about that. By my watch, it took them four and a half minutes. Ricki went down to answer the door and escort them upstairs.

Andrew entered the room first, bringing a blast of energy with him. Tagging along a few feet behind was a tall, concave-chested, Ichabod Crane sort of man, mid-thirties, lots of Adam's apple, buzz-cut hair, small wire-rimmed glasses and not much in the way of shoulders. In each hand, he carried an oversized satchel that could have contained almost anything, from computer gear to—I looked at Andrew's face—thumbscrews and a cat-of-nine-tails.

While Ichabod made a beeline for the computer, Andrew herded us all into a loose little circle. Towering over us as we fidgeted on our shabby chairs, he looked like a stock character in the rescue scene of a generic fairytale. Not the knight in shining armor. The dragon.

Hands on hips, shoulder holster showing against an impossibly white shirt, he let his wrathful gaze rest first on Bixie, then on me. Evan got just a glancing blow. Ricki had to endure only the slightest flick of his pale eyes.

"Karin, since you seem to be the...I won't say the brains behind all this. You start. And if I don't like what I hear, you and Bixie and the professor are all coming for a ride with me. To the station."

Giving Bixie and Evan a sideways glance and hoping they both felt the abject apology I was sending along with it, I took a breath and started in on my story. The same story I'd told him on the phone.

I was halfway through my fourth or fifth sentence when something in me gave way. "Andrew," I burst out, "there is no point in my going through this all again. The facts aren't going to change." His face was as still as stone. "I've told you. This was all my idea. It's my fault. And I know I was stupid and wrong and stubborn..."

I waited a couple of seconds for him to interrupt my self-abuse. When he didn't, I went on. "Ricki did absolutely nothing wrong. I told her to call me if anything came up, and so when she remembered the laptop, she phoned me. She had no idea it could be so important to the case." I shot Ricki an I'm-so-sorry look, which was completely wasted since she was staring at Andrew like a bird hypnotized by a snake.

I stumbled on. "And Bixie didn't do anything except give me moral support." Andrew snorted. "Same with Evan. He acted purely out of friendship. Truth is, he probably thought if he came over here, he could save me from turning this into a disaster."

"Which you managed to do anyway," Andrew interjected.

"Right," I said and felt my shoulders slump. Then a small flame rekindled. I straightened my spine and met Andrew's gaze full-on. "But I really don't see what the problem is."

Andrew re-crossed his arms. "Go on."

Hunger made it hard to concentrate. "Well, you have the evidence in hand. No harm done. And when they find out what's on that laptop, you're going to be a hero in the department."

I waited for an explosion. Nothing. I continued.

"I don't see why you can't treat Evan as an ad hoc police consultant. I mean, he just did the work that would have to be done anyway." I glanced over at Ichabod, who was bent over the laptop, his latex-gloved fingers burning up the keyboard. "And he probably saved you guys a small fortune, since it would have taken one of your computer honchos days to do what he did in just a couple of hours."

Evan opened his mouth to say something, then thought better of it. But the look on his face told me he didn't have a lot of faith in my Rumpole of the Bailey tactics.

Through clenched teeth, Andrew managed to say, "Uh-huh. And what about the fact that the evidence—extremely important evidence, I should point out—has been tampered with?"

"Well," I drew out the word, stalling for time.

"I shouldn't have done it." Evan's voice startled me. He gave Andrew a lopsided grin. "But once I got started, I couldn't stop. Blame it on academic curiosity, Lieutenant. My fatal flaw." He shrugged and grinned again, like the good-natured guy who gets jilted in an Italian opera.

Evan's outburst seemed to have a cooling effect on Andrew. He relaxed his military stance, uncrossed his arms, hooked one hand over his belt and used the other to rub his forehead. "Right. So here's what we're going to do."

He aimed his voice toward corner of the room where the laptop screen glowed softly and called out. "Jim, wrap it up, would you? Let's get all this stuff back to headquarters."

He turned back to us. "First, I'm heading out to the car for some more evidence bags." With a remarkably gentle look in his eyes, he turned to Ricki. "Ms. Christiansen, we'll need a statement from you. You can come down to the station later today, whenever you're ready." He handed her one of his cards. "Ask for me or for Sergeant Caldwell." When Andrew turned his head toward Evan, I caught Ricki's eye, shook my head frantically and mouthed the words, "Not Caldwell."

"Professor Bernstein. Bixie. Karin. You three are all going to the station to make your statements. Now." He nodded at Evan. "Professor, you can take your own car if you like. And I imagine our IT guys are going to want to spend some quality time with you. Better give your wife a call and let her know where you'll be."

Andrew hooked Bixie and me with his eyes. "Bixie, thanks to you I'm going to have to recuse myself from this case."

His sister looked down at the floor as if she were trying to find a crack large enough to crawl into. "Andrew, I am so sorry..." she began.

He cut her off and turned to me. I knew what was coming.

"You and your partner in crime here are coming with me. As soon as I have the evidence together, we'll head for the station. In fact, you two will be officially delivering this stuff to the department since I don't want to take the time to get a warrant. And while you're there, you will make full and complete statements, both of you."

He turned and walked toward the door, then shot back over his shoulder, "And I have a feeling it's going to take a long time before we get around to processing you both. In fact, if I can help it, you won't be seeing your happy little homes for quite a while."

While Ichabod loaded the last of the computer paraphernalia into his antique Corolla, Andrew loaded his sister and me into his Crown Victoria. Partly to distract myself from the hunger pangs that had by now reached epic proportions and partly to keep myself calm, I began scanning the traffic for stickers. They seemed to come in clusters. First, it was:

> *You Can't Be Pro-War and Pro-Life at the Same Time*
> *Which God Do You Kill For?*

Then for a few blocks, things got a little uglier:

> *Who Would Jesus Torture?*
> *Bad President! No Banana.*
> *Is It Vietnam Yet?*

Then thoughtful:

> *You Elected Him. You Deserve Him.*
> *The Republican Party: Our Bridge to the 11th Century*

Of course, mixed in with all the politics was the usual assortment of local favorites like *Visualize Peace, Perform Random Acts of Kindness, Free Tibet,* and *My Other Vehicle Is the Millennium Falcon.* But the hands-down winner of the afternoon was:

> *Frodo failed. Bailey has the ring.*

At the corner of Huron and Ashley, Amer's Deli was doing a brisk business. The lot was nearly full and customers in winter jackets and hats bustled in and out. A man in an Air Force parka was tenderly holding a large white plastic bag in both hands.

I thought of Amer's creamy hummus. His spiced-to-perfection pita sandwiches. His scalding coffee. His godlike baklava. My stomach gave a pathetic lurch. I turned to Andrew and touched his elbow lightly.

"I have a request."

"Oh yeah?"

"Could we stop at Amer's for something to eat? I haven't had anything since breakfast."

"No chance, Niemi." Was that a smile on his face? A sadistic little smile? "We'll get you something at the station. Something out of a vending machine maybe."

Son of a bitch. It *was* a smile, and he brought it out again as he began a hard right into the police station parking lot.

"Look at it this way. The sooner you get used to institutional food, the better. It'll be less of a shock to your system that way."

CHAPTER 44

Saturday – November 30

"But there's nothing left to tell," I reminded Paul hours later as I downed the last bite of a lamb pita sandwich. "You know everything."

After Bixie and I were finally allowed to make our statements, Andrew had refused to drive us back to Ricki's apartment and our waiting cars. I voted for a cab but Bixie insisted that we call Paul who, as it happened, was enjoying a rare Saturday night at home while David attended a dinner meeting.

Within fifteen minutes, our rescuer was at the station, bug-eyed with excitement and panting for details. And after more than five hours of being alternately ignored and intimidated, of sitting on hard benches and harder chairs, of breathing stale air, staring at dirty walls in shades of institutional green and tan, studying wanted posters, drinking coffee that had the consistency of molasses and the acid level of paint remover, and doing our best to ignore Moses B. Caldwell who kept staring daggers at us from his corner desk, Bixie and I were more than ready to vent.

Paul swirled the cabernet in his glass and studied the red film that formed briefly on the sides. "Everything?" he said in a sulky voice. "Not quite. I still don't know why you didn't call me after you heard from Ricki."

"Because I wanted to spare you," I snapped. "Would you have preferred spending the last six hours at the Ann Arbor Police Station?"

Bixie looked up from the far corner of the couch where she and Lew had been engaged in a prolonged love fest. "Karin's right. What good would it do to drag you into this... this..." She gave Lew a slow head-to-butt stroke. "This mess," she finished with a sigh. "And just for the record, Andrew made it clear we need to find ourselves a lawyer."

"Point taken," Paul conceded. Then he grinned. "But my God, this is so exciting. Who would have believed that Karin was right?"

"Thanks a lot," I mumbled.

"Well, you have to admit that your voting conspiracy theory sounded pretty far-fetched," Paul went on. "I mean, the whole plot line is right out of a Robert Ludlum novel."

As the stress of the day seeped in, I could feel fatigue creep through my body inch by inch. With her eyes at half-mast and her hands motionless on Lew's broad back, Bixie appeared to be in the same stupefied state. Paul, on the other hand, was just warming up. He poured himself another glass of wine and smiled expectantly. "So what happens next?"

"What do you mean?" I asked, not liking the direction the conversation was taking.

"What do you mean what do I mean? How about Grunwald Industries? And the Young Republicans and their advisors or handlers or whatever they are? Michael Madigan among them. Think about it, guys." As if we hadn't been thinking about it all day. "This is huge. Chaz Anderson may very well have hacked the vote. In a national election. Or at least a senatorial election."

Shaking his head at the immensity of it all, Paul gazed into the fireplace where a cheery blaze was throwing out currents of heat and making our shadows flicker against the wall, like figures in a Javanese puppet show.

"I don't know what to think," he pondered. "I can't believe the kid did the whole thing on his own. But it's going to be hard to prove that someone else was involved."

"Paul, what are you saying?" Responding to the edge in Bixie's voice, Lew lowered his ears, made himself as small as possible and skulked off the couch in search of Albert, who was visiting for the evening. Her eyes, sleepy no more, were burning with energy and reminded me uncomfortably of her brother. "Don't you get it?" she snapped. "It's over. O. V. E. R. From now on, Karin and I are going to concentrate on not getting ourselves arrested." She flopped back against the couch, picked up a pillow and hugged it tightly.

"Well excuse me," Paul snapped back. "So you're saying we just walk away? Forget everything we know, everything we've learned?"

"Yes, Paul." I said, as I collected paper debris and stacked styrofoam containers into neat piles. "That's exactly what we're saying. I know it's a radical concept, actually letting the police handle the investigation. But starting now, the main focus of our lives will be keeping ourselves out of trouble."

It was just after midnight when Albert and I unlocked the front door and let ourselves in. Exhaustion had made me fumble-fingered and, when I attempted to hang up my coat, it fell in a messy pile on the closet floor. I stared at the folds of grey wool for a few seconds, then shut the door. When I turned around, Albert was staring at me in what I assumed was disbelief.

After staggering upstairs, I stripped and pulled Terry's favorite bathrobe out of his closet, pausing for a moment to take in the faint scent of him that still lingered, ghost-like, among the clothes. Then I turned on the shower and stood under the blessedly hot water so long my skin began to pucker. By the time I came downstairs, toweling my hair, it was close to one a.m.

I was in the downstairs bathroom, combing the tangles out of my damp hair when the doorbell rang. After four seconds of heart-pumping panic, I crept into the foyer, turned on the porch light and glued my eye to the peephole.

"Andrew?" I said out loud.

After debating with myself for a few seconds, I opened the door about three inches and peered at my unwelcome guest, who was stomping snow off his shoes and looking incredibly dapper in a black wool car coat and burgundy scarf.

"Well?" he asked.

I opened the door about two inches wider and fought down a surge of anxiety at the thought that he was here to arrest me. "Isn't that what

I'm supposed to say?" I asked, grateful my voice wasn't shaking. "What are you doing here at this time of night?"

"I'm paying you a visit. Can I come in?"

"Andrew, please go away," I pleaded. "I promise never, ever to interfere with your work again. I'll even put it in writing. In the morning. Okay?"

He shook a skim of snow off his shoulders. "Just for a few minutes."

I felt like screaming. Instead, I opened the door, shuffled into the living room and pointed to the couch. "Drink?" I asked, hoping he'd say no.

"Sure, thanks. Scotch, light on the ice."

I walked into the kitchen resenting every step, made two drinks and delivered them to the coffee table before curling up in the big leather armchair with Albert at my side.

As he picked up his glass, Andrew seemed to be trying hard not to smile. It didn't take a rocket scientist to figure out why. Under Terry's robe I was wearing a tattered grey sweat suit paired with heavy wool socks and fleece slippers. I looked like the consignment shop version of an L.L. Bean ad.

I picked up my drink. "If I'd known you were coming, I would have put on a suit."

He did smile then. "Actually that outfit is very becoming."

I pulled the robe up around my neck and put one arm around Albert. "And you wanted to talk about what exactly?"

Andrew leaned forward, hands clasped, elbows on his knees. "I was just on my way home to try to get a few hours of sleep. I suppose you know I'm off the case, thanks to you and my sister?"

"I'm sorry," I said. "Really sorry."

"You should be. Anyway, before I took off for home, I had to stop by and ask you just one question."

I kept my attention on Albert, who was on full alert and staring at Andrew. "I've already answered every question you guys could possibly think of. I'm tired of questions. I may never answer a question again."

To my alarm, I realized that the odd pricking heat behind my eyes was—no, it couldn't be. Tears. I conjured up an image of Queen

Elizabeth and began my silent incantation. *I am the Queen of England, I am the Queen of England.*

"Just one, Karin." Andrew's voice was quiet and calm. In the dim light, he looked years younger. He stared at the floor for a second or two, then locked his gaze on my face. "Why?"

"Why what?" I asked. Albert, who had relaxed by degrees, was purring like an outboard motor.

"Why get involved in this case? And why keep pursuing it? You knew what you were doing was dangerous in a lot of ways. Yet you kept going. It's not about Isabel Lewis, not anymore, so don't tell me it is. And it's not about Bixie either. It may have started that way, but now it's about something else. So why? What was in it for you?"

Without warning, the stinging hot feeling behind my eyes started up again, stronger and more insistent. I fought back, and when I could trust my voice, I answered him. "People don't always know why they do things."

Andrew gave his head an angry shake. "Come off it, Karin. You know perfectly well why you did what you did. And I think, after everything that's happened, I deserve to know too. So... why?"

The question hung there in the air like a physical presence. An object that seemed to grow larger with every passing moment. I was horrified to feel a trickle of tears escaping from the corner of one eye.

"Because." I began, then stopped myself. From somewhere inside my head, a desperate voice told me I didn't have to answer. "Because, it..." Why was I doing this? There was still time to stop. Or at least to lie. I took a deep, ragged breath.

"Because," I blurted out, "it made me feel alive."

It was as if a dam had burst. I sat there in the oversized armchair, letting my tears flow, holding Albert with one hand, clutching Terry's robe with the other, wishing I had a box of tissues within reach and waiting for Andrew to say something clever or cruel.

Instead, he got up and walked around the coffee table until he was standing just a few inches from me. I thought I heard him say, "C'mere." Next thing I knew, he had me by the wrists and was lifting gently.

And the next thing I knew after that, I sobbing into his jacket lapel while he held me. I pushed against him. "D-don't," I hiccupped. "It... it will just make me cuh-cry more."

Andrew tightened his grip. "It's okay." I could feel the words vibrate in his chest as he spoke. "It's alright, Karin." He patted my damp hair. "Go ahead. Let it out."

A few minutes later, when my sobs had turned into snuffles, Andrew released me, reached into his inside jacket pocket and handed me a billowy white handkerchief. For some reason, the gesture brought me back to myself.

"I didn't think men used these anymore," I said wonderingly as I unfolded the big soft square of cotton. "Not since Cary Grant and William Holden."

He walked over to the couch and picked up his coat. "They do if they're married to Helen."

Right. Helen.

I watched him work the buttons. He paused briefly. "You alright?" I nodded. "You sure?" I nodded again. "Okay," he draped the wine-colored scarf loosely around his neck and started walking toward the door. "Then get some sleep. You're going to feel a whole lot better in the morning. Guaranteed."

I followed him into the foyer and, when he tried to open the door, I pushed it closed. "Just one thing, Andrew."

As he turned to face me, I realized how awful I must look. Not that it mattered, I told myself.

"This... What just happened. This is strictly between us, okay? No one else hears about it. Not Bixie or Helen or Caldwell. Or anybody." I let go of the door. "Right?"

Andrew pulled on the doorknob and let in a blast of icy air. He stepped onto the porch, turned and grinned at me. "I don't know what you're talking about." He winked. "I haven't seen you since you made your statement at headquarters."

After all those hot tears and heated exchanges, the cold air felt wonderful. I stood in the doorway and let it wash over me. When Andrew's taillights had disappeared around the corner, I went inside.

The clock on the mantelpiece chimed twice. Standing at the foot of the stairs, I reached into the pocket of my robe and pulled out the handkerchief.

Something told me it was going to be a long night. I pressed the soft folds against my face, still sticky and tight from dried tears.

A long night. Or a short one.

CHAPTER 45

Sunday – December 1

One thing I've noticed about guilt, Lutheran guilt especially. It's tenacious. Which is why, despite severe sleep deprivation and a powerful inclination never to show my face in public again, by ten the next morning I was standing on Evan's pleasantly cluttered front porch holding a grocery bag containing a baker's dozen of Barry's Bagels, half a pound of Zingerman's cream cheese, a package of absurdly expensive lox, a carton of orange juice with pulp intact and a copy of *The New York Times* so fresh I could smell the ink.

Given the fact that I might have inadvertently screwed up Evan's career for all time, I wasn't sure I'd be invited to cross the threshold. In that case, I'd shift to plan B, leave my peace offering foundling-style on the porch and spend the rest of the day behind locked doors, licking my wounds, worrying mightily, listening to the radio for every possible shred of local news and beating myself up for being such a balls-out idiot.

Plan B went by the boards about five seconds later when Evan opened the door. I noticed the puffiness around his eyes, the gristle on his cheeks, the fright-wig state of his hair and the fact that his Grateful Dead T-shirt was inside out.

After staring at me in silence for maybe three seconds, he said matter-of-factly, "You look terrible. In fact, you look worse than I feel."

"I have a lot of apologizing to do," I said. "Can I come in?"

He studied the bag. "Only if you've got onion bagels in there."

"Three onion," I assured him. "Three plain. Three roasted garlic. Three cinnamon-swirl. And one blueberry."

He nodded, backed up slightly and opened the door wider. "Come on in then, before you topple over. You can have the blueberry."

As we walked in silence through the wide, oak paneled hallway toward the kitchen, our footsteps made small echoes. It was an eerie sound in a house that was usually filled with music, chiming phones and top-of-the-lungs conversation. I glanced into the book-lined study, the living room, the dining room with its extra long table. Not a soul. "Where is everybody?" I asked, worried that Moira might have walked out in a towering rage and taken the kids with her.

Evan scratched his head as he trudged along, as if he found he question perplexing. "Moira decided to go to church this morning. She hasn't been to Mass in ages, so who knows what that's about. Could be she's praying for my soul. McKenzie decided to go with her. She kind of likes that new progressive Catholic stuff with the music. Also, she knows her mother isn't exactly thrilled with the fact that I was consulting with the police until dawn." His voice gave the word "consulting" an ironic twist. "Maybe she thought she could calm Moira down a little."

With one stockinged foot, he kicked at a skateboard blocking our path and sent it skidding through the open door of his study.

"Phillip took off with a couple of friends for a nature trek at Delhi. At this very moment, he's probably counting newts or studying raccoon shit."

I walked over to the sun-drenched breakfast nook and deposited the bag on the table. While Evan poured two cups of coffee and collected silverware, glasses and napkins from various locations, I took out the *Times* and set it next to his chair. Then I liberated some plates and arranged our impromptu brunch.

There was no attempt at conversation until we were both seated in front of toasted bagels and glasses of orange juice and our coffee cups were ready for refills. "Okay," I began, "on a scale of one to ten, just how pissed are you? And how many times will I need to apologize before you even think about forgiving me?"

Evan looked at me over the rim of his coffee cup, sipped and lowered it a few inches. "Well," he said in a weary voice, "being pissed at you never seems to do any good. So let's call it a two-point-five, which is where I am most of the time with you anyway." He forked a slice of lox onto his plate. "Actually, I wouldn't call it pissed exactly. Exasperated, frustrated, even a little amazed. Yes."

He draped the lox over an onion bagel already weighted down with cream cheese and looked at it pensively. "But I'd be lying if I said I wasn't worried about where all this is headed. I mean, for one thing, it's dead certain we're looking at an FBI investigation."

"FBI?" Suddenly the piece of blueberry bagel in my mouth had the taste and consistency of sawdust. While Evan chomped away, I chugged half my orange juice in an attempt to clear out the crumbs that had lodged in my throat.

"Of course the FBI," he said. "We're talking possible election tampering. A state mid-term election. One of the most bitter, closely contested elections since, well, since the last one. That makes it a federal case. Which means FBI. And who knows? It could even lead to a Congressional hearing and..."

"Enough," my voice betrayed the fear that was oozing into my brain.

With a calm I found infuriating, Evan took another leisurely bite out of his bagel. "Look. We've got to face facts." He swiped at his beard with a piece of paper toweling and a small shower of crumbs fell onto his shirt. "Depending on how the Ann Arbor Police decide to interpret our role in all this, we could find ourselves in a Senate chamber with reporters and cameramen crawling around our ankles while we try to explain what the hell we were doing hacking into a computer that was probably used to hack an election."

He glanced down at my plate. "Aren't you going to eat that? I thought blueberry was your favorite."

In my mind's eye, I imagined myself being grilled by grim-faced politicians, all playing to the cameras, all trying to outdo each other in the outrage department. "I think I'll just stick with coffee this morning," I said and pushed my plate toward the center of the table.

An hour and a half later, I drove impatiently through the peaceful streets, blaming Evan's high-test coffee for my growing sense of agitation. In an attempt to escape from my feelings of guilt, made worse by the fact that I'd missed church, plus anxiety at the prospect of facing the wrath of the FBI and possibly the U.S. Senate, I headed into the downtown area. Except for a few slow-moving pedestrians shuffling into the Fleetwood Diner and Café Oscar, the streets were deserted.

By the time I got home, it was nearly noon and my load of lousy feelings was heavier than ever. Albert had enough good sense and cat-type intuition to make himself scarce. I wandered into the living room to check for phone messages.

The first was from Andrew. I fast-forwarded. Next was Uncle Jalo who, in a thick Finnish accent, informed me that Aunt Ilsa was in church and he just called to say hello. The last message was from Bixie, suggesting lunch today.

With a sigh, I surveyed the living room and realized how much dustier dust tended to look in the ruthless light of early winter sunshine. There was no point in heading to my office since the likelihood of mustering a single creative thought was zero.

Determined to salvage some shred of what was promising to be a wreck of a day, I poured myself a large glass of spring water, nabbed a notepad and pen, trudged into Terry's study and sat down at the maple table that had served as his desk. Tucked under a window that overlooked the side yard, it was a perfect place for daydreaming. I remembered all the times I'd walked in and discovered him looking out that window, marveling at a bird or appreciating the lilacs or grinning at the backyard antics of Paul and David, who tended to be strenuous but unsuccessful gardeners. The memory made me smile.

"I love you," I whispered into the empty room. Then, wiping my eyes, I pulled out the old leather-seat desk chair that still held the memory of Terry's form, sat down, arranged the glass of water on a coaster and started writing.

When I looked up, disturbed from my labors by insistent hunger pangs, I was shocked to see that the small pewter desk clock read one-thirty. Notepad in hand, I trekked into the kitchen and built myself a turkey and cheese sandwich, stopping every now and then to glance at some of my scribbles.

Fifteen minutes later, I sat at the kitchen table flanked by a two-inch-thick sandwich oozing mayonnaise, an open bag of potato chips, a large glass of milk and—slightly to the right of my plate—the notepad.

Because the first bite of a sandwich is always the best, I gave myself a few seconds to savor it before turning my attention to the Benjamin Franklin-style grid that filled several sheets of paper.

Header, column number one: THEORY.

Header, column number two: PRO.

Header, column number three: CON.

First item. Allegra kills Dana, Chaz commits suicide.

Such a neat, tidy, deeply satisfying little theory, I just had to make it number one. Unfortunately, even though Allegra had access and possibly motive, I didn't believe it for a second. Under the "CON" column, I had written: Forget it. Allegra would never jeopardize her comfortable life. Besides which, being Allegra, she probably had the goods on Dana—some best-forgotten scandal or other.

On to theory number two: Dorey Goldstein kills Dana, Chaz commits suicide.

Once again, motive and opportunity were there, and probably means as well. Jealousy could be a powerful force. Even though Dorey struck me as all fluster and no malice, number two deserved a question mark because I didn't know enough about the Goldstein marriage or Dorey herself to be certain. And who could predict the vagaries of the human heart?

Number three I liked a lot: Michael Madigan plots election fraud with Chaz, learns about therapist Chaz is seeing, gains access by manipulating Mercedes into becoming a patient, panics, kills Dana, panics again, kills Chaz.

Great possibilities, this one. Except that all I had was guesswork. Yes, Mercedes was seeing Dana. But maybe that was pure coincidence or a desire to keep up with the latest trend in local therapy. And, yes, Michael knew Chaz, but so did a lot of other local Republican mentor-types, including my good friend George Popoulous. And then there was Michael's alibi for the probable time of Chaz's death, sealed with a kiss no less.

I sighed and moved on.

Number four: Chaz kills Dana and self.

It was such a sad, ugly thought I'd hated to even write it down. Still, it was a possibility. Here was a brilliant and desperate young man, in over his head. Way over. Here was a woman who may well have known his deepest, darkest, most dangerous secret. Chaz had access, motive and—with a little research and a little effort at local pharmacies—means as well.

But I couldn't believe the worst about Chaz. I'd been sharing my snug little West Side bungalow with Dana and him for some time now. There were never any bad vibes, no spectral conflicts. If liking figured at all in the afterlife, they seemed to like each other. And I refused to believe that Dana would be on such cozy terms with the ghost of her murderer.

I stopped and played back those last few thoughts. Bad vibes? Spectral conflicts? Good God. Had my brain finally turned to cosmic slop?

I dropped the pen and shook my head to clear out the mental miasma. At moments like this I began to worry for my sanity.

Leaving the dirty plate and glass where they were, I pulled the Ann Arbor phone book out of a nearby drawer, found the number I was looking for and glued my index finger to the spot while I walked over to the kitchen phone.

I punched in two numbers. Hung up. Dialed three numbers. Hung up. Took a deep, slow breath and let it out. Dialed all seven numbers and waited.

Charles Chang picked up on the third ring. "Yes?" he asked. Not "Hello." Not "Charles Chang here." But "Yes?" As if he'd been expecting something. But then, I reasoned, his work had probably taught him to always be expecting something.

"Mr. Chang?" I asked in a voice that didn't sound nearly as nervous or ridiculous as I felt. "We met last week. My name is Karin Niemi."

CHAPTER 46

Sunday – December 1

"Karin Niemi, I promised your father I would look after you for as long as I had breath in my body. And that is exactly what I intend to do."

Aunt Ilsa rarely lost her temper and, when she did, it was a wise person who didn't interrupt. This particular rant had gone on for several minutes and was still proceeding at gale force. I let my head sink into the wide leather chair back, next to Albert's languid form.

"So," my aunt continued, "I'm going to ask you again and I want the truth this time. What's wrong? Are you having money problems? Is that it?"

Good God, I thought, reaching up to separate Albert's paw from a clump of my hair, I'm a freelance writer. Of course I'm having money problems. "No, the money is fine."

"It is money, isn't it?" Worry crept into her voice, edging out the anger. "How many times have I told you, your uncle and I would be happy to help you out anytime."

"No it's nothing to do with money," I said, wishing I had a glass of water to help dissolve the lump that was suddenly living in my throat.

"You're not sick are you?"

"Me?" I asked, surprised at the question. "Can you even remember the last time I got sick?"

"Okay. Good. So what is it then?"

I decided this was probably a good time to trot out the truth, or some version of it. "It's Bixie, actually. A friend of hers was murdered."

There was a gasp. If murder was a rare occurrence in Ann Arbor, it was positively exotic north of the bridge. "And then another person, sort of a friend of that friend, was murdered as well. Or committed suicide. The police aren't sure."

"Oh my Lord," Aunt Ilsa breathed. "That's awful."

"It's been really hard on Bixie. She even moved in with me for a while. So…things haven't been exactly normal around here." And that was putting it mildly.

"Maybe you two should come up here for a week or so, get away from it all," Aunt Ilsa suggested.

A week in Marquette.

I thought about the tidy little three-bedroom ranch with its knotty pine paneling. About the sauna out back and the wood smoke that gave a permanent tang to the air. I thought about the fragrant coffee cakes delivered by neighbors in search of a good gossip. And the guest bedroom with its spare Scandinavian furniture and thick down comforter.

I thought about the cathedral-like Lutheran church on Third Street that would soon be decked out in garlands and Advent candles. I thought about fruit crisp baked with blueberries picked last August and stored in the freezer. I thought about how it would be to feel safe, to live in a house where the only spirits were in the brandy bottle Uncle Jalo kept in the kitchen cupboard next to the jar of Maxwell House coffee.

"Karin, are you there? Did you hear what I said?" Aunt Ilsa's voice cut through my reverie.

"Yes," I answered, giving myself a shake. "Thanks. It's sweet of you. But I know Bixie will want to stay put for a while. You know, see it through. The murder investigation, I mean."

"The murder investigation?" my aunt repeated. "But there's nothing either of you can do about that. You've just got to let the police do their work."

"Right," I agreed, about ten days too late.

After a few minutes of general gossip and a promise to send me a care package soon, Aunt Ilsa said good-bye, her worries temporarily eased. I sat where I was for half a minute, holding the phone next to my chest. Then, after replacing the receiver, I stood in my unlit living room, trying to recapture some of the serenity I'd felt in Charles Chang's house and trying very hard not to think about tomorrow and the day after that and the day after that and the day after that.

From my dark cocoon, I turned my head and gazed out the window. Directly across the street, in the shadowy semi-darkness between streetlights, a silver-colored sedan eased away from the curb, slithered up the street and disappeared around the corner at the end of the block.

I stared out at the empty street and thought back to Paul's question. Had I noticed a car prowling around the neighborhood? A silver-colored Volvo?

Nothing to worry about, Rational Self insisted. There are plenty of late-model cars around this town, some of them Volvos, some of them silver. So why shouldn't one of them be parked on a street in your little Westside backwater?

Parked on *your* street, Paranoid Self pointed out. Just opposite *your* house.

Realizing that Paranoid Self was going to win this round, I jerked the curtains shut and headed for the foyer, where I flipped on the porch light and double-checked the locks on the front door.

From there, I walked through the dark house into the kitchen, snapped the lock on the sliding glass door, reached behind the vertical blinds for the length of two-by-four that Terry had cut years ago and slotted it into the empty channel until it butted up snugly against the steel edge of the closed door.

Then, cursing Paranoid Self, I fumbled my way through the rest of the house, going from room to room in the dark, pulling curtains, closing blinds. Only when the last shade had been drawn did I turn on the big brass lamp in the living room.

A drink, I decided. What I needed was a good stiff scotch. For a second, I could almost taste it—rich, smoky, oily in the glass. But I didn't budge. Just stood where I was, listening to my quickening heartbeat.

The interminable hours of the night stretched ahead of me like a bad dream waiting to unfold. Rational Self was telling me to be brave but she was drowned out by the nervous whisperings of her paranoid twin. After a few minutes of indecision, I reached for the phone and dialed Bixie's number.

Half an hour later, having showered Albert with apologies and left extra bowls of water and food in his corner of the kitchen, I walked out the front door with a small overnight bag in one hand, my laptop case in the other, and my purse slung over one shoulder. After double-checking the front door and scanning the street for suspicious looking vehicles, silver or otherwise, I loaded my gear into Amelia and took off for Burns Park.

Bixie's house had never looked so good. That night, I burrowed under a hypoallergenic comforter, gazed around the moonlight-dappled room, said a few brief prayers and promptly fell into a deep sleep. By the time the juicer roared into action the next morning, I was seated at Bixie's kitchen table, sipping my first cup of coffee and working through what-if scenarios with my hostess.

What if the silver car belonged to the person who murdered Dana, or Chaz, or both? What if it belonged to an accomplice of the murderer? Or some thug hired by the killer as payback for my meddling? What if Chaz really had managed to hack Grunwald's software and rig the vote? What if the election results were contested? What if Senator Bailey was forced to step down? What if the Republicans turned their sites on the blundering amateurs who stumbled onto the damning evidence?

"What if they decide to swiftboat us?" Bixie asked as she loaded up a piece of toast with apple butter.

I reached for the jar of organic peanut butter next to her plate and transferred a large quantity to my cinnamon toast. "None of us are exactly tabloid material," I reminded her.

"Oh I don't know about that." Bixie's eyes were glittering as she slid two more pieces of bread into the toaster.

With elaborate casualness, she refilled her teacup from the pot on the table. "For instance, a clever party hack could take something as innocent as your friendship with Andrew and twist it into a torrid affair. If they did it right, they'd get a two-fer. Turn both your lives into media fodder."

At the sudden brrrrring of the kitchen phone, Bixie walked over to the counter, shifted a pile of newspapers, uncovered the receiver and picked it up. "Oh, I'm so glad you called," she cooed. "Did you get my messages? Listen, I'm really sorry about…"

After a brief pause, she turned to me with a chilly look. "Yes, as a matter of fact, she's right here. But how did…?" Another brief pause, and then she held out the phone to me without a word.

I took the receiver. "Andrew, what a surprise." And what lousy timing. "How did you know I was here? Am I being called in for questioning again?"

"I suppose that was for my sister's benefit." In the background, I could hear restaurant chatter followed by the unmistakable crash of crockery hitting the floor. "Hope that doesn't come out of her paycheck," Andrew commented. "Anyway, in case you're wondering why I called, I just thought you might be curious about where the case is going. Not that I can tell you anything important, having been reassigned to B&E."

I lowered the piece of toast I'd been nibbling. "I'm listening."

"Even though I can't pass long any hard facts, there are a lot of rumors flying around these days."

"Such as?" I prompted.

"Such as, I hear this might be a good time to sell your shares in Grunwald Industries. But of course that's just idle chatter. Also, word has it that the front page of tomorrow's paper is going to make for interesting reading, depending on how much the FBI decides to spill. Did I mention they've been called in? Are you still there?"

At that moment, I realized I was staring at the far wall of the kitchen, seeing nothing. "I'm hanging on your every word."

"Glad to hear it. One last thing. You might want to postpone that nose job you were planning. At least until Ann Arbor's favorite plastic surgeon has a little more time to devote to his practice. He's been very popular around headquarters lately."

"What?" I blurted out. "Has Michael Madigan been arrested?" Bixie stopped pretending to read last night's paper and looked at me, eyes wide and mouth open.

"No, nothing like that," Andrew said. "He's just a person of interest in the case. A lot of interest. Like you and my sister. Speaking of which, let me talk to her again. It's probably time we kissed and made up."

CHAPTER 47

Monday – December 2

"Well, that's a relief," Bixie declared after I told her the news about Michael Madigan. "Now I can stop worrying about you."

"You might want to keep a little of that worry in reserve," I suggested. "Aren't you forgetting about the silver Volvo?"

As I spoke, I swirled the remains of my coffee around in the porcelain mug the way I'd seen fortunetellers do with tea leaves. Unfortunately, nothing was revealed beyond a slight crack I hadn't noticed before.

"Paul saw the car," I reminded her. "Repeatedly."

Bixie pushed away from the table and smiled at me in a sweetly patronizing way. She'd been wearing that smile ever since she and Andrew had their little talk a few minutes earlier. She fluffed out her hair and adjusted the belt of her bathrobe.

"Coincidence," she assured me. "Ask around and you'll find that someone in the neighborhood has a friend or relative who owns a silver Volvo. Now I've got to get ready for my ten-thirty. If I don't see you before you leave, call me tonight."

Before I could say a word, she power-walked out of the kitchen and up the stairs. With a sigh, I started to clear away the dishes. "Easy for you to say," I muttered as I searched the cupboard under the sink for a bottle of dish detergent. "You're not going back to a haunted house and a drive-by stalker."

By ten o'clock I was back in said haunted house, but only long enough to check on Albert and pick up my grocery list. Desperate for distractions, I actually looked forward to the gridlocked mid-morning traffic, the parking wars and the legions of Whole Foods customers who even at this hour would be charging around the aisles as if grocery shopping were a blood sport.

I left the store a hundred and twenty dollars lighter and somewhat bruised from a collision with one of those cuted-up grocery carts reserved for toddlers. By the time I started hauling bags into the kitchen, it was nearly twelve-thirty.

Keeping a close eye on Elvis, I wolfed down a brie and turkey panini, threw a notebook and pen into my briefcase, filled my water bottle and headed out to my one-thirty. Normally, a new client meeting at Arbor Assisted Living wouldn't exactly make my heart soar. But today I felt both relieved and grateful at the prospect.

Truth is, I was ready to do almost anything, go almost anywhere and meet with almost anyone to delay the moment of truth. The moment, that is, when I'd be alone with my thoughts and those shivery little breezes telling me that Dana and Chaz were still in residence, still restless, still prowling the premises in search of peace or justice or vengeance or perhaps just some company.

By one twenty-five, I'd located the right building, claimed a visitor parking slot and found my way to a chilly teal and beige office suite. The marketing director was one Sara McDonald, medium-tall, medium-heavy, medium-pretty, somewhere in her late thirties.

I liked the fact that she was smart and well organized, friendly but not cloying. I liked that she had a clear, well-thought-out communications plan. I also liked the fact that when I showed her my samples, she asked intelligent questions about content and creative process and client input.

She must have found a few things to like as well because I walked out of the conference room with a handful of print projects and the promise of some web site work. Ah, I thought as I revved up Amelia and prepared to exit the parking lot in the direction of the nearest Starbucks, if only they could all be like that.

After rewarding myself with a café grande, which I insisted on calling a large coffee, I made my way through a maze of chairs containing bodies of every age and description, most of them attached to laptops, cell phones or crackberries. I found a small table in the corner next to a window and settled in for some quiet time.

I needed to think.

To help the process along, I pulled out my notebook and turned to a fresh page. At the top, I wrote: TO DO. With that as my inspiration, I numbered every line on the paper before backtracking to the first slot at the top.

Number one. I stared at the empty page and thought for a few seconds. Took a few sips. Then I scrawled out the words: Find a lawyer.

At the end of ten minutes or so, I had a list of seven items, none of which I wanted to tackle. I also had the rest of an afternoon and evening to fill. I flipped back to my pages of notes from the meeting. Fortunately, there was always work. And, I reminded myself, a hundred and twenty dollars worth of expensive groceries to play with.

It was nearly four when I rolled into the driveway. As I opened the front door, a gust of cold air ruffled my hair and stopped me in my tracks. I stood absolutely still for four or five seconds, holding the doorknob and hoping that the furnace was malfunctioning.

No such luck. I could hear a thrumming in the basement and Albert was sprawled across the nearest air vent, a sure sign that the heating system was in good working order.

Apparently, my ghostly guests were more agitated than usual. But why? Pondering that question, I tossed my briefcase and purse onto a nearby chair and hung up my coat and scarf. The police seemed to be moving in the right direction. And there was every likelihood that, eventually, they'd untangle the clues and find their way to the murderer. Or murderers.

I picked half a dozen envelopes off the floor near the mail slot, sauntered into the kitchen, put the kettle on to boil and fished Terry's antique dagger out of its drawer.

There was a card-sized envelope addressed in my mother-in-law's firm, elegant script. I slit open the top, set the envelope aside and moved on to the next piece of mail. That being the electric bill. Followed by the gas bill. Followed by an invitation to the Ronald McDonald House holiday fundraiser.

I had just opened the fifth envelope, and still no checks in sight, when Paul appeared at the sliding glass door. As I lifted out the wooden brace and unsnapped the lock, I wondered if he ever used the phone.

"My, how security conscious we've become," he chirped as he stepped into the kitchen, rubbing his arms from the cold. The turtleneck sweater he wore—ivory with little flecks of brown and green—told me he'd probably spent the day in the shop rather than his studio. "Had a busy day?" he asked.

"Just got back from a meeting," I said. "What's up?"

His eyes scanned the kitchen table and moved along the counters, searching in vain for the plate of cookies that's always out when I'm working at home. "Nothing much. Just wanted to see if you'd care to join me for an early dinner. I've got class tonight so I thought I'd have something light. David's working late and you know I hate to eat alone."

I considered the offer but realized I'd had enough of my fellow human beings for the day. "Thanks but I'll pass. I just bought a pile of groceries this morning."

"Okay," he shrugged and turned to leave. "Let me know if you change your mind. I'm cooking up a huge batch of seafood pasta." I weakened slightly at the thought of Paul's good-enough-to-patent clam sauce with artichoke hearts. But my resolve held. I waved him off just as the kettle began to whistle.

I brewed a cup of tea and settled down in the living room with the latest copy of *The New Yorker*, one of the last before Terry's subscription ran out. But none of the articles could hold my attention. I felt fidgety and restless.

Something made me glance across the room at the television. At that exact moment, the cozy twilight silence was shattered as the remote control flew through the air and crashed onto the floor, scattering batteries as it fell.

It took me about ten seconds to accept what I'd just seen. Once my startle response was under control and my heart had stopped hammering, I slammed the magazine onto the coffee table and stood up.

"That's enough," I roared into the apparently empty room. "Settle down, both of you, before you give me a heart attack. The police are going to figure this out. You just have to patient."

265

I unclenched my hands, crossed my arms and lowered my voice. "And scaring me to death won't accomplish anything." I took a deep breath.

I walked across the room and retrieved the remote, which had landed several feet from the television. With hands that shook only slightly, I reinstalled the batteries and pressed the on button. Maybe there was something they wanted me to see.

I channel surfed my way through the news. The Detroit stations hinted that Ann Arbor police were very close to making a major announcement relating to the deaths of Dana Lewis and Charles Anderson. One of the anchors mentioned that the FBI had been called in to assist.

The noise was comforting enough that I decided to break with tradition and leave the set on. I flipped over to PBS just in time for the start of the *News Hour,* turned up the volume and padded into the kitchen to explore my options for dinner.

Half an hour later, I was back in front of the screen balancing a tray on my lap. Albert seated himself next to me and stared, first at the tray, then at me. "You're right," I told him. "My standards are slipping."

By eight o'clock, the steak, green beans and sourdough bread had disappeared from my plate and I was feeling relaxed for the first time all day. Fighting off a nearly irresistible urge to sleep, I shuffled into the kitchen with my tray.

Eight-thirty found me back in my TV-watching chair, hoping that this wouldn't become a habit. PBS was running one of those harmless nature programs they do so well. The ones that make it so easy to drift off to sleep.

I would have stayed asleep if it hadn't been for the jangling crash that came from the kitchen, as if someone had dropped—or thrown—a telephone on the floor. My eyes snapped open and, once my brain had identified the sound and the likely location, righteous indignation propelled me out of the chair. Tossing the television remote was one thing. But smashing a phone was taking this poltergeist thing too far.

How dare they? I fumed. Who do they think they are, wrecking the place, abusing my hospitality this way?

Fueled by outrage and more than ready to give Dana and Chaz another verbal blast, I stormed out of the living room. Down the hallway. Past the study door. Through the kitchen archway.

And into the sites of an evil looking handgun that trembled in the two-handed grip of Mercedes Madigan.

CHAPTER 48

Monday – December 2

I've often wondered how I'd react in a life-or-death situation. Just me. Alone. Face to face with a murderer.

I knew I'd never have the bravado of V.I. Warshawski. Or the wily cop smarts of Arly Hanks. Or the dumb luck of Miss Seeton.

I hoped that I wouldn't be a bumbler or, worse, a coward. Secretly, I thought I'd be the type who disarms her attacker with brilliant arguments. But right now that didn't seem likely since all I could manage was one word.

"You."

"How convenient." The gun swayed as Mercedes allowed herself to gloat. "You've saved me the bother of searching through this charming little house for you."

She twisted her mouth into a horrifying leer. But then everything about her was horrifying. The belladonna eyes. The black watch cap that framed her taut, pale face. The thin black leather gloves. The form-fitting sweater, slacks and low-heeled boots, also black.

Suddenly I felt cold. Not weather cold. Soul cold.

"Mercedes, what are you doing here? What's this all about?"

Her entire body seemed to be vibrating. "Oh, I'm not really here at all." She pulled her lips back in another death's head grin. "When I open tomorrow's paper and read about your suicide, I'm going to be as shocked as anyone."

Suicide. The word soaked in slowly, with panic flooding in behind it. I let my eyes dart around the kitchen, hoping they'd land on something. Anything. An idea. A miracle. A weapon. A way out.

The day's mail was still lying on the kitchen counter next to the refrigerator, exactly where I'd left it when Paul dropped by earlier. In my mind's eye, I pictured the small dagger with the serpent handle that lay beneath the envelopes.

"Suicide?" My hands were sweaty and my heartbeat had become a blur. Suddenly, I knew that I'd do or say just about anything to delay the moment when she pulled that trigger. Or, given the fact that her hands were now shaking almost uncontrollably, when the damn thing went off by accident.

Shifting the gun to her right hand, Mercedes moved toward me in three slow steps. I matched each of her steps with one of my own—in reverse—until a kitchen chair ended my retreat.

"That's right. Sit down. You're going to kill yourself. One shot to the head with this." She wiggled the gun at me. "Not registered, of course. Or," she reached into the left pocket of her black slacks and pulled out a small bottle with a dropper top, "with poison. I haven't decided yet. In either case, you should probably be seated. It'll look more natural that way."

I've always been amazed at people who, under threat of getting shot, cravenly obey the orders of their whacked-out assailant by swallowing bleach or doing something equally unspeakable to themselves. No, I decided. No poison for me. It would have to be the bullet.

Don't provoke her, a female voice whispered in my ear. Play for time.

"I don't understand," I said, trying to stay in contact with whatever was left of Mercedes' mind. My breathing was shallow and my voice was unsteady. "Why are you doing this?"

She narrowed her eyes. "How can ask such a stupid question? Thanks to you, Michael and I are murder suspects." I couldn't take my eyes off her contorted mouth. "Murder suspects," she repeated in a near-shriek. "The police have been hounding us for nearly two weeks. Showing up at the house. At Michael's office." Her voice inched higher with every word.

"And now they're asking all kinds of questions about Charles Anderson. It's horrible. A nightmare. People are starting to talk. Michael's business is falling off. Soon, everything we've worked for all these years will be ruined." She moved the gun a few inches closer to me and I caught my breath. "And it's all because of you."

I licked my lips. "That's not true," I said. "The police figured everything out on their own."

"No," the word came out in a shriek. "No. It was you. You and your friend and her brother the cop." Surprise made my eyes open even wider. "Oh yes," Mercedes continued, obviously pleased with herself. "I know all about that cozy little arrangement. You'd be surprised how fast gossip moves in this town."

From somewhere deep inside me, a prayer went up. "If you know all that, then you also know that the police were aware you'd been seeing Dana."

"Because of you," Mercedes spit back at me. "Because of something you found out. Otherwise they would have never known. I made sure her appointment book disappeared and my file along with it."

As I struggled to take long, slow, measured breaths, I heard the voice again, the whisper in my ear. Time, it said. Give yourself more time.

Right, I thought, still focusing on my breath. More time. Or was I just kidding myself? Postponing the inevitable moment when Mercedes followed through on her threat?

"It wasn't me," I said, willing her to believe me. "I had nothing to do with it. Dana kept a back-up list of all her appointments on her computer. Didn't you know that? The police have a copy of the file."

I took a ragged breath and watched Mercedes' face collapse. "Mercedes, my name was in her calendar too."

"You're lying."

"No, I'm not," I pushed on. "I had an appointment with her. I'm a suspect too." Keep talking, I told myself. Don't stop. "And it's not all my doing. You're forgetting about Dana's neighbors. There had to be someone who saw you coming and going. Someone who recognized you and," I took a wild guess, "and Ms. Gibson. And maybe Michael as well. He dropped you off at least once, didn't he?"

Mercedes didn't say a word.

"And Michael's connection with the Young Republicans?" I kept reaching for the next sentence. "Common knowledge. A hundred different people could have told the police that Michael knew Chaz Anderson."

"Shut up." Mercedes studied my kitchen as if it were a map. "I warned you once that I'd do anything to protect my family. You should have listened. You should have believed me."

Her glazed, hate-filled eyes were like black pits. Looking into them, I realized that trying to reason with her was a fool's errand. I was talking to a crazy woman who wanted me dead.

Dear God, I prayed, I don't want to die. I'm not ready to die. Not now. Not like this.

Mercedes looked at me as if I were an insect. "I've decided. We'll use poison. In a glass of wine, I think. That seems like the right farewell gesture for someone filled with remorse for ruining so many people's lives with false accusations."

Reacting to the startled look in my eyes, she added, "Oh, yes. There will be a suicide note. Typed on your computer. Waiting for the police to find." With her gun hand, she gestured at the cupboards. "You must have a bottle of something around."

I nodded. "In the refrigerator."

"Good. Get it." She gestured again. "But do it slowly. And don't try anything because if I have to, I'll be happy to shoot you where you stand and let the police think this was just a break-in gone wrong."

I was afraid to speak but more afraid not to. "Mercedes, think about what you're doing." Why did every sentence coming out of my mouth sound like re-treaded dialogue from a B movie? "This isn't going to solve anything. You're going to get caught. And when you do, think of what it'll mean for your kids. For..."

"Shut up," she screamed. Good, I thought. Keep screaming. Maybe someone will hear. As if reading my thoughts, she lowered her voice. "Get the wine. Now."

I walked on wooden feet to the refrigerator. When I pulled open the door with my right hand, it shielded me slightly from Mercedes' view.

271

Quickly, before she could shift her position, I placed my left hand on the pile of mail.

Willing myself not to panic, I felt for the dagger, found it and grabbed the handle, pointing the tip toward my elbow. In one motion I angled it up my sleeve, wincing as the blade snagged the skin of my inner arm.

Except for ants and mosquitoes and flies and the occasional cockroach, I've never killed anything. I wasn't sure I'd be able to use a knife, even on someone who was intent on murdering me. Still, the feel of that cold steel against my lower arm sent a surge of hope through me.

"Quit stalling," Mercedes voice rang out from behind me. I made a production of shifting bottles and containers in the refrigerator. Finally, hands quaking, breath jagged, I reached for the half-empty bottle of chardonnay and pulled it out.

I could feel a sticky patch of skin where the knife had sliced my arm. Hoping that any blood would be camouflaged by my dark brown sweater, I turned around. Mercedes was facing me, her back to the sliding glass doors.

A flicker of movement outside drew my attention. Directly behind her on the tiny side porch, I saw something. A large shadowy something. It was…oh my God, could it possibly be?

A street light illuminated the space just enough for me to make out the form of a man. Wearing a dark jacket and white wide-legged pants.

Paul. It was Paul.

How much could he see from where he stood? Just the back of a black-clad figure. And me, getting wine out of the refrigerator.

I raised my voice to a desperate yell. "Mercedes, please don't kill me. Put the gun down, and we'll just forget about it. I know you've been under a lot of pressure lately…"

Mercedes let out a gutteral sound that might have been a laugh. "Don't be pathetic." With her gun hand, she motioned impatiently toward the cupboards. "Get a glass. Put it on the table with the bottle. And sit down."

I opened the cupboard next to the refrigerator. When I turned back to face her, glass in one hand, bottle in the other, Paul was hunched over the handle of the door. Of course. The key. Mercedes must have locked the door after she came in.

I wracked my memory, trying to recall what the door sounded like when it opened. I seemed to remember that it gave a metallic whoosh as it moved on its rollers. Too loud. Too noticeable.

As I walked back to the table under Mercedes' watchful eye, I deliberately tangled my feet, stumbled and lurched forward, sideswiped a kitchen chair and sent it crashing to the floor. Letting myself fall across the table, I released the bottle and glass and watched them topple. The bottle fell on its side with a heavy kerthump and rolled noisily across the floor. The glass shattered on impact, spraying shards everywhere and causing Mercedes to recoil.

At that moment, as they say, everything seemed to happen at once.

With one mighty shove, Paul pushed open the door, letting in a blast of cold air. Confused and slowed by the general mayhem, Mercedes hesitated before pivoting to meet the sound.

As she moved, Paul's body left the ground for a split second. His right leg shot out at ferocious speed and caught her on the shoulder. There was a scream as she fell sideways and crashed to the floor.

By the time I closed the distance between us, dagger out, Mercedes was splayed face down on the oak floorboards. She was making angry sounds, belly crawling, struggling desperately to reach the gun that was just a few inches from her right hand. I watched, horrified, as her fingers closed around the revolver.

In one seamless movement, Paul's right knee was on the floor, his left knee pressed against her spine. There was a whooshing sound of air being expelled, followed by a groan.

Paul reached over and twisted the wrist that held the gun. The hand went limp. The gun fell. Breathing hard, he stood up and gave a kick that sent the revolver skittering across the floor into the far corner of the kitchen. He placed one foot on Mercedes' neck. "Move and I swear I'll kill you."

Kneeling on the floor near them both, I placed a hand over my mouth and fought back an urge to vomit.

"Karin, call the police." Paul's words came out in short panting breaths. Still battling waves of nausea, I began crawling on all fours toward the kitchen phone.

"No need." The deep gravelly baritone voice that came from the direction of the open kitchen door was familiar.

Moses B. Caldwell stood just inside the door, badge in his left hand, gun in his right. "I happened to be passing and saw what appeared to be a break-in." He pointed the gun at Mercedes' unmoving form, then at Paul and me. "I've already called for back-up. Ms. Niemi, you and your friend make yourselves comfortable at the table and then you two can tell me what happened here." He gave Mercedes a brief glance. "I'll get her story later."

I tried to stand but couldn't. Paul, still breathing hard, pulled me to my feet. I could feel his hands shaking, either from shock or an overdose of adrenalin.

As I settled myself on one of the kitchen chairs, I was surprised to see Terry's dagger in my hand. I loosened my grip and the knife clattered onto the kitchen table.

I stared at it for a minute, shivering, teeth chattering, wishing I could cry. After rubbing my face hard all over, I looked up at Detective Sergeant Caldwell who was taking in the scene with Zen-like calm.

"I have a question for you," I said.

He cocked an eyebrow. "I'm supposed to be the one asking the questions. But go ahead."

"What kind of car do you drive?"

He smiled. "I drive a 2000 Volvo, Ms. Niemi." The smile widened. "Silver. But maybe you already guessed that."

CHAPTER 49

Wednesday – December 4

"Do you really expect me to believe you didn't know that Caldwell was spying on me in his spare time?"

I helped myself to another cherry oatmeal bar and realized, with only a tiny glimmer of shame, that I'd been playing the role of outraged victim ever since Andrew walked into Bixie's sun porch ten minutes earlier.

He loosened his tie and settled a little deeper into the ancient leather armchair. "We don't call it spying, Niemi. We call it surveillance."

He took a long pull at his coffee. "And you should be damn grateful he took it upon himself to keep an eye on you. If what's his name—David Carradine in drag—hadn't gotten there first, it would have been Caldwell who saved your life." He massaged the back of his neck. "I still can't believe that little…"

Bixie, who had just walked into the porch with a fresh carafe of coffee, stopped in her tracks. "Paul." Her voice was razor-sharp. "His name is Paul."

The two of them locked eyes. Then Andrew shrugged. "Okay. Fine. I still can't believe that *Paul* has a brown belt in judo."

"Truce time. Or take it outside." The words were out before I could stop myself. Brother and sister both gave me a who-the-hell-do-you-think-you-are look. But I wasn't interested in refereeing their snipe session. I wanted to get back to my questions about the case. And I had

275

a lot of them. Starting with why Mercedes Madigan would kill Dana Lewis.

"We don't know that she did," Andrew pointed out. "She hasn't confessed. The only thing she admitted to you was that she stole Dana's appointment book and her own client file. Her story is, she went to your house because she wanted to talk to you and maybe scare you a little. That's all."

"But..." I protested.

Andrew went on. "Her Bloomfield Hills lawyer is already arguing that she simply didn't want her relationship with Dana to become public knowledge. This dude is so slick, he'll probably end up suing you and what's-his-name for attacking her. And win the case."

Despite a few fresh creases above his eyebrows, Andrew looked more relaxed than he had in weeks. Of course, Bixie's back porch did have that effect on people. I should know, having spent much of the last day and a half bird watching, reading and napping on the very spot where he was now sitting. And it looked as if I'd be enjoying those same pursuits for the foreseeable future.

Over my objections, Paul had called Bixie as soon as Caldwell gave us permission to use the phone. Twenty minutes later, looking over the carnage that had been my kitchen, Bixie announced that I couldn't stay in such a tainted environment until someone named Sharon Gladstone had conducted an Ojibwa cleansing ceremony to drive out the dark energies.

Being in no condition to argue, I supervised the packing of a small suitcase and made sure that Albert was comfortably settled at Paul and David's house. By midnight, my overnight bag was living in Bixie's guest room and I was soaking my aching body in an Epson salt bath, wondering vaguely how an Ojibwa medicine woman wound up in Ann Arbor and whether her antics would disturb Dana and Chaz.

After downing a cup of cocoa and predicting that I'd be up all night, I slept heavily until just before noon and awoke with bruises and twinges in places I didn't even know existed. Refusing Bixie's herbs and tinctures, I took a Tylenol, ate lunch and staggered out to the back porch with a book. The last thing I remember is watching the antics of a male cardinal. I roused myself in time for dinner and fell asleep again during the evening news.

This morning, though, I made up for any sloth by launching myself out of bed at dawn's early light. Since then I'd been pecking away at my laptop, trying in vain to get some work done, replying to emails, scouring newspapers and listening to the radio for any scrap of news about Monday night's encounter.

The local radio stations were the first to break the story. It was odd hearing myself referred to in the third person, name withheld, the victim of an alleged break-in.

"But, Andrew, she threatened me with a gun," I protested. "Not to mention whatever was in that bottle."

"There is that," Andrew agreed. With the tip of his fork, he prodded the cherry oatmeal bar that lay on his plate. After a few seconds, he put the fork down and poured himself a fresh cup of coffee. "We figure her lawyer will argue that the gun was just a prop, to scare you into backing off, and that she had no intention of using it."

I groaned, he went on. "And they'll probably insist that the atropine—did I mention it was atropine?—is actually a prescription for her eyes and that she always carries the stuff around with her."

"But atropine is what killed Dana," I reminded him.

"Yes," he said with exaggerated patience "I know that. And so will the jury."

I shook my head in rage and disgust. "So what happens next?"

"The D.A. keeps collecting evidence. And the rest of us wait until there's a hearing and Mercedes' lawyer lays out their preliminary argument. In the meantime, there's the whole Chaz Anderson case to consider."

Andrew propped his feet up on a hassock that didn't quite match the armchair. "You two find yourselves a lawyer yet?"

"No," Bixie answered with fake sweetness. "There hasn't been a whole lot of time for researching attorneys in the last couple of days."

Not wanting to dwell on the prospect of lawyers—and their fees—I let my mind race on in its hectic way. "How do you think Mercedes and Michael found out that Chaz was seeing Dana in the first place?"

"Lots of possibilities," Bixie said. Wrapped in a paisley shawl, she looked almost as relaxed as her brother. "Dana could have scheduled back-to-back appointments with Mercedes and Chaz. In which case Mercedes would have seen him, either coming or going. And if Michael or Ms. Gibson went with her to the appointments, even just to drop her off and pick her up afterwards, they could have run into Chaz as well."

Bixie gazed off into space, where she was probably viewing an imagined encounter between Chaz and Mercedes, or Chaz and Michael. "Also," she went on, "Dana was notoriously casual about her appointment book. She'd leave it lying around. So anyone who was waiting could have found it, picked it up and leafed through it."

For a few moments, I mulled over those possibilities. But more questions kept popping into my head and since Andrew was in such an obliging frame of mind, I turned to him with the next one. "What about those pills Michael Madigan gave me? Any word from the path lab?"

Andrew shook his head. "No. I'm guessing they really are allergy pills. But on the bright side," he grinned, "it looks as if you might have been right about Madigan taking a phone call at dinner on the night Chaz Anderson died."

I slapped the fat, dusty arms of the chair I was sitting on and a storm of tiny particles danced in the light-drenched air. "I knew it. How long was he gone?"

"He supposedly took a call late in the evening, around ten-thirty or so, and was gone for about twenty-five minutes, give or take a few. Evidently, the drinks were flowing pretty steadily, so no one at the table can say for sure."

"Supposedly?" I asked. "He supposedly took a call?"

"His phone was on vibrate, or so he says," Andrew explained. I let out a small explosion of air.

"We have eye witnesses who saw him step away from the table and walk toward the rear of the restaurant, the men's room they assumed, talking into his cell phone. But..."

"But what?" I suddenly realized how invested I was in the notion of Michael Madigan being responsible, directly responsible, for someone's death. And held accountable for it.

I'd already decided that even if he hadn't actually put the poison in Dana's tea and remedies, he killed her by proxy. By infecting Mercedes with his fears, real or otherwise. He must have driven his half-crazy wife over the brink, harping on what Dana might know—and tell. Not only the deep dark secrets of Mercedes herself but those of Chaz Anderson and whatever Chaz might have spilled about Michael's role in the election hack.

"But what?" I repeated.

"But even if he did use those twenty-five minutes to meet with Chaz Anderson, we can't prove it. There are eight separate entrances to that parking structure. None of them well lit. The surveillance cameras they use are crap. And it turns out that half of them aren't even in working order."

"So," I interrupted, "you're saying there's no way to place him there."

I'd been sitting on the edge of my chair. Now I let myself collapse backwards. "And there's no way to prove he actually did anything to Chaz, even if he was there."

Bixie got up and, using her crossed arms to anchor her shawl in place, began pacing the perimeter of the porch. "That's right," she said. "If he did get a call from Chaz, Michael could say that he knew the kid slightly from the Young Republicans. He could say he was worried because Chaz sounded so upset and he thought he should do the responsible thing, try to help. So he agreed to meet him at the parking structure. They talked. And when Chaz seemed calmer, Michael went back to the restaurant. End of story."

Bixie took a few seconds to rearrange her shawl and her thoughts. "Obviously, it's not the sort of thing he'd mention to business associates. So he said nothing. The next day, when he learned that the kid was dead, he panicked. Cowardly but understandable. And then he decided not to incriminate himself by admitting he'd seen Chaz Anderson the night before, even though it was all completely innocent and well-meaning on his part."

"Very good, Bix," Andrew grinned at his sister. "You're starting to think like a cop. Or a lawyer. The fact is, even if we can place Madigan at the parking structure, any evidence would be circumstantial. Our crime scene guys didn't find any indication of a struggle."

"What about Grunwald?" I asked. "Was the software hacked? If it was, my God... all the election results would have to be nullified." I tried to imagine the turmoil that would ensue but couldn't seem to get my head around it. Some crises are just too big to contemplate.

Andrew stretched, yawned and stretched some more. "We won't know anything until the FBI has done their work and made their report. They don't play well with others."

Bixie had been staring out at a small flock of sparrows pecking for seeds in the garden. She turned her head slightly in our direction. "And of course, we all know there's no way the current administration would ever try to interfere with the FBI. Or manipulate the findings. For God and country, of course."

We all sat in silence for a few minutes. Magnified by the glass, the December sunlight was warm and soothing on my head and shoulders. A square of it rested in my lap. After all that sleep, how could I possibly feel so tired?

"What a mess," I finally said.

"You got that right," Andrew agreed. A buzzer went off. He checked his pager and stood up. "Gotta go." He straightened his tie. "Catch you later."

Halfway through the door, he stopped abruptly and spun around. "I almost forgot. I've got something of yours in the car, Karin. You left it at the station on Saturday night. Walk me out and I'll get it for you."

Bixie shot us both a squint-eyed look but said nothing. Puzzled and curious, I followed Andrew in silence through the house, out the door, down the walk.

As we approached the black Crown Victoria, he reached into the inside pocket of his camel hair blazer and pulled out an envelope. "Here. This is for you." I stared at the slim packet as if it were a letter bomb.

"What is it?"

"There's only one way to find out."

I took the envelope. Without another word, Andrew walked to the driver's side, got in and closed the door. Once the motor was going, he rolled down the passenger window and leaned over slightly. "Do me a favor, Niemi. Try to stay out of trouble for a week or two, will you?" As he drove away, he lifted one hand in a brief wave.

Shivering in the forty-degree air, I pried open the flap.

I'd expected a summons. An official something or other. Instead, what I pulled out was a bumper sticker. In bold white type on a blue background, it read:

Courage in women is often mistaken for insanity.

I stared at it for a long while. Then I put it back in the envelope. On a gnarled branch high above me, a female cardinal let out a long, bold chirrup. I watched her, silhouetted against a cloud, and wondered where her mate was.

After the stuffiness of the sun porch, the air was invigorating. I took deep slow breaths, two, three, four of them. Slowly, the hot feeling in my cheeks subsided.

I turned back and began moving toward the steps. Then I stopped, swung around and looked up at the cardinal again just in time to see her take flight.

Thinking how good it felt to smile, I walked back to the house.

EPILOGUE

Tuesday – December 31

Although the Marquette snowfall hasn't broken any records this year, at least not yet, it still takes some getting used to—especially for a troll like me who's more accustomed to the grey slush, occasional ice storms and timid snows that pass for winter below the bridge.

I hadn't intended to spend Christmas with Aunt Ilsa and Uncle Jalo. I just sort of dropped everything and ran. I didn't even bother to call ahead. Which explains why, when I turned up on his front steps the day before Christmas Eve, Uncle Jalo stood in the doorway for a few seconds, staring in disbelief as snowflakes collected on me and my luggage.

Then he scratched his head in an I'll-be-damned kind of way, gave me a wink and one of his best smiles, and yelled back in the direction of the kitchen, "Hey, Ilsa. We just got a special delivery Christmas present. You're going to like this one, I guarantee it."

They never asked why their favorite niece decided to appear two days before Christmas, unannounced. Or why she was noticeably thinner than the last time they'd seen her. Or why she seemed so jumpy and evasive. Instead, they fed me and hauled me around to church services and holiday parties and clucked over me when I needed attention and left me alone when I needed some space.

I couldn't, wouldn't tell my aunt and uncle about my overwhelming urge to get out of town and all that led up to it. But I did my best to reassure them that everything was fine.

And really, in a lot of ways, it was.

Michael Madigan, as expected, made no confessions and conceded no involvement whatever in either of the deaths. Turns out the call he got at the restaurant was from his secretary girlfriend. But as Bixie kept insisting, that didn't rule out the possibility of a pre-arranged meeting with Chaz on the top deck of the parking structure. Ever the optimist, she was waiting for an indictment which, she felt certain, could come any day.

Mercedes was arraigned on a charge of breaking and entering with intent to commit bodily harm. She'd been denied bail and was, in newspaper speak, awaiting trial.

The police were continuing their investigations and the D.A. was considering further charges against one or both of the Madigans including, possibly, murder. Officially, of course, Dana's death is still a big question mark. But I'm certain who did it. And I'm keeping my fingers crossed.

According to what I've gleaned from news reports, the FBI is still rooting around in the murky depths of Grunwald Industries, accompanied by the loud and expert protests of corporate PR types, lawyers, board members and shareholders. Somehow, though, my cynical self doesn't expect any shattering announcements casting doubts on the election.

During our consultation with a lawyer who looked barely old enough to shave but, according to reliable sources, was a barracuda in the courtroom, Bixie and I learned that—despite the dire warnings of certain police officers—the prospect of our being charged with anything was somewhere between highly unlikely and totally impossible.

It seems Andrew had neglected to mention that by willingly surrendering the flash drive containing Dana's schedule and the laptop that had belonged to Chaz, we fell into the camp of the good guys. In fact, we qualified as upstanding citizens. Bixie and I agreed that we'd never in our lives felt so good—positively euphoric, really—about spending so much money for an hour of someone's time.

Paul was a bit of problem.

Having saved my life, he couldn't seem to let go. He became a hovering, hand-wringing, perpetual presence. If the phone rang, it was Paul. If there was a knock on the door, it was also Paul, usually with a pot of soup or a casserole or a plate of cookies or an invitation to something or other. If I stepped out of the house, even to pick up the newspaper, he saw it. If I got as far as the car, he'd be standing next to me before I could turn the key in the ignition.

He seemed to believe that because he saved me, he was responsible for me, which was annoying in the extreme. Even after I pointed this out to him with superb discretion and angelic restraint, he didn't back off an inch. I decided my only option was to wait until a new obsession took my place. And for that, I prayed devoutly.

Andrew disappeared from my life and, temporarily at least, from Bixie's as well. All in all, a good thing—or so I kept telling myself.

It wasn't any of those realities that sent me and my credit card to the Northwest Airlines web site. Ironically, it was the exorcism that finally drove me out of the house, along with Dana and Chaz and whatever other uninvited spirits had taken up residence.

Of course, as Margaret keeps reminding me, it wasn't technically an exorcism. It was Rite One of the Burial of the Dead, as read from the *Book of Common Prayer.*

Margaret's friend Father Bart turned out to be a wonderfully kind and understanding man. Chubby and cheerful, balding and blue-eyed, wise and funny, he reminded me so much of G.K. Chesterton's Father Brown that I actually slipped not once but twice and called him by that name. Which seemed to delight him to no end.

It was comforting to have Margaret there throughout the ceremony, but not quite comforting enough. Before she and Father Bart arrived, I'd walked through the house trying to find Dana and Chaz. But wherever I went, there was only quiet. Complete quiet. Which was—in an odd way—much more disturbing than chilly wisps of air or objects hurled through space by invisible hands.

When I couldn't seem to locate them, I stood in the downstairs hallway and just talked. I explained what was going to happen or what I thought was going to happen and why. Trying to put myself in a Bixie-Dana mindset, I thanked them for whatever good they might have brought me and wished them well.

And then the doorbell rang.

as the usual idle chatter, the hello-thanks-for-coming stuff put everyone at ease and then, as we settled in our various ...ather Bart told us what he planned to do. Basically, after giving it a great deal of thought and prayer, he proposed to conduct the Episcopal service for the burial of the dead.

At first, I was startled by the idea of holding a funeral ceremony in my living room. The living room because, as I had explained to them both, that was where Dana first manifested to me—as a chilly little breeze where no breeze should be.

After receiving a nod from me, Father Bart donned his chasuble, crossed himself, blessed us all, including Albert who sat quietly at the priest's side, and began with the familiar opening lines:

> *I am the resurrection and the life, saith the Lord;*
> *he that believeth in me, though he were dead, yet shall he live;*
> *and whosoever believeth in me shall not die...*

At that point, Margaret dabbed at her eyes with a crumpled mass of tissues. Somewhat to my surprise, I did the same. Father Bart continued.

> *For none of us liveth to himself,*
> *And no man dieth to himself...*

It was only after the reading of a Psalm, during something called the Commendation, that things started to get truly strange. In a solemn, firm and surprisingly deep voice, Father Bart intoned:

> *Give rest, O Christ, to thy servants*
> *Dana Lewis and Chaz Anderson with thy saints,*
> *where sorrow and pain are no more,*
> *neither sighing, but life everlasting.*

Maybe it was just me feeling upset at having to say a final good-bye yet again, knowing I was asking the divinity to take charge of two souls, to remove their presence from my life, but the temperature in the living room seemed to drop fast and far. The air hung on me like a shroud. I hugged myself for warmth as Father Bart went on, half-talking, half-chanting:

Into thy hands, O merciful Savior, we commend thy servants
Dana Lewis and Chaz Anderson.

Panic welled up in me. Stop, I wanted to say. Stop now. This is a mistake. I've changed my mind. I was wrong. They can stay. Let them stay.

Receive them into the arms of thy mercy,
into the blessed rest of everlasting peace,
and into the glorious company of the saints in light...

And then I had a flash. Or a vision. Or a hallucination. Take your pick. I don't know what to call it. I only know that strange as it sounds, crazy as it seems, I saw Dana and Chaz. Actually saw them. Not with my eyes, and this is where it gets so bizarre, but with some kind of inner sight, some sense I never even knew existed.

Side by side, they were walking toward a blazing, beautiful, beckoning light. They were going Home, I realized. Home with a capital H. Pausing briefly, they turned toward me and raised their hands in farewell, then continued on their way.

Home.

Multiply the manifold blessings of thy love,
that the good which thou didst begin in them
may be made perfect... Amen.

The next day, haunted by a house that was suddenly silent and empty except for memories, I made my way to the Northwest Airlines web site and, miracle of miracles, discovered an empty seat on one of the pint-sized vintage planes they use for their remote northern routes.

The day after that, I was hunched over in that very same seat, pondering the vomit-like stain on the upholstery, nursing a glass of lukewarm water and wondering what level of turbulence could be y an aircraft that was in all probability held together by paper clips and prayers.

ow here I was. Standing at a picture window in a small living room that overlooks Lake Superior. Watching a northern Michigan snowfall at twilight. Waiting out the last hours of the last day of the year.

I suspected it would take a long while for me to process all that had happened. Or as Bixie would say, to integrate my experiences.

The new year would begin. My visit would end. I would go back to Ann Arbor. But what was waiting for me there, beyond the drama of a court case? How would I fill my days? How would I shape my life? Why had I been spared?

As if in response to an unvoiced prayer, a fragment of Father Bart's ceremony, a verse from a Psalm, floated down soft as a feather and lodged in my mind:

> *So teach us to number our days,*
> *that we may apply our hearts to wisdom.*

A car swung into the driveway, throwing circles of light that stretched into oblongs as they danced over my face, the couch, the wall. The lights disappeared. The front door opened.

It was Aunt Ilsa and Uncle Jalo, back from their last shopping foray of the year. I could hear them chattering as they stomped snow off their boots, heard the crinkling of grocery bags and the sound of jars and bottles and cans being unloaded onto the kitchen counter.

I took one final look at the blue-black sky, the streetlights furred by snowflakes, the New Year's Eve traffic crawling along the distant curve of M-28 while, just beyond, Lake Superior heaved beneath a sharp blanket of ice.

Then I closed the curtains, turned on the oversized lamp with the birch bark shade and walked into the bright, noisy kitchen.

∞ ∞ ∞ ∞ ∞

ABOUT THE AUTHOR

After graduating from the University of Michigan, Linda Fitzgerald worked as an advertising copywriter before launching her own freelance writing firm in Ann Arbor. While writing this book, she lived with her husband and, generally, at least one cat in the nearby town of Dexter.

Photograph by Steve Maggio, The Maggio Line